*Performing Identities
on the
Restoration Stage*

CYNTHIA
LOWENTHAL

Performing Identities on the Restoration Stage

SOUTHERN ILLINOIS
UNIVERSITY
PRESS
CARBONDALE AND
EDWARDSVILLE

Library of Congress Cataloging-in-Publication Data
Lowenthal, Cynthia.
Performing identities on the Restoration stage / Cynthia
Lowenthal.
p. cm.
Includes bibliographical references and index.
1. English drama—Restoration, 1660–1700—History and
criticism. 2. Theater—England—History—17th century. 3. Identity
(Psychology) in literature. 4. Body, Human, in literature. 5. Sex
role in literature. 6. Sex in literature. I. Title.

PR698.I33 L69 2002
822′.409353—dc21
ISBN 0-8093-2462-8 (alk. paper)   2002021677

Printed on recycled paper. ♻

The paper used in this publication meets the minimum requirements of
American National Standard for Information Sciences—
Permanence of Paper for Printed Library Materials,
ANSI Z39.48-1992. ⊗

For the Hevrons
Lynn, Ken, Parker, and
Elizabeth
AND
For the Lowenthals
Richard, Kim, Katie, and
Meagan

Contents

Acknowledgments

It is a pleasure for me to acknowledge the many debts I have incurred along the path of writing this book. My gratitude to Professor Susan Staves remains steadfast: she introduced me to new ways of thinking about Restoration and eighteenth-century literature, and because of her training I remain an eager student. I also offer my thanks to scholars of Restoration and eighteenth-century literature whose work and conversations along the way have helped to shape my thinking about early modern literature and culture: Michael McKeon, Bob Markley, Susan Owen, Jean Marsden, Doug Canfield, Laura Rosenthal, Jessica Munns, Katherine Quinsey, James Thompson, and Lennard Davis.

Friends and colleagues at Tulane University have been stalwart supporters and excellent readers. My first and most heartfelt thanks go to Teresa Toulouse, whose always insightful readings and productive suggestions made rewriting a pleasure. I also owe a debt of gratitude to the Office of the Dean of the Faculty of the Liberal Arts and Sciences, especially to Teresa Soufas whose friendship and generosity in sharing her knowledge of Golden Age Spanish literature with me and with our students enriched our understanding of early modern literature. I thank Linda Pollock for an always ready seventeenth-century citation, even an entire bibliography, whenever I asked for one. And where would any of us be without Gary McPherson's "numbers"? I am particularly happy to extend my special thanks to all who work in the office of the Dean of Newcomb College at Tulane University, especially Fran Hollingsworth and Cindy Taffaro. Knowing that the college was in such good hands allowed me to leave it for a few days in order to complete this project.

Acknowledgments

I am grateful to Southern Illinois University Press for securing two such fine and illuminating readers' reports, one from Kristina Straub and one from an anonymous reader. Their thoughtful and thought-provoking suggestions made for a much better book, and I thank them both. I also thank Elizabeth Brymer, Carol Burns, and Kristine Priddy of Southern Illinois University Press for all their help in seeing this manuscript to press.

Some of the material in this book has already appeared in print in other versions. Portions of chapter 4 appeared in "Portraits and Spectators in the Late Restoration Playhouse: Delariviere Manley's *Royal Mischief*," *The Eighteenth Century: Theory and Interpretation.* I thank the University of Delaware Press for permission to use a version of "Performing Nations on the Restoration Stage: Wycherley's *Gentleman Dancing-Master*," *The Clothes That Wear Us,* eds. Jessica Munns and Penny Richards and the University of Kentucky Press for permission to use a version of "Sticks and Rags, Bodies and Brocade: Essentializing Discourses and the Late Restoration Playhouse," *Broken Boundaries: Women and Feminism in Restoration Drama,* ed. Katherine Quinsey, 1990. I also extend my thanks to the British Library, especially the staff in the rare books collection for all their assistance and good advice.

I could never have written this book without the support of a whole host of friends. I especially want to thank Lee Heller, Bob Birkby, Lynne Rosenfeld, Renee and Marty Sachs, John Rouse, Janice Broder, and Jean Danielson. And, as always, my family has been extraordinarily encouraging. I extend my thanks and my love to my parents, Richard and Jeanne Lowenthal; and I dedicate this book to my siblings and their families: to Lynn, Ken, Parker, and Elizabeth; to Richard, Kim, Katie, and Meagan.

Performing Identities
on the
Restoration Stage

1 Introduction
New Identities on and off the Restoration Stage

THE FOURTH ACT OF APHRA BEHN's *Feign'd Curtizans* contains a dialogue that best represents the possibilities for the performance of new identities found on the Restoration stage. Cornelia, a young woman of quality destined for the nunnery by her brother, has along with her sister assumed the disguise of a courtesan. Galliard, dashing young English hero, has fallen in love with Cornelia—or, at least, with the woman he thinks is willing to sell herself to him. At the critical moment, when he is about to carry her away to his private chamber, she demurs, saying, "Stay, do you take me then for what I seem?" and he quite innocently replies, "I'm sure I do!" (4.2.434–35).

Encoded in this exchange are all the pleasures and all the anxieties necessarily provoked by performance, especially the possibility of mistaking *seeming* for *being*. But Behn takes the issue one step further. Once Galliard realizes *what* Cornelia is, that she is indeed an honest—that is, virginal—young woman, he is outraged by her *pretending* to be something other than what she seems, that is, her self-conscious projection of a false image:

> *Cornelia:* Stay and be undeceiv'd,—I do conjure ye.—
> *Galliard:* Art thou no Curtizan?
> *Cornelia:* Not, on my life nor do intend to be!
> *Galliard:* No prostitute! Nor dost intend to be?
> *Cornelia:* By all that's good, I only feign'd to be so!
> *Galliard:* No Curtizan! Hast thou deceiv'd me then? Tell me thou wicked—honest couzening Beauty!
>
> (4.2.454–60)

I

Cornelia's use of the verb "feign"—to produce a false appearance, to pretend, to dissemble—echoes the complaints about an essentially devious female nature common to the Restoration. But for actors, male and female, and for young, virginal heroines suddenly freed from male control, to "feign" can be as much a creative act as a deceitful one, for the art of acting is the confounding of "being" and "seeming," the self-conscious manipulation of the reader of signs by the producer of those signs, an act that produces a different but genuinely "honest" form of couzening beauty.

In *The Feign'd Curtizans,* this confusion of identity becomes so wonderfully complicated, so thorny, and so various that Galliard finally gives up, saying, "the game's too deep for me!" But Behn's game is deeper still. She dedicates the play to "Mrs. Ellen Gwin"— Nell Gwynn, one of the most famous Restoration actresses. In writing the dedication, Behn feigns again, this time by adopting the voice of a male admirer of Gwynn and dishing up compliments to her in nearly rapturous discourse: "you never appear but you glad the hearts of all that have the happy fortune to see you as if you were made on purpose to put the whole world into good Humour, whenever you look abroad, and when you speak, men crowd to listen with that awfull reverence as to Holy Oracles or Divine Prophesies" (86–87). Compliments fit for a Greek goddess are launched not only at a most accomplished Restoration actress but also at a performer infamous in the conduct of her personal life: as the King's publicly acknowledged mistress, she was called "the Protestant Whore."[1]

In these moments, the double bind of female identity, in particular, exceeds the theatrical space, for women's sexuality was never authorized to be a public spectacle, even though both Gwynn and Behn self-consciously exploited that prohibition. Jane Spencer makes explicit the equation of the actress and prostitute in the late seventeenth century: "the vizard or mask worn by the prostitute was synonymous with her: In the Restoration, a courtesan was a mask. So, of course, is an actor. . . . In the perception of the original audience, then, the feigned courtesan was being played by a real one" (98–99). As Laura Rosenthal has so elegantly pointed out, of course, the majority of Restoration actresses were *not* actually practicing prostitutes.[2] Instead a powerful and persuasive discourse, focused on the actresses' reputed sexual activity, was invested in publicly positioning them as "women for sale." Catherine Gallagher sees the same equation deployed against the female playwright: "the poetess, like the prostitute, is she who 'stands out,' as the etymology of the word 'prostitute' implies, but it is also she who is masked. . . . the prostitute is she who stands out by virtue of her mask" ("Masked" 22). In her compliment to Gwynn, Behn as usual manages to have it both ways: she positions a most notorious mistress as a goddess and an oracle, in a panegyric that both mocks and enacts the opportunity for the feigning of identity during the late seventeenth century.[3]

Restoration drama displays a very nearly compulsive interest in these kinds of newly minted identities. The degree to which the "natural" and the "performative" were intermingled in mid-seventeenth-century political discourse can be seen in Hobbes's famous definition of "a person," which has a decidedly theatrical cast:

> The word Person . . . signifies the disguise, or outward appearance of a man, counterfeited on the Stage; and sometimes more particularly that part of it, which disguiseth the face, as a Mask or Visard: And from the Stage, hath been translated to any Representer of speech and action, as well in Tribunalls, as Theaters. So that a *Person,* is the same that an *Actor* is, both on the Stage and in common Conversation; and to *Personate,* is to *Act,* or *Represent* himselfe, or an other. (112)

That identity can be shaped and changed, represented and acted, that it does not inhere in the very cells and fibers of the body, is a commonplace in scholarship of the last few decades.[4] Some scholars argue that disruptions in family in particular and in location more generally were the genesis of rapidly changing premodern notions about identity. In this model, an individual once had a defined and recognizable location in "all-encompassing and rigid social structures" like class and the family, according to Steve Pile and Nigel Thrift. When such traditional structures began to shift, however, it became a normal part of life to question identities, "to construct them reflexively rather than simply recognize them"; as a result, "social conflicts [were] no longer seen as just the epic clash of antagonistic social blocs but as a distributed deconstruction and reconstruction of social identities" (9). Stephen Greenblatt offers arguments drawn from historical and literary contexts to give us the powerful language of "self-fashioning" to describe the sixteenth century's "increased self-consciousness about the fashioning of human identity as a manipulable, artful process" (*Renaissance* 20), while Marjorie Garber's energetic *Vested Interests* provides a quite useful term to describe the moment that surrounds metamorphoses in identity, "category crisis"—"a failure of definitional distinction, a borderline that becomes permeable, that permits border crossing from one (apparently distinct) category to another" (16).

I contend, in the analyses that follow, that the Restoration theater responded to and provoked an extraordinary number of category crises throughout the period under examination here, 1656–1707. Through the constant manipulation of the signs of identity, playwrights and their characters disrupted, displaced, and transgressed a host of comfortable and commonplace assumptions about the stability of identity. That some scholars are quick to see these boundary crossings as subversive and liberatory is certainly attractive and often correct, but we must also be mindful that it is in the policing and reinforcing of the boundaries that the categories actually achieve their stability, if not their coercive rigidity. Thus, while boundary crossings may illuminate the edges of the frontier, they also serve to mark the walls that limit and sometimes exclude.

Theatrical Bodies:
Nation, Gender, and Status

My focus in what follows is identity as it is displayed, deployed, and enacted in the theater of the late seventeenth century, and that means a look at bodies. Bodies onstage move through space in a particular, controlled, and consciously deployed fashion; voices are inflected for the given moment; and gestures are offered up within a communally understood series of significations that accompany or create tension with the language offered by playwright.[5] But bodies themselves need to be situated within changing, and thus unstable, historical contexts—especially as these contexts had a powerful influence on questions of status and gender, definitions of Englishness, and even what it meant to be a person in the late seventeenth century. In this chapter, I look at the way identities are defined and contained by definitions of nation, gender, and status. Moreover, I investigate bodies—as they become objects acted upon by the newly powerful forces of cultural change—whose identity depends upon being disciplined, gazed at, and clothed in the early modern era. Most troubling and, for some, most potentially liberating are those identities whose bodily surfaces exist at odds with that individual's—reputed and invisible—interior life, an internal identity beginning to be valued as the only "authentic" identity, but an identity that loses its authenticity the moment it is articulated and thus brought to the body's surface.

Working from the premise that bodies generally are neither purely subject nor object—that they stand at "the threshold through which the subject's lived experience of the world is incorporated and realized," according to Lois McNay (98)—my analysis grows out of recent scholarship in literary theory, history, and anthropology, including the work of Norbert Elias, Mary Douglas, Pierre Bourdieu, Peter Stallybrass and Allon White, and most especially Michel Foucault, scholars who have taught us to denaturalize the body, to see it as part of larger cultural and historical processes.[6] These scholars, interested in what Lori Hope Lefkovitz calls the "changing cultural definitions of bodily limits, integrity, transgressions, sexuality, and violation" (12), each supply an element essential to the investigation.

Norbert Elias and Mary Douglas treat the issues of control and the "civilizing" of behavior—especially through the leverage of shame and impurity—of the early modern subject. Elias notes that, during the early modern period, the customs, behavior, and fashions from court were "continuously penetrating the upper middle classes." This in turn compelled those above to further refinement and development of behavior, while those below were required to increase their vigilance in policing "correct" behavior. The result was "an advance of the threshold of embarrassment and shame, as 'refinement' or as 'civilization'" (101). Indeed it is in body management, Foucault's powerful notion of "discipline," that early modern culture separates itself from previous eras:

> The historical moment of the disciplines was the moment
> when an art of the human was born, which was directed
> not only at the growth of its skill, or at the intensification
> of its subjection, but the formation of a relation that in the
> mechanism itself makes it more obedient as it becomes more
> useful, and conversely. What was then being formed was a
> policy of coercions that act upon the body, a calculated
> manipulation of its elements, its gestures, its behavior. (182)

Pierre Bourdieu extends our understanding of the processes by which such changes can occur when societies emphasize "the seemingly most insignificant details of *dress, bearing,* physical and verbal *manners*": by treating the body as a memory, societies "entrust to it in abbreviated and practical, i.e., mnemonic, form, the fundamental principles of the arbitrary content of the culture. . . . The whole pedagogic reason lies precisely in the way it extorts the essential while seeming to demand the insignificant"[7] (94–95). It is the body "at the threshold of cultural activity, of subject formation and signification," as Kelly and Von Mucke describe it, that requires further investigation; it is the body's material and discursive character, "subjected to the orders of civilization and discipline" and "its survival within that discursivity as a kinetic potential," that remains to be fully understood (4). I hope that through the analyses that follow—focused on approximately fifty years of theatrical representations drawn from plays written by both male and female playwrights and concentrating on the identities of aristocratic, gentry, or trading British men and women as well as the identities of national "others"—that our understanding of the ways early modern culture shaped, manipulated, distorted, and deployed the body in the service of identity will be extended and deepened.

An investigation of the late-seventeenth-century theater requires a look at identities within their particular historical context, and that means an understanding of seventeenth-century published plays, gossip about players, reviews of productions, and accounts—both historical and contemporary—of an era undergoing large-scale social, political, and cultural changes that created differences both ontological and epistemological for early modern individuals. These changes, which had a profound effect not only on the subjects treated by the theater but also on the audiences that frequented it, produced what I think of as a century of "increases": increased information about "new" parts of the world; increased knowledge drawn from a burgeoning "news" and print culture that supported the production of the first celebrity culture; increased wealth for a wide range of English citizens, especially wealth generated through rapidly expanding imperial adventures that gave access to the signs of status and cultural capital once exclusively possessed by the aristocracy to a newly diverse group of individuals; and increased mobility, especially a movement to cities, with the concomitant loss of an individual's local identity markers but with an increase in the possibilities for the feigning and fashioning of identity that newfound anonymity produces.[8] Theodore Leinwand describes the shift as a movement toward greater uncertainty and potential, "from status to contract, sacred to secular, ascription to achievement, finite to open, fixed to contingent, use to exchange, bounty to profit, feudal to (nascent) capitalist" (1), changes that disrupted the ways individuals conceived of themselves.[9]

"A seafaring nation has perforce an international personality," John Reeve proclaims (303). New notions about the elasticity of identity come, in part, from this new "place" of England in the European world and from the new cosmopolitanism that emerged in England during the time. In the years between the James I and James II, according to Margaret Ferguson, England went from being "a small island nation seeking to whittle away the monopolies that Spain and Portugal held on New World treasure—a whittling that occurred partly through the efforts of state-supported buccaneers such as Sir Francis Drake and Sir Peter Hawkins—to enjoying, in Eric Williams's phrase, an 'astounding commercial efflorescence' based on the Negro slave trade and Caribbean sugar production," trade that moved from England to Africa to the Caribbean and back again to England (163). As England's international personality took shape during the Restoration, the later stages of European imperialism—post–encounter and conquest, with its active forms of colonization, featuring all their concomitant violence—had a powerful influence upon the metropolitan stage, including the bodies that inhabited it and the texts they performed.[10] Bodies and embodiment, especially in relation to questions of power, take on special significance in this colonial context. Empire was "a significantly corporeal process," according to Leigh Dale and Simon Ryan, one constructed by the travelling of European bodies, the settlement of "new" places during and after Columbus's discovery, a movement that involved "the greatest migration of bodies ever recorded" and the attempted control, through observation and cataloging—and, I would add, sometimes the actual restraint and even murder—of indigenous bodies (2). During the Restoration, a second essential step in the colonial project was instantiated, one that requires that the conqueror return home, bearing not just material objects—the flora and fauna—that serve as evidence of a new world, but tales of human beings and their differences as they are encoded in those material objects, once wielded and worn by indigenous peoples and now returned to the metropolis as objects of scrutiny and even scientific inquiry. European bodies, as a result, experienced new sensations, and the indigenous bodies became sites of fascination, repulsion, and resistance to European invasion.

The bodies of less foreign "others"—more-local European imperialists—also took on greater significance during this time. In particular, Spaniards and Turks (who were often elided or confused with Moors who were themselves often elided or confused with American Indians) formed the locus of English anxieties about what constituted the proper imperial identity, although each is represented in a very different register. It is also in the representations of these national others that the differences between the imperialism of the English Renaissance diverges from the English colonialism of the Restoration. For instance, during the sixteenth century, Spaniards—"at once, an authority to be followed, a villain to be punished, and a rival to be bested" in New World imperialist ventures, according to Louis Montrose—were proximate figures of otherness. Catholic, Latin, and Mediterranean, Spaniards were "spiritually, linguistically, ethnically, and ecologically alien," while at the same time, England and Spain were equal participants within European systems of economic, social, and political structures and forces. Accordingly, their relationship complicated any simple binary distinction between Old World and New: "The sign of the Spaniard in English discovery texts simultaneously mediates and complicates any simple antimony of European Self and American Other" (194). Jean Howard sees the relations between these two countries during the early seventeenth century as antagonistic but fraternal: even though the Spanish were positioned as the antithesis of the English, they were "also constructed *in relation* to the English in a way that suggests a subterranean fraternal bond between the two nations, a bond defined precisely by rivalrous antipathy" (111).

Throughout the latter half of the seventeenth century, the Spanish remained figures of powerful interest and keen suspicion, even though their imperial might was clearly waning in the face of Dutch economic ascendancy, intense French imperialist activity, and growing British sea power. Michael Duffy's examination of eighteenth-century print culture is useful in this context. He claims that, during the first half of the seventeenth century, the Spaniard was "the foremost foreigner." Fears about Spanish imperial might held over from the Renaissance, even after the defeat of the Armada, still lingered. Especially lamented was the Spanish monopoly in the New World, reports of their cruelty promulgated in Black Legend discourses, and their suppression of the Protestant Dutch. More powerful was the standard complaint about Spanish aggression: they were perceived as dedicated to the creation of a "universal monarchy," and a Catholic one, that would allow them "whole possession of the world," according to Puritan pamphleteer Thomas Scott (23). These political threats translated into three Spanish character "deficiencies" most often cited by the English. First was their pride, especially as it was symbolized by their cloaks and ruffs, which themselves symbolized the Spaniards's being lost, mentally, in a world of their past grandeur. Second was their torpor, a laziness that contributed to their decline and allowed them to think they had a right to live off of plundering others. Third and last was their obstinacy, a refusal to admit a loss of power that often subsequently provoked Continental political instability—their allowing the Bourbons, for instance, to assume the Spanish throne (Duffy 26). Daniel Defoe, in 1730, is quick to point to these same Spanish deficiencies and to gloat a bit about the shrinking might of Spain: "the Spaniards tho' an indolent Nation, whose Colonies were really so rich, so great, and so far extended, as were enough even to glut their utmost Avarice; yet gave not over, till, as it were, they sat still, because they had no more Worlds to look for; or till at least, there were no more Gold or Silver Mines to discover" (*Plan* xii).

In the last days of the seventeenth century, however, conditions had significantly altered. Spain was a country with a king but no heirs, and the choice of the king's successor would affect the power structure of the entire continent, for the French Philip Bourbon was a leading contender. The specter of a unified set of French-controlled territories—territories that included not only Spain but also northern Italy, the Spanish Netherlands, as well as parts of Central and South America—filled England and her allied states (Austria, the Netherlands, various German states, and ultimately

Savoy and Portugal) with dread. Most important, however, Whig factions wanted to open up and protect markets blocked by the French, not only in Europe but in the Americas. Linda Colley reports on the success of the colonies during the first part of the eighteenth century, the growing value of their assets and thus the powerful inducement to keep markets open:

> Imports from North America increased almost fourfold in value in the first half of the century, West Indian imports more than doubled in the same period, while the amount of tea shipped into the country by the East Indian Company (as distinct from by the smugglers who brought in a great deal more) increased more than fortyfold from some 67,000 pounds weight in 1701 to close to three million pounds fifty years later. (69)

When in 1700 Louis XIV accepted Philip Bourbon as King Philip V of Spain, war was effectively ensured. British aims became to preserve Holland from the French, safeguard their own Hanoverian kings (Louis recognized exiled James III, "The Old Pretender"), and protect British trade with Europe and the Americas. Jeremy Black summarizes what was at stake this way: "for England, the Protestant succession was involved; for the United Provinces, the prevention of Bourbon control of the Spanish Netherlands; and for both, colonial and commercial considerations, especially West Indian trade" (51). The war ended in 1713, with the signing of the Treaty of Utrecht, which left Philip V on the Spanish throne, according to Hill, "with an assurance that the French and Spanish crowns would never be united. The Dutch recovered most of their barrier fortresses. France abandoned The Pretender and recognized Hanoverian succession. . . . English merchants were to trade with Spain on equal terms with French merchants" (Hill, *Century* 260). Thus while it might appear that a European matter— the Spanish crown—was the preeminent issue at stake in this war, a closer look reveals that the war was actually a contest fought over a global issue: control of trade to the New World and the colonies. In this the English were clear winners: as the "commercial victors [who] also gained a foothold in America through securing the slave-trade *asiento*," the monopoly on slave-trading in Spanish-held territories in the Americas, the British effectively assured conditions that would lead to the building of a global empire, according to Henry Kamen ("Spanish Succession" 697). Or, as Peggy Liss puts it, "After Utrecht, Britons would increasingly seek more, and direct, trade with Spanish America. Commerce, rather than territorial expansion, would become the official desideratum in regard to Spain's colonies in American and to Britain's own as well" (5).

Turkey, on the other hand, presented a different problem to the British. Not a remote country, strange to the English, Turkey was a place with which many Britons were well acquainted, according to Nabil Matar: throughout the period extending from the accession of Queen Elizabeth I in 1558 until the death of Charles II in 1685, the English and other Europeans met Muslims "from the Atlantic Ocean to the Mediterranean and Arabian Seas" (*Islam* 2). Europeans had traveled to Turkey for centuries, as pilgrims on their way to Palestine or, increasingly throughout the late medieval and early modern period, as traders and merchants.[11] Muslims were also "real" in a physical and linguistic sense to northern Europeans, according to Matar, for they represented "the most widely visible non-Christian people on English soil in this period—more so than the Jews and the American Indians, the chief Others in British Renaissance history"[12] (Islam 1). Thousands of Turks and Moors traveled to England during the early seventeenth century, and the English were acquainted with the literature, culture, and religion of Turkey through travel books and histories—especially monumental histories such as Richard Knolles's *Generall History of the Turks* (1603) and Paul Rycaut's update of that same text, *The Present State of the Ottoman Empire* (1666).[13] Indeed, Paul Coles has argued that sixteenth-century Europeans were much more eager for information about Turkey and the Ottoman Empire than they were for similar studies about the New World (152). In part because of the exotic allure in contemporary descriptions of Turkey, a group of men, called "rootless and socially disinherited" by Coles, was prepared "to cross the racial and, if necessary, the religious frontier" in pursuit of the profit and the power that Turkey seemed to promise:

The Turks practiced a high degree of religious toleration, whereas European governments did not. The Turkish military and economic systems provided men of obscure origin with avenues of rapid social and political advance, whereas Europe did not. The Ottoman empire was a lavish provider of booty for daring and resourceful employees. (154)

Beyond the sweeping survey of the important rulers in Turkish history—such as Tamberlaine, Bajazet, the Basses Ibrahim and Amurath—Richard Knolles includes in his history of "the glorious Empire of the Turks, the present terror of the world" (1), not only details of battles waged between Turks and Spaniards and other "Christians" but also more detailed and gruesome stories of Turkish bloodthirstiness:

> Whilst Solyman [the Magnificent] thus lay at Buda, seven bloudy heads of the Bishops and greatest of the Nobility (slain in the late battle at Mohatchz) were presented to him, all set in order upon a wooden step: wherat he smiled, to see his courtiers laying their right hands upon their brests, and bending their bodies as if they had done them great obedience, to salute them by name, and in derision to welcome them by the names of valiant Popes. (603)

Paul Rycaut, on the other hand, presents a somewhat more contradictory image of the Turks in the dedication of his *Present State of the Ottoman Empire,* written nearly 50 years after Knolles and containing a description of the Turks as both more barbarous and less savage than earlier descriptions would make them:

> This Present, . . . may be termed barbarous, as all things are, which are differenced from us by diversity of Manner and Custom, and are not dressed in the mode and fashion of our times and Countries; for we contract prejudice from ignorance and want of familiarity. . . . [the Turks, as] men of the same composition with us, cannot be so savage and rude as they are generally described. (qtd. in Heywood 40)

In part because of English familiarity with these kinds of images, the Turkish people, the Ottoman empire, and the Muslim religion together "formed an ever-present and fascinating or terrifying spectacle" (33) for early-seventeenth-century Europeans, according to C. J. Heywood.

Turkey also presented to the Western imagination powerful and very different images of women—both Turkish and "Christian"—

whose lives, while utterly circumscribed, were also reputedly shaped by the sensuous pleasures of the harems as well as the political power of their sultans, a mixture that always made for exciting and usually violent domestic turmoil and for stories eagerly consumed by Europeans. Richard Knolles records a typical narrative of one sultan's obsessive jealousy and the suffering of his innocent Greek wife. Carried by her first husband into battle "as his greatest treasure and chief delight," she fell into the hands of the Turks after he was slain. The Great Bassa, "surprised with her incomparable beauty" and seeing that she exceeded the rest of the captives "as doth the Sun the lesser stars," became "amorous": "Where finding her outward perfections no less graced with inward vertures, and her honorable mind answerable unto her rare features, took her to his wife honoring her far above all the rest of his wives and concubines." The honeymoon was short-lived, however, for "long lasteth not the summer fruit of wanton love, blasted most time in the blossom, and rotten before it be wel gathered": the Bassa, "after the manner of sensuall men," became insanely jealous of her. At length, she tired of his accusations and planned a secret escape, unwisely enlisting the aid of her eunuch who reported her plans to the Bassa. A bloody end followed: "[the Bassa] therwith inraged, and calling her unto him forthwith in his fury, with a dagger stabd her: so together with the death of his love, having cured his tormenting jealousies." And the tale ends with this cautionary verse:

> If feature brave thou dost respect, thou canst none fairer see
>> Nor in whose chaste and constant brest could greater graces lie.
> But whist mismatcht, she liv'd to mourne, inthral'd to jealous brain,
>> Unhappy she, with cruel hand was by her husband slain.

(557–58)

Unlike the Spaniards, with whom the British waged overseas wars, the Ottoman empire presented a very real, and abiding, military threat, much closer to home. As Bernard Lewis notes, the threat posed by the Turks was perceived as twofold: "a challenge to Christendom from the rival Muslim faith, and a menace to

Europe of conquest and incorporation" into the empire (72). In actuality, there were few European converts to Islam, and by the time of the Reformation most Europeans understood that the Ottoman empire presented a much greater military and political threat than a religious one. Historically, once the Turks entered the European mainland, they earned one military victory after another: from bases in the Balkans, during the fifteenth century, they could threaten Italy, and by 1529 they had laid siege to Vienna, an encounter that ended in a stalemate, even though the Turks occupied half of Hungary, including Buda. In part, it was because they *were* so successful that they had trouble running an efficient empire from a remote and central location. By the late seventeenth century, the time period that most concerns us in this study, the balance of power had begun to shift away from the Ottoman empire and toward Europe, even though the Turks were still engaged in some territorial expansion: in 1664, they took Crete and, in 1676, seized part of Poland. Beginning in 1682, they undertook a long war with the Russians, Poles, and Venetians, and even though, in 1683, they marched to the gates of Vienna, this time they were resoundingly defeated. Subsequently, they began a slow retreat that culminated in the loss of the Ukraine to Poland, Hungary and Transylvania to Austria, and Morea to Venice in the 1699 Treaty of Carlowitz[14] (Davidson 74–75). Paul Rycaut's *Present State of the Ottoman Empire* predicts just such a "decline" of Turkish empire: "This might body would burst with the poyson of its own ill humours, and soon divide it self into several Signories, as the ambition and power of the Governours most remote from the Imperial Seat administered them hopes and security of becoming absolute" (qtd. in Heywood).

Thus the Turks were a military rival equal to, and sometimes greater than, the European forces they encountered, and thus they were never perceived as a potential target of British imperial desires. As Nabil Matar notes, throughout the sixteenth and early seventeenth centuries—while the Spanish, Dutch, French, Portuguese, and British were conquering indigenous peoples from the Pacific to the Atlantic—Islamic military power "pushed the Ottomans and their North African satellites (the regencies of Tunisia, Tripoli [Libya], and Algeria) along with the 'Empire' of Morocco beyond the Mediterranean and as far as the wall of Vienna and into the English Channel" (*Islam* 2). Knolles complains in 1603 of just such Turkish raids in British territories:

> The Pyrats and Renegadoes of Algier, Tunes, and Sally (whose actions the grand Signior protecteth, though not their person, leaving them in that point of safety to them- selves has distasted [*sic*] the Christians of late very much, especially our English, by committing divers outrages on the Western coasts of England, as also on the South South West and West of Ireland, where they adventured to make some inroads, and have carried away much cattle and people for slaves, burning diverse Villages. (30)

Indeed in the 1620s and 1630s, British men and women were held captive in Ottoman territories—approximately 3,000 British cap- tives were held in Algiers—while the Turks continued to attack British ships in British waters: 1634 saw two barks captured off the Isles of Scilly, and in 1636 thirty-six ships from England, Scotland, and Ireland were taken, as well as four hundred captives. Even as late as the 1660s and 1670s, and after the British navy had become a real force to be reckoned with, still hundreds of captives re- mained behind in Algiers (Matar, *Islam* 3–7). Daniel Defoe, al- ways the greatest proponent of the benefits of trade—at least for England—will complain that "the Romans (like the Turks in our Time) were no Friends to Trade; they carry'd on their War for Glory" (312); he was probably remembering their successes in plundering British ships when he writes,

> The Turks have very little inclination to Trade, they have no Gust to it, no Taste of it, or of the Advantages of it; and being a rapacious, cruel, violent, and tyrannic People, void of all Industry or Application, neglecting all Culture and Improvement, it made them Thieves and Robbers, . . . they fell to roving upon the Sea; they built Ships, or rather, took Ships from others, and ravag'd the Coasts, landing in the Night, surprising and carrying away the poor Country People out of their Beds into Slavery. (319)

Looking at both Spain and Turkey together allows us to see more clearly the vital distinction that begins to develop during this time between "imperial" and "colonial" ventures. Imperial ventures produced "empires" that required, for their realization, adventurers possessed of a high degree of status or a class ranking above the middling sort. The English needed only to look south and east—toward Rome of old or the history of the Ottoman empire—to find the "romance" of empire. Spaniards, in more-recent days, *believed* that they could effect a New World empire in this old style, thus they called their New World holdings "kingdoms" and fashioned themselves as conquistadors. The English initially looked jealously, skeptically, and avariciously toward Spanish successes in building such New World empires. But, by the end of the seventeenth century, it was becoming clearer that even though the English had entered the *imperial* arena in a "belated" fashion, to use Louise Montrose's word, they were leading the *colonial* charge: merchants turned their gazes south and west as they worked to manage and administer colonial ventures dependent on capital generated by both aristocrats and merchants but vested in the hands of Citizens and bankers, men of middling, not aristocratic, status.

Africa and America present an even more interesting problem in this context, for they each held native inhabitants whose images were a source of anxiety and desire for Europeans, and thus both Moors and Indians play an important part in this analysis. Northern African and Moorish peoples were historically allied with Spain, as the first stop on Spanish crusades and in the constant warfare over Granada, but they are also inhabitants of the land that was to become one primary source of European slaves transported west to the colonies. Interest in Africa in the seventeenth century ran high in England, as evidenced by the lavish printing of John Ogilby's *Africa: Being an Accurate Description of the Regions of Egypt, Barbary, Lybia and Billedulgerid, the Land of the Negroes, Guinee, Ethiopie, and the Abyssines.* In chapters filled with promised details about the "customes, modes, and manners, languages, religions, and inexhaustible treasures" of Africa, Ogilby creates a portrait of Africa that moves, generally although not exclusively, from the Barbary North—a landscape filled with Muslim peoples of "tawny"-colored skin whom the author finds attractive and fascinating—to the tip of Africa and the Hottentots, whom the author finds physically unattractive, even repulsive, barbaric in their clothing and deportment, and possessed of very dark black skin. Thus the beginnings of a more modern form of racism can be traced to these kinds of distinctions.

A fascinating series of confusions and displacements—of geographical and national identities of Moors and American Indians—began to emerge during the late sixteenth and early seventeenth century. Once the English found themselves "operating within the Europe-North Africa-North America triangle," according to Nabil Matar, they turned quite naturally to the examples of the Spaniards for their descriptive discourses, since the Spanish, even though they were England's chief European adversary, were also its chief source of information about North America and North Africa:

> The Spaniards had partly defined their national identity through their encounter with the Moors and then the American natives. Because they had been well informed about the Muslims and their history, if only because they had been fighting them for centuries, once they began the conquest of America they applied their constructions of Muslim Otherness on the American Indians. (*Turks* 98)

The English, once in contact with Indians, followed the Spanish practice of superimposition, only this time they applied descriptions of Indians to Muslims (*Turks* 99). This mixing of geographical and ethnic differences makes sense once we understand that the English would have had the opportunity to meet both Moors and Indians, not only in their countries of origins but in one another's countries. Matar's description is worth quoting at length:

> [Britons] met American Indians in North Africa as slaves who had been carried across the Atlantic by the Spaniards and the New Englanders and sold into the Muslim markets; . . . Britons met Levantines in the Mediterranean who were on their way to the Americas, . . . Britons also met Moorish and Turkish captives of Spain in the Caribbean. . . . an English writer who was familiar with Muslims remembered and superimposed them on the American Indians while another who was familiar with American Indians remembered and superimposed them on the Muslims. Neither group was perceived autonomously—each was a predicate of the other,

although they originated half a world away from each other. (*Turks* 101)

In all, these unruly other bodies (New World, European, Levantine, and African) are more often than not contrasted with the controlled body—the classical body, as Bakhtin describes it, or the English body, as the English would, in their imaginations, have it. The disciplined body, as Foucault describes it, is an object to be worked on and molded: "The classical age discovered the body as [the] object and target of power. It is easy enough to find signs of the attention then paid to the body—to the body that is manipulated, shaped, trained; [the body,] which obeys, responds, becomes skillful, and increases its forces" (Foucault 180). And the disciplined body is most apparent when positioned *against* this unruly body, for in their difference, they are mutually constituative. The civilized body, according to Dale and Ryan, was celebrated for it ability "to rationalize and exert a high degree of control over its emotions, to monitor its own actions and those [of] others, and to internalize a finely demarcated set of rules about what constitutes appropriate behaviour in various situations"; the uncivilized body, on the other hand, was represented as constrained by few behavioral norms, quick to give "immediate physical expression to emotions," and eager to "satisfy bodily desires without restraint or regard for the welfare of others" (4).

Uncivilized bodies were often assumed to be female bodies, an essential element in the evolution of new, early modern definitions of appropriate male and female behavior. Shaftesbury and Joseph Spence, for instance, felt that the difference between "manly politeness and luxurious effeminacy" was principally a matter of excess, especially considering its connotations of luxury and self-indulgence, according to Michele Cohen, and thus "excess was in total contrast to frugality, simplicity, and self-discipline, characteristics of the virtuous citizen imagined by classical republicanism. . . . Excess positioned the gentleman as effeminate, 'self-control' posited him as manly"[15] (4–5).

In the analyses below, I will demonstrate that, on the late-seventeenth-century stage, especially powerful were those moments when the new freedoms and constraints on these bodies—English or foreign (whether the European and Fraternal Spanish, French, and Dutch or the more remote Turkish, Moorish, or Indian), classical or unruly, male or female, aristocratic or middling sort—created not only confusion of all sorts of identity categories, especially in terms of status, nation, and gender, but also opportunities to reify and instantiate new, clearer, usually exclusionary limits. While "race, class, and gender" form the traditional triad of identity categories for contemporary scholars, the early modern period presents students of drama with a slightly different focus. Most scholars conclude that it was during this era that the ideal body in England was being fashioned as white, male, and English, and I would agree that such is the *telos* of the change. During the Restoration, however, bodies were valorized when they were aristocratic, male, and Protestant, while the most intensely performative, aggressively veiled, and oft "discovered" bodies were always those of women. It is therefore my contention that both status identities and gender identities were underwritten and supported by new limits on national identities, and thus all three identity categories are interinflected, each with its own early modern distinction but serving to support and contain the others. For instance, race as it is represented and constructed during the early Restoration was as much a matter of religion and geography as skin color or genetic heritage, identifications clearly revealed in the cases of the Turks, Moors, and American Indians. Definitions of Englishness were drawn by juxtaposing proper Englishness to the disreputable behavior of women, and sometimes men, from "foreign" European climes. One important category in my analysis therefore is the forging and containing of national identity, both British and beyond, as it is complicated by and dependent upon the shifting definition of gender.

"Class" is another anachronistic term when applied to the Restoration, for "status" or "rank" are the concepts most alive in the seventeenth century, protocapitalist context. I subscribe to Michael McKeon's arguments, via Max Weber, about a "status-based" culture of the seventeenth century—that is, the "life fate of men that is determined by a specific, positive or negative, social estimation of *honor*"—and its slow metamorphosis into a class-based, that is, economically determined, system: "it is precisely during this period that the traditional, qualitative criteria of honorific status were being definitively infiltrated by the quantitative criteria of socioeconomic class" (162). And, as McKeon astutely points out, this change has a decidedly theatrical cast; "status values," like deference and paternalistic care that are commonly associated with aristocratic social relations, do not lose their force in the early modern period: "On the contrary, they undergo the more elaborate sort of 'theatricalization' that is likely to occur whenever social convention is raised to the level of self-conscious practice" (169).

In order to chart these changes, we first need to investigate the mechanisms that produced the changes, that allowed for the breaching of the traditional boundaries of status, nation, and gender. The Restoration stage gives us subjects who demonstrate that individuals could be "trained" to display or enact the valorized marks of various identities, performances achieved through repetition and rehearsal. Bodies could be disciplined to produce the "performative reiteration of cultural norms concerning bodily demeanour, gestures, dress, and other instances (not always conscious) of self-fashioning," according to Susanne Scholz (8). This training —and the attempts to secure new definitions for the boundaries for gender, status, and nation—fundamentally depended on new, early modern practices of looking and increased observation, the first and perhaps the most important element that underwrites the early modern fluidity of identity, for these activities contributed to the production of a culture of surfaces, a society of spectacle, and a cult of the artificial, as scholars have variously called it.[16]

An "increased tendency of people to observe themselves and others" is a new, early modern phenomenon, according to Norbert Elias: "the new stage of courtesy and its representation, summed up in the concept of *civilite,* is very closely bound up with this manner of seeing, and gradually becomes more so. In order to be 'courteous' by the standards of *civilite,* one is to some extent obliged to observe, to look about oneself and pay attention to people and their motives" (*Manners* 78). Foucault posits that the change is governed by a more coercive "panoptican": "The exercise of discipline presupposed a mechanism that coerces by means of observation; an apparatus in which the techniques that make it possible to see induce effects of power and in which, conversely, the means of coercion make those on whom they are applied clearly visible"[17] (189). Theater in any age demands that its spectators observe and look, of course, but the number of moments when looking and observing are *staged* on the Restoration boards, when looking is performed as a dramatic and self-conscious activity generating tension and complexity within the plot, leads me to suspect that something powerful is taking place. Perhaps one of the funniest of such moments occurs when Sir Fopling Flutter, the quintessential fop, chides Dorimant for not having a mirror in his dressing room: "A room is the dullest thing without one," he laments, and when alone "in a glass a man may entertain himself" and "correct the errors of his motions and his dress" (4.2.94–104). Fops, generally, in their shunning of violence and in their "refinement, civility, and sensitivity," as Susan Staves calls it, champion and even embody the new values of increased looking, management, control, and self-discipline of male, upper-class ideals, even though they are often criticized for importing excessive foreign (usually French) influences (428).

Most powerful are these very moments when individuals, such as Fopling, begin to see themselves as objects ripe for speculation, play, and performance. Opportunities for an individual's self-conscious manipulation of the external signs of identity are events that Restoration playwrights often, even compulsively, explore and/or lament. Emerging at this time was a new importance in the relationship between the surface of the body and identity for individuals other than aristocrats—whose bodies and signs of identity were part of a complex and hierarchical system understood by people of all ranks. When the body itself begins to function as "a symbol of worth and prestige," according to Brian S. Turner, the result is a more intense concentration on the surface, "to look good is to be good," and accordingly the role played by fashion, cosmetics, and body management increases in a world given over "to displays of personal status within a competitive society where narcissism is a predominant feature" (226). This notion of the self as an image is a particularly modern one that contemporary theorists locate within a "society of spectacle," but upon examination these kinds of cultures reveal themselves to have roots deep in the early modern era.

Simon During's work to establish "a non-filiative basis for personal identity" offers a very useful phrase for describing increasingly self-conscious manipulation of identity: "self-specularisation" or those moments when individuals might become objects of widespread public attention outside of religious, state, or legal ceremonies.[18] Such ceremonial behavior was common enough for aristocrats, as McKeon's "theatricalization" of aristocratic spectacle makes clear, but self-specular practices became progressively more private throughout the seventeenth and eighteenth centuries, During argues, when aristocratic men dressed up in exotic costume in order to have their portraits painted, or in a more extreme case when George Pzsalmanzar "became" a Formosan—by dressing and performing the part, even inventing an alphabet and a language—in order to gain access to the London literary scene (62).

I would like to qualify and extend During's very useful concept to suggest that self-specularization should include not only those moments when individuals chose to make themselves appear "exotic," in seventeenth-century terms, but also those moments when individuals began to regulate, control, and police their *own* images: when individuals became self-conscious about their *own* bodies as objects of speculation liable to manipulation on the surface. One of the funniest such theatrical moments occurs in Congreve's *Way of the World* (1700) when Lady Wishfort frets about how to present herself to a man she thinks is coming to make love to her:

> Well, and how shall I receive him? . . . I'll lie—ay, I'll lie down—I'll receive him in my little dressing-room; there's a couch—yes, yes, I'll give the first impression on the couch—I won't lie neither, but loll and lean upon one elbow, with one foot a little dangling off, jogging in a thoughtful way—yes—and then as soon as he appears, start, ay, start and be surprised, and rise to meet him in a pretty disorder—yes—oh, nothing is more alluring than a levee from a couch in some confusion.—It shows the foot to advantage, and furnished with blushes, and recomposing airs beyond comparison.
>
> (4.1.17–34)

These moments combine to demonstrate Lady Wishfort's sophisticated understanding that she is performing, even in the privacy of her own dressing room, an activity that demands that she turn her own body into an object of scrutiny in the same way her "audience" would.

This definition of self-specularization would also comfortably incorporate the productive possibilities in what Catherine Gallagher calls the "self-alienation" in Aphra Behn who presented herself as a person who sacrificed the ideal of the wholly integrated woman to create a new notion of identity predicated on multiple exchanges:

She who is able to repeat the action of self-alienation an unlimited number of times is she who is constantly there to regenerate, possess, and sell a series of provisionals, constructed identities. Self-possession and self-alienation, then are two sides of the same coin; the repeated alienation verifies the still maintained possession.[19] (24)

Cornelia and Marcella, the cross-dressing heroines of Behn's *Feign'd Curtizans,* deliberately, self-consciously, and with clear understanding violate the status norms of their culture in order to win a degree of freedom denied young ladies of quality. They understand and exploit a society of spectacle and a culture of surfaces, one that "recognizes" a person's identity by the signs written on the surface and judges that person's internal worth by the same standards. That these surfaces are, by the late seventeenth century, provisional, liable to manipulation, and subject to self-conscious and self-generated transformation—a series of metamorphoses particularly modern—is a cause for both joy and anxiety for playwrights.

In order for distinctions (which produce identity and which are subject to change) to remain strong, individuals need to know how to read and interpret the meaning of the visible signs they see on display on the external surfaces of the body. Thus clothing becomes another important external marker assigned to them a certain place in the social order based on their outward appearances, according to Susanne Scholz, a social order that did not associate sartorial splendor with effeminacy but with a pronounced masculinity and significant wealth (18).

Clothing is thus "a kind of discourse," Terry Castle argues, that speaks symbolically of the human being "beneath its folds": clothing can inscribe a person's sex, rank, age, occupation—"all the distinctive features of the self" (55). That is why Dorimant, in Etherege's *Man of Mode,* can so blithely say, "I love to be well dressed, sir, and think it no scandal to my understanding. . . . [But] that a man's excellency should lie in neatly tying of a ribband or a cravat! How careful's nature in furnishing the world with necessary coxcombs" (1.1.394–400). Clothing also encodes a powerful instability in its signs, a susceptibility to exploitation that may account for "that deep contempt" in which clothing has been held in Western culture. An abiding trope for the deceitfulness of the material world, clothing is "feminine in its capacity to enthrall and mislead, it is a paradigmatic emblem of changeability" (Castle 56). The seventeenth century marked the beginnings of a mass market in clothing, according to Jessica Munns and Penny Richards, who argue that, during this time, "England pioneered the alterations in material culture that led to the growth of mass markets"; simultaneously fashion emerged as "a national concern rather than a luxury system of expression limited to the elite," for once new groups of consumers were brought into the realms of "variable appearance" a massive destabilization of the markers of social hierarchy resulted (11, 13). Calling dress "the most fleeting of the arts," Aileen Ribeiro suggests that fashion is always "quite meaningless out of historical context," for it is subject to the arbitrary dictates of novelty, the whims of fashion: "What enraged critics of dress (artists and writers)—and it still does today—was the perpetual restlessness of fashion, its urgent imperative towards the new and its hedonistic consumerism" (3). In the late seventeenth-century exchange economy, the enactment of new sumptuary laws that might contain this fluidity of identity was out of the question, since it would impede the economic markets that depended on the mercurial nature of the "fashionable" and the desire for continual novelty, the repetition of an unsatisfiable consumer impulse. Recognizing this "hedonistic consumerism," Deborah Laycock has argued that the development of public credit and a fashion industry stimulated by credit themselves seemed to contemporaries "to threaten the bases of a stable identity of personality"[20] (128).

The new economy—with its increased wealth for an increasing number of citizens whose new buying power could purchase for them material items, especially fashions, that signified identities that were, in earlier times, out of the reach of average citizens— also provoked new questions about surfaces and depths, about the relationship between representations and their value, between what we see and what an object reputedly stands for.[21] James Thompson's compelling treatment of an analogous problem, that of money and its ability to represent changing and unstable values and worth, opens with the crisis that "severely debased" English coinage produced in the last decade of the seventeenth century. This crisis led commentators to ask fundamental questions about the nature of money, including the relationship of value to representation: "are gold and silver inherently valuable[?] . . . How do coins of both base and precious metal differ from bills of exchange, which also seem to represent value? What is the difference between a bill of exchange, which was a written document describing and transferring debt, and a banknote issued by the Bank of England, which was more like a check or a draft on its stock? (17). Coinage and later "disturbing new forms of paper money" (including bills of exchange in inland trade, goldsmith's notes, banknotes, and cash notes) provoked a "semiological crisis over the concept of value": What is value and where is it located? Does it reside in the signifier itself or in its referent? Or does value inhere in some signifying process that occurs in the act of exchange? (Thompson, *Models* 17). Fluid and changeable identities—like money, credit, and the "dangerously enabling capacities" of liquid assets (35) newly available to all sorts of people as a result of the new economy—provoke similar questions about individuals in this era: is identity inherent, visible without effort on the outside of the body? Is there an invisible referent that constitutes that identity? Or does identity inhere in a dynamic, social, and constantly evolving set of human relations?

These "dangerously enabling capacities" are represented most powerfully in the early-eighteenth-century figure of Credit in the form of an "imaginary figure of a young woman, whose beauty and desirability were matched by her pronounced delicacy and fragility" (1029), according to Terry Mulcaire's very persuasive argument, "Public Credit; or, The Feminization of Virtue in the Marketplace." She claims that the figure of "an autonomous male property holder" was less important to early liberal ideology than critics have argued; instead "a complex psychological and aesthetic investment in the imagined figure of a desiring and desirable but deeply volatile female identity" had much more influence (1030). Moreover, Credit was unregulated, and that made her much more attractive and much more potentially dangerous. Defoe's *Review,* for instance, recognizes Credit's power "to turn markers of value into objects of value," as well as its power to turn money into dross; thus "Credit's symbolic femininity represents this instability not merely as a frightening volatility but also as a potentially infinite resource"[22] (Mulcaire 1033, 1035).

This instability Beth Kowaleski Wallace has described as an "aesthetics of surface" and an "aesthetics of depth," a juxtaposition that asks whether there exists, underneath or alongside of the surface image, a stable, coherent, singular self—an invisible, interior, unrepresented, perhaps unrepresentable identity not available on the visible surfaces of the body but residing elsewhere and possessing a more powerful reality than the surface.[23] Scholars of Renaissance literature, including Catherine Belsey and Francis Barker, argue for a divided or fragmented early modern self, a consciousness in conflict that is best exemplified in Hamlet's response to his mother about a division between the internal and the external: "'Seems,' madam? Nay, it is. I know not 'seems'" (1.2.79).[24] Others have insisted that the idea of a nonessential, constructed self runs counter to much early modern discourse; Gill and DiPiero are representative: "In the seventeenth and eighteenth centuries, European critics and philosophers insistently sought to uncover precisely what their modern counterparts reject: the essential kernel of humanity, that part that remains unchanged when social trappings are stripped away" (5).

In the late seventeenth century, for all this insistence on the visible signs of the appropriately disciplined and classical body, a powerful belief about interiority and the self remained, especially the invisible and insubstantial nature of that self. More important for our discussion here, however, that unrepresentable, immaterial self takes on a gendered significance in the early modern context. In her groundbreaking *Body in Pain,* Elaine Scarry has argued that an important relationship between power and the representation of the body exists, for the materiality of the body represented in narrative is inversely proportional to the power that individual wields. Those without power are "deeply embodied," while those in power "can appear, if they wish, as disembodied (and hence invulnerable) voices" (DeRitter 19). This new configuration of power relations had the most significant implications for women. The female body's associations with "corporeality, plenitudinousness, and excess, all of which have been purged from the well-tempered body of the ideal (and implicitly male) subject" (70), according to Susanne Scholz, render it a part of nature, "an object to be mastered and domesticated by the male subject, who has learned to control his 'inner' nature by exterritorializing the instance of corporeality from the contained structure of his body" (70). As a result, in the discourses centering on the human body, "corporeality was ascribed to women exclusively, while the restructured male body was no 'body' any more" (70). The result was the relegation of corporeal woman to a lesser place of value.

To put the problem of surface and depth another way, one that more accurately reflects the dilemma faced by early modern subjects, both male and female, Michael C. Schoenfeldt writes, "despite Hamlet's eloquent and psychologically necessary articulation of his own inscrutability at the corrupt court of King Claudius, the real mystery is not to announce that one has 'that within which passeth show,' but rather to try to manifest what is within through whatever resources one's culture makes available" (2). It is just this problem of exhibiting or manifesting the self through these appropriate cultural resources with which Restoration playwrights and seventeenth-century individuals struggle. Because looking activates this kind of meaning, the surfaces of the bodies are preeminent: actors' bodies in particular—their spectacular function, their heavy materiality—provoke insistent calls to look or gaze. And yet, an audience would understand that both the character and the player would come accompanied by this visual spectacle and possessed of a reputed "interiority" or "inwardness"—a self that, in its insubstantiality, was unrepresentable, no matter how many times and in how many different ways playwrights try to stage it. Katharine Maus puts the paradox this way: "inwardness as it becomes a concern in the theater is always perforce inwardness displayed: an inwardness, in other words, that has already ceased to exist" (32). Beth Kowaleski Wallace finds that in the early-eighteenth-century works of Joseph Addison and Richard Steele, "an ascendant sensibility will link aristocratic display, ostentation, sartorial splendor, and performance to the *inauthentic* self, while decorum, modesty, restraint, and—above all—the absence of performative behaviors will come to mark an *authentic,* normative, and valued bourgeois subject" (474).

I will not presume to solve the "problem" of seeming and being, of the possibility that an individual might possess an interior at odds with an exterior, that appearance might not equal reality, for that is an issue that continues to plague and to delight artists and philosophers. Instead I offer in the chapters that follow an analysis of the changing early modern circumstances to which individuals were learning to respond: while the idea of an interior, consistent, and essential but unrepresentable self remains strong, onstage characters and offstage individuals simultaneously begin to exploit the variety and richness of external material signifiers, newly available to them and no longer the exclusive province of aristocrats and their display of status through wealth. These items, flowing into a more cosmopolitan England as a result of the globalization of trade, provided a plethora of identity signals that individuals could self-consciously manipulate and deploy in hopes of producing a wished-for effect, a variety that seemed to some to threaten the status quo and thus needed to be contained or a set of new possibilities that seemed to others to free them to explore positions ripe with potential. This manipulation does not mean that an individual could *actually* control the way the receiver interprets the external markers, then or now; it means rather that a heightened self-consciousness about the choices the producer had—and the increased variety of possibilities for signification—intensified during the late seventeenth century. I offer this study as a contribution to our deeper understanding of the way the categories of status and gender must draw on the category of nation for their efficacy. I also hope that in bringing together the issues of looking and value that the power of speculation will yield greater insight into the ways the external and internal, the biological and the cultural, combine to produces categories of identity that both constrain and liberate. I contend that this approach to the new lability of identity in the late seventeenth century will produce both a more accurate and a more compelling picture of the cultural dynamics at work in early modern culture and on the early modern stage.

Identity on the Restoration Stage

I have chosen four sites of analysis rich in moments that seek to support, subvert, or regulate status, national, and gender identities: unruly, savage bodies and British colonialism; more local but still unruly European national bodies and British mercantilism; discursive female bodies and the apparent impossibility of representing female desire; and the attempt to regulate female bodies through acts of sexual assault. I have chosen these four sites because they offer up very strong object lessons in the way identity both exceeds and moves within the normative categories set up for it. And, more important, in every case, violence—whether real or discursive—is the preeminent agent deployed to contain or erase the unruly, undesirable, undisciplined excesses of each category.

The chapter that follows this one, "Imperial Identities: Encounter, Conquest, and Settlement," examines the way European encounters with the New World are represented, especially Dryden's *Indian Emperour* (1665) and his figuring of conquest as romance: the wooing of New World women by the "proper" Old World suitors. Certain native figures, whom I call "the contested woman" and "the specular woman," play essential roles in the encounter and conquest narratives, as they quickly participate in their own colonization by falling in love with the "proper" male conqueror, who may be of Spanish origin but who acts exclusively like the perfect English gentleman. The essential violence in these encounters and conquests is sheared off once romance is allowed to drive the narrative. The chapter thus treats aggression in both its global and domestic forms and, while gender is never foregrounded as the instrument of conquest, it turns out to play the vital role. The same roles for native women and English men remain but metamorphose in later treatments of New World settlement and colonization, activities very different from encounter and conquest but demanding the same degree of violence. Here Behn's *Widdow Ranter* (1689) forms the focus of my analysis and the trope of the native woman loved by an Englishman becomes not a narrative of romance but a source of British anxiety, the fear of miscegenation overcoming the romance narrative that had earlier "married" European to New World blood.

The third chapter, "National Identities: Merchants on and off the Restoration Stage," takes up questions of European national types as they are offered up as negative examples of the deficiencies of all nations save England. External markers of identity—clothing, gestures, accents—are the focus of this analysis, especially as playwrights deployed the elements to secure a desired definition of proper Englishness for men, especially in the contexts of status and gender and especially in relation to fraternal European others. Here, I concentrate on three plays—Behn's *Dutch Lover* (1673), Wycherley's *Gentleman Dancing-Master* (1673), and Pix's *Adventures in Madrid* (1706)—each with a different approach to the "problem" national others presented in an era when increased trade meant increased wealth and when increased wealth meant the possibility for rapid upward mobility, a risky outcome, according to some of these playwrights, and a matter of some liberating potential for others.

The fourth chapter, "Discursive Identities: Actresses on and off the Restoration Stage," presents an examination of the way female identity exceeds the theater when encoded as part of a new print culture that helps to form and simultaneously to undermine conceptions of the female self. Beginning with a look at the extratheatrical discourses that surrounded the actresses, and very rarely the actors, I investigate how representations of female desire—in print; in the verbal portraiture of *ekphrasis;* and in a real, historical theatrical space—attempt to uncover and display an essential female nature. Manley's *Royal Mischief* (1696) stands at the heart of this analysis, as a bold attempt to represent the unrepresentable—female desire—on the late Restoration stage. Set in the exotic realm of Turkey and exploiting all the seventeenth-century stereotypes about lusty male Turks prone to violence, the play offers up a new figure: a Turkish princess reputedly equally committed to the pleasures of looking and equally filled with desire. In the end, this desire proves to be unrepresentable, except as it inheres in an essentialized female body. These representations also performed larger cultural functions: supported by the extratheatrical discourses concerning the actresses, they serve simultaneously to bolster aristocratic arguments about an essential and abiding aristocratic identity. The print discourses, like the theatrical representations, are fixated on the bodies of actresses and perform discursive forms of violence on women's bodies; more important, they serve as a site of displacement for the culture's fears about the performability of identity in the broadest sense, as the self-conscious deployment of controlled behaviors that could threaten upper-class claims to cultural and other capital not traditionally achieved by means other than birthright.

The fifth chapter, "Monstrous Identities: Excess, Sexual Assault, and Subjectivity," presents attempts to fix and contain female behavior through the figure of the monster—as a creature of excess, a breaker of boundaries, and a threat to culturally sanctioned norms. The word "monster" is often used throughout Restoration drama to refer to a host of excessive traits and behaviors, but most especially it is an epithet aimed at men guilty of sexual assault. On the surface, therefore, the figure would seem to present an attempt to contain male identity, a desire to prohibit the excesses of male sexual aggression. A deeper examination, however, reveals the way the monster serves as an attempt to contain female identity through the use of excessive violence and aggression. The end result is a series of moments that, like the extratheatrical discourse surrounding the actresses, promises the revelation of a woman's more genuine interior, hidden, and thus more authentic self, but it is an interiority written on the surfaces of a woman's body. In this case, however, her sexualized and traumatized body is the conduit through which an audience supposedly gains that access to that interior self as the memories of the assault force the victim into a performance of that wounded interiority. Thus the traumatized body of the private woman is turned into a spectacle in the aftermath of a sexual assault, itself a monstrous spectacle. Readings in this chapter refer to a number of plays that feature attempted sexual assaults, including Shadwell's updating of the Spanish Don Juan figure, *The Libertine* (1675), but this chapter ends with an analysis of the way two women playwrights, Mary Pix and Delariviere Manley, attempt to rewrite the terror of sexual assault in the Islamic and heroic worlds of *Ibrahim, the Thirteenth Emperour of the Turks* (1696) and *Almyna: or, the Arabian Vow* (1707).

Examined from a different perspective, I look in the first half of the analysis to Spain and colonialism, European mercantilism, and redefinitions of ideal British male behavior. I do so because nation and performance, when viewed together, help us to discover just how each category serves to bolster a fragile status hierarchy. Persons of "other races," including Muslims, Mexicans, North Americans, as well as Spaniards, Hollanders, French men and women, all at a far remove from England, function to create and contain English definitions of their own nation. The problem of appropriate national behavior in turn is dependent on the working through of appropriate gendered behavior as well, especially proper male behavior. So while an Englishman must make certain that his dress is not too effeminate, and that often means "not too foreign," he must simultaneously make certain that his behavior is not too masculine, and in the seventeenth century that usually meant not too Spanish. The first part of my analysis therefore looks at the controlled and disciplined male body, outfitted in the appropriate national attire and comported in a classical, regulated, and managed fashion.

In the second part of my analysis, I focus on plays set in Levantine and Muslim cultures, most especially Turkey, and turn my attention to ways women are represented within landscapes and cultural mores that are exotic and tantalizing to Europeans. Both on and off the Restoration stage, women's bodies are treated differently from men's bodies—as uncovered and revealed, rather than clothed in the appropriate signals of status and gender, and as unruly and traumatized, rather than as appropriately managed and contained. The Turkish settings are particularly fitting for playwrights who attempt a paradoxical examination of interiority, rather than the examination of material trappings of an exotic culture felt to be unfriendly to women, only to discover that female identity returns obsessively to the surfaces of the body. Women playwrights in particular struggle, unsuccessfully, to demonstrate such subjectivity, and when it does appear it is ephemeral and subject to charges of inauthenticity, because it is uncovered and revealed. Thus the argument—that early modern culture underwent processes that empowered men through progressive disembodiment, while it disempowered women through progressive embodiment—plays out in fascinating if not actually perverse ways in these plays: attempts to locate female identity in an interior realm almost always result in the further embodiment of female identity, producing an even further disempowered condition for women, since they become even more fully materialized and corporeal in the process.

I have chosen plays that span nearly the entirety of the era from the restoration of Charles II in 1660 to the death of Queen Anne in 1714, and thus I begin with an example of a genuinely heroic play about imperial adventures in the Spanish New World, a play penned by a man and almost instantaneously one of *the* most successful heroic dramas on the Restoration stage, Dryden's *Indian Emperour* (1665). It is a play that celebrates the possibilities for English colonial expansion based on a romance that results from a powerful act of looking, a great crowd-pleasing play that supports British colonial ambitions. This book ends with a later, failed heroic play by a female playwright about a strong woman under siege from the violent impulses of a Muslim sultan, Delariviere Manley's *Almyna: or, the Arabian Vow* (1707). It is a play that attempts to make chastity a valuable but invisible heroic virtue, one so potent that it can demonstrate persuasive power over a sultan, and thus it functions as a form of wish fulfillment updated as a new female heroic; it was, unlike *The Indian Emperour,* staged only once. This movement overall indicates an emptying out of the substance of the heroic, a seemingly inexorable movement from empire to colony and from aristocratic to bourgeois, with its concomitant movement toward an interiority not available, perhaps not even particularly interesting, to the 1660s—a subjectivity that will fail to secure authenticity by the eighteenth-century—a movement from love stories to rape stories, from controlled to uncontrolled violence.

I had no plan, as I began to write this book, to include in every chapter an analysis of a play written by Aphra Behn, but her work is so infused with the pleasures and the risks that remaking the self produces, with all the joy and all the terror that self-specularization brings, that her plays became an inevitable part of each chapter. I also found the works of the women playwrights of the 1690s of special interest: when competition between the two playhouses during the middle of the 1690s provoked a need for new plays and playwrights, Delariviere Manley and Mary Pix (who, along with Catherine Trotter, comprise the Restoration triumvirate of *The Female Wits*) stepped in and produced dramas as rich as Behn's in their presentation of female characters. The works of these three women playwrights allowed me to explore the ways new boundaries expand and contract to incorporate or to exclude new selves, especially in terms of the ways class and status influence gender and national character, and to examine the ways that the theater acted as one of many new regulatory agents in the early modern world.

Staging the body draws attention to the performativity of body and its regulation. But the difficulty of tracing such a phenomenon —the regulation of practices that constantly change, the mapping of boundaries that constantly shift—is immense. Theatrical subjects, especially as they help to reflect and create "real" subjects, are even more difficult to secure in their kinetic and ephemeral nature, for onstage, something truly transformative happens: as it did for Cornelia in the presence of Galliard, feigning can become "art," a trying out of a new, perhaps "honest," identity, one that might "couzen" but would always fascinate. More important, it was a transformation of identity available to *all* spectators: offstage, female spectators sometimes visited the Restoration playhouse masked, assuming the "indistinguishable" parts of lady and prostitute; dueling men sometimes performed their swordplay to the death in the pit, all under the watchful scrutiny of the audience. These people lived in a world where the onstage contingencies of identity were easily transferred offstage, performances that both inhabited and exceeded Restoration theatrical spaces. I intend the analyses that follow to contribute to our understanding of *how* the mechanisms that secured identity functioned on the early modern stage, and I hope that the methods I have employed—the four contexts I have chosen and the common issues threaded throughout, especially the on-going examination of the parts played by Spain and Turkey, the continuing use of violence to contain and secure identity in imperial and colonial contexts, and the deployment of gender in the service of securing the boundaries of status—make a particularly valuable contribution to our understanding of the various ways that the theater staged performances of identity, the ways identity exceeds and is contained, the ways the theater provided both the codes and the processes for performing identities.

2 Imperial Identities
Encounter, Conquest, and Settlement

ENGLAND'S LEAP INTO THE IMPERIAL ARENA was accomplished over and against, even in spite of, what Louis Montrose has called "the embarrassment of England's cultural and imperial belatedness" (193). This "belatedness" is especially apparent in relation to Spain, the enemy the English most feared and derided. All English accounts of the New World, at least until the 1590s when the English could produce their own eyewitness accounts, depended on prior Spanish accounts. Walter Raleigh, for instance, could only claim to be the first Englishman to explore the Orinoco basin; he could not claim to be the first explorer. And even to accomplish his own mission, Raleigh had to depend on—and often quoted in his own account—the descriptions of the timely (that is, not belated) Spaniards. But this tactic was not without its dangers, for the Spaniards whom Raleigh repeatedly represents as "cruel and deceitful" are also the authorities on whose reports he has undertaken his own discovery; the "epistemological and ideological destabilization" in Raleigh's account, according to Montrose, arises from his need "to ground his own credibility upon the credibility of the very people whom he wishes to discredit" (192).

In order to stabilize their own accounts, to create their identity as the "appropriate" imperialists, and to discredit their greatest imperial rival, the English began to devise strategies—political, literary, and rhetorical—to deal with their historical belatedness even as they were becoming the preeminent imperialists of their own day. They began to create narratives of discovery that actually *produced* the New World for European readers, "writing that conquers," as de Certeau would have it, writing that figures the New World as a "blank, 'savage' page on which Western desire will be written" (qtd. in Montrose 182). Or as Lennard Davis puts it, "the first contact between Europeans and Amerindians in the Caribbean basin . . . represents the first full-fledged attempt to transcribe a temporal set of events, to fashion those events into a variety of 'the real,' and to think of those events in terms of a larger narrative structure" (240).

I center my analysis in this chapter around a British instance of writing that conquers, Dryden's *Indian Emperour,* a play that concerns a truly monumental meeting: Cortés's arrival, in 1519, at the heart of Montezuma's Aztec empire. *The Indian Emperour* (1665) is one of Dryden's contributions to the whole European "discovery" series, but what he gives us is an English version—in the form of heroic drama—written 150 years after the real historical event the play chronicles, a play that contains a curious appreciation of alterity in some forms but an active eradication of it in others. Alongside my treatment of this play, I offer up by way of contrast three very different instances of plays set in the Americas. The first is William Davenant's 1656 masque, *The Cruelty of the Spaniards in Peru,* a generic oddity that functions as a thoroughly propagandistic, and thus ideologically naive, treatment of both Spanish and English imperialist intentions. The second is perhaps an unusual choice: Spanish playwright Lope de Vega's *Discovery of the New World by Christopher Columbus,* a drama that dates from the 1590s and one of the very few works to treat the first European encounter with native peoples. I have chosen this play in particular because it so clearly sets up some of the first and most fundamental European terms for encounter narratives and representations of indigenous inhabitants. The third is Aphra Behn's *Widdow Ranter* (1689), a play written long after the English subsequently represented the myths of the Americas—from encounter to settlement—and a play that looks at the processes by which colonization, and the administration of both Native Americans and colonists, was effected; it is an administration that supported the entrenchment of plantation economies, forms of newly minted wealth that themselves disturbed and refined English notions of identity.

English Imperialists

Dryden's *Indian Emperour* does not take as its subject a European power's first meeting with one of many isolated Caribbean tribes, as all discovery narratives must. Rather it represents the event that is Europe's first encounter with a heretofore unimagined empire. Inga Clendinnen writes of that unprecedented event: "The conquest mattered to Spaniards and to other Europeans because it provided their first great paradigm for European encounters with an organized native state, a paradigm that quickly took on the potency and the accommodating flexibility of myth" (12)—a meeting between two civilizations that was very likely an incident of "unassuageable otherness" (41). Fittingly, Dryden's play concerning such a momentous event dates from a time when there was renewed stability in England's internal politics: Charles II had been restored to his throne, the battles over his succession had not yet heated up, and members of Parliament in concert with British merchants were gearing up to engage in yet another trade war underwritten by burgeoning imperialist possibilities. Dryden's play grows out of not the energy and anxieties of discovery and encounter but the more powerful processes of colonization, more powerful because they were a more institutionalized form of imperialism.

Because they were also belated, the English hoped that their forms of conquest and colonization might avoid the mistakes made by the first conquistadors and might exceed the "success" Spain achieved. Spain had long occupied a place of anxiety in the minds of Britains and, as the quintessential villains in the drama of the last age, the image of the Spaniard performed powerful cultural work during the Restoration. What John Reeve calls "the Anglo-European seventeenth century" was preceded in the sixteenth century by intense concern about ever-expanding Spanish power:

> The wealth, power, and ambition of Spain cast a long
> shadow over English history which did not lift until the
> collapse of the Spanish monarchy in the 1640s. Spanish
> imperial power in the Atlantic, Spanish naval and military
> force in Europe, Spanish diplomatic leverage, and Spanish
> commitment to confessional religious conflict were unavoidable facts for England. (*Britain and the World* 304)

Anthony Pagden, too, provides some vital insights: during the first decades of the sixteenth century, the modern world "had been dominated by a struggle between the three major European powers—Spain, France, and Britain—for control of the non-European world. And the main theater for that struggle had been America"[1] (2).

37

Even though Cromwell's foreign policy of focusing his attention on Spain, rather than France, has been called out-of-date, it was the right policy for a country invested in overseas expansion, according to T. O. Lloyd: Spain's empire had become unwieldy, and if its defenses could be forced it provided opportunities "for trading and for snatching a few of the less well-defended colonies" (32–33). As part of that project, in 1655, an expedition was sent out to attack Hispaniola. Since this was the first time the English government had sent a naval expedition to seize the colonies of another European nation, the navy's lack of experience led to lack of success. After their defeat, Admiral William Penn and General George Venables pulled their forces together and, as a consolation prize, captured the island of Jamaica, an action that "indicated another approach to the art of colonization, in which the government took valuable colonies away from Europeans who had reached them first" (33). The consequences of these events helped to shift the balance of power between England and Spain, according to Christopher Hill: "It was the first of the Greater Antilles to be lost to Spain, and its seizure inaugurated a new epoch in English commercial policy. Between 1640, when sugar cultivation was introduced, and 1651, the slave population of Barbados rose from 1,000 to 20,000, most supplied by the Dutch. It had doubled again by 1673, but now slaves came from Jamaica" (158).

By the seventeenth century, the English and the French began to question what had gone wrong in Spain's approach to empire building—even though its empire was still the largest, most powerful, and longest surviving of all the European empires. Spain had become, in the minds of English men and women, "a model of what an empire should not be," according to Anthony Pagden, because, like the Turks to whom they were often likened, the Spanish came to represent "inflexible, illiberal and ultimately corrupting tyranny," mainly because they did not understand the power of free trade: "Because the Spanish imperium had been grounded upon the image of a single, culturally varied political order, ruled according to a codified body of laws and founded upon a unified set of religious belief, it had always been a closed society. Free trade meant creating a polity which was potentially open to foreign political influence"—and thus heresy. In this closed position, Spain began to be seen by most Europeans as trapped in something Pagden says that we might legitimately call premodernity (116–22).

And while the English and French voyages to the Americas were largely efforts to imitate Spanish successes (one needs merely to remember Raleigh and his obsessive interest in the Spaniards who paved his way), only the Spanish settlers "formally styled themselves conquerors, *conquistadores,* and only the native-born Spanish settlers *(criollos)* would, in the end, ground their claims to independence primarily upon their association with an aristocracy of conquest" (Pagden 65).

Because Spain had founded its colonies based not upon agriculture but upon conquest and because these produced only semisacred precious metals, Spain's territories were invariably described as "kingdoms," the "Kingdoms of the Indies" (Pagden 79). By the mid-seventeenth century, the British and the French colonies in America were, on the other hand, overwhelmingly bases for trade and the production of agricultural produce, colonies generating and exporting much that was new, and colonies requiring administrative structures and additional colonists. James Thompson has argued that the shift from the figure of the Spanish conquistador to the English colonial administrator can best be seen in the character of Amanzor in Dryden's *Conquest of Granada,* for he functions not as an epic hero—as a conqueror in the old Spanish style—but as "an emblem of the military conquistador who, under the demands of a budding colonial empire, must be replaced with or translated into a new type of hero, a prototype of the colonial administrator" (211).

Dryden's *Indian Emperour* follows on the heels of a virulent anti-Spanish Commonwealth foreign policy, which itself generated dramatic treatments that featured representations of wicked Spaniards intended to justify contemporary British imperialism— policies and dramas that depended on the demonizing of the very successful and thus very threatening Spaniards for Britain's own nationalistic use of force. The supposed difference between the behavior of the Spaniards and the English drew on the tradition of anti-Spanish and anti-Catholic propaganda, sentiments that "had been fuelled by stories of Spanish atrocities during the Dutch Revolt, and by the wide diffusion of Bartolome de Las Casas's *Brevíssima destrución de la relación de las Indias* (Short Account of the Destruction of the Indies) after 1583"[2] (Pagden 87). Thomas Scanlan has even argued that the publication of Las Casas's work in England could be said "to mark the beginning of the English attempts to fashion a national identity through colonial endeavor"³ (1). Stronger still was the repugnance the English felt for those government-backed Spaniards who slaughtered thousands of innocent Indians. Pagden claims that, as a result of such actions, "the Spaniards, like the Turks—with whom they became increasingly identified in eighteenth-century Europe—had only destroyed those whose ends they should have been protecting" (88).

One of the strongest English theatrical representations drawn from the Black Legends, one with powerful arguments about the colonialist intentions of the Protectorate, is Davenant's *Cruelty of the Spaniards in Peru,* a masque first performed in 1655 and obviously indebted to John Philips's *Tears of the Indians,* itself drawn from Las Casas's *Brevíssima Relación.* Philips's text was published complete with horrifying engravings of the bloodthirsty, barbaric treatment the Spanish leveled against the Indians and included are hair-raising images of human children being roasted over open spits, and—in a weird displacement of British anxiety—the Spanish and not the Indians are rendered as the New World cannibals. Such texts underwrote the British cause of anti-Hispanism, sentiments rampant in the mid-seventeenth century and carrying on long past the time Spain presented the most powerful threat to British imperial ambitions.⁴

Early in 1656, at the time of the first performance of Davenant's masque, the successes of Cromwell's imperialist designs in the West Indies were unknown. Two years earlier, in 1654, Cromwell had dispatched Admiral William Penn and General George Venables to the West Indies ostensibly to launch a surprise attack against the Spanish there. War officially broke out in late October 1655, and Cromwell's Council of State produced, as his defense, *A Declaration of His Highness, By the Advice of his Council; Setting Forth . . . the Justice of their Course Against Spain,* a document that cited Spain's violation of both English and Indian natural rights. Two years later, at the time of the performance of Davenant's drama, the British had failed to take San Domingo in Hispaniola and had endured the occupation of Jamaica, which was still threatened by Spanish guerrillas and attacks from Cuba. The defeats were so humiliating that, upon their return home, both Penn and Venables were imprisoned for deserting their posts (Jowett 112).

Thus Davenant's 1655 drama was performed within a context that suggested that British imperial might could be something less than mighty. Or, as Janet Clarke puts it, "Davenant's representation of the defeat of the Spanish and the collaboration of the colonized Indians with the English enacts the objectives, but not the outcome, of the Western campaign" (834–35). Davenant's piece was finally produced during the last months of Cromwell's Protectorate, when the attack against Spain was located not in the New World but in the Spanish Netherlands, indicating the various displacements at work in the final production: "Davenant dislocates the scene of colonization, suppresses the rhetoric of nationhood, and omits the nationalistic and providential dimension of the English expedition. The masque is thus ideologically and aesthetically distanced from Cromwell's colonial enterprises" (Clarke 836).

For my purposes, the most important moments in the masque occur in the final scene, when the red-coated British soldiers march into the New World, followed by Peruvians "known by their feather'd Habits, Glaves [*sic*], and Spears." The "Sixth Speech" opens with a lament for the initial kind welcome that the Indians had offered to the Spaniards: "We on our knees these Spaniard did receive / As Gods, when first they taught us to believe / They came from Heaven." But shortly thereafter the Spaniards revealed themselves to be "dark Divines . . . [who] hasten us below, / Where we, through dismal depths, must dig in Mines." In sharp contrast to the brutal Spaniards exist the "valiant English," who arrive ready to free the Indians from the yoke of Spanish oppression. The final chorus rings with joy for the arrival of their English saviors:

> *Chorus:* After all our disasters
>   The proud Spaniards our Masters,
> When we extoll our liberty by feasts,
>   At Table shall serve,
>   Or else they shall starve;
> Whilst th' English shall sit and rule as our guests.

The final gesture of the masque features a Spanish soldier bowing to these red-coated English "guests," who kick the Spaniard for his trouble, which causes him to bow even lower, "whilst the English and the Indians, as they encounter, salute and shake hands in sign of their future amity"[5] (114). The scene is a powerful instance of what Anthony Pagden has called the on-going anti-Hispanist, pro-English "propaganda" campaign waged in England: "The argument that the British would be welcomed by the Native Americans as liberators, as Raleigh claimed to have been by the inhabitants of Guiana, became a staple of the propaganda war waged against the Spaniards, and on behalf of almost every British colonization project" (Lords 88). In Davenant's vision, all of the actual hostility the British did indeed encounter in their New World exploits is shorn away to reveal only a grateful Inca nation joining hands with its "liberators" to celebrate the routing of the merciless Spaniards.

"The Romance of Conquest"

Only eight years later, Dryden places himself in a very different and much more difficult position in his representations of both the Spanish and the Indians, for his encounter narrative puts him in something of a bind: the "winner" in the historical context, and thus those who would be the nominal heroes, are the people who, in 1660s England, are figured as the cruel, the avaricious, and the Catholic Spaniards. The "losers" are the indigenous natives who had produced a vast empire of their own but whose continent the English desire to possess. Thus Dryden is faced with multiple dilemmas: how to present Spain as unqualified for the imperial task and, at the same time, to suggest that England is; and how to present the natives and their land in such a way that their conquest seems, if not just, at least not punitive. I argue that he accomplishes these tasks through a series of displacements, through structures that Montrose has called "oscillations" in European accounts of the New World: "an oscillation between fascination and repulsion, likeness and strangeness, desires to destroy and to assimilate the Other; an oscillation between the confirmation and the subversion of familiar values, beliefs, and perceptual norms" (182).

Complicating this oscillation and displacement, but very much a part of the process, is the problem of commensurability—the desire, even the seeming need, of European writers to create equivalencies between European and New World practices. These writers do so in order to produce a conquest that seems predicated on equity, if not actual beneficence. Often this takes the form, as we shall see, of representations of native inhabitants who are said to possess free choice in the matter of their conquest. As a result of this native free choice, the violence of settlement and colonization—in short, European imperialism—becomes not a matter of brute European force but an enlightened decision by the natives, a more comfortable

Enlightenment position grounded in European notions of possessive individualism. These oscillations characterize Europe's competing desires as they appear in discursive treatments of encounters
with the New World and function as a series of ideological sleights
of hand: images point to agents other than those that actually effect
change.

Dryden's *Indian Emperour* does indeed oscillate between the
poles of attraction and repulsion, an anxiety about conquest that
Dryden hopes to shear away by displacing the responsibility for
conquest away from the European and on to the native.[6] The opening scenes deploy two oscillating discursive strategies for positioning the New World between attraction and repulsion: the idealizing
and the demonizing of New World land and inhabitants. Scene 1
opens with the Spanish describing the new land they see—since it
is the land they have come to discover—and the descriptions celebrate those elements the Spanish (and, through identification, the
English) most wish to possess. Cortés, the nominal hero of this heroic, opens by remarking on the novelty of their discovery in an
allegory of rebirth and private genesis:

> On what new happy Climate are we thrown,
> So long kept secret, and so lately known;
> As if our old world modestly withdrew,
> And here, in private, had brought forth a new!
>
> (1.1.1–4)

Vasques joins in to elaborate a traditional Western depiction of
an Edenic landscape untouched by anything artificial, a natural
paradise:

> As if this Infant world, yet unarray'd,
> Naked and bare, in Natures lap were laid,
> No useful Arts have yet found footing here;
> But all untaught, and salvage, does appear.
>
> (1.1.7–10)

Such remarks—about the lack of art in the Mexican landscape—
seem initially puzzling until we hear Cortés's quick response:

> Wild and untaught are Terms which we alone
> Invent, for fashions differing from our own:

For all their Customs are by Nature wrought,
But we, by Art, unteach what Nature taught.

(1.1.11–14)

On the one hand, this statement functions to redefine "difference" as a culturally and linguistically dependent term—an instance of what Max Harris suggests is Dryden's ability to appreciate alterity, to acknowledge "the existence of multiple perspectives, and in some measure to call into question the universal authority of any particular perspective" (67). On the other hand, this contrast between nature and art more strongly locates the New World on the periphery, outside the boundaries of the metropolis and its culture and thus outside all the legitimated and celebratory values that inhere there.

Such a strategy makes the land doubly attractive in its vulnerable and unspoiled state. Vasques concludes his description with a remark reminiscent of the language in Shakespeare's *Tempest,* "Methinks we walk in dreams on fairy Land"—a charming enough statement until it is followed by this surprising trope:

Where golden Ore lies mix'd with common sand;
Each downfal of a flood the Mountains pour
From their rich bowels, rolls a silver shower.

(1.1.27–30)

An excrementary metaphor concerning the source of plenty in the New World is the perfect grotesque tribute to the "work" these conquistadors are about to perform.

Yet markers that serve to undercut the unspoiled nature of the landscape are also present in Dryden's text.[7] For instance, at just the moment that the Spaniards head inland to meet Montezuma, the supposed "unnaturalness"—that is, the culture, the civilization—of the Mexican empire is betrayed in a remark made by an Indian scout traveling with the company. When asked how far to Mexico, he replies:

Your eyes can scarce so far a prospect make,
As to discern the City on the Lake,
But that broad Causeway will direct your way,
And you may reach the Town by noon of day.

(1.1.44–47)

This clearly artificial structure—one so extensive that it will take the Spanish troops hours of marching to reach the city—bears the marks, not of an Edenic purity of nature but of an extraordinary industry, the marks of an advanced civilization.

With this image of a broad highway leading to a magnificent city resonating in the minds of an audience, the second scene opens with a presentation of the second European strategy for describing New World encounters: the demonizing of the native inhabitants. The stage directions cite "A Temple," and the theatrical evidence suggests that the elaborate sets of *The Indian Queene* were recycled for this production; thus an audience, prompted to imagine the Edenic quality of the land, would very quickly thereafter experience the spectacle of the human other: standing before exotic, painted scenes, the players perform in native costumes (Aphra Behn reportedly bequeathed to *The Indian Queene* feathers and an Indian dress brought back from Suriname). A high priest of the Indians speaks first by recalling the recent completion of a bloody ritual sacrifice:

> The Incence is upon the Altar plac'd,
> The bloody Sacrifice already past.
> Five hundred Captives saw the rising Sun,
> Who lost their light ere half his race was run.
>
> (1.2.4–7)

The bloodthirsty, human-sacrificing, clearly other character of the Indians themselves is thus superimposed over the idealized landscape, an otherness reinforced once Montezuma and his court enter. Leigh Dale and Simon Ryan argue that the defining of the civilized body "opened up a space for the rationalization of colonial and imperial processes as the imposition of a series of regulatory practices that took as their focus the body of the indigene, which was identified as the site of uncontrolled ferocity, laziness, savagery, disease, and stupidity" (5). Dryden's description of "a bloody Sacrifice" and the death of five-hundred captives does just that.

Guyomar, second son to Montezuma, hastily arrives with news full of wonder. Having traveled to "the utmost limits of the land: / To that Sea shore, where no more world is found," he describes the Spanish ships, the "dreadful Shapes," he saw moving toward the land:

The object I could first distinctly view
Was tall straight Trees which on the waters flew.
Wings on their sides in stead of leaves did grow,
Which gather'd all the breath the winds could blow:
And at their roots grew floating Palaces,
Whose out-bow'd bellies cut the yielding Seas.

(1.2.107–12)

Such a description—with its own confusion of the artificial and the natural—suggests that the Aztecs are an unsophisticated and technologically backward people who have not yet made the progressive transition to culture, a fact belied by the other marks of their civilization and by the rumors of vast wealth in gold and silver. When Odmar, the elder son, boasts of having felled a "double man," it is clear that Dryden has drawn on reports from the Spanish chronicles to suggest that the Indians thought a horse and his rider one creature. The younger Guyomar describes the Spanish guns in equally naive terms: "For deaths Invisible come wing'd with fire." Dryden's use of these descriptions, coupled with the initial images of bloodthirsty sacrifice, produces a powerful, if paradoxical, image of the Aztec natives as vulnerable but still dangerous children.

But the strangest tension in this scene, and one of the most telling instances of Dryden's refusing the natives an otherness he has otherwise insisted on, results from his own formalist imperative. It is one thing to hear the Spaniards, objects of English loathing and fraternal identification, speak in rhyming couplets but quite another to hear the same language from the demonized Indians—a disjunction especially emphasized when the language serves to offer a misinterpretation of Spanish military might, as it does in the lines above. Guyomar's couplets thus oscillate between the familiar and the strange, markers that characterize all New World accounts, a language here reinforced by the contrast between the feathers and finery of New World costumes and the rhyming sameness of Old World language, the most telling instance of the making commensurate that which is obviously incommensurate.

Stephen Greenblatt's analysis of the linguistic incommensurability in the speech of the Spaniard and the Indians, as it appears in the reports from the early chroniclers, is certainly accurate: "Arrogant, blindly obstinate, and destructive as was the belief that

46

the Indians had no language at all, the opposite conviction—that there was no significant language barrier between Europeans and savages—may have had consequences as bad or worse"[8] (*Learning* 26). Inga Clendinnen offers a splendid analysis of an instance of incommensurability, and of a "bad consequence," in her description of the miscommunication that flowed between Cortés and Montezuma. She writes that Cortés certainly understood his role as that of an ambassador, and as an ambassador he appears to have been received:

> But Moctezoma, like other Amerindian leaders, communicated at least as much by the splendor and status of his emissaries, their gestures and above all their gifts, as by the nuances of their most conventionalized speech. . . . Moctezoma's gifts were statements of dominance, superb gestures of wealth and liberality made the more glorious by the arrogant humility of their giving: statements to which the Spaniards lacked both the wit and the means to reply. (To the next flourish of gifts, carried by more than a hundred porters and including the famous "cartwheels" of gold and silver, Cortés's riposte was a cup of Florentine glass and three holland shirts.) (17)

A similar instance of commensurability, this time in pictorial representations of Europeanized Indians, can be found in DeBry's engravings that accompany Las Casas's text, according to Thomas Scanlan: "By Europeanizing the Indians, DeBry implicitly suggests that the process of transforming Indian culture is possible and that it has already begun. The Europeanization also suggests that the differences between the Indians and the English are ones of degree rather than kind" (60). But I think Scanlan's most powerful comment about these engravings concerns England's desires and fears about its own imperial identity, emotions played out in Dryden's attempts to fashion the perfect English colonial gentleman and invader:

> The English desired to imagine themselves in possession of orderly colonies. They desired to imagine themselves as loved by the native people. . . . The [also] feared losing control of themselves and the colonies. The feared being attacked by the native inhabitants. They feared the very strangeness of

47

them. . . . And probably most of all, the English feared that they would arrive in the New World and become the same monsters that the Spanish had become in their colonies. (60–61)

Dryden's impulse toward a leveling commensurability, intended to dampen these fears and cultivate these desires, discussed above in terms of linguistic likenesses, functions even more strongly in the complex love plots. David Kramer describes the situation this way: "In *The Indian Emperour* the Spaniards may have cannons and swords of steel, but the Aztecs have the desirable women, the richly worked gold, and all the good lines" (80). Yet Dryden's modern editor, John Loftis, has a different opinion, suggesting in a passage worth quoting at length that the love plots are not well integrated into the larger structure of the play:

> An arraignment of Spanish atrocity in America provides a principle theme of the play, and yet that theme is conveyed by way of dramatic action turning on a series of formalized love intrigues conducted within literary conventions shared by the French romances. To be sure, the complications in the love intrigues derive from the opposition of Aztecs and Spaniards, and they are all related to the conquest of Mexico. But the connection between certain episodes— those, for example, having to do with the rivalry of Odmar and Guyomar for the love of Alibech—and the conquest is not very close. Like most heroic plays *The Indian Emperour* is less notable for its thematic coherence than for the rhetoric of its isolated scenes. (318)

I would like to argue just the opposite, that the love plots actually perform the fundamental ideological work of conquest. In their very trivialization, the love plots serve as a most powerful ideological means of shearing off the essential brutality of the invasion, of eroticizing a bloody invasion, and of obscuring the magnitude of the conquest of an entire empire by locating the process in and through a domestication of "conquest"—an act of aggression reduced to the winning of a native woman's love.

And it is here that Lope de Vega's *Discovery of the New World* drama becomes useful. Dating from the 1590s, Lope's play is one of few theatrical representations of encounter and conquest. Even though the year 1492 saw not only the Spanish "discovery" of the New World but also the Spanish reconquest of the Old—the retaking of Granada and the securing of Spanish hegemony in southern Europe—almost no playwrights chose to represent the events, neither Spanish playwrights celebrating Spain's glories nor other European playwrights writing through their fears about Spain's ambitions and militarism.[9] Lope's *Discovery of the New World* is one such treatment; massive in scope, shifting from Granada to Spain to the New World and back to Spain again (including side trips by minor characters to Portugal and England), the drama is fraught with heroic military action, including the Spaniards's defeat of the Moors and their subsequent securing of the southern Continent. But of greatest concern is Columbus's discovery of a new, unimagined land inhabited by heretofore unimagined people. Lope thus places his encounter in a doubled imperial context: a New World discovery play accompanied by Spanish Continental victory, a presaging of the very worldwide hegemony feared by other European powers, themselves at the time without the Spanish conduits to the supposed riches of the West.

Moreover, the terms for conquest are set very early in the play and resonate in the work of subsequent playwrights, including Dryden. The conquest is often represented as a particularly male activity: European men venture forth, fight other men for, conquer, and win from other men these new territories.[10] But neither Lope nor Dryden represents the conquest in traditionally male, militaristic, and heroic terms. Each invokes "the romance of conquest," to use Doris Sommer's phrase in a different context, by locating the real victory within the domestic, by eroticizing the processes of both encounter and conquest and thus erasing the violence essential to the event. Peter Hulme's remarks about first encounters are relevant in this context: "the gesture of 'discovery' is at the same time a ruse of concealment" (1). In these plays, gender is the most important mechanism that serves to conceal both the reality and the brutality of the dispossession of native land. On the surface, religion in Lope's case or justice in Dryden's case might seem to be the force that secures victory, but two figures—whom I call "the specular woman" (one who sees and is seen) and "the contested woman" (one fought over, not by Europeans but by two native men)—carry the burden of ideological concealment in this formula: it is these women who actually create the conditions for conquest, and it is their efforts that secure European settlement as they become unwitting but active accomplices in the Spanish conquest. The seeing and seen "specular" woman plays a particularly important role, for this figure provokes questions central to the issue of knowledge and its relation to power: to what extent does the gaze control, and even produce, knowledge and thus to what extent does it secure power? Mary Louise Pratt's image of the "imperial eyes" is a very useful one, especially for pointing to the ways Westerners use seeing to mean understanding, the ways Westerners see and possess simultaneously. However, sixteenth- and seventeenth-century notions of empiricism and its relationships to power function differently from those that Pratt sees at work in nineteenth-century British travelers to Africa. The only images of distant strangers available to a Restoration audience came from an earlier set of Renaissance myths about fabulous and terrifying creatures inhabiting worlds elsewhere—figures illustrated in countless Renaissance texts that must have plagued the imaginations of the initial explorers. Later, with the conquistadors, settlers, privateers, and pirates, there came imperial monopolies, trading companies, and more trustworthy sea routes. But exploration, in the 1490s, meant risking the terrors of the unseen and unimagined.

Norbert Elias argues that the civilizing process depended on human beings becoming more intense observers, partly as displacement for their own stronger emotions, and partly as a means of scrutinizing their fellow humans for the signs of meanings encoded in their behavior:

> And this living-out of affects in spectating or even in
> merely listening . . . is a particularly characteristic feature
> of civilized society. It partly determines the development
> of books and the theater. This transformation of what mani-
> fested itself originally as an active, often aggressive expres-
> sion of pleasure, into the passive, more ordered pleasure of
> spectating. (202–3)

Elias uses as part of his proof of this turn from the sensual to the specular by citing lines from La Salle's *Civilite:* "Children like to touch clothes and other things that please them with their hands.

This urge must be corrected, and they must be taught to touch all they see only with their eyes," and thus it is "highly characteristic of civilized man that he is denied by socially instilled self-control from spontaneously touching what he desires, love, or hates" (203).

The intimate relation between seeing and possessing is nowhere more powerful than in the "romance of conquest," the act whereby the playwright displaces the processes of conquest from the actual invasion of territory to a more benign representation of the "conquest" of one's beloved, a conquest accomplished over and through the bodies of women. Indeed, the figure of the specular woman, the one who is seen and sometimes sees, appears in Lope's play as the very first native inhabitant the Spaniards actually encounter: she is a woman named Palca. Lope's representation of the first encounter is not a man-to-man, hand-to-hand contest but a chance meeting between a group of homesick and hungry Spanish sailors and a lone native woman. Columbus, upon spying the first inhabitant of this unimagined world, says to his men, "I shall try to make friends with her by offering presents"" (33). He then addresses her in a symbolically rich series of statements: "We are men; do you not see us? Speak! Take! Take these! Wait!" Her silence prompts him to question her ability to see, to understand: "Do you not see us?" And finally her stillness, her self-containment, goads him into impatient peremptory commands: "Speak," "Take," and "Wait" (33).

Palca, for her part, responds with sentiments that say more about European male fantasies concerning native women than about the sophistication of Caribbean inhabitants: "They are men, and fine looking; they appear worthy to be loved. They make signs. If they ask my name I shall answer . . . Palca" (33). To give Lope credit, he not only recognizes but also attempts to recreate the language barriers that existed between these entirely unfamiliar peoples. He "solves" the problem by producing a discussion whose *content* concerns the mutually incomprehensible speech between the Indians and the Spaniards:

Palca: If they ask my name I shall answer . . . Palca.
Bartholomy: Is it the name of a king, a man; is it the land? Is it war or peace?
Palca: Does the Senor ask for Cacique Dulcan-Quellin?

51

Columbus: We are not able to understand her, for, after all, it is a heathen language.
Bartholomy: Doubtless *Cacique* means they have something to eat; and *dulcan* that we will be well received. . . .
Palca: No doubt they are asking if there is another lord on the island as great and powerful. I shall answer: "Yes, Tapirazu."
Arana: She looks toward the interior of the country as if to say we would find something to eat. *(To Palca, making signs to her.)* You have something to eat, have you not?

(33–34)

This funny set of exchanges displays a deeper significance: Palca thinks that all the statements the Spaniards make refer to questions of her *cacique,* her chieftain, so she thinks they are engaged in a discussion of questions of authority and power. The Spaniards, on the other hand, all surmise that her statements refer to food—since they are ravenously hungry after a long sea voyage. In the end, signs and gestures, and an odd dialogic quality that produces only dissonance, suffuse this first encounter.

Columbus, less concerned with his body's hungers, wants to feed his curiosity. In that desire, he positions himself as "the seeing man": "This woman will bring us other natives of the country. I should like to study their customs, their power" (34). As the seeing man, Columbus assumes the empiricist's imperative: to study, to look, to learn through seeing; as the seeing man, his "imperial eyes passively look out and possess" (Pratt 7). The seeing man also functions as the main protagonist of what Pratt's calls "anti-conquest" narratives: that is, "strategies of representation whereby European bourgeois subjects seek to secure their *innocence* in the same moment as they assert European hegemony" (7). Columbus's eagerness to study the natives' customs appears benign, while his desire to scrutinize their power registers a potentially more sinister intent.

But then, in one of the strangest moments of the play, he commands Palca to perform on *herself* the very activities he intends to undertake. While commenting to his sailors on her naivete, he hands her a *mirror:*

Now show her a mirror; give it to her, and a string of bells.
[To PALCA] Take it, look at it.

She is not very clever at handling it; she looks at the back of
it. Turn it on this side, and see yourself in the light.

(34)

This scene functions, through the symbolic power of a theatrical
prop, to suggest that the natives, brought into European light, will
finally see who and what they really are. The inevitable conclusion
an audience must reach is that the identity of the natives is not
something the Europeans need ask for—as Palca presumes they
will. It is rather something the Spaniards come bearing as a gift.
This "specular woman," seen and made to do the seeing, paves the
way for Spanish settlement when her initial fear gives way to interest in her conquerors, an interest reinforced after she is presented
with and after she sees a new vision of herself.

In Dryden's case, the conventions of heroic drama, coupled with
the complexity of the love plots, make the process of "domestic
conquest" seem less ideologically transparent than Lope's, even
though the displacement performs more powerfully for it. The
Indian woman who functions as Dryden's "specular woman" is
Cydaria, daughter of Montezuma. She emerges as the immediate
object of desire during Vasques's reading of the *Requerimiento* and
carries the burden of the idealizing and Edenic descriptions usually
applied to the land.[12] During the reading of the legal document
that justified, in the minds of the Spanish, their invasion because it
was based on the legal fiction that Spain had—by virtue of its
evangelical mission—the right to dispossess the natives of their
land, Cortés approaches Cydaria according to these stage directions:
"While Vasquez speaks, Cortés spies the Ladies and goes to them
entertaining Cydaria with Courtship in dumb show" (1.2.265).
Even after Montezuma kindly rejects the Spaniards's offer to take
over his land, change his religion, and rule his empire, he allows his
daughter to remain and speak alone with Cortés.

"Looking" is central, almost obsessive, in this "love match." The
stage directions emphasize the point: "Cydaria is going, but turns
and looks back upon Cortés, who is looking on her all this while"
(1.2.248). The power of her beauty, he claims, actually robs him of
his sight: "Like travellers who wander in the Snow, / I on her
beauty gaze till I am blind" (1.2.252). The idealizing of Cydaria's
love—immediately recognized by Cortés and his valuing of her—

places her in such close proximity to the larger debates about possession, ownership, and conquest that she *becomes* the Mexican land described in the first act; or, as James Winn has noted, Cortés lays claim to her in the same way he lays claim to the land (154).

The most telling moment in the play comes when Cortés turns the debate upside down by positioning himself as the conquered territory in the typical and exaggerated discourse of European courtship—a discourse that traditionally positions him as the conquered one:

> But my complaints will much more just appear,
> Who from another World my freedom brought,
> And to your conquering Eyes have lost it here.

> (1.2.362–64)

In a genuinely imperial context, the trope of "love as conquest" performs a powerful ideological function: it serves here, more emphatically than in Lope's drama, to erase the larger and more troubling questions of ownership, violence, and subjugation that real acts of imperial aggression necessarily provoke. Indeed, the asymmetry between these two "colonial" enterprises, the invasion of a continent and the conquest of one's beloved, is easily lost once the love relationship is substituted as the significant, meaningful battleground. When Cydaria immediately returns Cortés's love, she functions both as a means of exchange between hostile forces and as a conduit of continuity between past and present. She represents the Edenic and idyllic female equivalent of the land her father rules—and thus the "real" colonial enterprise is accomplished through her cooperation, a benign partnership supposedly based on mutual affection and gain.[13]

Cortés, however, presents something of a problem for Dryden, especially in the quest to produce a model imperial identity that is both male and English: Cortés is a Spaniard who must function as the kind of hero with whom an English audience will identify, the kind of hero who possesses virtues the English might recognize as their own and with which they will identify. Thomas Scanlan has written that the English sought to repress their desire to subjugate native populations or at least to narrate that subjugation "as something other than the desire for domination and economic gain"; but that repression was largely due to their "*conscious* attempt to fashion a colonial identity that would stand in stark contrast to that of the Spanish. To be sure, the effect of the English determination not to reproduce the rapacity and cruelty of the Spanish was to generate colonial ideology that allowed its adherents to avoid confronting their darker motives" (18–19). Thus Dryden's task is to present the right kind of hero who can provide significant justification for the invasion, without revealing that darker side, and he accomplishes that feat by contrast. Cortés is presented in ways different from the other Spanish characters: he is less motivated by a generic Spanish avarice (represented by Pizarro here) or by Spanish sexual rapaciousness (symbolized by Vasques) than by a concern for the justice of such an invasion. For instance, when Cortés, the Taxallans, and the rest of the conquistadors arrive in the heart of the city, they burst onstage in a cloud of violence—a flurry that ends when Cortés actively rescues Montezuma from the even bloodthirstier Taxallans.[14] The Mexican emperor, amazed that his fierce native rivals have been so quickly subdued, "naturally" concludes that Cortés must be a god and so kneels to him and calls him "Patron of *Mexico,* and God of Warrs, / Sonne of the Sun, and Brother of the starres——."[15] This gesture, the image of a splendid Aztec emperor kneeling to a Spanish conquistador, iconographically reinforces Cortés's status as the self-controlled hero of this invasion.[16]

Cortés's fine qualities echo Renaissance English discourses that sought to differentiate English claims to empire from those of the Spanish by locating the difference between these nations in an essential moral difference: the English represent themselves as filled with impulse-control and moderated male desire, unlike the Spanish who are represented as excessive and hypermasculine. Or as Norbert Elias might phrase it, "all forms of pleasure [including cruelty and joy in the destruction and torment of others], limited by threats of displeasure, gradually come to express themselves only indirectly, in a 'refined' form" (192), which results in "the necessary restraint and transformation of aggression cultivated in the everyday life of civilized society" (202). In the case of Raleigh's *Discoverie,* for instance, Louis Montrose presents this argument about appropriate masculinities:

> One of the central ways in which Ralegh attempts to
> obfuscate this predicament of dependency upon and iden-
> tification with the enemy is through an absolute distinction

of the Englishmen's sexual conduct in the New World from
that of the Spaniards. . . . In the case of Englishmen, however, masculine sexual aggression against the bodies of native
women has been wholly displaced into the exploitation of
the feminized new found land. Indeed, the Englishmen's
vaunted sexual self-restraint serves to legitimate their exploitation of the land. (192, 195)

Dryden provides Cortés with these same positive characteristics
and thus allows an English audience to ignore the Spaniard's national difference and to identify with his moral excellence.

The obscuring of Cortés's national identity is only one of many
such sleights of hand. Dryden also obscures the relationship between choice and conquest in his treatment of the political and
militaristic dimensions of the invasion itself, in his reconfiguration
of the power dynamics of justice, force, and free will. Cortés begins the debate about invasion with this powerful rationalization
offered to Vasquez:

> By noble ways we Conquest will prepare,
> First offer peace, and that refus'd make war.
>
> (1.1.52–53)

Cortés later disabuses the emperor of his mistaken assumption that
Cortés is a returning god by describing himself instead as "Ambassadour of peace, if peace you choose, / Or Herrald of a Warr if
you refuse" (1.2.250–51). The specific conditions of such an imperial "peace" are here neither defined nor interrogated; instead, the
speech allows Cortés to claim "nobility" for himself and more importantly to suggest that the outcome of this first encounter—
peace or war, cooperation or violence—is somehow *Montezuma's
choice,* a displacement of responsibility for potential violence onto
the native inhabitants, rather than the invaders, and a strategy intended to produce innocence for this group of well-armed conquistadors.

The same strategy works in the sexual economy. Dryden tips
his ideological hand just once in that context, but it, too, is a powerful moment. When Montezuma's son returns to take his sister
home, Cortés urges her to go quickly by saying, "Turn hence those

pointed glories of your Eyes," or "I shall turn ravisher to keep you here" (1.2.385, 388). The last words of act 1, the first encounter, ring with threatened sexual violence but masquerade as love. It thus becomes an act that ends focused on the threatened rape of a native woman, but a rape that is figured as the inevitable result of a powerful visual attraction. Fixating on these love problems allows an audience not to see the violent penetration of the Aztec empire by European conquerors but instead to wonder at the power the specular woman appears to wield.

Such violence is particularly evident in the second iconic figure used by both Lope and Dryden: the contested woman. While "the specular woman" creates the conditions for encounter, it is "the contested woman" who creates the conditions for conquest. She, too, functions as the site of displacement of European hostility and thus as the repository of claims for European innocence. Both Lope and Dryden accomplish this displacement by predicating their dramas on *internal* native tensions that predate the arrival of the Spaniards. This a priori conflict is generated out of native hostilities arising from a native woman's being claimed and fought over by two native men, not hostility and bloodshed caused by invasion. According to Peter Hulme, "in America, the language of savagery was honed into the sharpest instrument of empire," a language of savagery that demanded European intervention. Hulme concludes that "the topic of land is 'dissimulated' by the topic of savagery" (3). In Lope's *New World* drama, we can add to the dissimulation "the contested woman" in a plot that involves Tacuana, daughter of a Haitian cacique, who is stolen, before the play opens, by the leader of a neighboring village and whose theft appears to demand Spanish intervention to produce justice.

Unhappy with her captivity, she goes to a Spaniard to ask for his *help* in returning her to her home. She speaks to him not about the fact that perfect strangers have entered her homeland, seeking gold and the religious conversion of her people. Instead, she asks for his protection from those she describes as her real enemies: other natives. She compliments the Spaniards, calling them "valliant," "children of the sun," and "godlike," and expresses sentiments the Spaniards want to hear: "may you see this land subject to your laws and may your God and Christ triumph over our gods" (46). But she ends with this powerful, almost irresistible invitation:

Bring your sons here so that they may marry our daughters and mix their blood with ours and all the Indians will become Spaniards!

(46)

Lope takes the real source of New World conflict—Spanish invasion—and turns it into an internal native problem that actively requires Spanish "assistance" of the kind that thereafter opens the door for Spanish control of native affairs. It invites memories of the famous drawing, widely reprinted in the late sixteenth century, that features Vespucci's discovery of America, a scene whose center of interest has been described this way by Louis Montrose: "[A] recumbent [female] figure, now discovered and roused from her torpor, is about to be hailed, claimed, and possessed as America" (180). This image of America has special resonance in Lope's play, for the iconic figure is made doubly "real." Initially, like Palca, the figure rises not only to meet but to see and be seen by Europeans, to have her very identity written anew and reflected back to her. And then, like Tacuana, she invites the conquerors to mingle their blood with hers and thus to subsume her identity into a category not of her making.

Dryden takes on a more complex representation of the contested woman by displacing the most powerful imperial questions to the love triangle between Alibech and the two sons of Montezuma. Again the rhetoric of war is displaced from the actual, ongoing, violent clash of forces to a purely internal, domestic love affair. And again the bigger issues of imperialism—questions of claims to land, justifications for birthrights, Lockean ownership based on use of land—are worked out as two native brothers fight over the desired object, the native woman. In the same way an English audience is being asked to see a fraternal link between the Spaniards and the English, with the Indians as distant, truly other creatures (Cortés as the perfect English hero), it is again asked to accept the metonymic link between the Indian woman—as a site of conflict, vulnerable, unspoiled, beautiful—and the land.

The powerful difference in Dryden's treatment of this now familiar trope is his brutally honest representation of the utter destruction of the Aztec empire that results from the encounter. He rejects the happy ending of Lope's drama and shuns the simple fantasy that concludes Davenant's masque. But that does not mean that he accepts European responsibility for the massive death and destruction of a New World empire. Indeed, in line with his presentation of the kinds of European innocence that he produced elsewhere, he cites internal native tensions and royal interfamilial strife as the causes of the annihilation of thousands of New World citizens.

The native love affair in *The Indian Emperour,* not the European invasion, is positioned rhetorically as imperial from the moment it is first mentioned. When Montezuma asks each son to name his beloved and when both Odmar and Guyomar profess their love for the same woman, Alibech, a debate erupts between the brothers as to who has the better claim, arguments made explicitly in the language of imperialism. Odmar begins by insisting on his longer-standing claim to love:

> Some respect to my birthright due,
> My claim to her by Eldership I prove.
>
> (1.2.138–39)

To this, Guyomar responds, "Age is a Plea in Empire, not in love." Prior claims, Odmar's "Eldership"—and by extension, in the terms of the larger drama, the native inhabitant's right to possession—are described in positive terms: his love "took deepest root which first did grow" (1.2.164). But the rejoinder of the younger Guyomar is also legitimated: "That Love which first was set will first decay / Mine of a fresher date will longer stay" (1.2.166). Guyomar is the nontraitorous brother left alive in the fifth act, the brother positioned as the laudatory figure and representing the legitimated newcomer's claim to the desired object, and he represents the position the English want to assume. Here, competing claims to possession are not worked out in the "upper" conquest plot, as when Cortés and Cydaria instantly fall in love, or even as the plea for rescue as we find in Lope. Instead, it is again dissimulated, worked out over the contested body of a native woman that produces a protracted and devastating siege. As in the plays of both Lope and Davenant, the existence of internal strife paves the way for conquest, a native schism that opens a door to describing the event not as war but as a foreign policy meant to bring peace to warring natives.

Given the choice between a birthright to possession and a more passionate and abiding attachment, Alibech refuses to choose:

For to my self I owe this due regard
Not to make Love my gift, but my reward.
Time best will show whose services will last.

(1.2.159–61)

Refusing her active agency, she is positioned as the ideal native: passive in the midst of a vital choice, she becomes the reward for the victor. And yet, like Montezuma, she is *forced* to choose. The difference is that she is aware of the disingenuous nature of this forced choice, a disingenuousness she is quick to point out to Cortés: she tells him that the gods have given him the power of life and death, and his old argument about Montezuma's choice—in his words, "That pow'r they to your Father did dispose / Twas his choice to make Us Friends or Foes"—cannot conceal the unequal power relations:

Injurious strength would rapine still excuse,
By off'ring termes the weaker must refuse;
And such as these your hard conditions are,
You threaten Peace, and you invite a War.

(2.2.20–24)

Thus the essential nature of the conquistadors' conquest is finally unmasked, not as choice but as force—as an unsatisfactory, threatening peace or as an "invitation" to war. Either way, the Indian way of life—including its government, its religion, even the use of its land—will be forever changed.

But Dryden does not stop there. To the specular and the contested women of Lope's play, Dryden appropriates a third figure—Lope's demon—and turns it into the energetic, anti-imperial woman: Almeria, beloved by Montezuma, who scorns him for the past wrongs he did to her mother, the Indian Queen of Dryden's earlier drama. Presented as wronged and vengeful, haughty and fierce, she bears the burden of the demonizing discursive strategy. An audience is instructed to read her as the least attractive of the three women because she is the most outspoken, even hysterical. For instance, in the pivotal third act, when Cortés has been captured, Almeria wants to exact revenge on the Spaniard by executing him on the spot: "Give me a Sword and let me take his head" (3.4.70). And when events move too slowly for her, she insists, "Either Command his death upon the place, / Or never more behold

Almeria's face" (3.4.81–82). In the end, tired of the family conflict Cortés's capture has produced, she falls to urging immediate revenge: "Make haste, make haste . . . See, see, my Brother's Ghost hangs hovering there / O're his warm Blood, that steems into the Air, / Revenge, Revenge it cries" (3.4.119–23).

But it is she alone who truly understands the magnitude of the threat in the Spaniards's arrival. Thus she utters the strongest anti-imperial arguments to Montezuma:

> Go, go, with homage your proud Victors meet,
> Go lie like Dogs, beneath your Masters Feet.
> Go, and beget them Slaves to dig their Mines,
> And groan for Gold which now in Temples shines;
> Your shameful story shall record of me,
> The Men all crouch'd, and left a Woman free.
>
> (3.1.65–70)

The powerful threat that fierce native resistance presents to colonizers and potential colonizers, especially as it resonates as a form of protonationalism for the Aztecs, is a source of genuine and well-founded anxiety for the British, an anxiety that Dryden contains here in part by locating it in a demonized, hysterical, and thus marginally less dangerous native, a *woman*. But, in a reversal just as stunning for modern readers, Dryden contains the entirety of that threat, indeed he utterly erases it, when his anti-imperialist voice of doom succumbs to the erotic power of her conquerors: in a plot reversal that only the dictates of heroic drama could produce, Almeria falls passionately and hopelessly in love with Cortés.

Almeria is reminiscent of the most disturbing character in Lope's play: the Demon, who is also given the best anti-imperial speeches and who is also resoundingly defeated at the end of the play. The conclusion in Lope's drama contains a moment just as miraculous as Almeria's conversion, not a love match but an instance of Christian transcendence that underwrites the larger cultural discourse deployed by Spain to justify its imperial designs. In the last act, the Demon arrives to tell Dulcan—leader of the tribe who has stolen the contestable woman—that a Spaniard has effected Tacuana's escape, a fact that leads to words a modern reader would call the truth of the conquest: the Demon says, "Oh! The fool, to believe in the friendship of these Spaniards! They covet your gold, so they make themselves saints and pretend to be decent Christians, and meanwhile others will come and take away all your riches and carry them back to Spain" (57). As a fight ensues, a cross, which had been planted very early in the drama, is pulled down, only to be miraculously replaced by another cross that slowly rises in place of the first; the promise is that, were it to be felled again, another cross would again take its place. This miracle leads to an end of hostilities when Tacuana and her husband accept the Spaniards, metonymically equated with the power of miracles: "Today, sacred wood, you are to rule over our people. Forgive us again, oh cross!" (59). Columbus returns to Spain, bearing the wonders of America, to be hailed as "the man who arrives with a world!" (59). Lope's supernatural demon-creature metamorphoses into Dryden's Almeria—the shrill-voiced harridan, a native Cassandra, silenced finally when she "recognizes" and responds to the near miraculous erotic power of her conqueror.

It is thus not surprising that the last act of *The Indian Emperour* features the protracted siege and the horrifying famine that were themselves horrifying historical realities.[17] The splendid city of abundance metamorphoses into a spectral landscape of destitution and want:

> Famine so fierce, that what's deny'd Mans use,
> Even deadly Plants, and Herbs of pois'nous juice
> Wild hunger seeks; and to prolong our breath,
> We greedily devour our certain death:
> The Souldier in th' 'assault of Famine falls;
> And Ghosts, not Men, are watching on the walls.
>
> (4.2.33–38)

Alibech describes the citizen's plight in a moving simile, comparing them to defenseless birds left abandoned after the death of their mother—a feminizing, and in this case, maternalizing, of the now ruined Aztec landscape:

> As Callow Birds———
> Whose Mother's kill'd in seeking of the prey,
> Cry in their Nest, and think her long away;
> And at each leaf that stirs, each blast of wind,
> Gape for the Food which they must never find:
> So cry the people in their misery.
>
> (4.2.39–44)

Unlike the "winning" of Cydaria, who capitulates to her conqueror immediately and who therefore appears to find in her lord a gallant lover and a strong protector, the continuing contest over Alibech produces utter disaster: the complete destruction of Indian resistance (in the figure of Almeria and her suicide); the demise of claims to birthright and the legitimate rights to the territory (in the death of Odmar, the older brother); and the final surrender of the land (in the expulsion of both Alibech and Guyomar, the younger brother, from the domain of Aztec civilization).

Dryden paints a pathetic portrait of destitution and loss, as David Bruce Kramer notes, "Dryden's almost unfailing sympathy with the weaker culture is one of the constant pleasures of the drama; simple conquest over the merely brutish other is never lauded. There is always sorrow, imaginatively expressed, at the necessity to conquer and destroy one's noble adversary" (75). Yet beyond the sorrow in the ending, the contemporary English audience was offered this imperial lesson: native acquiescence to European colonization is the only productive choice, since it will generate peace and plenty. Both Cydaria's capitulation to Cortés and the ending of Davenant's masque promise peace and plenty, but only for those Englishmen with the appropriate imperial identity: those who arrive ready to "assist" warring natives and to "love" native women whom they spy with imperial eyes. Native division and resistance, not European incursion, inevitably result in want, destitution, and famine as Dryden's particularly moving final act demonstrates.[18]

Even in the last scene of *The Indian Emperour,* the play refuses to surrender the free choice paradigm. When Cortés offers joint leadership to the defeated Guyomar—"Live and enjoy more then your Conquerour: / Take all my Love, and share in all my Pow'r"— Guyomar rejects the offer, pointing out the pitiful fact that there is no more city to rule. Then in a move reminiscent of the end of *Paradise Lost,* the Indian lovers prepare to depart paradise—only this time they leave behind an utterly annihilated Eden to head for a place even less hospitable:

Northward, beyond the Mountains we will go,
Where Rocks lye cover'd with Eternal Snow;
Thin Herbage in the Plains, and Fruitless Fields,
The Sand no Gold, the Mine no Silver yields:

There Love and Freedom we'l in Peace enjoy;
No *Spaniards* will that Colony destroy.
We to our selves will all our wishes grant;
And nothing coveting, can nothing want.

(5.2.368–75)

Against the images of exile and despair, Guyomar celebrates the native's only recompense in the banishment: freedom from colonial avarice within a bleak landscape and a barren peace. But against these powerful sentiments, Dryden still gives Cortés the final celebratory lines, sentiments that describe both his love and his imperial enterprise: "Thus doubly blest, with Conquest, and with Love" (5.237–9).

The Indian Emperour was a hugely popular play, especially with Court society (the Duchess of Monmouth was said to have acted a part in a private production), and it remained in repertory for over fifty years. Its success, in some measure, depended upon English nationalism: the play "proves" that conquest—in the old Spanish mode—is a terrifying and brutal phenomenon but, in a benign English fashion, produces cooperation and peace. It satisfies the moral conscience, first by maintaining a fiction of commensurability: Montezuma appears to have power and thus, the play suggests, it is his choice whether Cortés acts as "Ambassadour of peace" or "Herrald of a Warr." Simultaneously, Dryden manages to keep other categories, such as the stealing of native women, from collapsing into the same, the stealing of land: subjects and objects are inverted, shifted in order to secure an innocence otherwise unavailable to the invaders and the playwrights. Moreover, as we have seen above, the "romance of conquest" serves to secure European innocence by positing that it was the native women who actually effected the conquest when they loved at first sight and used the Spanish to settle their internal domestic struggles. Or as Margaret Ferguson puts it, "the colonizing of the New World was figured as a project of erotic possession" ("Juggling" 224). What we come to understand is that these women participate in a New World version of the oldest form of European property transmission: the bodies of women, metaphorically linked with the land, are transferred from native to European control in a conquest that appears as benign as it is effective.

Colonial Identity

In the remainder of this chapter, I take up the systematizing and institutionalizing of some of the forms of violence we have already examined and the appearance of new forms of violence that erupted alongside of or because of the on-going wars with native inhabitants. In other words, I will examine *colonization* as James Thompson defines it: "the legitimating and the systematizing of a formerly episodic rapine" (218). It is the process of controlling the signification of such episodic rapine that concerns me in these last pages.

Aphra Behn's *Widdow Ranter,* a play produced approximately twenty-five years after Dryden's *Indian Emperour* and featuring not encounter or conquest but occupation, best represents this next step in the resistance, violence, and institutionalization of conquest.[19] In this later play, there is no need to stage an encounter, for the English already constitute a force of occupation in the Americas. Among these colonial subjects still exist the demonized, the specular, and the contested woman, but the figures take on a very different appearance. In addition, as the British continue to attempt to legitimate, excuse, and justify their occupation, they begin to work through the issues not just of gender, as we have seen in the Dryden play, but also the relationship between gender and status as these categories are being formed and formed anew in the colonies, signifiers that very strongly and insistently define the ideal, even the acceptable limits, of "appropriate" colonial rule.

In Lope's and Dryden's plays, all the conquerors, whether they were born so or not, act like aristocrats. In Behn's play, lower-class knaves and criminals occupy positions of power and claim to possess honor and gentility. In the earlier works examined in this chapter, all the heroes were Spaniards. In Behn's play, all are transplanted or transported English men and women. Thus Behn faces no need to entice an English audience to identify with a national other, since there are plenty of sympathetic and/or heroic characters with whom the British might identify. In Dryden's and Lope's plays, the means to power was war—invasion and conquest, an interloper's staking a claim to some part of the landscape. In Behn's play, land is power—land already invaded and conquered, and thus disingenuously "owned." Altogether these issues add up to the production of a "plantation economy" that opened up seemingly infinite possibilities for the colonists to recreate themselves and to redefine their status and identity through the manipulation of the distance from and the products of empire.

The Widdow Ranter, produced posthumously in 1689, two years after Behn's death, contains a double focus: an upper, heroic plot involving love, violence, and war; and a lower, comic plot involving love, marriage, and property. Nathaniel Bacon is the hero in the upper, heroic plot, and the actual events that took place during his "uprising" are worth recounting here. In 1676, Nathaniel Bacon, in pointed defiance to the Virginia government, organized a volunteer army of "indentured servants, African slaves, dissatisfied soldiers, and the laboring poor" (266), according to Margo Hendricks, in order to wage war against the Indians. He was very successful— so successful that he began to be seen as a threat as much to the local government as to the Indians. Had he not died in that same year, shortly after capturing Jamestown, he might well have acted on that threat but, as it was, the rebellion collapsed without its leader.[20]

As the dashing outlaw in Behn's play, he is a hero in the old heroic mode, a character with imperial ambitions and cast in the old aristocratic mold. The initial forms of conquest, especially those engaged in by the Spanish, held the promise of acquiring for its conquistadors not simply a quantity of riches but an equal share of the exaggerated honor in the old feudal sense. The desire for territorial expansion through conquest was, according to Anthony Pagden, bound by a code of aristocratic values that had played "a crucial role in the creation of all the earliest overseas empires": "For overseas expansion promised to those who engaged in it not only trade and, if they were lucky, precious metals, it also offered the promise of glory, and with glory a kind of social advancement which, before the mid-eighteenth century, could be acquired by no other means" (64). Bacon seeks that same glory.[21] His companion, Friendly, uses a series of adjectives to describe him, in language reminiscent of a feudal hierarchy, or an identity with an aristocratic essence:

You have named a Man indeed above the common Rank,
by Nature generous, brave, resolv'd and daring; who studying
the Lives of the Romans and great Men, that have raised

themselves to the most elevated Fortunes, fancies it easy for
ambitious Men to aim at any pitch of Glory. I've heard him
often say, Why cannot I conquer the Universe as well as
Alexander: or like another Romulus, form a new Rome,
and my self ador'd?"

(1.1.113–15)

Having no official commission as general of the army, Bacon is
nonetheless the darling of the frightened colonists because he has
single-handedly taken over the defense of Jamestown.

In the world of Behn's play, the abiding power of the New World
tropes we saw developed in Dryden's work is again apparent: internal strife among the native inhabitants is positioned as the source
of hostilities. But, this time, it takes the form of a curiously exter-
nalized love plot and a fight for the contested women—Bacon's
desperate fight, outside of all legitimate bounds of authority, for
the love of the Indian Queen. Margaret Ferguson cites an important historical difference that distinguishes this narrative from
those earlier encounter romances: "[the colonial project was] rife
with fantasies of miscegenation—a mixing of ostensibly distinct
categories that was just beginning, in the mid-seventeenth century,
to be legally prohibited in the American colonies and which was
for that reason acquiring a new erotic charge" ("Juggling" 224).
What we saw in earlier narratives was a marriage, of sorts, at least
in the old aristocratic sense of the merging of dynastic fortunes: in
Dryden, Europe "marries" the New World when Cortés takes Cydaria's hand. In Behn's later treatment, there can be no marriage in
the offing, since the Indian King stands as the immovable obstacle
to Bacon's desires. As a result, love between a native woman and a
European man in this later version translates into the European
form of illegitimate desire—adultery—and love becomes a baser,
illegitimate emotion, lust. The result is the prohibition of miscegenation couched in moralistic terms.

Like Cortés, his Spanish predecessor, Bacon professes his love to
the queen in the old style, in the loftiest language of heroic love.
When the Indian Queen asks him "what is the God of Love?" he
offers this extravagant reply:

> 'Tis a resistless Fire, that kinddl'd thus *(Takes her by the hand
> and gazes on her)* at every gaze we take from fine Eyes, from
> such Bashfull Looks, and such soft touches—it makes us

sigh—and pant as I do now, and stops the Breath when e're
we speak of Pain.

(2.1.131–134)

The other colonists, however, are less generous in their description
of the "match," and they suggest that his love is just part of his
larger ambitions: he "fancy[s] no Hero ought to be without his
Princess," they say (1.1.113–15). Thus Ferguson can argue that
"The 'white' male hero Bacon . . . looks politically dark to his
countrymen—indeed indistinguishable from the enemy Indians—
in part because he prefers an Indian lady to one of his own people"
("News" 164).

But the Indian Queen returns Bacon's love, just as Indian women
onstage had done before, and it is again the power of sight that
wins her over. She says, "at twelve Years old——at the Pauwomun-
gian Court, I saw this Conqueror. I saw him young and gay as
new-born Spring, glorious and charming as the Mid-day's Sun; I
watch'd his Looks, and listened when he spoke, and thought him
more than mortal" (5.3.177–80). "Watching his looks" is one of
the activities native women best perform, it appears, since these
plays so often figure them as mesmerized by the beauties of non-
native men. But in this case, the Indian Queen claims that the
power of Bacon's visual image is matched and perhaps exceeded by
a new element—his formidable storytelling powers:

> The more I gaze upon this English Stranger, the more Con-
> fusion struggles in my Soul: Oft I have heard of Love, and
> oft this Gallant Man (when Peace had made him pay his idle
> Visits) has told a thousand Tales of dying Maids; and ever
> when he spoke, my panting Heart, with a prophetick Fear
> Sighs reply'd, I shall fall a Victim to his Eyes.
>
> (2.1.38–42)

Thus, in one sense, the contested woman remains a site where the
comfortable conventions of love and honor, rather than rape and
rapine, can be worked out in yet one more dramatic instance of
the formula. But, in another sense, the central place of the native
woman is lost because she is only half of the double plot Behn
employs. This is a profound change. The Indian women present in
the earlier dramas were part of a larger, heroic, glory-filled conquest of land that held infinite potential. Behn writes in the mode

68

of comedy *after* the glory days of conquest, when the British—without Spain's self-styled mandate from God—know that they will need to depend on commerce and agriculture as the result of their labors, a "modern" form of colonization that does not bespeak the values of an old, aristocratic, glory-filled, but feudal, "premodern" heroism. James Thompson writes about this important shift in the definition of heroism itself, a new choice between "military and mercantile conquest," that by the 1670s involved the following: "The choice is not only a choice between Catholic or Protestant models of government, but it is also a choice, on the one hand, between the French example of crude and brutal exploitation of feudal adventurism—primitive accumulation at its crudest—and, on the other hand, the highly efficient and systematic colonization of Holland" (220), England's model for a colonialist mercantile structure. And the death of this native woman, and not her marriage to her colonizer, functions as one of the most powerful symbols of the aftereffects of the shift from encounter and conquest to colonization: her death clears away any native resistance to the colonists' imperial ambitions and functions symbolically as a harbinger of the more massive forms of genocide to come.

The "problem" of the Indians is laid at the feet of the British by one of the young heroes of the comic plot: "For at this time the *Indians,* by our ill Management of Trade, whom we have Armed against Our selves, Very frequently make War upon us with our own Weapons; Tho' often coming by the Worst are forced to make Peace with us again, but so, as upon every turn they fall to Massacring us wherever we lie exposed to them" (1.1.95–99). Indian resistance is strong and violent, with the weapons of warfare being continually supplied to the Indians by bad British management, in a seemingly infinite cycle of violence.[22] By the mid-seventeenth century, however, the British have also fashioned complex justifications for their colonial encroachments. A moment in the second act that features Bacon's meeting with the Indian king and queen contains one such British rationalization. Bacon bows to the King who initially observes the courtesies: "I am sorry Sir, we meet upon these terms, we who so often have embrac'd as friends" (2.1.1–2). The King then goes on to complain about British imperial ambitions: "Yet tho I'm young, I'm sensible of Injuries; And oft have heard my Grandsire say—That we were Monarchs once of all this spacious World, till you an unknown People landing here, Distress'd and ruin'd by destructive storms, Abusing all our Charitable Hospitality, Usurp'd our Right, and made your friends your slaves" (2.1.10–14). The King's speech, quite naturally, employs the discourse of politics in his complaint: the conquistadors unlawfully "usurped" power, and they did so by force (and "made" the Indians slaves).

Bacon's reply, however, rehearses a strange new definition of English property laws, a redefinition that describes the outright stealing of New World land as a sin of his forefathers, but one that somehow does not taint him or subsequent colonists. More important, it does not prevent him from inheriting what was stolen: "I will not justify the Ingratitude of my fore-fathers, but finding here my Inheritance, I am resolv'd still to maintain it so, And by my sword which first cut out my Portion, Defend each Inch of Land, with my last drop of Bloud" (2.1.15–16). Note that in the competing discourses of legal property transmission and genteel social behavior, "ingratitude" succumbs to "inheritance" in New World conflict. Thus, in Bacon's new definition, occupation equals inheritance, which in turn equals possession by rights. Rightful possession, of course, *forces* him and all of the English settlers into a violent defense of the land that this "logic" tells him is rightfully his.

Thus, on the surface, war again appears to be the active agent of settlement. The Indians are represented as fiercely resisting British incursions and as fighting the construction of additional settlements (even though a contemporary British audience, having heard the news of the Jamestown uprisings and Bacon's routing of the Indians, would rejoice at the spectacle of the Indians's defeat). This upper plot, by focusing audience attention on the danger, the heroism, and the potential erotic connection between an Englishman with imperial ambitions and an Indian Queen, functions to conceal, displace, dissimulate the real forces of colonization. That phenomenon is in fact effected in Behn's play in the lower plot and not by the violence of encounter but by the power of money in marriage, settlement, and occupation—themselves the agents that allow for the growth of new settlements and the on-going administration of already extant colonial towns. So while it seems that colonization is accomplished through the winning of the Indian wars—in the old, heroic fashion—it is actually the actions of British administrators, commercial and governmental, that secure the land and ensure continued occupation.

While the suggestion in the earlier plays was that land could be secured through war and the conquest of an Indian woman, here, according to Bacon's legal fiction, ownership of land has already been transferred from Indians to settlers. Existing plantations are now "owned" through inheritance and expanded, in part, by war and by occupation—or through a more powerful intermediary: money. And money is secured through merchant daughters and widows, where the extravagant possibilities for upward mobility of women in the New World—an upward mobility that is most easily, if temporarily, effected through lying, especially about one's own identity, and more permanently through marriage—must have been disturbing to a contemporary audience. When Flirt says, "For I my self am a Gentlewoman: my Father was a Barronet, but undone in the late Rebellion—and I am fain to keep an Ordinary now, Heaven help me" (1.1.187–89), Timorous responds, "Good lack, why, see how Virtue may be bely'd—we heard your Father was a Taylor, but trusting for old *Oliver's* Funerall, Broke, and so came hither to hide his head" (1.1.190–92). Flirt's very name more than suggests lower-class origins, and Timorous's accusation that her support for the Commonwealth, always a grave sin in Behn's predominantly Tory mind, caused her family's demise.[23] Nabil Matar has written that the "voluntary self-fashioning" practiced by Europeans reveals that aristocratic identity fashioned itself *against* the other, while the European commoner was willing to transform himself *into* the others, and he argues that so many of them fashioned themselves into the other that "they caused deep anxiety in their home communities" because these "renegades" became committed to their new communities and even abandoned their Christian names and adopted Islamic or Indian names (95).

Behn's new world is filled with lower-class characters who have taken advantage of the opportunity to remake themselves—tinkers, excisemen, and pickpockets who metamorphose into Virginia planters, "men of rank," justices, and leading citizens. Margo Hendricks cites the anxiety such New World refashioning must have caused an English metropolitan audience: "In an age preoccupied with identity, needless to say, the ability to 'put on' an identity as easily as one puts on a coat is troubling. The success of men such as the Justices visibly undermines the class-based assumption about who is capable of ruling"[24] ("Civility" 229–30). In the end, however, it is clear that Behn presents those *not born* to rule as being too self-interested, too ignorant, and too blind to rule. Friendly articulates this essentialist position: "This Country wants nothing but to be People'd with a *well-born Race* to make it one of the best Collonies in the World; but for want of a Governour we are Ruled by a Councill, some of which have been perhaps transported Criminals, who having Acquired great Estates are now become your Honour, and Right Worshipfull" (emphasis mine; 1.1.105–09). The ending of the play sees the replacement of lower-class council members by "real" Englishman—men with class-appropriate status, gentlemen newly arrived and willing to fight valiantly and to govern more intelligently.[25] Wellman says of them, "Places in the Councill shall be supply'd by these Gentlemen of Sense and Honour. The Governour when he comes shall find the Country in better hands than he expects to find it" (5.1.388–91). The parochial planters—those knaves and tinkers who once ran the settlement—will go back to doing what they do best: indulging themselves into a stupor from the local pleasures of the senses. Timorous, for instance, says "Gad zorrs, I never thriv'd since I was a States-man, left Planting, and fell to promising and Lying; I'le to my old Trade again, bask under the shade of my own Tobacco, and drink my Punch in Peace" (5.1.395–97). Thus, in the end, the class structures created and maintained in England are replicated in the New World.[26]

Women in the New World, however, present a different story. The eponymous Widdow Ranter is the most important character whose identity has been utterly transformed in Virginia. Indeed, the language Friendly uses to describe her original identity is that language usually reserved, if not for indentured servants, for slaves:

> Thou wilt find a perpetual Visiter the *Widdow Ranter,* a Woman *bought from the ship* by *Old Colonel Ranter;* she serv'd him half a year, and then he Marry'd her, and dying in a Year more, left her worth Fifty thousand Pounds Sterling, besides Plate and Jewells: She's a great Gallant, But assuming the Humour of the Country Gentry, her Extravagancy is very Pleasant, she retains something of her Primitive Quality still, but is good-natur'd and Generous.
>
> (1.1.78–85 [emphasis mine])

The colonel purchased the widow, as he would any slave, upon her arrival in Jamestown. This practice of buying British women was commonplace, according to Janet Todd: "Many immigrants had the cost of their passage paid on arrival by someone needing a servant, for whom they would then work without wages until they had paid off the cost of their fare and keep. Convicts and the poor were often auctioned to bidders" (452).

Thus the widow possesses "primitive qualities," like the demonized native women in encounter dramas, but her primitivism is drawn from English class biases and is produced for comedic effect.[27] Because that primitive quality positions her as an important figure in Behn's redefinition of the limits of acceptable womanhood and acceptable New World citizenship, it is thus with deliberation that Behn distinguishes the English Widdow's character—and most particularly her act of cross-dressing—from that of the Indian Queen. Both are "primitives" who don the garb of "masculine" heroes and fighters for their respective sides, and each produces a pivotal plot effect. But discerning the differences between them allows us to comment on Behn's notions of appropriate "primitivism," including its use in the redefinition of the boundaries of acceptable New World behavior for women and the ideological and political forces driving each character.

The Widdow cuts a wonderful figure of a man. She smokes; she drinks; she fights fiercely; she is a tireless companion for her fellows in arms. She is not, however, so masculinized by her clothing that she forgets her mission: the winning of Colonel Dareing's heart, a feat she accomplishes by the close of the final act. Not having been fooled for a moment by her masquerade, Dareing expresses his happiness with his new, cross-dressed bride: "Give me thy hand, Widdow, I am thine—and so intirely, I will never—be drunk out of thy Company. . . . prithee let's in [to my tent] and bind the bargain." When the widow suggests that they wait until the end of the war, Dareing replies, "Nay, prithee take me in the humour, while thy Breeches are on—for I never lik'd thee half so well in Petticoats" (4.2.277–79). Thus the Widdow's cross-dressing is figured merely as a disguise, and one easily seen through at that. It causes little anxiety because she uses it to further the "right" British cause in America; indeed, it functions comically, for it is no more a ridiculous garb for her than that of her normal role: a servant masquerading as the wife of an army officer. Most important, she uses her cross-dressing for entirely "feminine purposes": to get her man. A profound lability of identity is the hallmark of the Widdow's life in the New World, a movement from indentured servant, to wife and then widow, to swashbuckler and finally wife again. On the surface, Behn's drama positions British efforts to colonize as the agent that creates new possibilities for the radical shifting, even the redefinition, of identity. Margo Hendricks argues that while such redefinitions may have been feared by the English at home, they were actively embraced by the colonists: "In the minds of the transported, the colonies represented an opportunity to 'fashion' an identity" (229). Margaret Ferguson too claims that Colonel Dareing and the Widdow Ranter are only marginally subversive characters: Dareing because he fights for Bacon's cause and the Widdow because "she is openly unchaste, has money of her own to spend as she sees fit, and uses it to achieve respectability and also to gain sexual satisfaction with a younger man who enters into the institution of matrimony with jovial cynicism" ("News" 173).

These two characters are less subversive and less anxiety-provoking than the real threats in the play, Bacon and the Indian Queen, who are truly dangerous because they break too many social laws to be allowed to live: "One might indeed argue that the Widdow and Daring acquire their license to live at the price of their doubles' deaths" ("News" 173). No such lability of identity is available to "real" primitives; the crossing of the real borders of miscegenation Behn prohibits. The Indian Queen's cross-dressing, for instance, has no comedic power. It produces only anxiety, for she dons her Amazonian attire as an act of war, a primitive, therefore punishable, act of aggression against the British.[28] She has put on men's clothing so as to avoid being captured and dragged to the British settlement. Behn describes the scene this way: "Enter Queen dresst like an Indian Man, with a Bow in her hand, and Quiver at her Back" (5.1.159–60). She is also surrounded by a dozen Indian protectors who fail to beat back Bacon's charge. Just as he enters the stage and just as her protectors are about to shoot poisoned arrows at him, she cries, "hold" just long enough to allow him full access to her. He rushes onstage, fails to recognize her, and then stabs her mortally. Unlike Colonel Dareing, who immediately recognizes his beloved widow, Bacon brutally murders his unrecognizable queen. He subsequently kills himself by drinking poison, while saying he has, "Secur'd my self from being a publick Spectacle upon the common Theatre of Death" (5.1.293–94). An audience understands that, for all his ability to wield the extravagant discourses of Western passion, in loving the queen Bacon has "gone native": the violence he displays, his refusal to acknowledge legitimate authority, and his adulterous lusts for a native woman position him as "savage."

The irony of the Indian Queen's masquerade, the fact that it makes her unrecognizable by utterly confounding her identity, is that it causes her death. In so doing, it becomes a comment on the lability of Indian identity: it more than points to the dangers of miscegenation; it effectively secures the impossibility of assimilation.[29] In the end, this Indian Queen cannot be saved. Lope's Palca participates in an encounter narrative; she greets her new European visitors with kindness and eagerly looks into the European mirror in order to redefine herself. Dryden's Cydaria similarly participates in a conquest narrative; beginning as an emperor's daughter, she ends the legitimate wife of the new colonial ruler. Even Almeria, Dryden's demonic queen and speaker of anti-imperialist discourses, falls in love with Cortés, the conquistador. But Behn's Indian Queen can neither fight for her people nor marry her beloved European (unlike Lope's Tacuana, who invites the Spaniards to mingle their blood with hers). Once encounter gives way to settlement—once discovery is systematized into colonialism—even this less-than-satisfactory option disappears. Once possession is effected, unassimilable, the Indian Queen cannot participate in the "romance" of conquest; unassimilable and demonized, she dies on land no longer her own.

3 National Identities
Merchants on and off the
Restoration Stage

A *True-born Englishman's* a Contradiction
In Speech an Irony, in Fact a Fiction.
A Banter made to be a Test of Fools,
Which those that use it justly ridicules.
A Metaphor invented to express,
A man *a-kin* to all the Universe.
—Defoe, *The True-born Englishman*

THE EPILOGUE TO WYCHERLEY'S *Gentleman Dancing-Master,* performed in 1673 on the eve of the Third Anglo-Dutch War, is spoken by the actress who plays the character of Flirt, a prostitute who "wins" herself an exorbitantly Frenchified English lover at the close of the play. Gendering her compliments to the audience, while simultaneously making divisions according to rank, she first addresses the "City damsels," ironically suggesting that—unlike the heroine of the play—"real" City women do not dissemble. She then offers an even more ironic compliment to the "good men o' th' Exchange":

On whom alone
We must depend when sparks to sea are gone,
Into the pit already you are come—
'Tis but a step more to our tiring-room,
Where none of us but will be wondrous sweet
Upon an able love of Lumber Street.[1]

This reference to the merchants' upward mobility, occasioned by war and the military service of gentlemen, is put into theatrical terms: now that trading men have entered the playhouse, it is only a small step to the actresses' "tiring-rooms."

She then proceeds to catalogue the differences between the gentlemen and the goldsmiths and bankers of Lombard Street by contrasting the clothing that identifies each—not an unexpected occurrence in a play concerned with the ways fashion is read and misread as character:

You we had rather see between our scenes
Then spendthrift fops with better clothes and miens;
Instead of laced coat, belts and pantaloons,
Your velvet jumps, gold chains and grave fur gowns;
Instead of periwigs and broad cocked hats,
Your satin caps, small cuffs and vast cravats.

The gentlemen who have gone off to fight may have more money, better clothes, and handsomer features, but merchants are the only men left in town—a fact that leads to Flirt's final prediction that makes explicit the sexual "threat" implied above:

Then you are
Fit to make love, while our houzas make war,
And, since all gentlemen must pack to sea
Our gallants and our judges must you be.

This "appeal" to the men of the City is obviously less than flattering, primarily because Wycherley names the problem: mere merchants may attempt to assume the rights and privileges left unattended by aristocrats, especially those that allow trading men access to women players and, by extension, to all women. Like the tinkers and excisemen of Behn's Virginia, these bankers are not born to entitlement, but they could, in the absence of the restraining influence of aristocrats, obtain access to desirable women, especially if they look the part. And yet this threat is simultaneously mitigated by the categorizable group identity of merchants: their satin caps and fur gowns are immediately recognizable; their self-chosen vestimentary difference sets them visually apart. No one will be fooled.

Or will they? That is the central problem Wycherley sets up in *The Gentleman Dancing-Master* (1673)—how to read the outward signs of fashion and behavior as the measure of character and worth. His solution to the problem, as seen above, is entirely conservative: his play reconfirms the belief that identity itself is stable, consistent both on the surface of as well as underneath the fashion signs one might temporarily don. Others, including Aphra Behn and Mary Pix, approach the subject of identity as if it is more elastic, as if the possibilities for refashioning European identity have less to do with the essential and more to do with a potential. It is the ways that identities are produced, determined, and overdetermined—both theatrically and socially—that form the subject of my investigation here. Specifically, I am interested in the ways national identities—in this case, Dutch, Spanish, French, and English— become (or at least come to seem) essentialized, even though this phenomenon is accomplished through clearly nonessential means. I will be looking at the ways these playwrights reify and deploy material items, especially the gendered fashions unique to a particular culture, and thus I'll be reading gendered bodies, national bodies, and bodies as texts. Some are "masked," their identities seemingly denaturalized and questioned; others are "unmasked," revealing essentialized categories that remain uncontested. I argue that this theatrical phenomenon of masking and unmasking—of denaturalizing and essentializing—was a necessary component to the larger cultural and political processes that worked to establish a late-seventeenth-century definition of "Englishness," a national boundary that was itself a necessary accompaniment to burgeoning British expansionist projects.

Frontiers and Boundaries

That various geographical regions produce unique material signifiers—food, costumes, and gestures—is not news. One need only look at a recent series of IBM commercials to see the persistence of such images: Italian nuns wander through convent halls discussing the Internet or elderly French gentlemen ponder the speed of processor chips. IBM's intention, of course, is to represent the realization of the global village—with all of us linked by modem and machines. The advertisers accomplish this, however, through the exploitation of convenient and abiding national stereotypes. In another example from the IBM series, we are offered a combination of familiar national elements: Greek deep-sea divers climb back into their boat and agree to "do lunch"; the spot ends with one diver asking, "Sushi?" The humor resides in the Mediterranean fishermen's plans to dine in the mode of Hollywood executives and their anticipation of the pleasures of a Japanese culinary specialty.

Something of this same cosmopolitanism was at work in late seventeenth- and early-eighteenth-century England. Along with it came the belief that one culture could know another, especially through the external "signs" of a nation. Linda Colley, whose work more than suggests that the English had ample opportunity to meet and know their Continental neighbors, firmly rejects the description of the British as an insular people: "For most of their early modern and modern history, [the British] have had more contact with more parts of the world than almost any other nation —it is just that this contact has regularly taken the form of aggressive military and commercial enterprise" (8). At the same time, these imperial contacts—both military and commercial—helped to underwrite early modern British definitions of other national characters: "Not so much consensus or homogeneity or centralisation at home, as a strong sense of a dissimilarity from those without, proved to be the essential cement" (Colley 17).

Clearly then national images suggest boundaries, but boundaries that can be breached in signs that can be read. Clothing is, of course, one primary signal. Anthropologist Terence Turner argues that within a society the adornment of the body is distinctive in that it is the medium "most directly and concretely concerned with the construction of the individual as social actor or cultural subject" (36). Because this concern is fundamental to all societies and social groups, "the imposition of a standardized symbolic form upon the body . . . invariably becomes a serious business for all societies, regardless of whether their members as individuals take the matter seriously or not" (36). In this context, he quotes Chesterfield's advice to his son: "Dress is a very foolish thing; and yet is a very foolish thing for a man not to be well dressed, according to his rank and way of life" (16). Turner therefore suggests that "the surface of the body seems everywhere to be treated not only as the boundary of the individual as a biological and psychological entity but as the frontier of the social self as well" (15).

This language of "frontiers" and "boundaries" is echoed in the works of political theorists, especially those interested in questions of nationalism as an early modern phenomenon. Anthony Gliddens, among others, has pointed out that premodern nations have frontiers: that is, vague, loosely agreed upon geographical locations that become progressively less visible the farther one moves from a strong center (45); Peter Sahlins describes frontiers as possessing "zonal qualities" within a broad, social context (4). Modern nations, on the other hand, have borders: precisely demarcated geographical divisions that may be understood to have a center somewhere but are less dependent on it for definition. Or, as Peter Sahlins puts it, a nation has "a precise, linear division, within a restrictive, political context" (4).

The shift from zone to demarcation was an evolutionary one that slowly occurred from the seventeenth through the nineteenth centuries. A movement from territorial sovereignty into political nationalism was accompanied by a shift in public rhetoric, especially in the content of patriotic discourses. Gerald Newman, concerned with the rise of English nationalism, argues that it is useful to distinguish between patriotism and nationalism. He suggests that patriotism is a relatively primitive feeling of loyalty to one's nation, often connected with military matters, an attachment to the country's prestige in the context of foreign relations. Nationalism, on the other hand, is "a much more complex, programmatic and historically conditioned elaboration of this simple feeling [patriotism] into *patterns and demands of actions* deeply affecting group policy. . . . it takes all the nation's affairs, internal as well as external, into its compass" (Newman 52, 54).

A similar evolution in the content of English patriotic rhetoric accompanied this shift from territory to nation. Peter Furtado's work adds an important dimension to this issue, primarily because he locates the difference in political rhetoric in a relatively precise historical moment, one that points to important changes in England's status as a potential worldwide trading and imperial power. He writes that, before the late seventeenth century, loyalty to the monarch or support for the Protestant Church took precedence over loyalty to anything called a nation; during the late seventeenth century, however, "the language of patriotism became firmly established in the repertoire of English political rhetoric" (1.44), especially during the Commonwealth and in a time of national emergency. His interpretation of this change emphasizes its uniqueness:

> The crucial event in this [enthusiasm for an active secular national foreign policy] was the First Anglo-Dutch War of 1652–4. . . . Though the war was followed in detail in the

news-sheets of the day, it was not accompanied by an out-
burst anything like jingoism; instead, it seems that this war
was unusual for its day in being *only* comprehensible in
terms of a clash of calculable national interests, for there was
none of the more familiar background of dynastic, religious
or traditional xenophobic animosities. The rewards of victory,
beyond the tonnage of enemy ships captured, comprised only
the assertion of English hegemony over the Narrow Seas,
and thus the abstract exaltation of national honour. (1.51)

The First Anglo-Dutch War thus clarified England's perception of
itself as a separate, secular nation with particular national interests
at odds with other nations' national interests.

After 1660 and the restoration of the Stuart monarchy, patriotic expressions took on an important internal political function,
one related to the traumas of the recent civil war and to the
continuing tensions within the country: patriotism was used for
"the sublimination and exteriorisation of the conflicts of mid- and
late-seventeenth-century English society" (Furtado 47). This is a
particularly powerful insight, for such a combination of genuine
political rhetoric coupled with the sublimination of internal difference can be found in some of the literature of the late seventeenth century, specifically in Mary Pix's *Spanish Wives* (1706). Two
excerpts that celebrate English freedom will illustrate. In a love
song, a Spanish lover listens to his English beloved sing to him a
description of the liberties of English wives:

> Ere I submit to be your Wife
> Listen to an English Husband's life:
> With Sparks abroad I'm every day,
> Gracing the Gardens, Park, or Play,
> Hearing all the pretty things they say,
> Give and take Presents, and when that's done,
> You thank the Beaux when I come home.
>
> (19)

In the second excerpt, the character of the gentle Spanish Governor (who finally does indeed allow his wife more liberty than the
average Spaniard) is willing to speak of men's compensatory pleasures if such womanly liberty leads her astray:

—Phough! I have been in England.——
There they are the happiest Husbands——
If a man does happen to be a cuckold,
Which, by the way, is almost as rare as in *Spain;*
But, I say, if it does fallout, all his Wife's Friends
Are his; and he's caress'd—nay, godszooks, many times
Rises to his preferment by it.

(2)

Obviously, when played before an English audience, patriotic sentiments in scenes like these can have the force of argument and produce persuasive power—but only when they exist in contrast to a negative, repressive, or in some other way lamentable set of social conditions. And Pix creates just such an environment by choosing to set her drama in Spain, long looked on with suspicion by the English for its repressive treatment of women.

Equally important, however, is Pix's status as an English *woman.* In that context, the celebratory speeches above can be read as much as ironic complaints, based on gender differences, as genuine political statements. Thus she may, on the surface, criticize Spain by suggesting that the average Spaniard's sense of honor blinds him to the active benefits of English cuckoldry—the possibility that he will have even greater access to women, an action described, in a lovely pun, in the language of political upward mobility. But such statements are clearly false. Pix's comedy therefore serves as much as a lament for the oppressive circumstances for women in her own country as a criticism of foreign practices. A theatergoer, however, listening to such speeches, would be more likely to hear the humor rather than the complaint in the remarks, and the result is the displacement of the tensions between the genders in England onto the repressive behavior of Spaniards. An internal problem is exteriorized, and its solution satisfies because it appeals to a citizen's relatively secure sense of patriotism and not to the anxiety of gender inequity.

Such displacement can occur only when there is an equal or greater perceived benefit to be had elsewhere. Furtado argues that this benefit was the nation: "For patriotism to serve as a means of sublimating internal conflict, it must be able to appeal to a universally understood entity or image of the nation, in relation to which all citizens, of whatever social rank, must be equally submissive" (49). As a result, patriotism could function within an increasingly secularized political world not only as a way to position England's interests against that of a foreign other but also as a means of producing England's definition of Englishness; the result is Newman's nationalism: an elaboration of patriotism into patterns of actions affecting group policy. We saw this phenomenon emerging in the earliest performances of Dryden's *Indian Emperour* and its presentation of the good and worthy English imperialist, a man who functions not as the rapacious conquistador but as the sophisticated lover of a beautiful woman and the land she represents.

The "universally understood entity" that subliminates and appeals, in Furtado's terms, became Britannia, whose main characteristics by 1700, other than epitomizing national pride, included Britain's close identification with liberty, its hegemony over the sea, and its imperial destiny (49). Even this image, to function productively, had to have the power to attract widespread allegiance, and Colley argues that such attraction was found in the idea of the island as a nation, an entity that promised special profit for individual Britons:

> Great Britain was forged in the way that it was after 1707, and to the extent that it was, in part because different classes and interest groups came to see this newly invented nation as a usable resource, as a focus of loyalty which would also cater to their own needs and ambitions. From patriotism, men and women were able to anticipate profits of some kind. (55)

Thus the creation of national identity passes through an evolution from territory into nation, one supported—in the case of England—by a secular patriotic rhetoric that celebrated the excellencies of the island in contrast to the deficiencies of foreign powers while it simultaneously contained internal anxieties and strife. But that very act of creation, "imagining" a nation as Benedict Anderson would have it, is fraught with anxiety, a fact Peter Stallybrass recognizes:

> While the nation is inscribed within geographical boundaries which separate inlaws from outlaws, brother from others, it is not only a spatial entity. The nation has to be

invented or written; and written, what is more, in the crucial
and troubling knowledge that it could be written otherwise.
It is because the nation could be written otherwise that the
act of writing must be forgotten, transformed instead into
the act of reading a pre-given past. (3.200)

Each play analyzed below contributes in its own way to the inven-
tions of England and Englishness, a category of identity being re-
written according to changing economic and social conditions,
both at home and abroad, during the late seventeenth century.

Essential Identities:
Behn's *Dutch Lovers*

In that context, I begin with Aphra Behn's *Dutch Lover* (1673), a
play set in Madrid and involving primarily Spanish and Dutch but
also German and Belgian characters.[2] On an English stage, English
actors played the parts of national others, but they do so in a traditionally theatrical way; that is, they mimic in order to impersonate, not to draw attention to and criticize the "foreigners." All do
so, that is, except the title character, the Dutch Lover. He is the only
one who is positioned as the object of national ridicule, for it is his
"Dutchness" that provides the grounds for comedy. My interest in
such a presentation resides in what Raphael Samuel calls "national
fictions":

> National fictions might be considered not as reflections of
> ideology, whether at second or third remove, but as compo-
> nents in it, an imaginative underpinning, or disguise, for pre-
> cepts which are common currency of political debate. . . . in
> dealing with the figures of national myth, one is confronted
> not by realities which become fictions, but rather by fictions
> which, by dint of their popularity, become realities in their
> own right. (xix, xxvii)

This process of making fiction into reality is clear in Behn's play
as she appeals to an abiding set of English prejudices concerning
the Dutch (a concurrent production in that season was Dryden's
virulently anti-Dutch *Amboyna*). Eighteenth-century prints provide
a wealth of material evidence, as Michael Duffy's *Foreigners in England* demonstrates. Called by Britains "cheese-worms," "maggots,"

and "hogs," Hollanders were presumed to be motivated by avarice, cowardly when drunk, and willing to let others fight for their freedoms. Their connection to the Commonwealth rebels also made them suspect low republicans. These prejudices grew out of the often intimate historical relationship between these two countries. During Elizabeth's reign, as a response to Spanish aggression, the English strengthened their ties with the Dutch. Economically, the countries were linked because Holland was a center for fishing and for the distribution of English woolen exports. There were Protestant religious ties between the two nations, and thus a free Holland was valued as a buffer against a Catholic Spanish invasion, a fact that worked to strengthen political ties. In times of peace, the English could admire such character traits as Dutch industry, neatness, and social welfare (Duffy 27–31).

By the mid-seventeenth century, however, English attitudes began to change, primarily because the Dutch had proven themselves to be such adroit traders that the English began to fear the possibility of a Dutch trade monopoly. Fernand Braudel, calling Amsterdam "an urban centre with an imperial vocation" (235), argues that the Dutch had indeed created for themselves the most advantageous trade circumstances:

> The warehouses of Amsterdam could absorb and then disgorge any amount of goods. There was an extraordinary volume of property, material, goods, and services on the market, all available at a moment's notice. At a given command, the entire machine went into action. This was the means whereby Amsterdam maintained her superiority—an abundance of ever-ready goods and a great mass of money in constant circulation. When they belonged to a certain class, the merchants and political leaders of Holland could hardly fail to be aware, through their day-to-day practice, of the immense power they wielded. (236)

It is therefore not surprising that during the years 1652–54, 1665–67, and 1672–74, England and Holland waged three violent wars. The first, Cromwell's war, was popular, for it netted booty from the Americas and increased England's economic position. The second, Charles II's first war, was less lucrative, but it still had the power to stimulate such celebratory and patriotic verses as Dryden's *Annus*

Mirabilis—a poem that ends with the prophecy that London, not Amsterdam, would henceforth become the universal center for trade:

> 297
> Now, like a maiden queen, she will behold
> From her high turrets, hourly suitors come;
> The East with incense and the West with gold
> Will stand like suppliants to receive her doom.

> 300
> The vent'rous merchant, who design'd more far
> And touches on our hospitable shore,
> Charm'd with the splendour of this Northern Star,
> Shall here unlade him and depart no more.

> 301
> Our power'ful navy shall no longer meet,
> The wealth of France or Holland to invade;
> The beauty of this town, without a fleet,
> From all the world shall vindicate her trade.

> 302
> And while this fam'd emporium we prepare,
> The British ocean shall such triumphs boast
> That those who now disdain our trade to share
> Shall rob like pirates our wealthy coast.

By 1672, however, Charles II's decision to create an alliance with the Catholic French in order to wage war against the Protestant Dutch proved to be generally unpopular and provoked public resistance.

During the late seventeenth century, while Spanish imperialist ambitions and power waned, the quite genuine and growing threat posed by both the Dutch and the French intensified. Their figures, too, haunted British imaginations, as bodies defiled by food unpleasant to English palates (including the eating of frogs, a part of French cuisine) or as avaricious drunks featured in eighteenth-century print caricatures of the Dutch. The real threat posed by the Dutch was thus less predicated on money and more on status: the English were afraid of being outwitted by a group of social inferiors. "This feeling," writes Michael Duffy, "that the Dutch were not quite gentlemen, was reflected in a marked lack of upper-class travel in Holland [as] compared to France in the seventeenth century (although there was a remarkably large lower-class flow to learn trade and service), and by the representation of the Dutch in prints from the early eighteenth century onwards in plain burgher costume" (29). Behn's play therefore takes on special meaning when set within this contemporary political situation: the Third Anglo-Dutch War (1672–74), well underway at the time the play premiered and supported by Charles II (and by Behn's own well-established Tory sentiments), gave her broad license to bolster royal foreign policy and to make England's current enemy the object of scorn.

But the play is supremely odd in many respects. The multiple love plots range from a case of seeming incestuous love, to the debauching of a young Spanish woman, to an ingenue couple's outwitting of a coercive father by foiling the arranged marriage with the Dutch lover. The plot abounds in mistaken identities, potential and real violence, guilt, passion, and disguises, not just anti-Dutch sentiment. Indeed, as Jacqueline Pearson points out, the play offers a wide range of especially fluid national positions: "The Dutch Haunce van Ezel is half-Spanish, the Flanders colonel Alonzo discovers that he is really Spanish, Spanish Hippolita adopts disguise as a Venetian, and Spanish Alonzo disguises himself as a Dutchman" (229). It is just these instances of cross-national dressing that interest me here, impersonations that serve as relatively straightforward assaults on England's current enemy and thus as a theatrical confirmation of English prejudices. More important, the play and its presentation of these national others also participate in the larger process of establishing a very particular identity for those other nations—the production of a "national fiction" through the ideological force of theatrical impersonation. Behn accomplishes this task, to position the Dutch as worthy of continued English loathing, through ridicule and exaggeration, the standard tools of satire. She also manages to shear off some of the anxieties about a fearsome military enemy, to reduce, deflate, and confine its potential threat. But the strategy she employs does more than suggest that the Dutch are essentially different from the English; it works to subliminate internal class tensions—between merchants and gentleman—by exteriorizing them in the form of national conflict.

The ridicule centers on the Dutch lover, Haunce van Ezel—a character generally agreed to be "half man, half fool." We are not, however, initially introduced to him but to one of the Spanish heroes—Alonzo—who impersonates the Dutchman in order to fool Euphemia's father into allowing him access to her. Thus this double, a performing "Haunce," initially carries the burden of the anti-Dutch sentiment. The cross-dressed national impersonator enters, "dressed ridiculously," while his friend cautions him that in order to be believable as the foppish and awkward "Haunce," he must be "very rude, and very impertinent." Of course, an English actor's impersonation of such bad Dutch behavior as performed by a Spaniard would readily delight an English audience, and "Haunce" readily complies—by constantly interrupting, lasciviously demanding to see his intended, and just generally refusing to observe any social signs of disapproval. His activities produce the desired result: he wins Euphemia's father's displeasure and disdain for the oafish Dutch suitor.

When the "real" Haunce makes his first onstage entrance in act 3, scene 2, we are not disappointed, even though Behn's stage directions provide no specifics as to the ludicrousness of his attire, only that he wears *"a fantastical travelling habit."* Sick from the journey—"a pox of all Sea-voyages" are the first words out of his mouth—he swigs brandy and staggers about as his servant offers a useful suggestion: "Sir, if I may advise, take t'other turn in the Grove, for I find by my nose you want more airing" (3.1–5). Haunce responds with his own more vigorous warning: "Do not name a storm to me, unless thou wilt have the effects on't in thy face" (3.2.11). His first appearance thus confirms many English prejudices about the Dutch: he is drunk and unpleasant, he stinks from the voyage and from his sea sickness, and he is completely unaware of his own repulsiveness. Such a representation is good and traditional grist for the comedy mill: he is a standard unselfconscious comic character, whose servant has more insight and sensitivity to nuance than he does. But the most pointed satire of his character is located in a more threatening and meaningful political and economic context—in the issue of his class status as merchant and his desire to escape the confines of that status through mimicking the fashion of his "betters."

It is commonplace in Behn scholarship to acknowledge that

while she will question essential identities for women—witness the number of plays where the "categories of women" breakdown (*The Rover, The Second Part of The Rover,* and *The Widdow Ranter* are three such examples discussed in this book)—she is generally willing to essentialize status. *Oroonoko,* early cited as an example of Behn's admirable abolitionist impulses, is now generally looked upon as her complaint about the treatment of a royal person, no matter his country of origin. Status thus often overrides other considerations, especially for her male characters. Haunce van Ezel is no exception. For example, when he insists to his servant that Euphemia will love him once he goes home, cleans up, and dresses the part, his servant tells him "none but a Cavalier ought to be soundly drunk, or wear a sword and feather; . . . a cloak and band were fitter for a Merchant" (3.2.42–44). Haunce rejects this advice, and the status location that positions him below his desires, by demanding that he has as much right to "any sort of debauchery or gallantry" as any man. By Behn's lights, his quest for upward mobility is bad enough; worse still is his flawed notion of gentlemanly character, one that is entirely superficial, for it translates only into the external signs of clothing and unattractive social excesses.

When his servant then reminds him of his usual attire at home, his "essential" foulness is confirmed. It is a passage worth quoting at length:

> Do you remember, Sir, how you were wont to go at home? When instead of a Periwig, you wore a slink, greasy hair of your own, through which a pair of large thin souses appeared, to support a formal hat, on end thus— . . . A Collar instead of a Cravat twelve inches high; with blew, stiff, starcht, lawn Band, set in print like your Whiskers; a Doublet with small Skirts hooked to a pair of wide-kneed Briches, which dangled half way over a leg, all to be dash'd and durty'd as high as the gartering. . . . Your hand, defil'd with counting of damn'd durty money . . . A cloak, half a yard shorter than the Breeches, not through lin'd, but fac'd as far as 'twas turned back, with a pair of frugal butter-hams.
>
> (3.2.48–63)

This description not only fails to insult Haunce but actually pleases him, so much so that he laughs throughout his servant's description and responds with this retort: "And dost thou not know when one of those thou hast described, goes but half a league out of Town, that he is so transform'd from the Merchant to the Gallant in all Points, that his own parents, nay the Devil himself cannot know him?" (3.2.75–78).

Haunce names the real threat here: that a merchant might indeed transform his status—and therefore fool a vulnerable public —through a quick change of clothes. Such a possibility was quite real in a society without strong sumptuary legislation. Frances Elizabeth Baldwin, calling the reign of Elizabeth I "the zenith of sumptuary legislation in England," reports that James I repealed all of the existing sumptuary laws; this act "proved to be a death-blow to English sumptuary legislation," so much so that not even during the Commonwealth was new sumptuary legislation passed (248–49). Charles II made half-hearted attempts to regulate only one "style" of dress—burial clothing: "no one whatsoever shall be buried in any shirt, shift or sheet made of anything but wool, or put into a coffin lined with anything made of flax, silk, hemp or hair." But such laws were obviously intended less to regulate personal display than to encourage the wool industry (265). Thus if insufficient public vigilance fails, and by 1673 merchants did indeed have easy access—through plenty of ready money for wardrobe changes—to the "real" signs of a rank not their own, then the possibility for misreading the signs and the blurring of the "real" boundaries of rank becomes powerfully threatening.

Behn therefore takes pains to make clear Haunce's "real" nature as unfashionable, cheap, and dirty. His essential identity as social inferior, as a trading man, is confirmed time and again—not through his clothing, but through his character deficiencies. For instance, when drunk, he willingly enters into a dangerous situation and actually fights to defend Hippolita. When sober—that is, in his "real" character—he is the complete coward, so much so that he actually cries when later confronted by Alonzo. Moreover, his hope that his own status-boundary can be breached leads to a general and more threatening "identity confusion," one that Behn especially emphasizes when it spills over into a "confusion of women."[3] This occurs when Haunce first encounters Euphemia and Olinda, his intended and her serving maid. Haunce cannot identify the status difference between them: "Ay, one of these must be she: but 'tis a wonder I should not know which she is by instinct" (4.1.71).

Worst of all, according to Behn's standards, he sees women in an exclusively mercantile context—commodities and items to be bought and sold with as much interest or commitment as he would give a shipment of wool. When Euphemia's brother threatens to break off the match, he responds in the passionless jargon of business transactions: "Why should I run my self into a premunire when I need not; your Father is bound by agreement to mine, to deliver me the wares (that is, his Daughter) safe and sound; and I have no more to do, but to protest against him in case of non-performance. 'Twill be a dear commodity to me at this rate" (4.2.53–57). If the item in question is not delivered in good order, he will simply initiate a standard civil breach-of-contract suit.

In the final scene, these questions of identification come to a head when the impersonating "Haunce" meets the "real" Haunce. When Euphemia's father demands to know the identities of the two identically dressed men before him, the "real" Haunce reaches the outermost limits of his understanding concerning identity categories as they are encoded in the signs of fashion—so much so that he is willing to sacrifice his own "real" identity altogether: "I know no more than the great *Turk,* not I, which of us is me; my hat, my feather, my sute, and my Garniture all over, faith now; and I believe this is me, for I'l trust my eyes before any other sense about me" (5.2.81–83). This is Behn's comment on the worst possible outcome of unfixed and unreadable identities: the "real" Haunce goes so far as to surrender his own identity when he seeks status position superior to the one he deserves.

In the end, when he bumbles into a marriage with Olinda, Euphemia's maid, he confirms an English audience's desire that he get his just deserts—and, more important, their desire that he marry a woman befitting his status position. Insensitive as always to the necessity, as Behn sees it, of maintaining status boundaries, Haunce blithely and happily celebrates the match: "Now do they all expect I should be dissatisfied; but, Gentlemen, in sign and token that I am not, I'll have one more merry frisk before we part, 'tis a witty wench; faith and troth after a month 'tis all one whose who" (52.191–93). While it may indeed be "all one" to Haunce, Behn strongly rejects this attempt to level or even status difference by dropping the curtain on this final vision: the essentially lower-class Dutchman dances sprightly with his fitting serving-class maid.

It is Behn's clever use of the cross-dressed national, both a real and an impersonating Haunce, that allows her to make these essentialist arguments. The doubling of Haunce's identity confirms a performed versus a real identity. And yet, in a larger context, an audience knows that it is an English actor playing the Dutch Haunce. His "realness" is only as real as the actor's skill in mimicking the audience's national prejudices. But onstage, the doubling performs a double ideological function: on the surface, it exploits an external conflict and thus serves to contain English anxiety about the war, promote patriotic spirit, and deliver a "just" reward to a repugnant national other; less transparently, it also models and solves an internal problem—by presenting the possibility of a too-permeable English status boundary in the form of a threatening national other, Behn's punishment of the threatening foreigner inevitably spills over on the upstart homegrown merchant.

Performing Nations:
Wycherley's *Gentleman Dancing-Master*

Wycherley's *Gentleman Dancing-Master* (1673) would seem, on the surface, to present a very different case: unlike Behn's *Dutch Lover,* this play is set in England and features only English characters. But Wycherley presents a more complex presentation of the problem of national others because he does so in an even more explicitly mercantile context, and thus I want to investigate the part he played in rewriting not only the definition of other national characters but also the limits and degrees of acceptable Englishness.[4] The title, lifted from Calderon's *El Maestro de Danzar,* points to a gentleman, Mr. Gerrard, as the nominal hero. His problem in the play is that he is forced by circumstances to impersonate not a national other but a gendered other—a dancing-master—in order to win time alone with and woo the heroine, Hippolita. Thus he is forced, unlike Haunce, to "dress down" in terms of his social rank. We know that he is a gentleman because he is willing to engage in amorous adventures and to display a hearty manliness. But this manliness must be tempered when he accepts his role as dancing-master: he must perform a gentler, more repetitive masculinity, one that smacks of female "accomplishment" and lacks the bravado he displays with his male friends. Yet we also know he is a "good" Englishman from an early scene when he insists to his drinking companions at a tavern that they sing no foreign songs, only "Arthur of Bradley" or "I am the Duke of Norfolk," two traditional and very English ballads.

The impediments to his match with Hippolita are not the fact that she is a fourteen year old who has been continuously cloistered throughout her youth. Instead, two family members, who are experiencing "identity confusion," act as the blocking characters. These men, however, bear the burden of a particularly pernicious form of the disorder, for they suffer from "nation confusion." The first is her father, Sir James Formal. As an Englishman having lived in Spain for fifteen years, he returns home thoroughly enamored of all Spanish customs: he insists on being called Don Diego, dressing in the Spanish fashion, and muttering oaths in Spanish. He is also especially keen to maintain the family honor in the Spanish tradition, by preserving his daughter's chastity. In quest of that, he has decided to marry Hippolita off to the second obstacle to her happiness, her cousin Nathaniel Parris, or Monsieur de Paris, as he wishes to be called. This Englishman, having visited France for only three months, has returned home thoroughly Frenchified—so much so that he speaks broken English, cannot recall the names of London landmarks, and cultivates all of the fashion excesses of the French. Obviously the necessary ingredients for national stereotyping and patriotic ridicule are present.

And, indeed, Wycherley makes much of the standard English complaints of the times about the Spanish and the French. As Michael Duffy's examination of eighteenth-century print culture has revealed, during the first half of the seventeenth century, the Spaniard was "the foremost foreigner." Spanish imperial might, dwindling precipitously after the Renaissance, still could provoke powerful emotions in the English, especially their monopoly of New World trade and reports, like those of Las Casas, that detailed in specific and horrifying ways their cruel treatment of native inhabitants. The standard complaint persisted—that Spain was dedicated to a Spanish, Catholic universal monarchy—while new complaints about Spanish habits and "essential" national characteristics took on new power. According to Duffy, the English were quick to complain about Spanish pride, symbolized in their cloaks and ruffs, which themselves symbolized the Spaniards's being lost, mentally, in a world of their past grandeur; a Spanish laziness that provoked them to live off of what others had earned or plundered; Spanish obstinacy and their refusal to admit a loss of power that subsequently led to contemporary political instability (26).

Similar print treatments of Spanish deficiencies of character abound. A 1599 text, called *A Pageant of Spanish Humours*, contains chapter titles that run this way: "A Signor is an Angel in the Church," "A Devil in his Lodging," "A Woolfe at Table," "A Hogge in his Chamber"; on occasion, the author is less loquacious and indicates Spanish character only as "Avaritious," "Ambitious," or "Bloodthirstie and Tyrannous." A somewhat later account, the 1624 *Spaniards Perpetual Designs to Universal Monarchie* (translated from the French), draws on Las Casas for its descriptions of the Spaniards's "monstrous, outrageous, and new devised cruelties, which these devilish and tyrannous Spaniards have inhumanely practiced amongst the simple and innocent" peoples of the Americas (31). *The Character of Spain: Or, an Epitome of Their Virtues and Vices,* published in 1660 and obviously derived from Black Legend sources, is representative in that its references are mainly exaggerated accounts of Las Casas's *Devastation of the Indies*; this 1660 author insists that "the blood they spilt would over-poise all the gold [the Spanish] ever fetch from [the New World], if it were counter-ballanced" (35). In 1656, John Phillips (nephew to John Milton) published an account of Las Casas called *Tears of the Indians,* a text that contains extraordinary engravings featuring the burning alive of native inhabitants—including the incineration of an infant—as well as suggestions that the Spaniards, not the Indians, actually practiced cannibalism. Davenant's *Cruelty of the Spaniards in Peru* (1658) employed elaborate painted scenes, music, and spectacle to tell the story of innocent native inhabitants abused by Spaniards to call for the English to intervene and free them from "the Yoke of the Spaniard." Thus old fears of Spanish imperialism —tales of cruelty, rapaciousness, and greed—lingered, even though the might of the Spanish Empire had dwindled precipitously.

By the 1660s, however, a change in English attitudes toward the Spanish was underway, primarily because a more powerful and what would prove to be more consistent and abiding fear of the French began after Charles II's return. If the English feared the Spanish because they presumed to desire "universal monarchy" and if they feared the Dutch because they were ambitious to own a "universal trade," then the French were doubly feared—for they were seen not only as desiring but also perhaps capable of obtaining both. Many English merchants especially began to feel that the country should make peace with a weakened Spain and war with the much too successful mercantile Dutch; even more strongly they argued that England should turn its military attention to the "real" enemy, the French, who were blocking trade both in Europe and in the Americas and injuring, through the imposition of high tariffs, the English woolen market. A decisive turning point came, in 1667, when Louis XIV seized territory in the Spanish Netherlands, an event that illuminated the fact of a very strong French military presence throughout the Continent; these fears were confirmed when France effectively overran Holland in 1672, the year before Wycherley's play premiered.

The English attempted to contain their anxieties about French military and commercial might through ridiculing the habits of its citizens. Peasants, for instance, were represented in eighteenth-century prints as poverty-stricken and abject, and thus they were featured eating food, like frogs and snails, disgusting to the English palate. Moreover, the French were presumed to be incapable of appreciating and, therefore, of fighting for political freedom; hence, their acceptance of an absolutist government. And finally, these assumptions combined to create a picture of an aristocracy too full of levity and folly, too indulgent in the superfluities of life, and thus too effete to appreciate a more vigorous English liberty: "They were [represented as] a naturally subservient people, too concerned with their own pleasures. They fiddled and danced while being plundered by their own king" (Duffy 31–35).

Thus Wycherley's two national "others" in *The Gentleman Dancing-Master* are set against each other as representatives of past and future imperial threats. They also serve, however, to delineate the differences between the visible traits of Spanish implacability or French decadence and the soundness of an English constitution. The first, Don Diego, is the quintessential Spaniard. In his *gravitas* and his great readiness to fight for his honor, he reveals an intransigence too extreme for an Englishman. He describes it this way: "Now in Spain he is wise enough that is grave, politic enough that says little and honourable enough that is jealous, and though I say it that should not say it, I am as grave, grum and jealous as any Spaniard breathing" (2.1.38–42). Monsieur de Paris is, of course, just the opposite. He is far too willing to change according to the fashion whims of the moment, a fact he reveals in the following dialogue:

> *Monsieur:* And do I speak agreeable ill Englis' enough?
> *Gerrard:* Very ill.
> *Monsieur:* Veritablement?
> *Gerrard:* Veritablement.
> *Monsieur:* For you must know, 'tis as ill-breeding now to speak good Englis' as to write good Englis', good sense or a good hand.
> *Gerrard:* But indeed, methinks, you are not slovenly enough for a Frenchman.
> *Monsieur:* Slovenly! You mean negligent?
> *Gerrard:* No, I mean slovenly.
> *Monsieur:* Then I will be more slovenly.
> *Gerrard:* You know, to be a perfect Frenchman you must never be silent, never sit still, and never be clean.
> *Martin:* But you have forgot one main qualification of a true Frenchman: he should never be sound, that is, be very pocky.
> *Monsieur:* Oh, if dat be all, I am very pocky, pocky enough, jarnie. That is the only French qualification may be had without going to Paris, mon foy.
>
> (1.2.148–68)

Gerrard even goes so far as to say that "in three months at Paris you could renounce your language, drinking and your country . . . and come home so perfect a Frenchman that the draymen of your father's own brewhouse would be ready to knock thee in the head." (1.2.136–41). Thus the Spanish Don Diego is presented as the potential perpetrator of violence, while the French Monsieur is presented as the pocky object of violence.[5] Each character is positioned as different in spirit and in character.

And yet, both are *Englishmen* suffering, as Wycherley would have it, from the delusion that their nationhood can be taken off or put on as easily as a new set of clothes. The situation raises an opportunity for Wycherley to question and define the limits of English national character; it also raises, for modern readers, an opportunity to examine and interrogate the means by which Wycherley accomplishes this definition.

Because both Don Diego and Parris are obsessed with the clothing of their adopted nation, it is fitting that fashion becomes the ground upon which these cross-dressed nationals wage their most furious battle. For Don Diego, character is good, proper, and worthy only when it is visible in the "signs" of the Spaniard: "And I will be a Spaniard in everything still and will not conform, not I, to their ill-favoured English customs, for I will wear my Spanish habit still, I will stroke my Spanish whiskers still and I will eat my Spanish olio still and my daughter shall go a maid to her husband's bed, let the English custom be what 'twill" (2.1.44–50). He therefore insists to Parris that he may marry Hippolita only if he will do so attired in the complete Spanish fashion.

The funniest moments in the play concern the fight over this process of Parris's transformation into Don Diego's version of a Spaniard. With great pride in and vanity about his Frenchness, Parris asks his future father-in-law, "Have you not the admiration for my pantaloon, Don Diego mon oncle?" The Don replies, "I am astonished at them *verdaderamente;* they are wonderfully ridiculous." This provokes a hymn to the French signature garment from Parris:

> Redicule, redicule! Ah, 'tis well you are my uncle, da.
> Redicule, ah! Is dere anting in de universe so gentil as
> de pantaloons? Anyting so ravisaunt as de pantaloons? Auh,
> I could kneel down and varship a pair of gentil pantaloons.
> Vat, Vat, you would have me have de admiration for dis out-
> ward skin of your thigh which you call Spanish hose. Fie,
> fie, fie, ha, ha, ha.
>
> (3.1.185–195)

Each "reads" the other's outward appearance—the frontier of the social self—as though it signifies transparently. Of course, the obstacle to Don Diego's plan is that Parris will not cooperate with his Spanification, for he, too, shares the Don's profound faith in the inextricable connection between fashion and character.

Much of the rest of the action therefore concerns Parris's being slowly shorn of his beloved French garments, events that provide a perfect example of Garber's "category crisis"—"a failure of definitional distinction, a borderline that becomes permeable" (16). A moment in act 4 carries these illuminating stage directions:

Enter MONSIEUR DE PARIS without a peruke, with a Spanish
hat, a Spanish doublet, stockings and shoes but in *pantaloons,*
a waist-belt and a Spanish dagger in't and a *cravat* about his
neck. Enter HIPPOLITA and PRUE [her maid] behind, laughing.
(4.1 [emphasis mine])

Laughing, indeed, for the Monsieur is a hideous amalgamation of
cross-national signs. When the women suggest that his identity as
a Spaniard is less than convincing, Hippolita asks the essentialist's
question: "But where's your Spanish beard, the thing of most consequence?" Parris replies with the constructionist's answer: "Jernie,
do you tink beards are as easy to be had as in de playhouses? Non.
But if here be no ugly, long Spanish beard, here are, I am certain,
the ugly, long Spanish ear [earrings unpopular in both France and
England]" (4.1.14–19).

In such a moment, Wycherley has created a scene whose elements could have allowed him to interrogate the nature of identity
itself—identities located in beards and bodies, as opposed to national fashions presented in social performance. Instead he constructs this scene, indeed the entire drama, *not* to interrogate or
undermine the notion that identity categories themselves are essential but to reassert and reinscribe the limits of acceptable Englishness, a moment that cultivates what Colley calls the "strong
sense of dissimilarity from those without" (17). The scene thus
conspires to point only to the ridiculousness of an Englishman's
refusing his birthright and heritage by choosing instead to make
himself a spectacle through dressing cross-nationally.

The last scenes of Parris's transformation even more strongly
emphasize this point. The stage directions read "Enter MONSIEUR in
the Spanish habit entire only with a cravat and followed by the
little BLACKAMOOR with a golilla in his hand" (4.1.124), the golilla
being the stiff, wired collar that stands up behind the neck, the
signature garment of Spain. When Don Diego commands the
young man, "Come, sirrah black, now do you teach him to walk
with the *verdadero gesto, gracia* and *gravidad* [the countenance, grace,
and seriousness] of a true Castilian" (4.1.163–65), the rest of the
scene is taken up with action that is especially theatrical—that is,
its effects are primarily visual and dependent on gestures and motion: a young black man, whose status (as a Spaniard, a Moor, or a

slave) is not clear, is given the task of instructing, by gesture and invitation to imitate, a foolish Englishman pretending to be a Frenchman about the social niceties demanded of a Spaniard.[6]

Depending on the way the scene is performed, the young man could be shown to be at least as adept at imitating a national other as is Don Diego; we can certainly see from the text that he is a better Spaniard than Parris is a Frenchman. And when Monsieur dubs him "my walking master," Wycherley's point is even more strongly made: here, onstage and in front of an audience, the absurdity of imitating what one *is* not, according to Wycherley's definition, is made doubly powerful with the introduction of the visual difference of race. Again, the scene conspires not to emphasize the general arbitrariness and artificiality of national categories, a conclusion a modern reader is almost forced to acknowledge; instead it contains a moment whose visual impact—especially in the spectacle of the nearly mute but extraordinarily adept Spanish "Blackamoor"—insists on the absurdity of breaching national boundaries. Even though we recognize that Wycherley has accomplished this comment through choreographing arbitrary and culture-bound social performances, the scene works—by insisting on this absurdity—to define national identity to be as natural, as inevitable, and as different as seventeenth-century definitions of race.

These elements alone make Wycherley's play a fascinating example of early modern British attempts to define essential national characters, and to build national boundaries, by locating them in material differences. But the play also premiered in the midst of the Third Anglo-Dutch war, a military endeavor that displayed England's willingness to fight to promulgate and protect its commercial interests and its burgeoning expansionist projects. Yet even as the English "discovered" and returned to their island the products and novelties of imperial expansion, they simultaneously sought out and invited into their now cosmopolitan homeland the "contamination" of foreign culture, events that signalled the beginnings of a new global economy that allowed for and helped actively to produce the radical change in England that Neil McKendrick calls the "consumer revolution."

Although McKendrick locates this revolution in the eighteenth-century, he acknowledges that it could not have occurred without "the pre-existence of many preparatory conditions dating back to the seventeenth century and some even deeper into the past" (14). Early in the seventeenth century, luxuries were equated with "foreign 'exotiques'" and thus were a danger to the balance of trade. By the 1690s, however, "mere consumption" had lost its pejorative meaning, and citizens had begun to accept the overall benefits of an elasticity of demand. Wycherley's 1673 play then is located between these moments of anxiety about importing foreign goods into England and recognition of the economic benefits of expanded trade opportunities.

By the eighteenth century, real social change had taken place. McKendrick's description of the new economic realities is worth quoting at length:

> More men and women than ever before in human history
> enjoyed the experience of acquiring material possessions.
> Objects which for centuries had been the privileged posses-
> sions of the rich came, within the space of a few generations,
> to be within the reach of a larger part of society than ever
> before, and, for the first time, to be within the legitimate
> aspirations of almost all of it. . . . What men and women
> had once hoped to inherit from their parents, they now
> expected to buy for themselves. What were once bought
> at the dictate of need, were now bought at the dictate of
> fashion. (1)

Even the possibility that changes such as those described above might occur in England produced discomfort for those gentlemen, like Wycherley, invested in maintaining the status quo. That once-unattainable material goods—luxuries owned exclusively by the upper classes who, as a result, also exclusively controlled their signification—could be placed within easy reach of anyone with sufficient capital also seemed to provide an easy and seemingly uncontrollable route for middling- and lower-class upward mobility.

McKendrick points out that the social organization of English society—"the potential it offered for social mobility, the social competition bred by its closely packed layers" (20)—provided a rich breeding ground for those committed to elevating their class status. In that context, fashion proved to be a particularly vital force: "In England where there was a constant restless striving to clamber from one rank to the next, and where possessions, and especially clothes, both symbolized and signalled each step in the social promotion, the economic potentialities of such social need could, if properly harnessed, be immense" (20–21). Dress, in particular, "was the most public manifestation of the blurring of status divisions which was so much commented on" (53).

Wycherley's play responds then, in its obvious obsession with dress and fashion, to these new possibilities and to the anxieties caused by potential boundary-crossings. These include the dangers of confusing or, worse still, making illegible the social significance of material goods that should serve, according to Wycherley, not just as signs for national divisions but for status distinctions as well. Thus, like the rhetoric of patriotism, Wycherley's play seeks ostensibly to define Englishness, but it does so through "the sublimination and exteriorisation" of internal, English status-conflicts. This anxiety, and Wycherley's means of containing it, are most intense in the closing scenes of *The Gentleman Dancing-Master,* when the romantic entanglements of the drama are placed in an explicitly mercantile context. In terms of national identities, the conclusion is rather tidy. Hippolita and the English gentleman Gerrard marry, with Don Diego's fortune if not his blessing. And Parris, in a proviso scene that presages (albeit in an ironic way) Millamant and Mirabell's similar negotiations, comes to an "understanding" with Flirt the prostitute, a bargain weighted heavily in favor of her personal and financial freedoms. The two cross-national dressers are humiliated in the process of learning their lessons about what Gerrard calls "imitating what we like": each is punished with the loss of or the loss of control over his fortunes.

When the suggestions about merchant Don Diego's less-than-ancient family lineage are made explicit at the close of the play, however, the audience learns an even more complex ideological lesson about the proper uses of English trading wealth and the proper ways of transferring it from one class to another, lessons that seek to contain the possibilities for upward mobility based on newly available material signifiers. We find out, in the last act, that the class status of Don Diego, Sir James Formal in England, is a recent acquisition. When Don Diego draws his sword on Gerrard for dishonoring "the grave, wise, noble, honourable, illustrious, puissant and right worshipful family of the Formals!" he begins to sputter about his family origins:

Don Diego: We are descended, look you . . . I say, we are
descended. . . . My great-great-great-grandfather, I say,
was—
Monsieur: Well, a pinmaker in—
Don Diego: But he was a gentleman for all that, fop, for he
was a sergeant to a company of the train-bands [citizen mili-
tia] and my great-great-grandfather was—
Monsieur: Was his son . . .
Don Diego: He was, he was—
Monsieur: He was a feltmaker, his son a wine-cooper, your
father a vintner, and so you came to be a Canary merchant.

(5.1.446–64)

The upward movement of the Formal family, from pinmaker to
wine-cooper, has culminated in the Don's status as a Canary merchant.[7] As such, he would have been involved not only in the wine
business but also in a wide range of West African trade, and his
"Blackamoor" servant at least suggests that human beings as well
as wine could have been counted among his importable and ex-
portable goods.[8] It is this fact—his status as an only-recently-
wealthy merchant and not just his compulsion to value all things
Spanish—upon which the play turns. His fifteen years in Spain
may have allowed him to amass a fortune, but when he exports
himself back to England he becomes only a figure of ridicule; his
current wealth will always be tainted by his humble family origins.[9]

All the more powerful, then, is the epilogue with which I
opened this chapter. Merchants such as James Formal would have
populated an audience that sees the monetary benefits of expanding trade and initiating the production of an imperial system.
Indeed, as Colley has argued, "a cult of commerce became an
increasingly important part of being British" (56). But she also
points out the social and political resistance to such upward mobility: "trade was the mainspring of Britain's economy and a vital
part of its identity, yes. But in terms of wealth, status and power,
men of trade in this society came a long way behind men of land,
and continued to do so for a long time" (56). It is just this lesson
about rank and status—that for Wycherley does not include easy
upward mobility for merchant men, even if they bring home the
wealth acquired through imperial ventures—that an audience must

learn. An English trader is an English trader, with a stable identity based on his family status, whether he affects the gravity of the Spaniard or not.

The play provides only one—standard and traditional—means for upward mobility: the transference of wealth through a daughter to a gentleman. In this case, the wealth goes not to a Frenchified dandy insensitive to the dangers of the erasure of national boundaries but to a decidedly English gentleman, one incapable of dissembling his essential Englishness (as his ridicule of his rival and his future father-in-law suggests), his essential masculinity (as his inept performance as a dancing-master displays), or his essential gentlemanly character (as his recognition of "the value" of Hippolita and her abilities, cleverly, to dissemble illustrates). In act 5, then, when Hippolita is handed to Gerrard, a fortune made in foreign lands is transferred back to England where, the play suggests, it belongs. The ultimate promise is that Don Diego's money will go on to produce, through his English daughter and her English gentleman, an abiding English fortune—one that may have been gotten in the "old" Spanish manner but one that is returned to England, and not handed to France, to be transmitted through a woman for cultivation and expansion.

Only one final irony remains: for all the play's ridicule of Don Diego's and Parris's readings of others based on the outward signs of their national fashions, it is clear that, under scrutiny, Don Diego is indeed as stiff-necked and unyielding as his golilla; and that Parris, under his cravat and pantaloons, is also truly an idiot. Both, it turns out, are reading the other entirely correctly: their adopted national fashions do indeed signify their essences. But as we have seen, the drama functions to deliver just the opposite message: the foreign excesses of these cross-national dressers serve not to suggest that Englishmen are capable of being insensitive and unyielding, blustery and foolish; instead they prove that English prejudices about the Spanish and French, and not internal anxieties about class and status, are just and true—a comfortable and self-satisfying message for any theatergoer engaged, if only tangentially, in the on-going wars, both military and commercial, fought in the 1670s. Defoe may be able to call the English "a Metaphor invented to express / A man a-kin to all the universe," but Wycherley is invested in approaching border crossings only as a means of marking and containing their limits.

Nation and Gender:
Mary Pix's *Adventures in Madrid*

Similar to the changes we saw in the presentation of colonial and national identity in Behn's *Widdow Ranter*, Mary Pix's *Adventures in Madrid*—which premiered in 1706 and against a backdrop of new social and political realities, especially the on-going War of Spanish Succession—treats gender and nation in ways qualitatively different from their treatment in *The Dutch Lovers* and *The Gentleman Dancing-Master*.[10] At this historical moment, the possibility of French hegemony is the problem that most vexes the British imagination. But Pix does not meet the French threat head-on. Instead, she too taps into old fears about the Spanish—tales of Spanish cruelty, rapaciousness, and greed—and into new fears focused on Spain and the Spanish empire as paradigms for the failed modern empire: a country that had made grave mistakes, in its quest for world dominance, mistakes that the new imperial nations were very anxious to avoid. In part as a means of displaying just why the Spanish had to be rejected as models for imperial power and in part as a means of shearing off public anxiety about the current War of Spanish Succession, Pix's play works out the problem of nation through gender, again with special attention to appropriate male behavior.

Pix also writes in a social climate different from that Behn and Wycherley faced, for by the 1700s changes in gender politics and gender identities had begun to shift generally toward the "feminine": that is, both men and women were rewarded for increased restraint, greater passivity, and deeper reflection—all virtues beginning to be associated with women. For women, that meant moving more into the invisibility of the domestic sphere, but for men it often meant choosing new ways to solve conflicts. Richard Steele's *Tatler No. 25*, for instance, urges men to put up their swords and to give up the practice of dueling on city streets, "so fatal a folly" he calls it. Thus Pix presents us with characters who allow us to see that the limits of nationhood and gender, rather than nationhood and status, are much more explicitly delimited, especially as they are presented as actively co-constituative—categories that point to the appropriate and reject the inappropriate nations and genders for the imperial project.

Like Behn's *Dutch Lover*, *The Adventures in Madrid* is set in the

Spanish capital, but Pix employs only Spanish and English characters in her comedy. Still, national differences abound, as they do in both the Wycherley and Behn dramas, and the first two scenes of *The Adventures in Madrid* work through one way that nation and gender are interdependent. In act 1, we meet two English heroes, one of whom is dressed as a Spaniard, and their very first exchange concerns the wearing of the fashions of another country, an act immediately linked to questions of gender. Gaylove, spotting his friend Bellmour "Equipt . . . a la Mode D'Espagne," exclaims, "I'd as soon change the Habit of thy Sex and wear the Women's Furbelows as these Dam'd Golilia's" (1). As shocking as it might seem to a modern audience, Gaylove's remark indicates that he would prefer a English*man* cross-dressed as an English*woman* to an *English*man cross-dressed as a *Spanish* man, a remark that more than suggests that if both positions—nation and gender—are performable, then nation overrides gender.

Bellmour, himself wearing glasses in the Spanish mode, resists that too easy argument and retorts with a remark that situates him as the predatory male: claiming that spectacles in Spain are "a Proof of Manhood not of Age," he points out that "not a Hero of fourteen durst pretend to a piece of Gallantry without these Magnifying Glasses, adorn'd his Nose" (1). Entering into the joyful spirit of this game, Gaylove then suggests that they transport the glasses back to England to help a "Decay'd Beauty" of his acquaintance in her patching, and Bellmour chimes in that the Spanish "close Collar" would also help to hide the wrinkles in the lady's neck (1–2). These lines contain a rather complex maneuver and a revealing ideological lesson: after an initial gesture that attempts to belittle and feminize an English *man* (a suggestion that a man's national fashions are more important than his gender), together these Englishmen come up with a better idea: transport all Spanish *men's* fashions back to English *women* for their improvement. Thus, in a few short lines of dialogue, national identity is simultaneously hierarchized and gendered: Englishness can contain either gender, while Spanishness is fit only for women—and old women at that.

Gaylove, still chafing against the vision of his friend's Spanification and not quite willing to give up on his ridicule, then insists that his design is to see Spain and not inhabit it, and thus he refuses the "Formality of their incomprehensible Dress" (2). Bellmour responds again as the ever-hopeful lover: he answers that he has donned the habits of Spain—"their formal Gate, set Speech, and stiff Behaviour"—only to increase his odds of snaring a Spanish woman (2). In characterizing the Spanish in this way, Pix clearly articulates descriptions of Spanish character alive in England at that time. For example, she may actually have read an account of life in Spain published two years before, in 1704, for it contains the same ridicule of spectacles: "it is [a] very Comical Show to see a mixt Multitude of Boys and Girls, Men and Women, Young and Old, with all their Noses . . . Yoak'd with Spectacles of different Sizes and Colours, altho', perhaps, not one of them but sees as well as I do" (5). This account, supposedly written by an Officer in the Royal Navy, has a title that says it all: *A Trip to Spain: or, A True Description of the Comical Humours, Ridiculous Customs, and Foolish Laws of that Lazy, Improvident People the Spaniards*. This naval officer's complaints about "the Spanish character" are typical ones—pride in their family lineages, arrogance about the beauties of their cities and their women, and avarice and covetousness in general: Spain is "a large Garden of Butter-Flies, or rather a Hive of Idle Drones, where neither Wit nor Industry is encourag'd" (3) and where the Spaniards refuse to invest their money and live off the interest, but instead spend the principle and die poverty-stricken (7). But this text also displays a near-compulsive impulse to catalogue Spanish dress, adornment, and fashion. Typical for instance are the following: all a Spaniard needs is "a Snuff box, a Tooth-Picker, a Dagger at his Postern, a Spado at his Side, an Old Cloak, and a Trencher Crown'd-Hat" and he fancies himself as great as the Prince of Condi"; or "He parts his Hair in the middle of his Crown, and tucks it behind his Ears; He wears . . . a pair of Breeches that have need to be got on with a Shoing-Horn, Shoes without Heels, and Yellow Stockings that cover a wonderful pair of Legs, of the Irish fashion" (3). Like Wycherley, the naval office presents Spanish material culture in the form of the empiricist's catalogue of external phenomena, and he expects his readers to equate difference in fashion with difference in essence.

But Pix's presentation is not quite that simple. In the scene that directly follows the Englishmen's conversation about clothing, we see a similar problem of fashion and identity worked through very differently in the case of women, a problem that at least appears to question the equating of fashion with essence. In this scene, we are introduced to the Spanish heroines in the play. Lisset, the cross-dressed friend of Clarinda, has bought her way out of the prison that the old, myopic, and abusive Gomez has forced her into. The old Spaniard, who controls the lives of all the women in this play, is not above plotting to kill any impediment to his schemes for making or stealing fortunes in the Americas, and thus when in the midst of the reunion scene among the once-separated women Gomez blunders in and spies "a thing in Breeches," the potential for violence is high. When he demands of her, "what are you ha?" she provides him an enigmatic but potentially benign response: "What am I Sir—I am a Man and no Man, I bear the outward Figure of a Man, but in Reality am an Eunuch——." His reply, worthy of any good Lacanian, is wonderfully funny: "An eunuch, good lack" (11)."

Comforted by this explanation and no longer feeling threatened, he listens to her invented stories of eunuchs, Turkish seraglios, harem-guarding, and female intrigue-spoiling. Shortly convinced of the efficacy of this Turkish practice (in lines a young actress friend of mine has said are bound to be the hit of the show), Gomez stalks the stage, exclaiming, "why have we not Eunuchs in Spain? Oh 'tis an admirable Custom and useful Policy, . . . Why han't we Eunuchs in Spain? I say, why have we no Eunuchs" (12). This theatrical fantasy, of castrating the hypermasculine bully, must have had a powerful appeal for members of a British audience seeking not to make the same mistakes as the first generation of Spanish imperialists.

Pix's descriptions of the fashions and habits of Spanish women and English men would seem to locate national and gender identity outside of the essential and within social and cultural practices of adornment: Lisset successfully plays the eunuch, and Bellmour artfully impersonates the Spaniard. Yet Pix's descriptions of Spanish men suggest the opposite, for they appear to have little room for a fluidity of identity. As we saw earlier, when Gaylove and Bellmour describe Spanish men's fashions as best suited for English women, Pix aligns Spain with the feminine. This is an odd and disjunctive ideological occurrence in an English culture that generally makes much of Spanish men's violence—their jealousy, their fear of cuckoldry, and their abuse of the powers they hold over sprightly, ingenious, and inventive Spanish women (characters an

English audience would readily read as English heroines). Even the English heroes, when dressed as Spaniards, are too quick to draw their swords, usually against each other. Upon examination, however, this act of feminizing a Spanish man turns out to hold the key to the central, most powerful ideological conflict in this play: the way gender is deployed to displace and secure a national identity.

This deployment and displacement resonate most powerfully in the character of Gomez, who is, on the surface, a quintessential example of the hypermasculine Spanish male: he has ordered the death of Clarinda's brother, Don Philip, so that he can marry her off to his loathsome twin and thus keep her fortune in the family. Even as his plan begins to unravel, he plots for an escape to Mexico where he can, as he says, "Tyrannize at pleasure" and increase his fortune, he hopes, exponentially.[12] Complaints about Spanish hypermasculinity, and its counterproductivity in conquest, had historical roots in earlier English discourses. As we saw in previous chapters, Louis Montrose's reading of *The Discovery of Guiana* makes the point that Raleigh insists that only an English form of manliness—that is, an impressive impulse control and an appreciation for delayed gratification (also good merchant sentiments)—will win the imperial day. We have seem similar complaints about Spain's mishandling of its conquest of the Americas. Thus Spanish men, whom Gaylove mocks for "their formal Gate, set Speech, and stiff Behavior," are represented as adhering to an older view of heroic action: a premodern notion of honor found in an abusive masculinity and a coercive employment of an arbitrary power. On this broader cultural level, Gomez is positioned as the wrong kind of gender and the wrong national character for the building of empires. He must therefore be punished.

The ending of the play does not disappoint. For the heroes and heroines, the conclusion mirrors an ideological "return" of the kind both Behn and Wycherley presented. Lisset and Bellmour, the crossed-dressed characters whose identities appear to be the most fluid and changeable, since both live on the frontiers of gender or national identity, are brought back into line. First, Lisset's essential femaleness is secured in her marriage to the faithful Guzman. Second, Bellmour is "reformed": he and Gaylove, who were early in the play infected by the violent atmosphere and the fashions of Spain, have learned Raleigh's lesson about the art of self-discipline by the end of the play. They have come to value the manly English virtues of self-control, and they have mastered delayed gratification. Secure in his match with his Spanish beloved, Bellmour returns to England, the perfect English gentleman, married to a woman whose brother has plans for fortune-hunting in the West Indies.

Only Gomez is punished. Outwitted and outmaneuvered by the young men *and* the young women he tried to control, Gomez' plan to abscond to Mexico, where he would act out his lascivious desires on his unprotected niece, is thwarted; hauled in front of The Inquisitor, he is judged guilty of "most Notorious Crimes"— including the attempted murder of Don Philip and an attempted incestuous marriage to Clarinda—and as part of his punishment he is forced to turn over all his money to those whom he had injured. In the end, revealed to be an impotent Spaniard and failed imperialist, he is left stripped of both his social and his erotic power.

This unveiling of Gomez' true "nature" is reminiscent of another incident found in the naval officer's *Trip to Spain,* one that presents an image of Spain as all surface and no substance. The anecdote opens with a criticism of the Spanish for their voracious spending habits—even though their stiff-necked honor keeps a "Person of Quality" from haggling with a shopkeeper or even accepting change from a piece of gold. As a result, the nobility actually live in a state of near poverty (a theme threaded throughout the account). Thus a penniless nobleman, in order to maintain appearances, will go so far as to "buy [the] *legs* of fowls, [and] fasten them to hang down so it appears to others that he has purchased a whole bird" (7). This nobleman's wealth, like Gomez' masculinity, is a facade. Only an absence, hidden under the nobleman's cloak, hangs below his belt.

At the end of Pix's play, as Gomez marches off with The Inquisitor to an unknown fate, his performance as a man is revealed to be as illusory as the body missing from the legs of the fowl, a truth now visible for all to see. Similar to the endings of *The Dutch Lover* and *The Gentleman Dancing-Master,* which serve to exclude vulgar mercantilists, *The Adventures in Madrid* concludes by drawing boundaries to exclude the hypermasculine Spanish. Most important, for all the freewheeling possibilities that cross-national dressing might present, breaches in the boundaries of status, nation, and gender are finally contained when all the desirable women and all the promises of wealth and material good fortune in the New World are transported out of the hands of an emasculated imperialist and into the safekeeping of Englishmen who possess appropriate imperial identities.

4 Discursive Identities
Actresses on and off the Restoration Stage

THE LATE RESTORATION PLAYHOUSE was filled with women—women spectators, women playwrights, and women performers. David Roberts disturbs many of the old assumptions about the nature of the late-seventeenth-century audience when he constructs a full picture of the Restoration playhouse that was "rich indeed": in attendance could have been lady's companions and maidservants; female relatives of members of parliament, professional men, and merchants; royal mistresses, duchesses, and the wives of the aristocracy; and a "conspicuous minority of women of all classes" who disguised themselves at the theater[1] (94). The powerful influence of these female spectators, especially upper-class women, is discernible in constant references in epilogues and prologues to the "Ladies" in the house, women appealed to, as does Thomas D'Urfey in *Trick for Trick* (1678), as the arbiters of taste: "The poet now the ladies help does crave, / That with a smile or frown can damn or save" (qtd. in Roberts). The power attributed to these women is both royal and sexual because the lady, regal in her critical detachment, is also, according to Roberts, "potentially alluring in her command of the favourable nod or glance" (34–35). More important, such appeals locate the "Ladies" in a particularly theatrical position: in such moments, they themselves become the theatrical objects of view.

By the mid-1690s, these same spectators would have had the opportunity to see the two most famous female performers on the late Restoration stage, Elizabeth Barry and Anne Bracegirdle, actresses who had become so famous—who were perceived to be so much a part of the repertoire and whose performances were so stylish and memorable—that a satire, *The Female Wits* (a 1697 rehearsal drama), targets the onstage behavior for which they were renowned: parodied, for instance, were Mrs. Barry's penchant for stamping her feet during ranting speeches and Mrs. Bracegirdle's elegant manner of weeping onstage. The fact that such personal attacks were launched at these female performers is evidence of their "star" status, a theatrical phenomenon begun thirty years earlier from the moment women players were first introduced to the English stage. We need only recall Pepys's enthusiastic responses to "my Lady Castlemaine" or the gossip surrounding Nell Gwynn's liaison with the King and her success in comedy to see just how quickly and powerfully the women players became objects of speculation and specularization.

Barry's and Bracegirdle's star status, however, generated for them both power and hazards: because they participated in an event that displayed their bodies onstage, this visual availability, so essential to their representations of characters, translated into a communal, extratheatrical discourse filled with speculations about the offstage activities of their bodies. This chapter begins by examining these discourses to determine the ways the bodies of the Restoration actresses were read—as representations of ephemeral characters moving through an onstage space and as "known" objects, especially "familiar" bodies, moving through an offstage discourse. I then place this issue of female identity as a visual and/or sexual spectacle in a dramatic context in a reading of Delariviere Manley's *Royal Mischief,* a play set in Turkey and thus suffused with issues of sexuality, power, and intrigue—and the greater possibility that a woman might successfully participate in all three activities —in order to see whether it is possible for a woman to escape the gaze or to deploy it for her own purposes. I finally take up the ways such extratheatrical discourses performed a larger and more powerful cultural function, one drawn from the subtle interdependence of class and gender definitions: by locating an essential female identity inextricably linked to the body, the discourse about the actresses served to reinforce aristocratic claims to an equally "essential" aristocratic identity, one that worked to separate "the Ladies" from their common but equally spectacular counterparts.

Public Women:
Actresses and the Private Body

Colley Cibber, writing in 1740, calls the public's interest in the lives of the players "natural": "A Man who has pass'd above Forty

Years of his Life upon a Theatre, where he has never appear'd to be Himself, may have naturally excited the Curiosity of his Spectators to know what he really was, when in no body's Shape but his own." He concludes that the public has "a sort of Right to enquire into my Conduct" (1, 4). Such an inquiry took shape, in the late seventeenth century, beyond the ephemeral form of communal gossip, in printed histories of the theater, verse satires, unauthorized biographies, and even Tom Brown's *Letters from the Dead*. Thomas Postlewait sees this confluence of interest as a "concern for the complex relation between intrinsic and extrinsic identity" that, in the eighteenth century, concentrated on "a perceived gap between public behavior and private selfhood, between the artifice of social manners and the integrity of personal sentiment" (250). Information supposedly filling that gap allowed an audience to believe that it had some special access to, some "knowledge" about, the performer that could indeed describe what an actor "really was." Yet even though Cibber attempts to create a difference between an authentic self and a role by pointing to the body as the source of the distinction, "when in no body's Shape but his own" (1), his *Apology* goes on to present the discourse of a likable, charming—if often disingenuous—persona, a "Cibber" who is quick to cite his failures and successes in his public roles as theater manager and poet laureate.

For women working in the theater, both women players and playwrights, such access was almost singularly constituted by knowledge about their private, sexual lives—knowledge that supposedly located and revealed an authentic self. Aphra Behn, whose specter hovered over all subsequent women writers, actively exploited this seventeenth-century inability to separate the professional woman from the prostitute. The culture heard very distinctly the "public" in "publication," according to Angeline Goreau, and believed that a woman could not preserve a private body if she put her mind on public display; Catherine Gallagher elaborates, "The woman who shared the contents of her mind instead of reserving them for one man was literally, not metaphorically, trading in her sexual property. If she were married, she was selling what did not belong to her, because *in mind and body,* she should have given herself to her husband" (23). Gallagher concludes that Behn intentionally sacrificed the ideal of the "totalized" woman in her aggressive assumption of identities dependent on multiple exchanges: in "literalizing and embracing the playwright-prostitute metaphor," Behn chose to "regenerate, possess, and sell a series of provisional, constructed identities"[2] (27, 24).

As we might expect, a Restoration audience found it doubly easy to equate the actress with the prostitute: her job demanded that she present her body, feign desire, and display this divided female identity; her profession required that she regenerate, possess, and sell a series of provisional selves.[3] John Hill makes that easy equation when he writes, in 1750, for instance, that an actress must guard against, even empty herself of response to her own "trivial, domestick affairs," because "the mistress and the actress have only this in common, that it is more easy to them to affect a passion, as they are less under the influence of its opposite one" (26). But it was not simply that an audience failed to distinguish between a woman's staging of her own reputed desire—as in prostitution—and a woman's participation in a theatrical event that *itself* stages a character's sexual desire. It is the very fact of female presence that evidenced pretense, generated tension, and confirmed the fear that a woman was capable of division or multiplicity. As Peter Stallybrass has noted, the relationship between "speaking" women (harlots, whores, and other public women) and their "silent" counterparts (chaste women, invisible within the domestic sphere) began during the Renaissance:

> The connection between speaking and wantonness was common to legal discourse and conduct books. . . . The signs of the "harlot" are her linguistic "fullness" and her frequenting of public space. . . . The [ideal wife], like Bakhtin's classical body, is rigidly "finished": her signs are the enclosed body, the closed mouth, the locked house. (126–27)

Of course, Restoration actresses were, by definition and by necessity, such "speaking" women. Worse still, they painted themselves with cosmetics and donned apparel not identical to their essences, activities that Jonas Barish has so ably demonstrated functioned to fuel the antitheatrical prejudices of the day: William Prynne, a prolific antitheatrical writer, rants, for instance, against "the common *accursed hellish art of face-painting*," which "*sophisticates and perverts the workes of God, in putting a false gloss upon his creatures*" (Barish 93).

Yet similar claims for prostitution and implied division did not attach themselves to male actors, as Katharine Maus has elegantly pointed out (603). The public had not been particularly interested in the offstage lives of the earlier Renaissance actors such as Brubage or Kempe, nor was a Restoration audience particularly concerned with the offstage activities of the bodies of male actors. Kynaston, for instance, could have aroused similar interest: famous for playing women's parts in the pre- and just post-Restoration theater, he is described by John Downes as being "a Compleat Female Stage Beauty, performing his Parts so well, especially *Arthiope* and *Aglaura,* being Parts greatly moving Compassion and Pity; that it has since been Disputable among the Judicious, whether any Woman that succeeded him so Sensibly touch'd the Audience as he" (19). Kynaston was often gathered up by ladies of quality after a performance, still in his female dress, to be paraded around St. James Park, and there is evidence that he was himself "kept" by women in his offstage life (Cibber 72). Even Joe Haynes—who became notorious for once riding an ass onstage to speak an epilogue—was celebrated, not condemned, for his unsanctioned offstage behavior. Tobyas Thomas's *The Life of the Late Famous Comedian Jo. Hayns, Containing his Comical Exploits and Adventures, Both at Home and Abroad* (1701) excuses Haynes's antics by apologizing for his irregularities this way: "His Frauds were rather to be call'd his Frolicks; Deception more then Deceipt [*sic*] . . . his Designs and Strategems, aspiring more to an Aiery Feast, the pleasure of a Light Jest, than from any sordid hunger after an Avaritious Cheat" ("To the Reader"). Thomas describes Haynes's sexual escapades as giving him "a little too much of the Libertinism," even though the text contains a story (intended as comic, but horrifying to a modern audience) of Haynes's attempted rape of a young, mute serving girl—charges dropped after Haynes claimed to be secretary to the Duke of Monmouth and after the young woman herself was physically unable to speak as his accuser (12–14).

Restoration actresses, however, were burdened with this additional definition established through a discourse concerning the private activities of their offstage bodies and their sexual, rather than theatrical or technical, "virtuosity."[4] Thus the problem of female duplicity—always in danger of erupting in the case of women generally—was even more strongly reinforced when the "speaking" woman becomes "spoken of." Barry and Bracegirdle, who acted together in at least 20 new tragedies during the reign of William III, lived with such discursive definitions. Descriptions of

Barry's rise to fame always cite her father's falling fortunes and her guidance, first, under Mrs. Davenant, who introduced her to the "company of the best sort" so that in time she was "soon Mistress of that Behaviour which sets off the well-bred Gentlewoman" (Betterton 13). Her second mentor, Lord Rochester, reportedly wagered that he could make her the finest player on the stage, and through constant rehearsal, especially of her voice (which was said to be flat and monotonous), he is credited with helping her to achieve the Restoration definition of the best actor: she could *become* the person she played (Betterton 14–16).

Cibber praises her for being "gracefully Majestic" and for creating "a Presence of elevated Dignity" in characters of greatness, while Gildon's *Life of Betterton* recounts her onstage actions as "always just, and produc'd naturally by the Sentiments": "She indeed always enters into her Part, and is the Person she represents. Thus, I have heard her say, that she never said, *Ah! poor* Castalio! in the *Orphan,* without weeping. And I have frequently observ'd her change her Countenance several Times as the Discourse of others on the stage have affected her in the Part she acted" (39–40). This becoming a self *to* the self creates a version of female unity that might lessen the anxiety of a spectator who, perceiving the difference between the actress and her character, is convinced of female duplicity.

Yet "becoming" the part also meant that an actress had to convince her audience to forget, momentarily, the public discourse that subverted the onstage sympathy. In Barry's case the obstacles to overcome were mighty, for contemporary accounts of her offstage life were often harsh, abusive, and even obscene. In *The Playhouse, A Satyr,* Robert Gould calls her a "Drab" and "a Hackney Whore" and specifically equates her with a prostitute:

> So Insolent! there never was a Dowd
> So very basely born so very Proud:
> Yet Covetous; She'll Prostitute with any,
> Rather than wave the Getting of a Penny.[5]
>
> (qtd. in Summers 311–12)

Tom Brown is equally specific: "Should you lie with her all Night, She would not know you next Morning, unless you had another five Pound at her service" (3:39). While Anthony Aston paints her as a "shining actress," with dark hair and light eyes, of a slightly plump "middle-size," he describes her mouth as opening "most on the Right Side, which she strove to draw t'other Way" (6–7); Curll's Betterton claimed that this irregularity resulted in "A peculiar *Smile* . . . which made her look the most genteelly malicious Person that can be imagined" (19). This same physical characteristic, however, was also used as a sign of her reputed sexual promiscuity and forms the basis of a contemporary attack on her personal character: "With mouth and cunt, though both awry before, / Her cursed affectation makes 'em more"[6] (Wilson, *Court* 78).

Such discourse concerning Barry's life accompanied her performances as much as Bracegirdle's reputed and much-discussed chastity. The most tragic consequence of Bracegirdle's legendary purity was the death of actor/playwright William Mountfort, who was killed while attempting to abort Captain Richard Hill's real-life abduction of Mrs. Bracegirdle. Of her stage representations, Cibber claims that no other woman was "in such general Favour of her Spectators," because she was not "unguarded in her private Character," a discretion that made her "the Darling of the Theatre." He goes on to say that because she was "the Universal Passion, and under the highest Temptation," her resistance served "but to increase the number of her Admirers." It was, he adds candidly, a kind of fashion to lust after her (101).

Yet even these contemporary accounts also clearly focus on the activities of Mrs. Bracegirdle's body. And they too go beyond merely reporting the "remarkable" absence of her sexual activity to inscribe meaning on her body itself, this time in signs of her virginal status. Cibber claims that, in her youth, she threw out "a Glow of Health and Chearfulness" (101), while Aston describes her beauty as a conventional kind of loveliness: she had dark brown hair and brows, "black sparkling Eyes," and fine, even white teeth. He goes on, however, to concentrate on the beauty of her involuntary physical responses, signs on her body that mark her sexually: she had "a fresh blushy Complexion" which, when she exerted herself, flushed her neck, face, and breast (9). Yet for all the celebration of her chastity, not even she escaped charges of sexual license. In one of Tom Brown's *Letters from the Dead* (1702), a fictionalized Mountfort intimates that he and Bracegirdle were lovers: complaining of a backache, he cries, "pox on you, says he, for a bantering Dog, how can a single Girdle do me good, when a Brace was my Destruction" (*Works* 2:224).

Thus, when Peter Holland writes that in the Restoration theater "the actor precedes the role" (79), he points to a similarity shared by Restoration performers and modern celebrities whom Michael Quinn has described as possessing an overdetermined quality that keeps them "from disappearing entirely into the acting figure[s] in the drama" (155). They come equipped with such a powerful intertext—a conjunction of life and art, and a continuity of sequential roles—that it is difficult and perhaps even impossible to separate "the personal from the referential" (158). The Restoration actress, as such a celebrity, was always, at the same time, a body onstage (a visual phenomenon), the character she played (a representation in the minds of an audience), and an individual woman whose life in the "real world" came as part of the theatrical event (a verbal construct).[7] But unlike the castrati, whose bodily difference was more than metaphorically inscribed, whose physical difference could be seen and heard, the bodies of the actresses were perceived through a different veil of "knowledge": through an offstage discourse with a life of its own, a discourse often entirely unanchored, without a traceable source, and perhaps even an outright fabrication.[8] It is the very fact of its public existence that endowed it with the power of "truth" and with the status of a stable signifier. Thus, as Quinn has argued of all celebrities, the actress is both a sign object and a sign producer (157). Through the discourse, an audience essentialized the actress according to her sexual behavior as a means of coping with the lack of female unity her role-playing displayed on stage.

When Quinn goes on to argue that the celebrity phenomenon appeals to a culture that "creates, maintains, and apparently requires celebrity actors to feed its desire for an aesthetics of familiarity, recognition, and fulfillment" (160), he sounds curiously like the author of the *Players Tragedy,* an anonymous 1693 work that references the "Actress, whose Reputation, as well as Person is exposed for the Pleasure, and Diversion of the Audience" (10). Reputation, like familiarity, works to establish the "exposure" of the actress's "person" through an interest in her onstage beauty and her offstage body, both as a sexual commodities in communal discourse and as the source of pleasure. Thus in the inevitable erotics of theater performance, visual spectacle read through an extratheatrical "knowledge" of female performance both confirms and disturbs notions of female identity.

Representing the Unrepresentable:
Female Desire

I want to investigate the problem of power relations within this context of extratheatrical discourse, visual spectacle, and the production of erotic response by examining the construction of female identity as it emerges in the problem of representing a "new" female interiority. This investigation will focus on a work written by one of the first English women playwrights, Aphra Behn's *Rover; or, The Banish'd Cavaliers* (1677), and more thoroughly as it is subsequently modified in Delariviere Manley's *Royal Mischief* (1696). Such an investigation reveals the means by which two female playwrights participate in and comment on the problematics of looking, including the seeming gendering of the spectatorial economy, by bringing to light the mediating force the theater exerts in allowing and prohibiting the representation of female desire. Manley's work allows us to see how Turkey serves simultaneously to undercut and to bolster the problematics of this gendering, for it functions on the surface as a setting that resonates with erotic potential in the minds of English audiences, while it simultaneously presents a place where not only female desire is reputedly invisible but also women themselves are said to be locked away from any penetrating gazes. As such, Turkey becomes the perfect site in which to interrogate the placement of women as the objects of view within a voyeuristic economy, to conceive of a place from which women might return the look.

The most problematic character in Behn's *Rover; or, The Banish'd Cavaliers* is Angellica Bianca, a courtesan renowned for her beauty and infamous for her trade.[9] The extraordinary changes she undergoes through the course of the drama—from controlling her heart and body to exploding into violence against the lover who scorns her—is the singular, near-tragic part of the comedic plot that Behn never successfully resolves. One reason that audiences perceive Angellica Bianca as both too fascinating and too sympathetic for the more rollicking comedy that surrounds her is that Behn presents a character who forces an audience to examine the ways it "reads" women, to be self-conscious about the relationship between representation and reality as it functions to construct female identity.

Before she ever takes the stage, the courtesan's fame is touted in a communal discourse predicated on mutual "looking." Belvile tells his friend Willmore that she is known and adored by all the youths of Naples who "put on all their charms to appear lovely in her sight . . . while she has the pleasure to behold all [who] languish for her that see her" (1.2.323–26). The multiplicity as well as the mutuality of the exchanged gazes are evident in the acts of viewing Belvile describes. Willmore, the Rover/hero who has yet to see the courtesan himself, is so thoroughly convinced of the reports that he already imagines his arms "full of soft, white, kind woman" (2.1.16). But he goes one step further in making his rather free-floating desires concrete: he wishes that he could see her likeness, because even a representation would produce the pleasure found in "the shadow of the fair substance" and "a man may gaze on that for nothing" (2.1.20). When the courtesan's bravos enter and attach beneath the balcony one large and two smaller portraits of her (each accompanied by an advertisement stating the terms of her purchase—a thousand crowns a month), "Angellica Bianca" takes the stage, replicated three times and in various sizes, but at one remove from the "real." Yet even these "shadow[s] of the fair substance" are so powerful that they provoke Willmore to remove one of the smaller portraits, kiss it, and clutch it to his breast. Thus mutual looking becomes solitary male gazing on the representation of the female body, looking that moves a man to action.

That Behn introduces Angellica Bianca not by revealing her in the boudoir or engaged in her "occupational" activities but through her painted substitutions suggests Behn's larger and more self-conscious comment on theatrical signification generally. In staging this display, Behn acknowledges the way that likenesses can provoke erotic responses in any spectator, but she simultaneously and even more forcefully demonstrates the division, the lack of a unified female identity, that such a display "proves." And although the portraits function practically to indicate the courtesan's sexual availability, Elin Diamond has gone further and argued quite persuasively that Angellica Bianca is *doubly* commodified, first because she puts her body into exchange, and second because her body is equated with the art object: Willmore understands that "the appeal of the paintings is precisely that they are not the original but an effective stand-in"[10] (534, 531). In taking her portrait, kissing it, and clutching it to his breast, he makes visible not only the commodity status of paintings and their models but also—by metonymic extension—the commodity status of the painted actresses and painted scenes.

This metonymic connection between the performers and the scenes is central to Diamond's arguments about the "dreamlike, seductive, and commodity-intensive" nature of the Restoration stage. She suggests that underlying the seventeenth-century suspicions about the theater is a Puritan notion built on the Platonic condemnation of mimesis as the making of counterfeit copies of true originals; thus "the nature of theatrical representation, like the 'nature' of woman, was to ensnare, deceive, and seduce" (523). Contributing to the atmosphere of seduction and illusion in the Restoration playhouse was the new configuration of the Restoration stage: the forestage platform that allowed for audience interaction with the players, especially during comedies, was now accompanied by painted screens that could be rolled away to reveal an upstage, "internal" or "discovery," space. Such an arrangement provided the possibility for a "new scopic epistemology," for a new "spectator-fetishist" who took "pleasure in the ornaments that deceive the sight, [and] whose disavowal of material reality produc[ed] a desire for the 'delightful Magick' of exotic and enticing representations'" (522). As further evidence, Diamond recounts an incident where the rolling away of one painted scene to reveal yet another painted scene had its real-life equivalent in Pepys's backstage travels. The painted actresses moving through the scenes onstage—those women who so enthralled him—were revealed, backstage, to be painted women again, just another, and this time disappointing, illusion: "[Pepys] hoped to separate the pretty woman from the painted actress, but it was the actress he admired—and fetishized—from his spectator's seat" (523). For scholars, therefore, one "lure of the sign" in Angellica Bianca's triple portraits is that they make visible this "metonymic connection between painted female performers and painted scenes" (524).

While I fully agree with this insightful analysis, I would go further to suggest that the problem of resolving Angellica Bianca's character resides not simply in the metonymic connection between her beauty and her painted body displayed for sale but in another such connection: a metonymic extension from an upstage —internal, revelatory, and discovery—space to its promise of a more genuine, interior identity. Thomas A. King brilliantly analyzes the tension in the actress's two bodies—the body of the character she played and the body of the "actress" and the demand to conflate the two—as necessary in the kind of theatricality instituted in the late seventeenth century and predicated on exploiting a new interest in spectatorship as part of what King calls "Western ocularcentrism" and the production of bourgeios subjectivities: "neither body that the actress presented may have possessed the kind of authenticity with which we credit the self today: both 'layers,' that is, were *performed*" (81). King's argument—that an idea of an authentic underlying or inner self existed beneath the performance of an actress during the Restoration may be "open to negotiation during the Restoration proper" (82)—is a good one. Indeed, I would argue that this negotiation begins to take place the moment actresses stepped onstage in the 1660s. King's suggestions that an interest in the lives of the performers may be connected to the eighteenth-century interest in "consciousness" or "sensibility" and that "the project of negotiating properly gendered subjectivities for both men and women" begins in the Restoration theater (81–2, 88) are both facets of playwrights' increasing emphasis on interiority—a fact that will emerge more forcefully in the next chapter's examination of female trauma and female playwrights' wish to represent the unrepresentable, especially an unrepresentable female desire, a process we will investigate in the remainder of this section.

A paradigmatic moment that displays the tension between the material body and an uncovered interiority, an interiority that will come to be seen as possessing more authenticity than the material body one can see, features Angellica Bianca and her downfall. It begins at the moment when she claims to possess an interiority at odds with her representation, when she "falls in love with" Willmore:

> Put up thy gold, and know,
> That were thy fortune large, as is thy soul,
> Thou shouldst not buy my love,
> Couldst thou forget those mean effects of vanity,
> Which set me out to sale;
> And as a lover, prize my yielding joys.
> Canst thou believe they'l be entirely thine,
> Without considering they were mercenary?
>
> (2.2)

Diamond argues that Angellica Bianca's attempt to place herself in a state of nature—so that she labors not for money but for love—is an act intended to "demystify and authenticate herself" (533). But this is precisely the problem: Angellica Bianca is finally doomed because she proffers an authenticity that seeks to transcend the paint and the commodification, those conditions so forcefully represented in her introduction, by locating it in an interiority that *cannot* be represented. Thus her final lament, after she has terrorized Willmore with a pistol, can initially be read in the traditional manner as an acceptance of her weaknesses and the loss of her "honour":

> But when love held the mirror, the undeceiving glass
> Reflected all the weakness of my soul, and made me know,
> My richest treasure being lost, my honour,
> All the remaining spoil cou'd not be worth
> The conqueror's care or value.
> Oh how I fell like a long worship'd idol,
> Discovering all the cheat!
>
> (5.1)

But it can also be more productively read as Behn's poignant complaint that spectatorial relations are such that there is no possibility of a woman's ever transcending her representation: Angellica Bianca, once indeed such an "idol," is brought down by a different kind of "cheat"—a belief in an interiority that she cannot represent, even in that revelatory upstage space.

Twenty years later, Delariviere Manley was fully aware that she was writing within a particular historical tradition, specifically in the footsteps of Behn.[12] The celebratory verses attached to the 1696 published version of *The Royal Mischief* include Mary Pix's laudatory pronouncements about Manley's likeness to the great women writers of the past, including the eloquent "Afra":

> You snatch the Lawrel with undisputed right,
> And Conquer when you but begin to fight;
> Your infant strokes have such Herculean force,
> Your self must strive to keep the rapid force,
> Like Sappho Charming, like Afra Eloquent,
> Like Chast Orinda, sweetly Innocent.

Manley's presentation of an analogous but competing use of por-traiture in *The Royal Mischief* provokes comparison.[13] Performed in 1696 at Lincoln's Inn Fields by the Betterton, Barry, and Brace-girdle company in a respectable six-night run, the play includes the use of portraits both as onstage props and in the form of *ekphrasis,* a term art historian Jean Hagstrum defines as "that special quality of giving voice and language to a mute art object," a reasoning grounded on the etymology of the word—the Greek *ekphrazein* means "to speak out," "to tell in full" (qtd. in Meltzer). Manley's is a particularly intriguing case because she complicates Behn's use of the portrait by reversing the genders: her play invokes the image of a life-sized portrait of a man gazed at by a woman who experi-ences a powerful erotic pleasure in looking. Such a reversal—a woman looking fetishistically at the image of a man—problema-tizes the historicity of the reification of women in the theater and the moments that supposedly gender the spectatorial economy be-cause Manley makes visible the mediating force the theater exerts in the production and erasure of a female interiority as it is repre-sented as female desire.

Manley creates a play set not in the carnival atmosphere of Naples but in the more exotic realms of Islam. As we saw in the first chapter, Britons would very likely have been acquainted with visitors from Turkey who traveled to England by the thousands during the seventeenth century. English merchants and traders would also have journeyed to Turkey in search of new markets and new goods. Images of Turks and Moors provoked feelings, not of imperial aggressiveness—indeed, there is no talk during this era about attempting to invade or colonize any part of the Ottoman empire—but of awe, anxiety, and not a little fear. By the 1690s, however, what has been called by some scholars "the decline" of the Ottoman empire had begun, according to Justin McCarthy, in part, because unlike European nations, the Ottoman Empire did not experience a Renaissance: "nor did they take part in the edu-cational, scientific, philosophical, economic, and industrial revolu-tions that followed upon the Renaissance in Europe" (148). Mod-ern technologies of warfare bypassed the Turks: they continued to build galleys rather than powerful sailing ships, and more impor-tant for our purposes they failed to adopt modern structures of command for their cavalry units, a structure that required the "drill-ing of men to achieve a unity of action," according to McCarthy

(149)—in other words, they failed to produce a modern, disciplined, Foucauldian body for the common, cavalry soldier. Previous imperial successes also actually contributed to Ottoman difficulties: communications from the center were nearly impossible to effect over such an immense empire, and thus they were slow to react to changes. Most especially, the European discovery of the New World, and the return of Spanish silver to European coffers, increased inflation throughout the West, creating shifting economic conditions to which more flexible European economies could adapt but with which the fixed economy of Turkey struggled to cope.

Thus at a time when the military and economic power of the Ottoman empire was on the wane, Manley exploits what may have been the most powerful European perception of both the Ottomans and all Islamic countries: their exoticism and sensual excess, especially as a sites where women's lives were reputed to be markedly different and where Turkish men of status were slaves to their excessive sexual desires. Or as Bernard Lewis describes it, "What chiefly aroused, in varying degree, the astonishment, reprobation, and envy of Western visitors were the institutions of polygamy and concubinage, and the processes by which the personnel of the harem were recruited and replenished," while "the image of the Turk as an insatiable sensualist is the best known and most widespread of all the stereotypes" (83). In Western imaginations, then, the harem could denote a place where women were remarkably powerful or remarkably vulnerable. The mothers of the sultans, for instance, were reputedly always the real power behind the throne. Since the sons of sultans were emotionally removed from their "illustrious fathers," the power of the mother increased exponentially if her son rose to the sultanate. McCarthy describes these mothers as "a focus of court intrigue" and as "leaders of palace factions and active participants in political battles" (162). Simultaneously, Turkish women were also reputed to live remarkably sequestered and limited lives: enclosed in harems, unavailable to view, they lived in a place where women's desires—whether real or not—were always veiled. Lady Mary Wortley Montagu's report of her visit, in 1717, to a Turkish bath, narrates an event that would have occurred twenty-one years after the premiere of Manley's *Royal Mischief*.[14] In this account, she positions her reader as a voyeur who glimpses images of Turkish women in their most vulnerable state, a vision forbidden to outsiders but available to Lady Mary because of her womanhood (the word "harem," according to Lewis, is drawn from the Arabic word *haram,* meaning forbidden or off-limits):

> The first sofas were cover'd with Cushions and rich Carpets, on which sat the Ladys, and on the 2nd ther slaves behind 'em, but without any distinction of rank by their dress, all being in the state of nature, that is, in plain English, stark naked, without any Beauty or deffect conceal'd, yet there was not the least wanton smile or immodest Gesture amongst 'em. They Walk'd and mov'd with the same majestic Grace which Milton describes of our General Mother.
>
> (1.313–14)

Manley chooses a Turkish setting—one ripe with intrigue, male sexual rapaciousness, female sensuality and political power, a culture whose initial stages of decline and even decadence had begun to emerge—for a plot that centers around a strong, sexually responsive, and villainous princess, Homais (played by Elizabeth Barry), a woman locked away in her castle, while her husband wages war abroad. Her desire for her husband's nephew motivates an action filled with violence, including the possibility that the virtuous Bassima (played by Anne Bracegirdle) will have her eyes gouged out and her hands, nose, and mouth cut off as punishment for a supposed adultery with the vizier Osman.[15] His punishment for the same supposed adultery is to be shot—alive—out of a canon. His wife, Selima, risks personal immolation as she roams the plains picking up the "smoking Relicks of her Lord, / Which singes, as she grasps them" before throwing herself on his pyre, "bestowing burning Kisses / And Embraces on every fatal piece" (46).

Aided by her faithful eunuch Acmet and by the political ambitions of her ex-lover Ismael, the princess achieves her desire—only to be found out and stabbed in the last act by her husband. She dies, but not before performing a thrilling ranting scene in which she calls her husband a "Dotard, impotent in all but Mischief" and exclaims, as she flings her blood about, "Thus I dash thee with my gore, / And may it scatter unthought Plagues around thee" (45). And even though her husband offers forgiveness and understanding about his nephew's sexual transgressions, the young man—overcome by guilt—falls on his sword and dies. The eunuch is racked, Ismael is executed, and Bassima dies after drinking poisoned sherbet. At the final curtain, five of the seven major characters are dead, and the Prince stands alone to exclaim, "O horrour, horrour, horrour! / What Mischief two fair Guilty Eyes have wrought"[16] (47).

The play is predicated on a Cartesian division between an external reality and some inner "nature"—the long-standing complaint about the theater updated in contemporary Puritan suspicions concerning representation and illusion and about to explode in the Jeremy Collier controversy. The duality, as it is defined in *The Royal Mischief,* provides women with two mutually exclusive and equally unsatisfying positions. The wicked Ismael announces the first premise in terms of traditional male fears about female identity—that a woman's beauty only disguises her lack of virtue:

> Virtue in [women's] Souls is like their form,
> Only exterior Beauty, worn to deceive
>
> . . . .
>
> But when they meet a Lover to their wish,
> They gladly throw the borrow'd Veil aside,
> And naked in his Arms disclose the cheat.
>
> (10)

The veil, for Ismael, is part of a manipulable system of signification that a woman can exploit when she is without desires, when it suits her to "veil" herself in "virtue." This hidden and thus virtuous character is only a garment "borrow'd" temporarily, for a woman easily casts her veil and her virtue aside when, "naked" in the arms of her lover, she discloses the "cheat."

The princess's husband, however, provides the second premise as he laments this culturally sanctioned, duplicitous, female division in terms of a woman's "lack":

> O pity, Nature, thou
> So much should'st Err; so far bestow thy utmost
> Cost upon the Case, and leave the Building Empty;
> The lovely Frame exhausted all thy Store,
> And Beggar'd thee so far, thou could'st not look
> Within, to aid her Wants. Hence monstrous Forms,
> And unimagin'd Ills inhabit there.
>
> (37)

Even as he imagines nature's being spent in the creation of her beauty, the prince also allows the competing and paradoxical suggestion that she is, in fact, left full of "wants." Because his imagination fills this lack with "monstrous Forms" and "unimagin'd ills" that incapacitate her for any stable identity, he can only wish to be "well dissembled with"—to be presented with the false but pleasing representation of the loving wife:

> Wert thou but truly kind,
> What Worlds of bliss could'st thou not give?
> Thy Eye, thy Lips, thy thousand Beauties,
> Were too Divine a Feast for Mortal taste;
> O let me be but well dissembled with.
> And I will lie for ever in thy Arms,
> Nor never wake to find the fond illusion,
> But think it all substantial shining treasure.
>
> (7)

Thus there is no positive, empowering, or ennobling identity for women; they may either dissemble well and succeed or feign poorly and fail.

The play also describes portraiture in a similar fashion: like women, paintings are essentially empty, simple ornaments for the production of a viewer's personal spectatorial pleasure. This idea, too, is voiced by the cynical Ismael. In his attempt to convince the vizier to cultivate an illegitimate passion for Bassima that will topple him from power, Ismael uses his understanding of the self-contained pleasures of representations to devalue such "private" indulgences. He asks the lovesick vizier:

> What, do you doat upon a new found species?
> I thought you lov'd her; as she was a Woman,
> As nature bids us love, not with Platonick
> Nonsense; when you have reckon'd all her
> Beauties up, the Sex is lovelyest in her:
> Bate that Circumstance and a fair Picture
> Does the Work as well.
>
> (10)

In urging the vizier to love Bassima as a woman—according to "nature" and not some "Platonick Nonsense"—Ismael locates the only stable female identity in the body. Like paintings, he insists, women are beautiful outside but lack any "genuine" interior: "Bate that Circumstance, and a fair Picture / Does the Work as well." The

"Platonick Nonsense" of spectating lies at its being one remove from the "real"—that is, the body. Thus doting on the illusory, the merely represented, can bring only a second-order, unresponded-to pleasure. The arguments of art historian Richard Brilliant about the nature of portraiture are relevant in this context, for he writes about the ways that "portraits stifle the analysis of representation": more than any other form, the impact of the portrait can be understood only though an acknowledgment of "the necessary incorporation of the viewer's gaze into the subject matter of portraiture" (8). This "necessary incorporation" is precisely the point Ismael makes: he insists that the vizier must not remain content with spectating, with the "secondary" pleasures that viewing generates.[17]

Bolstering these suspicions about the empty or deceitful nature of paintings and female identity is the play's obsession with images of the eyes "guilty eyes," "beauteous eye," eyes "so bright" that they "dazzle the sight," "lustrous" eyes that "sparkle" and "eclipse" the natural light. Eyes have active power in this drama obsessed with the question of looking, an activity central to the illegitimate love plot. In the first scene of the play, we discover that the princess is distressed for the unrequited love of her husband's nephew. Yet in a surprising revelation, we also learn that the princess has never actually seen the young man. The source of her desire is a portrait. Acmet, the eunuch, explains:

> [Her husband], to
> Help the fatal mischief on, made her the
> Present of his Nephews Picture———
> By which she so indulge'd her fond desire,
> That soon her reason fled and left her heart
> A prey to Passion, nor cou'd her Stars resist it.
>
> (14)

Seventeenth-century portraiture, according to Erica Harth, was cast in an aristocratic mold of analogue, where representations glorified and celebrated a royal or noble subject; "[t]he dimensions of art were heroic; the tone was elevated" (17). This idealization of the represented image was intended to produce positive social and moral results, as Timothy Murray suggests: "Whether painted or written, a portrait's depiction of ideal models of comportment,

virtue, and behavior are said to provoke contemplation and ultimately (what could only be an attempt at) emulation by the viewer"
(109). Yet in Manley's version, the result of gazing at a painted version of the human form is not the princess's meditative contemplation on some disembodied aristocratic notion of virtue but a passionate response that produces her own sexual desire.

This powerful personal reaction to painted likenesses is a phenomenon recognized by art historians and theorists. Brilliant writes
that portraiture owes its "high reputation and enormous popular-
ity" to "the intensity of the viewer's engagement with the portrait
image at a much deeper level of personal involvement and response
than is usually encountered in the experience of visual images"
(19). As an example, he cites the picture of a soldier, away at war,
that can inspire an intense scrutiny in any viewer who fears for the
young man's safety. But he goes on to claim that portraits have an
additional, real-world power: portraits elicit responsive *behaviors*
from viewers—as if the art works presented themselves in the form
of a proposition, "this is so and so," and the viewers then behaved
accordingly. He cites the overturning of Stalin's statues as an example of such responsive behavior, and we remember Willmore's
being moved to kiss Angellica's portrait. The result of the "immanent power" of the "double nature" of portraiture is that "for some
viewers the portrait was not art object but a living being"[18] (24–
25). David Freedberg goes so far as to describe such viewing as an
"enlivening" process: "There is a cognitive relation between looking and enlivening; and between looking hard, not turning away,
concentrating, and enjoying on the one hand, and possession and
arousal on the other" (325).

Thus Homais, imprisoned in her castle, looks at a portrait and
experiences a desire based on the heroicization implicit in the form
of portrait painting, a look that equates the representation with the
person and that enlivens the object into a subject. In reversing the
genders—in the princess's gazing at a man's full-length portrait—
Manley acknowledges that women, too, respond powerfully and
erotically to likenesses and to pleasing images that demand an intense scrutiny and provoke action.[19] The situation, on the surface,
also suggests that Manley *could* work from a position that allows the
presentation of an active and erotically charged female spectatorship that fetishizes and enlivens—through embodying—the male
image.

But complicating the potential empowerment of this female spectating is Manley's larger comment on the "veiled" status of female desire. The princess's response to representation is apparently so invisible that even her closest companion, Acmet, cannot see it:

> None has approacht your Royal sight,
> Fit to give Love, or to create desire,
> Or if there had, I soon had markt the Man;
> For love like yours, in absence may be hid,
> In presence never!
>
> (2)

The princess's husband, hoping to make certain that she would not —indeed *could* not—desire, makes her a captive: he imprisons her and thus removes her from any active engagement with the world. And even though the veil she wears is intended to insure that no woman will provoke male desire, it also performs an even more powerful and opposite function: it veils the reality of female desire from prying public eyes.

Thus when Manley goes on to display what occurs when those who have responded to images actually meet in the flesh, the problematic nature of female desire is more powerfully conceived. In what must be the most striking scene of the play, we watch as Acmet, the eunuch, actually "seduces" the nephew—by proxy—for the princess. In doing so, it is clear that he can function in ways she cannot—as her mobility, her freedom, her access to the world. He *becomes* her agency. Yet, in ways fundamentally paradoxical, as her substitute, he is also the means to replenish her "lack"—even though, of course, he is himself the preeminent symbol of masculine "lack." As a form of detachable power, which is itself already detached, even absent, he becomes the degendered link between the genders. Thus the princess sends out that "part" of herself that can freely move, that part that—in its cultural near-invisibility—is her most powerful weapon: she sets loose her desire into the world.

Understanding the power of representations and the force of beautiful images, Acmet first attempts to persuade the nephew to attend on the princess by showing the young man her portrait. Like Willmore, the nephew finds her image arresting—he looks hard and responds, equates, and enlivens. Finding her beauty finally overpowering, he, like Willmore, is moved to act on the representation, to kiss her likeness:

Then she is sure above all Mortal Frame,
Her Eyes have Rays, her Face a Glory thro'
The whole, that strikes full at my Heart;
Now when I put the Colours to my Lips,
My Heart flew at the touch, eager to meet
Her Beauties; I'le gaze no more, there's Magick
In the Circle.

(17)

Pulled between his desire for the princess and his duties to his uncle and to his new wife, the nephew is able to resist the initial power of the representation as he thrusts the portrait aside: "I'le gaze no more, there's Magick / In the Circle."[20] He appears to understand the difference between person and representation, the copy and the original—at least to the extent that he is able to resist any action.

So Acmet employs a second strategy, the creation of another portrait—but this time in the form of *ekphrasis* or verbal portrait painting. His description concerns the princess's powerful and supposedly private response to the nephew's *own* portrait. Acmet tells the young man that his picture is the "chief Ornament" of the princess's rooms, positioned so that it is the first thing she sees when awakening each morning:

How often have I seen this Lovely *Venus,*
Naked, extended, in the gaudy Bed,
Her snowy Breasts all panting with desire,
With gazing, melting Eyes, survey your Form,
And wish in vain, 't had Life to fill her Arms.

(17–18)

Although here, in one sense, the princess is positioned as the spectator—she gazes at her nephew's image—it is finally clear that we have double portraits, doubled instances of gazing, for the princess is finally positioned as the delimited object of view within Acmet's portrait.[21] Her pose could suggest the posture of what Carol Duncan calls the femme fatale in the world of art, a woman who "looms over the male viewer, fixing him with a mysterious gaze and rendering him will-less," but it is also an image that Duncan acknowledges implies victimization: images of raised arms, in the modern world, are emptied of their classical connotations of "defeat with dignity" and instead become almost exclusively a female gesture—"a signal of sexual surrender and physical availability"²² (63).

Thus for all the seeming activity in this passage—the motion in the verbs "panting," "gazing," and "melting"—female desire is finally enclosed within a frame that itself invites spectating. Within that frame, the nephew views a woman's highly charged erotic response to representation, a response she "proves" through an open display of her nakedness. Such a voyeuristic presentation of appropriated female nakedness is reminiscent of the scenes of rape and violation that Kristina Straub claims functioned to "veil" the eighteenth-century realities of domination and submission, for the actress's sexuality was "perceived as threatening enough to require violent containment. Rape is, in a sense, an attempt to exclude the idea of feminine control from the spectacle of feminine desire" (104). Here, it is not the *violence* of rape that controls female desire, but a different and even more veiled, and thus more powerful, device: the framing of female desire within a portrait that appears to transfer control to the nephew himself.

The result of Acmet's strategies is that the nephew ultimately succumbs, of course, but he agrees to the encounter only in part because he is motivated by the beauty of her likeness. The truly powerful force in this seduction is his being convinced of the princess's mutual desire—a notion he comes to accept through the eunuch's description of her private responses, a mediated and discursive view of an interiority to which the eunuch's degendered eyes have reputed access. And most importantly, that interiority returns to the nephew himself: his desire is generated through the "magic" of "gazing" in his mind's eye on the [verbal] representation of a naked woman whose sexual arousal is dependent on her viewing his [visual] representation. So he is himself revealed to be the source of his own desire.

It is therefore not surprising that the next act opens with the princess gazing at her own reflection in the mirror. As she waits for her young lover to arrive, she bids her doubts be gone:

Ay, see [my doubts] flee before this Lovely Face,
My Hopes glow in my Cheeks and speak my Joy,

My Eyes take fire at their own Luster, and
All my Charms receive addition from themselves,
Pleas'd at their own Perfection.

(19)

While these comments serve as simple complaints about female
vanity, they also suggest that the princess—who has yet to see the
object of her desire in the flesh—understands that the fundamental
source of desire in representations returns, narcissistically, to the
spectator.[23]

The lovers' long-awaited and fateful meeting takes place upstage,
in that space for revelation and interiority, with kisses so powerful
the princess faints dead away. And as the nephew sinks sympatheti-
cally to his knees, it is left to Acmet—once again performing his
mediation, standing slightly downstage between the lovers and the
audience—to rejoice in the magical powers of the eye: "He's caught,
as surely as we Live, / Her Eyes have true Magick" (22). This part
of the plot concludes, not with the opening of the screens for reve-
lations and discovery but with Acmet's drawing the painted screens
between the audience and the lovers, refusing them that "real" representation of the discursive bodies he himself created through a
metaphor of the veil:

We'll not intrude into a Monarch's Secrets,
The God of Love himself is painted Blind;
To teach all other Eyes they shou'd be vail'd
Upon his Sacred Misteries.

(22)

It is useful, at this point, to return to the question of the female
spectator and to ask just what a woman, sitting in the late-Resto-
ration playhouse, might have made of these events. The easy answer
is that such a spectator, within her own metaphorical confinement,
would surely have experienced the thrill of illicit pleasure in iden-
tifying with the princess who not only experiences desire but is
able to detach a part of her self and send it out into the world with
a picture in hand. But Manley accomplishes a subtler and more
subversive comment on the problems and the power that representation of desire creates for women playwrights, players, and
spectators. She understands that no woman—no princess or female
spectator—can own her desire publicly at this time. And so she

does so through Acmet. He accomplishes the seduction by present-ing *both* a provocative visual image and a verbal record of a female interiority filled with erotic response. Thus the nephew "sees" both the object of his desire and her discursive interiority, but only through thoroughly mediated structures—paint on canvas and the descriptive powers of the eunuch: an apparently neutral (and, spe-cifically here, a "neutered") apparatus.

By placing Acmet in this position, Manley suggests that the theater itself acts as such a mediating force. But what it mediates is *female* desire—not simply in the form of representation but most powerfully in the promise of this particular kind of interior female response. Female desire, which Islamic and early British culture de-mands be as veiled and as nearly invisible as Acmet, turns out to be, once loosed in the world, as powerful and as real as he is (if also as vexed in its power position as he is in his gender condition). I do not mean to suggest that *all* spectating everywhere and at every time is therefore mediated by female desires, only that in this play Manley was free enough (and all the evidence about Manley her-self suggests that she was tenacious enough) to insist that a female playwright can and will expose one *process* by which the theater produces the "magic" that makes female desire visible but also forces it back into an invisible—discursive—interiority. Thus it should not surprise anyone that Manley was publicly criticized, in print, for presenting this play because it contained so much "warmth," charges she responds to by insisting that even Dryden himself cre-ated characters that were warmer still. She concludes that it is not her play but her sex—a woman's making female desire visible— that is the source of the displeasure.

But even this is finally "magic." Just as Acmet convinces the nephew of the princess's interiority through a portrait unanchored in any real authority (we don't know whether the princess ever really displayed such an erotic response), the theater works through a similar sleight of hand: it is the princess's *body*—exposed, naked, and erotically charged, but only discursively available—that sig-nifies this interiority, a hidden reality available only in its greatest exteriority. Thus Manley's play suggests that spectators are not se-duced and deceived by the paint and the illusion in the Restoration playhouse—they are not fooled into believing that Barry *is* a prin-cess.[24] The power of the playhouse's seduction goes beyond the me-tonymic connection between the painted women and the painted scenes, so that the "magic" comes from the part the theater itself plays in purporting to provide a means *past* the paint: when the "invisible" (female desire) is made "visible" (by and through the eunuch) in a discursive moment—itself not representable—an audience believes it has a way past the princess, past the paint even, and to Barry herself. After all, it is *her* body the audience imagines "panting" and "melting" with discursive desires and *her* body a late seventeenth-century audience would have thought itself acquainted with through extratheatrical discourses obsessively interested in the sexual lives not just of the actresses generally but of Mrs. Barry in particular.[25] Thus the *real* "magic" in this circle is that, when Manley throws the veil of female desire aside, she works to disclose yet another, and this time even more powerful, "cheat": an "unveiled" discursive interiority whose signs are visible only when they inevitably return to reinscribe female identity in representations of the sexualized female body.

Essentializing Discourses: Gender and Status

In its consistent essentializing, the discourse concerning the bodies of the actresses plays an important part in larger cultural and political attempts to locate the sources of identity: to determine where it resides, how to recognize it, and how to represent it. The "real-world" objects of multiple gazes were, of course, the aristocrats whose public performances displayed a power and an identity inextricably linked to a theatrical kind of presentation and spectacle.[26] Lawrence Stone, in *The Crisis of the Aristocracy,* cites conspicuous consumption as one aristocratic strategy used for securing an upper-class identity. Such display included the expensive maintenance of pomp and circumstance in royal service, the cost of attendance at Court in the hope of office, the pleasures and vanities of London (and the "rounds of dissipation that undermined both the health and fortune"), and the necessity "to keep open house to all comers, to dispense lavish charity, to keep hordes of domestic servants and retainers; to live, in short, as a great medieval prince." Such upper-class excess not only served a social function, "as a symbolic justification for the maintenance or acquisition of status," but also erected a strong barrier against "the lower orders," a means of keeping outsiders from encroaching on aristocratic privilege (184–87).

Yet, as Christopher Hill has observed, the "new" roles available for aristocrats after 1660 were precarious. Before 1640, the aristocracy had a discernible social significance, if only as mediators working the court to procure monopolies for merchants; the restored aristocracy of the post-1660 generation, however, found itself playing a largely decorative role: "the aristocrats who regained their privileged position after 1660 had no significant role to play in the reconstructed social order. Flocking to court, they ceased even to take their traditional part in local government; and at court their role was decorative rather than functional" (Hill, *Collected Essays* 301). Even though courtiers, like Rochester, were free to indulge their passions, this only emphasized their social irrelevance, a situation that resulted in the condition of the "alienated aristocrat." Thus, Hill claims, after Charles I's execution, tragedy was replaced by heroic drama "in which kings concern themselves with imaginary points of honour in love and war because real political issues have become too hot to touch" (*Collected Essays* 326).

Such conclusions are supported by Michael McKeon's claims that the eighteenth-century aristocracy's "increasingly defensive awareness" that social hierarchy and exclusive class identity were "under assault" resulted in an increasing "theatricalization" of social performance (151, 169). He cites Defoe's attack on the supposedly essential identity of the aristocrat—"as if there were some differing Species in the very Fluid of Nature . . . or some *Animalculae* of a differing and more vigorous kind"—as an instance of a new philosophical ridicule of the aristocratic notion that honor is "biologically inherited" (154). The resulting attempts to naturalize aristocratic ideology take on not a biological but a theatrical component: status values that we commonly associate with aristocratic social relations—such as deference and paternalistic care—undergo an elaborate sort of "theatricalization," one that is "likely to occur whenever social convention is raised to the level of self-conscious practice" (169).

This theatricalization of aristocratic social performance and the increasingly self-consciousness practice of aristocratic identity may account for the fact that the "real-world" result of some actresses' display of their "reputations" and "persons" was a movement from playhouse to town house, or even to country house, when they were courted or kept by the aristocrats for whom they played.[27] As Lesley Ferris acknowledges, "It was the expected custom for the men of the court to keep a pretty actress—just one of their many expenses in an age of public display" (70), a phenomenon that is perhaps a late-seventeenth-century sign of aristocratic, conspicuous consumption. Two of the most famous examples, of course, are Nell Gwynn and Moll Davis, each of whom became mistress to Charles II; Gwynn also gave birth to a son of the king, the first Duke of St. Albans. Margaret Hughes was the mistress of Prince Rupert; Anastasia Robinson was reported to have married Lord Peterborough; and Hester Davenport was tricked into a false marriage by the Earl of Oxford when he dressed one of his servants as a parson to "marry" them.

The actresses' apparent upward mobility—the shift in their status and their extratheatrical assumption of a new social identity—had its analogues in the larger cultural play, and display, of a fluidity of identity. Late-seventeenth-century English culture was self-conscious about the possibilities for performance in nontheatrical spaces, for masking and spectacle, for newly representing the self in nontheatrical realms. Terry Castle's extraordinary documentation of the eighteenth-century masquerade provides ample evidence of this theatricality in a culture vacillating between the pleasures and anxieties in the play of representations, the possibilities and the problems inherent in unitary notions of identity. At the masquerade, the large-scale cultural equivalent of the theatrical performance, "New bodies were superimposed over old; anarchic, theatrical selves displaced supposedly essential ones; . . . The pleasure of the masquerade attended on the experience of doubleness, the alienation of inner from outer, a fantasy of two bodies simultaneously and thrillingly present, self and other together, the two-in-one" (4–5).

Yet when Katharine Maus calls the actresses' upward mobility "unorthodox" (609), such a claim *is* true only if we think of class barriers as impermeable and of common women as barred—not just from wealth but from the cultural capital of the social graces, manners, fashions, and trappings of the aristocratic class. It is clear, however, that in important ways women onstage enacted and embodied these aristocratic imperatives: in tragedy especially, actresses took the parts of aristocratic and even royal characters, queens and princesses; like ladies of quality, they costumed themselves in finery, marking themselves as extraordinary in the same fashion as their more genteel counterparts. This question of fashion

—as an external sign by which identity is marked—had powerful class implications in the late seventeenth century, as we saw in a previous chapter. Castle comments on the problematic nature of fashions and the "massive instability of sartorial signs" that accounts for the contempt for clothing in Western culture: "Clothing has always been a primary trope for the deceitfulness of the material world—a mutable, shimmering tissue that everywhere veils the truth from human eyes. Inherently superficial, feminine in its capacity to enthrall and mislead, it is a paradigmatic emblem of changeability" (56). She concludes that underlying the early-eighteenth-century sumptuary laws and anti-masquerade literature was the fear that when a commoner wore the clothes of a higher rank, even in jest, it incited in the wearer a desire to join that rank and receive its rewards: "Luxurious costume might invest the lower orders with delusions of grandeur. Worse, it could lead to the revolutionary notion that rank itself could be altered as easily as its outward signs" (92). Jessica Munns and Penny Richards point to the new transformative powers of clothing as a particularly seventeenth-century phenomenon: "The combination of affordable textiles and fashion-book patterns made innovations in appearance, once exclusive to the highest court circles, available to aspiring provincials in a matter of months" (12), and it was the power of this new reality that threatened the status quo.

This anxiety about the performative quality of aristocratic signs is reflected in stories about Restoration actresses who had to be warned by theater managers not to wear their costumes outside the theater, reputedly on pain of being charged for their laundering. J. H. Wilson reports that some of the clothing worn on stage came from "the castoff suits or dresses of ladies and gentlemen too proud to wear the same outfit more than once," and he calls the extra-theatrical display of such costumes a "compensation" for the female players: "There was always the chance of slipping out after the play wearing one of the company's 'French gowns a-la-mode' or some other finery." The companies frowned on this practice, however, and complained that "their clothes were 'Tarnished and Imperelled by frequent wearing them out of the Playhouse,' and fined the culprit a week's pay if they caught her in the act" (Ladies 33–40).[28] Such managerial fiscal responsibility may be one practical reason for the injunction, but the prohibition also masks a deeper anxiety. Onstage, actresses, like aristocrats, were aware that they were always being watched; however, when both actresses and aristocrats paraded on public display the fashions that set them apart from lower-class spectators, clothing itself drawn from aristocratic models of ideal style, such fashion marked the wearers outside the theater with a particular status. Moreover, both actresses and upper-class women knew that their finely costumed bodies were commodities that might be "purchased" *outside* the theater in an aristocratic market: like the discourse recounting the private sexual activities of actresses, letters among aristocrats and gentry detailed not only the marriages but the scandalous sexual relationships of upper-class women. The sexual liaisons of both aristocratic women and actresses were, in some measure, "public" property.

On an even larger scale, the English had been engaged in recent and turbulent cultural dramas, to use Hobbes's theatrical metaphor, of their own. These spectacles could have provoked serious questions about the nature of royal and aristocratic identity: King Charles I had been beheaded, the rightful James II had been overthrown, and the foreign William III had been installed on the throne. Kingship was obviously subject to religious and political demands, and the old imperative—for an essential, traceable genetic royal line—had already given way to contemporary expediencies. Yet the notion that the "part" of the king had been played by a series of "substitutes" enters the discourse only as a means of confirming the status quo: the only "Pretenders" to the English throne were the family of James II, whose lineage should indeed have secured him the role but whose unpopular political and religious activities resulted in his replacement by a more congenial Dutch understudy.

Thus when the theatrical questions of display, identity, and unity are applied to aristocrats, they take on a very different resonance.[29] The reasons are manifest in questions of class imperatives linked to notions of class essentialism. First, and most simply, people of rank did not join the theater: Cibber recounts the sad story of a young aristocratic woman who, as a result of being thrown out of her family after an "indiscretion," comes to the theater for a job; her relations prohibit her taking the stage by interfering behind the scenes, and Cibber concludes there was "more dishonor to the family for her to be on stage as to sell patches and potatum in a Bandbox" (46). Second, and more powerfully, such dishonor can occur only because there was little acknowledged symbolic distance between a Duke, for instance, and some separate, private self: he *was* his rank. And while some aristocratic behavior was indeed attacked—for instance, Steele (himself Sir Richard) despairs of the excessive affectation and the violence inherent in the male, upper-class codes—such writing rarely suggests that aristocratic men, in particular, were merely role-playing, acting as substitutes in a larger cultural drama. The discourse of the era allowed them a simultaneity of identity: the Earl of Rochester, whose "real" name was John Wilmot, is essentially Rochester.

So when an aristocrat—and even a monarch—lent his or her robes to an actor for a particular part (an event guaranteed to increase the box office), Restoration discourse did not publicly proclaim this as the division of aristocratic identity, the conclusion a modern audience immediately jumps to, or an undermining of aristocratic, or even royal, essentialism, an interpretation obviously available to the seventeenth century audience.[30] Instead it located the suspicion, the distrust, and the pleasures of divided identity in the playhouse, a difference that could be highlighted when the player wore the monarch's robes.[31]

Thus, if Restoration theater performance offered a representation of "ideal" behavior in its fashions, voices, and gestures, then it served as a mediating element operating between the force that established certain behaviors as ideal—and, in the seventeenth century, that meant the aristocracy—and its application in the larger culture, as a shaping force in an audience's self-definition and behavior.[32] Jessica Munns and Penny Richards acknowledge the powerful part that literature played in the circulation of these ideals when they write that "Literary works did not merely comment on fashion; they also created fashion . . . if actors on stage represented the manners and appearances of the elite, the elite in turn dressed their hair a la [Hester] Santlow and carried with them fans and snuff boxes decorated with images from the plays" (13). The beautiful fashions, cultivated speech, and formalized gestures of the late-seventeenth-century actors, drawn from such aristocratic dictates of style and decorum and functioning as indicators of the proper emotional response required from an audience, served actually to reinforce an audience's belief that a *separable* self for the actor existed independent of the plot. And as we've seen, for women, that separable self was described in the discourse as a sexually available body. So while the stylized performances of seventeenth-century actors cultivate and constitute the fiction, they also create a transparent structure through which an audience can replay the narratives of an offstage reality "masquerading" as a deeper "truth."

Only a naive reader of performance is tricked. Aston recounts the story of Betterton and a country gentleman's experience at a fair: the country gentleman thinks the puppets in the puppet show are real, and only after much convincing does he come to believe, as Betterton insists, that the players are "Only Sticks and Rags" (5–6). That night, after Betterton had taken the gentleman to see his own production of *The Orphan,* when asked whether he liked the performance, the country fellow replied, "Why I don't knows, . . . it's well enought for *Sticks and Rags*" (5–6). The lesson is clear. A naive reader first experiences an epistemological and ontological problem: he fails to distinguish between the player and the part, entering wholly into the fiction of the spectacle; then, he encounters an aesthetic dilemma—how to distinguish a genuine performance from its poor imitation.

Readers of seventeenth-century culture, however, were put in an analogous but more precarious position: they had to enter wholly into the fiction of aristocratic spectacle; otherwise they might suspect that the bodies and brocade so visible in the upper ranks might be merely the sticks and rags of a cultural construct. Such questions of identity are instead displaced to the safer territory of the playhouse, a space where differences were said to be leveled. As a watering hole for aristocratic men, who often sat on the stage and "contributed" to the dialogue, it was also a place where aristocratic women frequently attended performances dressed like the onstage princesses or masked in the same fashion as prostitutes. Pepys recounts a telling incident in this context, one concerning Frances Jennings (sister to the Duchess of Marlborough and resident in the house of the Duchess of York) and her attendance at the theater "disguised" as an orange-wench, an impersonation finally unmasked only by a too spectacular item of fashion: "What mad freaks the Maids of Honour at Court have: that Miss Jennings, one of the Duchess's maids, the other day dressed herself like an orange-wench, and went up and down and cried oranges; till, falling down, or by some accident, her fine shoes were discerned, and she put to a great deal of shame" (21 February 1665). It is precisely this confusion of "women" that becomes the crucial issue: in the playhouse, ladies of quality could play down their rank, while the status of the common, woman player (and one powerful seventeenth-century meaning of the word "common" meant "shared") rose onstage, even to the heights of majesty, an event the dominant class both demands and fears and thus the dominant ideology must enact and resist.[33]

And thus the contemporary accounts indicate that Mrs. Davenant did indeed train Mrs. Barry so well that she was "soon Mistress of that Behaviour which sets off the well-bred Gentlewoman." "Gracefully Majestic" in displaying the "Presence of elevated Dignity," Mrs. Barry becomes a target, as the satirical barb complains, precisely because she cultivated a carriage so noble that her mean birth was in danger of being obscured.[34] The late-seventeenth-century discourse about actresses' sexual activities disguises this larger cultural anxiety—that the traditional, "essential quality" of the aristocratic class might not be distinguishable from those persons who could so excellently, and so convincingly, mimic it—an anxiety worked through by essentializing the identity of the female players through the activities of their sexualized bodies as a means of confirming a class status quo. In the same way that discourses on masculinity functioned to contain the upward mobility of a rising merchant class in Wycherley's *Gentleman Dancing-Master* and Behn's *Widdow Ranter,* discourses concerning the sexual activities of the actresses serve to support and undergird aristocratic claims to an essential—and thus exclusive—upper-class identity.

5 Monstrous Identities
Excess, Sexual Assault, and Subjectivity

RESTORATION THEATER FEATURES A veritable plethora of monsters trooping across the stage. Sometimes these monsters are "real," excluded from the human community because of their "race" or their physical features; the extraterrestrial creatures of Behn's *Emperor of the Moon* (1687) are one good example. Sometimes the monsters function metaphorically and discursively, revealing themselves in the end to be not monsters at all, but too thoroughly human: the increasing numbers of sexual predators and rapists that appeared on the Restoration stage fit into this category. And sometimes monsters become monsters because they've been preyed upon by other monsters: the victims of these rapists are made monstrous as a result of the sexual assault.

Monsters deviate from agreed-upon social and cultural norms. As we have seen in the plays examined so far, difference most often functions to exclude: playwrights used difference to secure an inside that was "safe" from and impenetrable to those represented as "other"—a New World dominated by self-controlled English imperialists or an England populated by Englishmen and Englishwomen appropriately attired and disciplined, for instance. In highlighting difference, the monster marks the *limits* of a culture's self-definition and the consequences of transgressions, according to Michael Uebel: "identity emerges through exclusionary means, over and against the monster who is posited as radically other; yet the monster, residing in interstitiality, also leads back to, and comes to inhabit, the intimate place of identity" (281).

This interstitiality, however, is precisely what makes the monster so dangerous, for in returning to that intimate place of identity it simultaneously functions as an equally powerful inclusionary force

—an inclusion that depends on the monster's capacity to breach walls, transgress boundaries, invade spaces not its own. Most important, the monster *always* infects with monstrosity everything that it touches, and so both the rapist and his victim will label themselves—and will be called by others—"monstrous." In that, the monster possesses the power of an annihilating form of sameness, for as all students of Restoration drama know the victim of sexual assault must die. One unexpected consequence of the production of that likeness, however, especially in the aftermath of sexual violence, is an explosive, if short-lived, discursive subjectivity for the victim, trauma that leads her to exteriorize her pain and attempt to perform her wounded interiority, even as her body—like the bodies of the actresses presented for public scrutiny both on and off the stage—becomes public spectacle, this time in the aftermath of a monstrous sexual assault.

"Clarifying Examples"

Excess, in the seventeenth century, was the stuff of monsters. We need only recall Ambroise Paré's very popular, sixteenth-century book of marvels that features engravings of three-legged men, women with floppy rabbit's ears, and faces with a third eye to remember that all of these creatures possess an excess—extra hands or legs, extra heads or eyes.[1] The *OED* cites the root meaning of the word "monster" as the Latin *monstrum,* "something marvelous, orig. a divine portent or warning"; later the meaning includes "an animal afflicted with some congenital malformation, a misshapen birth, an abortion," and later still we see "a person of inhuman and horrible cruelty or wickedness." Katharine Park and Lorraine Daston trace a similar line of development from sixteenth-century monsters as prodigies, drawn from the realm of religion, to eighteenth-century monsters as medical pathologies. The category of the monster thus moves from the divine portent, warning, and message to the aberrant, the abnormal, and the nonrepresentative (23–25).[2]

The seventeenth-century scientific interest in monsters was keen, a fact recognized by Helen Deutsch and Felicity Nussbaum whose recent groundbreaking work, *"Defects": Engendering the Modern Body,* cites new modes of scientific classification that produced a discourse of the normative body, any deviation from which was presumed to be a defect, imperfect, monstrous. Frances Bacon is a good example of the scientist who viewed monstrous births not as omens or portents but as "a point of reference that allows the naturalist to identity the overreaching regularity of the rest of organic life" (1), according to Andrew Curran and Patrick Graille. The century saw a proliferation of cabinets displaying curiosities that contained both monstrous animal and human remains, and according to Stephen Pender this collecting and displaying of monsters occurred during "an age of curiosity" ("Bodyshop" 97), a time of "a readjustment of scientific investment in singularity" from an attention to objects and bodies themselves to "an emergent focus on the ways in which such 'ethnographic objects' conformed to taxonomies": "In other words, the display of human beings gradually came to depend on both ontological categories (on the difference between the normal and the anomalous) and the frisson of the freakish" ("'No Monster'" 150). Dennis Todd's recent study of eighteenth-century monsters reports that the volume of literature about monsters was immense, spanning everything from popular ballads and broadsides to recondite treatises: "Some of it was religious, seeking to find in each singular birth a portent or sign. Much of it was a more profane character, trading off an uncritical fascination in the marvelous, often collected in profusely illustrated, encyclopedic volumes"[3] (44).

Whether as "an abjecting epistemological device basic to the mechanics of deviance construction and identity formation," as Jeffrey Cohen has called it, or as a "powerful clarifying example," as Katharine Park and Lorraine Daston have argued, the monster in the late seventeenth century was held up against normative examples as unnatural and nonrepresentative even as it was simultaneously offered up as a too fascinating model of excess. It is instructive to look at the figure of the monster in three of its more benign contexts to see how pervasive the notion of an aberrant human identity actually was and to see how the excessive bodies or energies of these creatures, producing anxiety, are positioned as outside the norm before moving on to more malevolent monsters who, because they demand victims, demand containment.

My analysis begins with Behn's *Second Part of The Rover* (1681), a play that features two very "real" seventeenth-century monsters: a giant and a dwarf.[4] Dennis Todd writes that the two types of "monsters" most popular with London viewers at Bartholomew

Fair were giants and dwarfs. One giant, on display at Southwark Fair in 1684, remarked in his handbill that "his late Majesty was pleased to walk under his Arm, and he has grown very much since." More popular still were dwarfs, especially those who were "well-proportioned" and possessed of intelligence and the ability to interact with the audience (146). Anne Lake Prescott has come up with a figure she calls *Gargatom,* a combination of the gigantic and the minuscule, based on the consistent juxtapositions of Gargantua and Tom Thumb in early Stuart literature, a creature who raises questions about the relation of size to status—or the relation of "the immense to the nugatory, of plethora to dearth, *ultra* to *citra,* and in what this might say about tumescent pride, misused language, and social confusion" (75–76). Yet Prescott is wary of too ready judgments: "Giants and pygmies are ambiguously monstrous: strange 'here' but normal 'there,' where their species is at home, whether Scythia, Africa, Brazil, Lilliput, or Brobdingnag" (75).

Behn's "monsters" are equally ambiguous. She brings them on-stage together only once during the course of the drama (the Giant makes an appearance alone in the fifth act), and they appear most centrally in the opening scene of the third act when Fetherfool and Blunt, two English suitors, decide to woo and win the new-comers and so draw lots for the Giant and the Dwarf.[5] When they arrive, both men are tongue-tied, confounded by the women's sizes. When the Giant asks, "What, does the Cavalier think I'le devour him?" Fethererfool responds, "Something inclin'd to such a fear." The Dwarf, perceptive about the oddity of the situation but not the least bit shy, pronounces the most intelligent assessment of the whole situation by assuming that it is *her* suitor who suffers from a abnormal physical condition: "Sure, Segnior Harliquin, these Gentlemen are dumb."

That the monsters exceed the boundaries of scale produces much stageplay for the male suitors. For instance, when they must approach their "intendeds," the suitors slowly and with great trepidation approach, quickly speak, and scurry away like the frightened bunnies they are; when they must make actual contact, Fetherfool runs up and down a ladder to salute the Giant. Excessive size also produces much extravagant rhetoric exchanged by the potential "lovers" and much cynical discourse offered up by the Giant who will not be wooed by such fools:

147

Fetherfool: Whe then, Madam, without inchanted Sword or
Buckler, I am your Man.
Giant: My Man! My Mouse. I'le marry none whose Person
and Courage shall not bear some proportion to mine.
Fetherfool: Your Mightiness, I fear, will die a Maid then.
Giant: I doubt you'l scare secure me from that fear, who
Court my Fortune, not my Beauty.
Fetherfool: Huh, how scornful she is, I'le warrant you
{aside}—whe I must confess, your Person is something
Heroical and Masculine, but I protest to your Highness, I
Love and Honour ye.

(3.1.70–77)

Beyond the possibilities for this kind of farcical comedy, the
"monsters" function in more profound ways to comment not only
on questions of "the immense to the nugatory," as Prescott would
have it, but on questions about what constitutes real value and
genuine worth. Fetherfool, who is as flighty as his name implies,
describes the value markers of the young women this way: "two
Monsters arriv'd from Mexico, Jews of vast fortunes, with an old
Jew Uncle their Guardian; they are worth a hundred thousand
pounds a piece——Marcy upon's, whe 'tis a sum able to purchase
all Flanders again from this most Christian Majesty" (1.1.169–74).
This sentence shocks in many ways, and upon reflection serves
only to complicate rather than to clarify the problem of the monster. The origins of the women's monstrosity, which initially appear
to be the singular excess of their size, turn out to be multiple.
Could it be their ethnic difference, their Jewishness, that excludes
them and makes them monstrous? Or is it a national difference,
that they come from Mexico?

Economic difference—wealth so vast that they could by themselves rescue Flanders from the tyranny of Spain (itself a very
strange possibility when one considers that Mexico was fully allied
with Spain)—turns out to be the key. Blunt, who moves from the
first part to the second part of *The Rover* even more firmly committed to revenging himself on *all* women, no matter their size,
immediately begins to calculate his plans for getting even (although he utterly fails to ask any of the questions a rational person
would when told that monsters have come to town: what kinds of
monsters are they? what do they look like? how big is the giant?).[6]

Blunt instead quickly injects this query, "But harkye, Lieutenant, are you sure they are not Married?" (1.1.176), and thus he locates the women's "real" value not in their freakish sizes but in their freakish economic status—over one hundred thousand pounds a year.

Of the Giant and the Dwarf in this play, Jacqueline Pearson has written that, beyond providing a grotesque comedy in keeping with the harlequinade element in the play, they are also allowed to suggest "the monstrousness of a system of money marriage" in which women attain significance only in terms of their economic value, and she concludes that the "lady Monsters" are not only treated with sympathy as individuals but are also "the vehicle of images of monstrosity which ultimately apply not to women, foreigners, Jews or the deformed, but to foolish men, oppressive hierarchies, and unjust political systems"[7] (223). This is a familiar, if powerful, theme in Behn's work, even though it functions here through two of her strangest characters. But Pearson has another, more interesting explanation for the monsters' presence: of the sexual economy of the play in general and of its relationship to categories of identity, she argues that all the central romantic relationships consist of a Spanish woman and an English man, and "the difference in nationality lightly and effectively dramatizes not only the potential Otherness of men to women, but also the fact that this very Otherness is what makes possible harmonious heterosexual relations"[8] (221). The Dwarf and the Giant are yet two more instances of difference that enable sexual union.

These are all certainly powerful differences, but they are finally relegated to secondary status by a most telling moment of exclusion that occurs during a revealing discussion about size and value, one that culminates in Behn's treatment of one of her favorite issues—status:

> *Beaumond:* Marry'd, who the Devil would venture on such formidable Ladies?
> *Fetherfool:* How, venture on 'em, by the Lord, *Harry*, and that would I, though I'me a Justice o' th' Peace, and they be Jews, (which to a Christian is a thousand reasons).
> *Blunt:* Is the Devil in you to declare our design?
> *Fetherfool:* Mum, as close as a Jesuit.
> *Beaumond:* I admire your courage, Sir, but one of them is so

little, and so deform'd, 'tis thought she is not capable of Marriage; and the other is so huge an overgrown Gyant, no man dares venture on her.

Willmore: Prithee let's go see 'em; what do they pay for going in?

Fetherfool: Pay—I'de have you know they are Monsters of Quality.

(1.1.177–88)

Fetherfool is aghast at the suggestion that these women are freaks in a sideshow, since he is willing to let "Quality" override all other characteristics. Behn takes her usual conservative position about status in this instance: though she may be willing to play with the possibility of gender-crossings and to flirt with the possibilities of miscegenation in many of her works, she likes her status-based hierarchies and even goes so far as to inscribe them as essential. Thus to present us with "Monsters of Quality," women excluded from the norm because of their wealth and status, is not a deviation from Behn's usual position, as Pearson suggests, but rather her strongest insistence that even monsters, naturally excluded because of their size, are welcomed into polite society, not as interstitial creatures but as full-fledged members of the community—when they are wellborn.

More threatening are the metaphorical monsters found in two of Shadwell comedies, *The Woman-Captain* (1679) and *The Virtuoso* (1676), characters who are made monstrous not in their exceeding the boundaries of their size but in their breaching of sanctioned boundaries of gender roles.[9] In the first instance, Mrs. Gripe, wife to an ascetic usurer who keeps her and all his domestic goods locked up, takes on the identity of her brother (a captain in the army) and stages an escape by masquerading as a military officer. Her part was played by Elizabeth Barry who, as we saw in the previous chapter, lived with a public "star" status that was both supported and undercut by an extratheatrical discourse eager to reveal her private sexual activities; an audience would thus enter the theater "knowing" that such a woman was fully capable of transgressing the sexual norms of her culture and thus was right and appropriate to play the breeches "part." Called "this vile Monster of Woman-kind" (3.11) by her husband, she thoroughly chafes against his tyrannous treatment of her, barring her from all public life, actions described by Sir Humphrey this way: "she can never be seen but out of a Window, which is no bigger than the hole of a Pillory" (1.199–200). To this, Wildman replies, "He locks her up, and always carries the Key about him" (1.201). Sir Humphrey, however, holds the choicest piece of gossip about the Gripes: "Nay, at Night he sows his Shirt and her Smock together, that upon any violent motion the twitch may wake him: There's a Horn-preventing Design" (1.202–4).

Once unstitched from her husband and dressed as a soldier, "Captain" Gripe soon learns how to comport herself, not only as a man but as the best kind of military man. Initially, she learns that strutting about in a fine uniform and berating all the men under her "command" have positive effects: "I shall strut, look big, and huff enough for a Captain, I warrant you" (3.489–90). With additional instruction from her sergeant, she learns the proper body management demanded of a man: self-discipline, self-control, and self-restraint. Once she masters those masculine virtues, she takes on the task of teaching three upper-crust wastrel boys how to be upstanding, honorable—that is, moderated and internally disciplined and appropriately masculine—young men. When they fail to understand that they have signed away their freedom to the military and say, "Come Captain, you have done enough with us . . . let us go, we'll go to the *Temple* or *Alsacia* for refuge till the Business be over" (5.277–78), she responds with a gentle reminder about their duty, a reminder real men would not have needed: "Come, Gentlemen, no fooling; you have receiv'd the King's Money, and his Cloaths, and I will make you know you are my Souldiers— Stand to your Arms all!" (5.293–95). She turns swiftly and easily to violence, however, when they fail to follow her commands, and she cudgels them, twice, saying, "shall such Rascals as you think it enough to be Drunk, and Swagger, beat Bawds, kick Drawers, squabble with Constables and Watches, break Windows, and triumph in Drunken Brawls and Street-quarrels, and never serve your Countrey?—If you have Valour, I'll make you turn it that way" (5.315–20). This physical abuse, plus threatening to shoot them and finally tying them up at the neck and heels for mutiny, subdues the worst of the town bullies—activities all done within the view of, but outside the understanding of, her husband, the miserly Gripe.

In accomplishing this task, she certainly does nothing to eradicate violence. Indeed, she herself perpetuates it, but the play more than suggests that she does so for the greater good: to teach wild and unruly young men a lesson about the limits of an explosive masculinity and the necessity for the tempering of that violence. She enters a potentially dangerous arena to perform a socially necessary act of containment, and in the end she positively tames the three wild creatures of pleasure by harnessing their violence for legitimate uses: she makes soldiers of them, the perfectly self-controlled early modern male body.[10] The play more than suggests that men and violence are natural companions; indeed, it is violence left unchecked that produces the three wastrels. It also suggests that violence is never erased; it can only be correctly harnessed and deployed. It takes "this vile Monster of Woman-kind," who uses force to subdue force, to harness excessive behavior for legitimate purposes—the turning away of violence from its random applications and toward its use in systematic, programmatic forms.

These lessons and the power that goes with them ultimately allow the woman-captain to trick her husband into giving her the money she deserves, and in the end it is canny intelligence coupled with disciplined violence that ultimately produces for her the real power she needs: she abandons her captain's role in order to assume the responsibilities of a free, married woman—in possession of a separate maintenance. If this play could be said to model appropriate gender roles, then an excessive, monstrous *woman* turns out to be the best model of a moderated *man,* for she displays a control of violence for strategic purposes and disciplined emotion deployed in the service of a clever ruse; for that, she is rewarded with a man's freedom and economic security.

Shadwell's *Virtuoso* features an even more disturbing incident of cross-dressing, one that explicitly couples violence with sex and provokes the label of the *monstrous.*[11] This violence involves Sir Formal Trifle, an orator and would-be wit, and Sir Samuel Hazard, a self-fashioned ladies' man and coxcomb. The plot commences when Sir Trifle so tries the patience of young Miranda and Clarinda with his endless speechifying that they trick him into standing on the trapdoor where he "sinks" below, the stage directions tell us. Meanwhile, Sir Samuel Hazard cross-dresses in order, he hopes, to create greater access to these same young women, whom he fancies. He is punished even more severely, for not only has he donned an absurd female costume but he performs his "parts"—both male

and female—very badly, and so he too is tricked into the vault below.

When the naive and unworldly Sir Nicholas Gimcrack, the eponymous hero of the piece, hears that Sir Formal, whom he thinks
is a disciplined and virtuous man, is trapped in the company of a
lewd woman (the cross-dressed Sir Samuel), he reacts with horror.
Miranda tells him, "Sir Formal is privately shut up with this lewd
woman, and has been this hour" (4.3.79–80); Sir Nicholas responds,
"*O monstrum horrendum!* Is my friend, that seeming virtuous man,
fall'n into the snare?" (4.3.84–85). What Sir Nicholas does not
know is that his friend is "seeming" virtuous indeed, for Sir Formal, actually the *monstrum horrendum* of this moment, is about to
launch a sexual assault against the cross-dressed Sir Samuel.

Once trapped below ground, Sir Formal almost immediately
gives in to his amorous impulses: "I can no longer contain myself.
This lady, join'd with darkness and opportunity (the midwife of
vice as we may so say), has so inflam'd me that I must further attempt her chastity. I am confident she must be handsome and no
mean person by her silken garments" (4.1.1–3). When rhetoric fails
to move Sir Samuel, Sir Formal offers "her" his purse; to this, Sir
Samuel replies, "I'll take the rogue's purse whate'er come on't"
(4.1.24). Rhetoric finally gives way to actual assault in this absurd
exchange:

Sir Formal: Thou hast provok'd my gentle spirit so it has
become furious, and it is decreed I must enjoy thy lovely
body—
Sir Samuel: Out upon you! My body! I defy you. I am an
honest woman; I scorn your words. I will call out for somebody to protect my honor.
Sir Formal: Your honor cannot suffer. None can see us, and
who will declare it?
Sir Samuel: Out upon you! Get you gone, you swine. I will
not suffer in my honor. I am virtuous. Help! Help! A rape! A
rape! Help! Help!
Sir Formal: Be not obstreperous; none can hear you. You have
provok'd me contrary to my gentle temper—even to a rape.
Come, I will, I must, i'faith I must.
Sir Samuel [aside]: 'Sdeath! The rogue begins to pry into the
difference of sexes and will discover mine. I must try my

strength with him—Out lustful Tarquin! You libidinous goat,
have at you.
[Sir Samuel beats Sir Formal, kicks him, and flings him down.]
Sir Formal: Help! Help! Murder! Murder!
Sir Samuel: Be not obstreperous; none can hear you.
*Sir Formal:*Upon my verity I think this be an Amazon! Well,
I can bear this, but—
Sir Samuel: Do you again attempt my honor? I'll maul you,
you lascivious villain.
Sir Formal: Hold, hold, I beseech you. I humbly rest con-
tented. I acquiesce.
Sir Samuel: Get you from me, lustful swine. Be gone.

(4.1.50–80)

The humor in this scene depends on the assumption that no real
harm can come to either of these characters—since apparently no
seventeenth-century audience member was worried about the
violence in male-on-male sexual assault.[12] In comedy, this "safe"
assault is doubly funny, for its source is a double degeneration of
male behavior: first, after a man "sinks" into the feminine, it is a
short step to degenerate into the animal, as can be seen in both
men's hurling the animal insults of "swine" and "goat" at one another. One of the greatest fears monsters invoke in us is our anxiety about just such degeneration—about the possibilities of blurring the boundaries between the animal and the human. Dennis
Todd reports that the third most popular attraction at eighteenth-
century fairs were those creatures that "blurred the distinction between men [*sic*] and beasts." Included were apes and monkeys who
mimicked human actions, dancing dogs, and a number of "Clever
Mares." More disturbing still were those humans who seemed to
have degenerated into animals: a boy covered with fish scales or the
bristles of a hedgehog, a "cannibal Indian" from South Carolina, or
the "Tall Black Wild Man," exhibited in London in 1711, who had
been "taken savage in the Woods near Bengall in the East Indies"
and had a body covered all over by thick, black hair (148).

In the scene above, Sir Formal and Sir Samuel—no matter the
gender of their external garments—have degenerated into a goat
and a swine, the lusty and the loathsome, and thus metaphorically
the *monstrum horrendum* of this scene depends not just on the surrender of one's gender identity but on the loss of humanity that

accompanies the degeneration into the animal. At the conclusion of the play, each is punished when the woman he fancies rejects him for a more appropriately masculine suitor: that leaves the "lustful swine" Sir Formal tricked into marriage with Clarinda's maid Betty, while the cross-dressed Sir Samuel loses a good bit of his money and nearly all of his dignity.

"Unnatural Rapes and Murders": Monstrous Excesses

All students of seventeenth-century drama must eventually confront the real monster on the seventeenth-century stage: rapists and perpetrators of sexual assaults of much more threatening and traumatic forms than those described above. Modern scholars are not quite certain what to do with the problem of sexual assault on the Restoration stage. Susan Owen suggests that Restoration dramatists both took for granted and actively altered the trope of rape as social corruption, as it was found in the late Jacobean period: "Both Whigs and Tories use rape as a trope of the monstrous, associated by Tories with rebellion, and by Whigs with popery and arbitrary government" (*Restoration* 175). Other arguments often depend on whether the focus is the rapist or his victim. Presenting an indictment of the sexual rapaciousness of men and thus focusing primarily on the rapist, some scholars have argued that rape functions as a criticism of the larger patriarchal culture, especially for attempted rapes in comedy (Behn's *Rover; or, The Banish'd Cavaliers,* and the criticism, in this case, of cavalier culture, for example). Anthony Kaufman's analysis of Behn's play is especially good in this regard. He argues that "the impulse to rape is seen not merely as the gauche actions of an obvious fool, but as a constant threat in the best male characters" (3), and he forces us to admit that Willmore, the hero of this drama, acts on his desires to rape as often as the foolish Blunt.[13] Still a third approach, focusing primarily on the victim, constitutes a "scopic economy" reading of rape: the presence of newly introduced actresses—living, breathing, real British women onstage—helped to fuel the nearly insatiable desire of audience members to see (quite literally "to see") the nakedness of the vulnerable and victimized woman player.[14] Elizabeth Howe's reading is representative: "the most striking manifestation of sexual exploitation in tragedy is its portrayal of rape. The [introduction of] actresses caused rape to become for the first time a major feature of English tragedy," because rape "became a way of giving the purest, most virginal heroine a sexual quality" (43). We need only remember the extratheatrical discourse that surrounded Mrs. Barry and Mrs. Bracegirdle, that focused on a reputed "knowledge" about their private sexual behaviors, to realize just how powerful an effect their introduction to the stage produced. As we saw in the last chapter, this discourse took on additional power when coupled with the staging of a female desire inscribed upon and incessantly returning to a female body "discovered" through the moving shutters and the new technologies of the Restoration stage, a body, such as we saw in Manley's *Royal Mischief.* Elizabeth Howe also recognizes the power of the movable shutters to open and reveal nearly naked, or at least severely disordered, women on-stage after their rapes have been verbally recounted, often quite explicitly; such "discovery" scenes situate the actress's body as an offering to the audience, "as a piece of erotic entertainment—a kind of pornographic painting brought to life"[15] (46).

Any one of these three kinds of readings will certainly shed light on a particular piece, and together they go some way toward explaining why so many rapes suddenly "appear" in the late seventeenth century. But I would like to offer a reading that more forcefully acknowledges the pain experienced by the female victim. In this reading, I will attempt to account for the sheer excessiveness of the act of rape—for the energy, for the cruelty, and for the trauma—of sexual assault by focusing on its most powerful source: not sexual desire but a compulsive search for "novelty." This destructive form of desire arises alongside and in conjunction with the larger culture itself that produces and imports "novelties" at an increasing rate, a desire that provokes an insatiable consumption that produces waste in the form of the discarded bodies of the rapist's victims. Within this cycle of consumption—attraction, violence, repulsion, and new attraction—the victim experiences an explosive, if short-lived, compulsion of her own: the need to speak her trauma, to articulate a wounded interiority, a subjectivity that insists on a female identity that exceeds the surfaces of her body. In other words, I look to monsters.

I argue that violence is both inherent in the monster and, lamentably, the product the monster produces: the victim, feeling the taint of the monster, must die, while the culture from which the monster emerged is revealed to be both its source and its sustenance. I begin my examination of sexual assault by taking up yet another Shadwell play, *The Libertine,* based on a Spanish character with a long stage history and presenting yet another instance of bad Spanish behavior, but this time behavior so excessive that neither contemporary audiences nor modern scholars have known quite what to make of it.[16] *The Libertine* is the paradigmatic Restoration rape play featuring the era's most monstrous protagonist, the play that by my count contains more references to more separate rapes than any other play of this era—perhaps more references than any other play in history—and that features as its eponymous "hero" a man who is both a serial murderer and a serial rapist.

The play displays a degree of violence unprecedented on the seventeenth-century stage. By my count, Don Antonio raped and impregnated both of his sisters; Don John killed his father, primarily because the elder man, governor of Seville, had kept Don John's aunt from his violent sexual attacks; and the men brag about having ravished two nuns and wounded a third because "they were uncivil" (28). Indeed, the quotation that heads this section comes from Maria, a woman tricked into sexual contact with Don John and who subsequently follows him throughout the drama, trying to revenge herself upon him and to warn others about Don John and his cohorts—whom she calls "greater Villains that the Earth e'r bore"—and whose horrid actions have come in the form of "Revenge, Revenge cruel, unnatural Rapes and Murders. They are Devils in the shapes of men"[17] (70).

The single idea guiding the despicable actions of Don John and his cohorts is a perverse, if fascinating and historically vexed, notion of "natural" behavior. We discover as early as the first lines of that play that, when Don John and his cohorts call themselves "natural" men, they mean men who indulge their impulses, what they call "pleasure": Don John begins the play with these words,

> Thus far without a bound we have enjoy'd
> Our prosp'rous pleasure, which dull Fools call Sins;
> Laugh'd at old feeble Judges, and weak Laws;
> And at the fond fantastick thing, call'd Conscience,
> Which serves for nothing but to make men Cowards;
>
> (25)

Don Antonio thanks Don John for having dispelled the "fumes" of religion and moderated behavior from their minds:

By thee, we have got loose from Education,
And the dull slavery of Pupillage,
Recover'd all the liberty of Nature,
Our own strong Reasons now can go alone,
Without the feeble props of splenatick Fools,
Who contradict our common Mother, Nature.

(25)

Like Rochester, Don John would have it that "nature" means no restraint of any appetite, and his discourse echoes Rochester's remarks to Gilbert Burnet: Rochester insisted that it was unreasonable to suppose natural appetites "were put into a man only to be restrained, or curbed to such a narrowness," and he included in these appetites the free use of wine and women[18] (qtd. in Staves, *Players' Scepters* 257).

Libertines themselves, however, justify their actions in discourses about freedom, and especially its relationship to nature and culture, that were alive in the late seventeenth century.[19] It is therefore useful to look at the concept of nature as it was being scrutinized in the late seventeenth century and as Don Juan and his cohorts constantly deploy the term throughout the play, usually in contrast to the repressive dictates of "custom." Susan Staves's extensive analysis of authority, and its relation to the conflict between custom and nature as it unfolded in the late seventeenth century, is relevant here. Staves argues that one immediate consequence of the distinction between custom and nature is that the things that are not natural become stigmatized as "only customs or mere conventions" and seem to have less authority than they did before: "*physics* ('nature') and *nomos* ('conventions, custom, law') begin as opposites" (*Players' Scepters* 254). Staves notes that many Restoration writers were also fascinated by this same question, whether the law of nature bound every man to a conventional morality—"obedience to civil magistrates and parents, faithfulness to oaths and covenants, respect for property, and avoidance of murder, adultery, incest, sodomy, fornication, and suicide" (260). Playwrights were also eager to take up these questions by speculating about the lengths to which natural passions and ambitions might go if there were no such thing as natural morality or natural obligation. Staves muses, "It may seem paradoxical to say that the most characteristic acts [of] these heroes who claim to live according to nature are unnatural, but their 'unnaturalness' depends upon assuming some moral order in nature that disallows incest, matricide, and so on . . . and it was precisely this assumption that was being questioned" (298).

Jean-Marc Kehres, examining a later text—Sade's *Justine*—acknowledges that Justine is quick to identify the "monstrous vitality" of the Sadeian hedonist as "conceptually other," but many of the libertines present themselves not only as part of nature but as "its most accomplished exemplars": "Indeed, [Sade] claims to fulfill nature's primary goal, namely experiencing pleasure through the infliction of pain" (101–2). The Sadeian libertines have also borrowed a page from Don John when they insist on the naturalness of their aggressive emotions. Kehres argues that, throughout *Justine,* Sadeian libertines profess to be "free from the alienation of social conventions": according to many of the libertines, their sexual practices can only be "natural" since "Nature would not allow such actions to exist if they did not obey its dictates" (107). In this context, Shadwell presents a libertine so excessive that he functions as "the unrepentant libertine" who, according to Andrew P. Williams, refuses any "reformed" version of his identity, preferring instead to hold fast to a masculine identity "that defined manhood within a relatively rigid sphere of characteristics"—including "voracious sexual appetite, a permanent state of skepticism," and "the pursuit of pleasure and power"[20] (95). Or the libertine could be said to function as an exemplar of "moral monstrosity," a condition that James A. Steintrager sees as "the inversion of the deep value of the century: it turns pity into the malicious enjoyment of another's pain"[21] (115).

I would argue, however, that the voraciousness of the libertine's sexual appetite is not driven by nature, as he himself would insist, but by a force much more modern and gaining significant power throughout the last years of the seventeenth century: a new British love affair with novelty. Marina Bianchi argues that novelty is anything that disrupts a previous set of individual experiences and that, within certain boundaries, produces pleasure: "novelty is pleasurable provided that its degree is not so high, nor so low, as to make it either unsettling or boring" (3). More importantly, novelty and consumption are inextricably linked, since consumption produces an insatiable "taste" for the desirable object. Don John says, after stumbling upon a house in the street, "Let me see, here lives a Lady: I have seen Don Octavio haunting about this house, and making private signs to her. I never saw her face, but am resolv'd to enjoy her, because he likes her; besides, she's another Woman" (31). "Another" woman is a new woman, a "novel" woman, one as yet "unenjoyed," a fact Don John himself recognizes fully: when chastised by another cast-off woman for making her miserable, he replies, "Miserable! Use *variety* as I do, and You'll not be miserable. Ah! There's nothing so sweet to frail humane flesh as *variety*" (emphasis mine), and "What an excellent thing is a Woman before Enjoyment, and how insipid after it" (40–41).

An important, even intimate, relationship exists between novelty and repetition, especially in terms of pleasure and power. J. S. Peters's arguments about the impact that a newly emerging, early modern print culture had on seventeenth-century citizens provides an enlightening context for this problem of repetition: "A print world creates a play about rehearsal, about repetition, because it is conscious of the repetition of its own material forms, because (in a world in which knowledge is easily storable on the page) it cannot be certain that life is bettered by the repetitions that once served preservation" (173). The lives of Don John and his cohorts are composed of nothing but this kind of repetition, a numbing sameness of activity that never satisfies, a new world of unfulfilled desires: "The problem with the system of rapid obsolescence and plentiful supply (of fashions or bodies or books)," also according to Peters, "is that it confuses the nature of desires: it is hard to know what one 'would have' when one is constantly in the process of having something new. The multiplication of objects obscures both the identity of that thing appetite wants and the fact that appetite has no particular object" (180). Or, as Andrew P. Williams puts it, "Like an empty bottle of sack, females are easily discarded by the libertine once their potential for providing sexual pleasure has been realized" (102). Don John and his gang are so committed to this "process of having something new"—new rapes, new murders, and new mayhem—that they end up suffering from a confusion of desires, appetites that soon devolve into the state of *having* "no particular object," for it is the activity alone that becomes self-sustaining.

The final result of this state of rehearsal, repetition, and objectless appetite is waste, which itself produces a perverse sort of pleasure: "This circulation of waste makes novelty impossible. Waste is what novelty tries to exclude; waste is what repetition, reiteration (rehearsal) generate; waste is what happens when the libertines waste the bodies that fall across their paths—the Mrs. Loveits or Bellindas" (Peters 182). And waste is the product Don John and his friends create when they cultivate "only their pleasures," their senses, and their appetites in a discourse that itself encodes the repetition of their behavior.²² At one point in the second act, Don John is encircled by six of his wives, all demanding to be named his legitimate spouse; his "solution" to the problem is to attempt to hand each wife over to one of his friends with this remark: "I hate unreasonable, unconscionable fellows, who when they are weary of their Wives, will still keep 'em from other Men. Gentlemen, ye shall command mine" (45). When wife number four physically resists being given to Don Lopez, Antonio says, "A mettl'd Girl, I like her well: She'll endure a *Rape* gallantly. I love resistance, it endears the pleasure," and this exchange sets off a chorus of repeated "ravishes" that is chilling in the directness of its threat, for they appear to chant themselves into a nearly hypnotic trance in their celebration of "ravishment."

> *Don John:* Vertue and Honour! There's nothing good or ill, but as it seems to each man's natural appetite, if they will consent freely. You must *ravish* friends: that's all I know, you must *ravish!*
> *Antonio:* Ladies, you shall fly, but we must *ravish* first.
> *Don Lopez:* Yes, I assure you we must *ravish*————.
>
> (45 [emphasis mine])

The series ends only when wife number four exclaims, "No, Monster, I'll prevent you," (45) and stabs herself to death in the presence of the entire company. This moment is not an aberration, for an equally chilling moment occurs in the second act, when the men sing another hymn to rape:

> *Don Lopez:* I dogg'd my new Mistriss to her Lodging; she's *Don Bernardo's* Sister, and shall be my Punk.
> *Don John:* I could meet no willing Dame, but was fain to commit a Rape to pass away the time.
> *Don Antonio:* Oh! a Rape is the joy of my heart; I love a Rape, upon my Clavis, exceedingly.
> *Don John:* But mine, my Lads, was such a Rape, it ought to be Registered; a Noble and Heroick Rape.

Don Lopez: Ah! dear Don John!
Don Antonio: How was it?
Don John: 'Twas in a Church, Boys.
Don Antonio: Ah! Gallant Leader!
Don Lopez: Renown'd Don John!

(32)

Dead bodies and broken spirits litter the paths these men travel.

Don John's own demise offers little by way of cathartic release of the anxiety he and his actions produced, for he goes to his death entirely unrepentant. Dying in front of a church and next to the suddenly enlivened statue of his father, Don John's demise is engineered by the ghost of Don Pedro, who urges his son to "Repent, repent, all your horrid crimes: / Monsters, repent, or Hell will swallow you" (89); his father is also attended by the ghosts of many of the men and women killed by Don John who "cry for vengeance" (89), according to the statue of Don Pedro. Enveloped and embraced by a host of devils, Don John is finally swallowed up in a cloud of fire, unrepentant to the end: "These things I see with wonder, but no fear" (91).

Some scholars, such as Christopher Wheatley who has produced one the best and most recent books on Shadwell's work, argue that the libertine is finally defeated in the end, not by the intervention of God but by being rendered absurd in his excessiveness.[23] But that very excessiveness paradoxically and perversely endows the libertine with positive features: the very act of representation—an act Shadwell must perform in order to criticize the libertine as something vile, immoral, despicable, and excessive—simultaneously and inevitably confers on the libertine all the theatrical powers conferred on the character who occupies center stage. Such a finely discriminated and energetically detailed presentation of the actions of a rapist, even if the intention is to reject and revile him, serves simultaneously to legitimate him. Once he is thus spotlighted, he becomes a theatrical object of desire—even as he rips through the world in the most unruly, uncontrolled, and unholy fashion. Or, as Michael C. Schoenfeldt has argued of such bodies, "It is the disordered, undisciplined self, subject to a variety of internal and external forces, that is the site of subjugation, and the subject of horror" (12), and I would add the site of that perverse desire. Even the libertine's death does nothing to wipe away the pain and mayhem he leaves behind; indeed it could be argued that his stoicism and unwavering adherence to the single-minded pursuit of pleasure would, in a different context, represent an admirable strength of character.

The monstrous rapist fully encodes the powerful and contradictory emotions of attraction and repulsion found in monsters generally. As such, the figure serves as "a monster of prohibition," a character Jeffrey Cohen argues "polices the borders of the possible," interdicting some behaviors and actions, incorporating others: "The monster of prohibitions exists to demarcate the bonds that hold together that system of relations we call culture, to call horrid attention to the borders that cannot—*must* not—be crossed"[24] ("Monster Culture" 13). Or, more bluntly put: "The monster embodies those sexual practices that must not be committed, or that may be committed only through the body of the monster" (Cohen 14). Monstrous acts of sexual assault, acts that "must not be committed," paradoxically, increased in frequency on the Restoration stage. The act that demarcated uncrossable borders "rapidly became a standard part of the dramatic formula, most often used for a titillating combination of violence and eroticism," according to Jacqueline Pearson (*Prostituted Muse* 96). The most troubling consequences in the increase in the representations of rape and of the standardization of the rapist's excessiveness are the wasted and broken bodies of women. Don John's actions deny any semblance of selfhood to the victims of his crimes, especially to the female victims of sexual assault who are relegated to the status of "anonymous, faceless, biological entities whose existence is verified solely in terms of their commodification and violation," according to Andrew P. Williams (103). The bodies of women become merely objects of the repeated and never satisfied appetites for variety of the monster of sexual assault—the worst case example of an early modern phenomenon that increasingly materializes and embodies women even it simultaneously, and as a result, strips women of the power and agency they might possess.[25]

Victims, Trauma, and Monstrous Subjects

Stephanie Jed has argued that fathers train their daughters to understand that a rape narrative proceeds according to this sequence: a movement from chastity, to rape, to corruption, and finally to self-castigation. On the Restoration stage, however, there is one, truly final step: the death of the raped woman. Sometimes she is murdered, sometimes she commits suicide, but nearly always a rape requires a death.[26] These deaths are preceded by haunting forms of trauma that provide insight into the nature of the early modern self riven by violence and struggling for coherence. Such a woman's broken mind and body reside in the heart of Nicholas Brady's *Rape* (1692 and 1730): traumatized and stigmatized by actions not her own, the doomed heroine provokes a set of questions not only about difference, as we have seen above in Don John's obsessive quest for novelty and variety, but about likeness and equivalence— about what happens when a victim's boundaries disappear as a result of violence, about the consequences for women when trespass becomes invasion, and about the annihilating sameness that produces the traumatized self.

The heroine, called Eurione in the 1692 version, is the eldest Gothic princess held captive by the Vandal king. She is intended for the king's "son" Agilmond, who is actually a young woman brought up as a man. "His very soul's a Woman" (4), we are told, and "his" mother tells him to "offer such Love / As tender Sisters to each other bear" (23). Eurione returns the love of the young "prince," but she falls prey to the lascivious desires of Vandal Genselaric, who becomes obsessed with her once he learns that she will wed her womanly "prince." In a play stunning in its fascination with the violence of the attack and in a play that comes closest to actually staging an onstage rape, the discourses concerning this violence are themselves extreme. The night before the rape, Genselaric the rapist relishes the act of violence in his imagination:

> Thither we'll haste, and, shrouded from all eyes,
> Expect her coming, seize the trembling Prey.
> And rifle all the Treasures of her Beauty:
> Then if the Prince feasts on her Sweets to Morrow,
> He shall have but the leaving of my Riot.
>
> (21)

His anticipation is couched in traditional language of self-justification and falsified female resistance: "Methinks I see already / Her dying Looks, her seeming faint Resistance, / And feel the might Transport of hot love!"[27] (21).

The act of rape itself occurs in a darkened offstage arbor, and the audience is made aware of it only by Eurione's offstage shrieks.

But then the scene draws to reveal the arbor, and the stage directions read as follows: "The Scene draws, and discovers Eurione in an Arbour, gagg'd and bound to a Tree, her hair dishevel'd as newly Ravish'd, a Dagger lying by her." The whole assault and the representation of its aftereffects happen very rapidly and with powerful impact, made all the more so when we realize that the part was originally played by Mrs. Bracegirdle, who was legendary for her purity and chastity, as we saw in the last chapter, and who was thus likely to produce intensified empathy for anyone witness to the aftermath of the assault. After Eurione is untied, we hear her first description of herself as a victim, as an excluded member of her family and society:

> Here's she that was Eurione
> Now she is nothing but a Loathsome Leprosie,
> Which spread all o'er the Gothish Royal Blood,
> Infect the Noble Race.—
>
> (25)

She describes her wounds as internal: her body is represented not as one that has had violence perpetrated *on* it but as a body now filled with disease *inside* it, and once again spectators seem to have special access to private, unseen, hidden recesses of a woman's identity. In representing her own person as a plague, one who needs to be kept away from human contact, she calls for quarantine beyond the borders of civilization. These remarks point not only to the reality of a society where venereal disease was rampant and incurable but also to a contagion that has spread beyond the body to infect the psyche. Having been permanently breached externally, she suffers an equally permanent internal change, one that can, even through minimal contact, infect and distort all who come near her: "come not near me; I am contagious sure, / And all chaste hands will blister that but touch me" (25).

Filled with self-disgust, Eurione's alienation becomes a self-loathing so extreme that she sees herself as monstrous: "I cannot bear their eyes; already see / All turn and gaze, as if they saw a Monster" (53). Cathy Caruth has argued that the history of the traumatized individual "is nothing other than the determined repetition of the event of destruction" and that "it is the experience of waking into consciousness that, peculiarly, is identified with the reliving of the trauma" (34). Unlike Don John's repetitive acts of violence, acts external to him and perpetrated on another, Eurione's repeated memories are relentless, personal, and oppressive, so overwhelming that they produce a self-loathing so extreme that Eurione can only wish to be removed from the searing gaze of others. Infected with the monster's touch, she loses her singularity and coherence. Francis Barker has argued that

> the dividedness of the [early modern] subject—both within and from itself (as well as from 'the other,' 'the social,' 'the world')—disables it radically as an active agency. Indeed, it constitutes, rather than what has frequently been seen as the bearer of a progressive liberty, the potential instead for a very profound subjection. (*Tremulous* vi)

Just such a disabling of agency is discernible in Eurione's lament.

Part of the trauma we see in this heroine is also encoded in a linguistic shift in the evolution of (even the reversal of) subject and object in the uses of the words *rape* and *ravish,* uses familiar to scholars interested in sexual assault. Kathryn Gravdal notes that the original definition of *rape* required that a man abduct a woman, literally "steal" her away. Over time, this requirement vanished, leaving the terms *ravir* and *ravissant* free to become figurative in their use: "When *ravis* was literal, it was the male who ravished (carried away or abducted) the female. When the term soars off into the realm of the figurative, it is the female who is ravishing, who causes the male to be 'carried away' and [who] is responsible for any ensuing acts"[28] (5). This shift in meaning, especially in the context of the monster's erasure of difference and the infecting power of his likeness, implies a significant shift in the responsibility for the act of being raped, ravished, or carried away: no longer the victim in the crime, the woman becomes, linguistically at least, the subject—indeed the cause of the crime—and thus the focus of responsibility for actions men could now be said not to be able to control. In one sense, it would seem that she has therefore breached the boundaries of gender: her sameness is his sameness. But, in fact, each has entered the realm of the monstrous: the rapist's excessive energy—an monstrous agency unbounded and extreme—translates to women as an excessive consciousness of loss, a monstrous disabling agency in its way equally unbounded, equally extreme, and equally repetitive.

And the difference is discernible in the language the rapist and the ravished victim use. Genselaric, the rapist in Brady's play, simply crows with remembered pleasure in his retelling of the act; he feels no qualms about his act of violence:

> Methought, in one short moment I possess'd
> The crowded joys of a long life's delight;
> As if some friendly Power by Chimic Art
> Had Drawn the Spirit of an Age's pleasure
> Contracting all into that happy Minute
> To make the Cordial rich—
>
> (27)

Even his friends are appalled by his coarseness: "My Lord, your joys / Have made you wonton, but methinks 'tis strange / That Pleasure forc'd shou'd give such vast delight."[29] Eurione can only lament "come not near me; I am contagious sure."

Of this loss, Jean Marsden has noted that "the repeated exhibitions of Eurione's violated virginity link the sexual with the monstrous, a kind of sexual freak show in which the violated woman becomes the monster, fascinating but unwholesome and ultimately unnatural" ("Rape" 192). I would like to quibble a bit with the argument that the play dramatizes Eurione's "violated virginity," for such a violation is not actually demonstrable. Eurione can only *speak* about the trauma, can only acknowledge the violation and recognize the loss. Madness, like trauma, "necessitates its externalization as spectacle, as theater," according to Veronica Kelly, since mad subjects must "somatize and perform their symptoms by means of anti-social acts and opinions, or by physical disorders. These must be embodied, narrated, costumed; in short, performed" (169). In Eurione's case, it is not her violated virginity that is paraded on-stage as freakish and monstrous; it is a traumatized consciousness that must be embodied and performed—a wounded interior self, whose perceived loss can only be communicated through language and gesture.

Wounds, according to Cynthia Marshall, serve as "tokens of the self, even as gateways to it," as "evident and unassailable facts of personhood" (100). In the case of Shakespeare's Coriolanus, for instance, his refusal to display his wounds—his insistence that they remain hidden—is an action that functions as his attempt to "retain control as 'author of himself'" (100, 103), and this leads Marshall to conclude that "when human identity is understood as inescapably bound up with an unruly and vulnerable body, notions of a free, whole, and coherent self are impossible to support" (114). This fact is even more powerfully demonstrated in the identities of rape victims, whose bodily wounds are different—internal and undemonstrable—but whose psychic wounds demand exteriorization. Unlike the malaise and world-weariness exhibited by Don John, emotions that spur him to greater violence, rape victims are forced into the repetition of the memories of pain and terror, moments they perform in an attempt to ease the trauma.³⁰ As such, theirs is an inwardness made visible, a paradoxical process that Katharine Eisaman Maus has described this way: "inwardness as it becomes a concern in the theater is always perforce inwardness displayed: an inwardness, in other words, that has already ceased to exist" (*Inwardness* 32). This paradox of the traumatized self, as it is both performed and lamented, displays an inwardness provoked violently, painfully, and horribly into view.³¹

For my purposes, the process also comments on the limits of identity for women. We have seen women in comedies dressing in cross-gendered fashion to secure greater freedom for themselves—the Widdow Ranter, Lisset as a eunuch, or the woman-captain—all cleverly manipulate the gender distinctions in their culture for their own benefit. The women in these tragic rape narratives emerge into view as a result of their performance of the symptoms of their internal trauma, symptoms written in the material—their disordered and disheveled clothing—and in the kinetic and discursive. For women, then, the question returns, as always, to the body: how can the body that has been breached, wounded, and invaded survive? The answer Restoration drama provides is that it usually doesn't. The monster—the destroyer of coherence, the carrier of difference, the one who confuses, conflates, and incorporates what should remain distinct—is the bearer of a sameness that annihilates: his victim is made monstrous as a result, urged to speech, to a voice available momentarily to those who suffer from the disastrous effects of the promiscuous commingling of differences. Unable to reside in that monstrous interstitiality for long, the victim finally abandons her momentary agency to the silence of oblivion.

I want finally to turn to two plays, written in the form of heroic drama, by two women playwrights—Mary Pix's *Ibrahim, the Thirteenth Emperour* (1696) and Delariviere Manley's *Almyna: or, the Arabian Vow* (1707)—to see whether a woman playwright who controls the rape narrative will handle the pressures of the conventions that onstage rape demands in the same way as her male counterparts do, whether she will attempt to contain or to exploit the same kinds of excesses, and whether she will treat the victim in the same way, breaching boundaries and collapsing the categories. In other words, I want to see whether a woman will imagine the same kind of monsters.[32]

My contention is that, in a 1690s and early 1700s climate more friendly not only to women playwrights but also to strong female characters, the propagation of rape narratives allows and perhaps even provokes these two women playwrights to attempt to produce something different—a new, female heroic, different from the manly sort with its emphasis on the clash between love and honor, because it attempts to present an antidote to the pathetic victims of sexual assault of the kind we have seen above. And while the female heroic erupts as a doomed form of resistance within the very structures producing the forces that will ultimately subvert it, this form of the heroic simultaneously opens up the possibilities for heroines to use their own extreme strategies—both rhetorical and physical—in their much more active attempts to ward off sexual attacks. Subsequently they themselves breach boundaries, commit transgressions, and define the culture's limits; in short, they take on many of the excessive qualities of the monster.

A powerful difference exists, however, between these monstrous women and the monstrous rapists: these women do not require a victim; indeed, in their attempts to *protect* other victims, they come to symbolize a form of monstrous vitality: seeking to maintain the purity of their minds as well as their bodies, these heroines work to secure justice for the violence done to them and to others, even as they hope to produce new political tranquility in their societies. There is no threat of an annihilating sameness in their actions; indeed difference has a positive valuation in this sequence *not* dependent on repetition and the waste it produces but on interrupting that cycle. And even when it becomes clear that their liminality cannot ultimately protect them from assault, it can at least lead them to be active participants in modes of resistance, subjects who speak before being traumatized and from outrage and principled resistance.

In order to understand Pix's and Manley's choices, I want first to look at one of Pix's most memorable rapists, Ibrahim, the Thirteenth, a man who is not the hypermasculine, superaggressive, sexually predatory monster that Shadwell's Don John or Brady's Genselaric was but an effeminized sultan drawn to sexual violence in large part because, as the man who controls the political power of his nation, he can.[33] As we saw in the preceding chapter, Turkey occupied a special place in the imaginations of seventeenth-century Britons. In this case, Pix draws on discourses that positioned Turkey as a place of dangerous tyranny to create the character of the Sultan who falls prey too easily to the persuasive argument of others, especially when they promise him personal pleasure.[34] The Sultan is aided by his ex-lover, Sheker Para. In a role reversal that complements the figure of the effeminized sultan, we have the much too masculine evil villainess: it is this woman who actually convinces the sultan to rape; indeed she seduces him into raping the beautiful and chaste Morena, so that she, Skeker Para, might seduce and secure for herself Amurat, Morena's beloved.[35] Sheker Para's too sexual, too aggressive nature—her feminine insufficiency—is displayed in crowing proclamations of this kind: "I look down on the Sultana Queens, despise their Pregnancy, and want of power" (11), and thus she functions transparently as a male-directed, woman-hating, negative model of female excess.

One of Pix's most interesting arguments in this play couples the violence of rape with the problem of luxury, a form of economic excess that leads to personal degeneration. Early in the first act, the Mufti complains about the sultan's "gaudy Pageantry, Ill acted Scenes of Pomp and show," instead of real greatness, for this sultan treads on Persian carpets, not on the necks of Persian Kings (1). He is also described as surrounded, encircled, even enveloped by women, "softness and ease / Flatterers and Women, fill alone our Monarch's Heart; / Women enough to undo the Universal World / . . . whole useless hundreds" of women command his attention, the Mufti laments (1). Worse still, the great collection of women he keeps in the seraglio are bad for business:

> The Vultures deckt in Painted Plumes,
> So eager are for their vain trappings,
> That soon as a Merchant Ship salutes the Port,
> His goods are seiz'd, and brought to the *Seraglio*
> Without Account, Value, or Justice, yet at this

The Pander *Visier* winks, whilst the poor Owner
Waits in vain for Answer or Redress.

(2)

Even for a sultan, Ibrahim's love of luxury is extreme; he proclaims,

As Heaven hath given me a Despotic
And unbounded Power: so shall my Pleasure be.
But oh! The Earth's too little; and its Pleasures
Too few! I cannot keep my mind
In a continued Frame of Joy.

(18)

Like Don John and his companions who are unable to satisfy their
need for novelty and pleasure, soon he too allows Sheker Para to
lure him, with vivid descriptions of Morena, into committing violence against this innocent young woman. Sheker Para says,

Whilst within your own Royal Gates
Of this *Seraglio* lives a Helene, whose
Lovely fact strikes Envy dumb,
Late I saw her at the Baths;
But, Heaven, such a Creature
My astonish'd Eyes ne're view'd before.

(18)

For all these descriptions of her beauty, we soon discover that
Morena is potentially a new kind of heroine: smart, courageous,
and bold, she uses both rhetoric and action in her attempts to ward
off the sultan's assault. In the scene with the greatest tension—
when Morena is brought before the Sultan and when it is clear that
he will use force against her—she attempts to dissuade him first
through her rhetorical skills with a reminder of the debt he owes
her family: when the sultan was a child, Morena's father begged for
his life and saved him from being put to death by his predecessor.
She thus can legitimately claim a debt of honor at the moment he
will have her dragged off:

Tear out my eyes, stab, mangle my face;
Till it grow horrible to Nature
And the amazed world gaze with terror,

Not delight: Burn me! heap torture
Upon torture! and if I murmur a complaint
Fulfil the bitterst curse—Release,
And bear me to your bed!

(23)

But when the sultan will not relent—too filled with images of "unknown delight" and "something Poignant, that will relish Luxury" (24)—the scene becomes progressively more violent, including the sultan's stabbing and killing one of his eunuchs for failing to carry out his orders. When Morena fully realizes the gravity of her situation, she does not stand idly by. She shouts, "Murder, and Rapine! / What a horrid place is here! / My turn is next—," and the stage directions read "She catches hold of the Sultan's naked scimiter" and "draws it through her hands"[36] (24). In a scene filled not just with violence but with gore, she lifts up her bloody hands and snarls a direct threat to the sultan:

Do [drag me away] Tyrant! but 'tis thy last of mischiefs
If thou dost not kill me—
With dishevell'd hair, torn Robes, and
These bloody hands, I'll run thro' all thy Guards
And Camp, whist my just complaints, compel rebellion!

(24)

Seemingly, this is a heroine not to be paralyzed into immobility by the threat of violence; indeed, she promises to foment rebellion and cultivate internal political strife in order to bring him down. But in the end, Morena is undone by the conventions of the seventeenth-century rape narrative: she swoons. As a result, her inert body is carried away, while the Sultan ends the act exulting in her capture,

Threatening Danger shall never bar my way,
I'll run through all, and seize the trembling prey:
Rifle her sweets, till sense is fully cloy'd;
Then take my turn to scorn what I've enjoy'd.

(24)

Pix then produces a series of discovery scenes that further undercut the more daring discourse of her heroine. Emphasizing the trauma of sexual assault, Pix works from the same scopic economy as her male counterparts, presenting multiple scenes of female trauma as coded in a woman's deshabille and her hysterical lamentations. The next act opens with Morena's father, the Mufti, onstage and with stage directions that read "Enter Morena . . . , her hair down, and much disorder'd in her dress" (25). Her father experiences the sight of her traumatized body as his own punishment:

> Answer me Prophet, Author of our Law,
> What have I done, what horrid crimes committed,
> That my aching Eyes are punish'd
> With this doleful sight!
>
> (26)

Morena is barely able to speak, saying only that "Ruine, Despair, and Death my Lot," and hoping that "The Grave will hide me" (26). The second and most pointed verbal description of the rape is offered by the Mufti and delivered to Amurat, her beloved. The Mufti tells him that Morena was "dragged" from her father's protection, that the sultan's eyes were "fiery," and that his cheeks "glow[ed] with Lust" (28). Even as she offered up prayers, tears, cries, and "wounding supplications," her bloody hands only dyed "her white Arms in Crimson Gore" while the "savage Ravisher" twisted his hands:

> In the lovely Tresses of her hair,
> Tearing it by the smarting Root,
> Fixing her by that upon the ground:
> Then—(horrour on horrour!)
> On her breathless body perpetrate the fact.
>
> (28)

At this point, Pix produces a third discovery scene in stage directions that read "The Scene draws, and discovers Morena upon the ground disorder'd as before" (28). Three times she offers up such scenes—two visual and one verbal—and the three scenes together support the conventional elements of rape narratives: a strong erotic content in a scene predicated on female resistance and male attack, the mixing of violence and blood.[37]

But staging the scene three times also has resonance where trauma is concerned. In the final scene, when Morena's mind becomes the focus and source of her anxiety, she takes the stage dressed entirely in white, although very likely stained with gore, and laments the fact that these persistent and horrifying memories will not release her, that the damage resides in her memory:

> Drest in these Robes of Innocence,
> Fain wou'd I believe my Virgin Purity remains,
> But on! Memory the wretched'st Plague,
> Still goads me with the hated Image of my wrong.
> My Soul grows weary of its polluted Cage,
> And long to wing the upper Air, where
> Uncorrupted Pureness dwells.

(38)

The play follows the sequence Stephanie Jed finds in rape narratives: chastity, rape, corruption, self-castigation, and death, the only difference being that when this heroine takes up arms against her attackers she ends up wounding only herself in this act of violence. In the end, with her unified being shattered, she becomes a person without a coherent sense of self.[38]

The truly surprising element in Pix's play, however, is her hero—a man possessed of two important, traditionally female traits: an excess of sentiment (he is not sentimental, merely capable of deep affection for his beloved) and an excessive, almost exquisite understanding of the conflicted "value" of female chastity. Rather than displaying the usual lamentations and breast-beating one expects from men who describe themselves as "wronged" when a daughter, a sister, or a beloved is raped, this hero speaks to his suffering wife-to-be with great tenderness, calling her attacker "the monster," and in an act that allows the boundaries of difference between them to stand, he blithely dismisses the importance of Morena's loss of chastity with this beautiful question, one focused on the purity of her mind and not on the corruption of her body:

> Shall I forsake the Christal Fountain,
> Because a Rough-hewn Satyr there
> Has quench his Thirst? No! The
> Spring, thy Virgin Mind, was pure!

(40)

More unexpectedly and quite outside of the normal conventions, this beloved—even after he is promised the throne and future empires—cannot face life without her, and in a final, extraordinary, and excessive act, he stabs and kills *himself* out of grief for his lost love. (It is left to Morena's father to seek and secure an appropriate revenge: the janissaries join forces with him, they are the victors in the rebellion, and ultimately the sultan is murdered.[39]) Thus Pix may not be able to pen a narrative that allows the raped woman to escape the assault and live, but she can imagine a world where women take up arms and where men understand that a woman's value resides not in her unbreached body but in her strong and unsullied mind.

More radical is Delariviere Manley's *Almyna: or, the Arabian Vow,* a play that features another woman celebrated for possessing a "virgin mind."[40] And its villain is an even more despicable, power-hungry, rapacious rapist-sultan whose rash vow sets into motion the whole course of the drama. The sultan, angered by his first wife's adultery, has vowed never to be hurt or humiliated again. Yet he also insists that men have "needs"—"as Man, our Appetites are keen" (11). His solution is to marry a series of virgins whom he orders killed the morning after each marriage to assure his and their "honor." The play opens with the Vizier lamenting the slaughter of so many young women:

> I was not form'd to murder helpless Women,
> Under the sacred name and veil of Marriage.
> What is it else but Murther? Horrid Murther?
> The Shrieks, and Dying Groan, of the poor Queen!
>
> (1)

A significant portion of the play is taken up with attempts to disabuse the sultan of his notion that women have no souls, one of the reasons that he can so blithely murder all his young brides in this hugely excessive act of annihilating sameness. The vizier explains that the sultan believes that women are only the equivalent of beasts:

> Hence he expounds, that frailer Womankind,
> Have mortal Souls in common with the Brutes:
> So are they born to Dye, to perish ever.
> Not to Immortal Life, ordain'd as we.
>
> (2)

And the Sultan himself speaks of the worthlessness of women:

To fix thy Joys in Air:
In less, in nothing; for no more are Women:
Form'd as our Prophet says, without Soul,
By Nature bad, by Chance, if ever Good;
Their Shining out-side but a gawdy bait,
To make us take the toyl from Nature to our selves,
And do her drudgery, of propagation.

(9)

Into this hostile environment, Manley introduces Almyna, a woman of tremendous learning and great rhetorical skill, a warrior willing to participate nonviolently in her country's empire, and a believer determined to prove to the sultan that, unlike the beasts her likens her to, she does indeed have a soul. This energetic and heroic part was given over to Elizabeth Barry, whose task it became to convince the sultan that her character was one possessed of a virtue as heroic as any man's, in this case an heroic chastity. Abdulla, in an attempt to convince the Sultan to relent in his view about women, celebrates Almyna's virtues:

She is not only Fair, but Wise and good:
Her Vertue fixt, upon a sure Foundation;
Well has she too Emply'd her early Years,
Join'd Art to Nature, and improv'd the Whole.
What ever Greek or Roman Eloquence,
Egyptian Learning, Philosophy can teach;
She has, by Application, made her own.

(10)

Her own speeches, filled with exalted rhetoric, demonstrate her worthiness and her passion for greatness:

But I to Glory have resign'd my Life,
That Spiritual Pride of Nobel hearts!
And not to be as Love, Cloy'd with Possession.
Glory the strongest passion of great Minds!
Which none but Souls enlarg'd, can entertain
Uncommon, wonderful, and Excellent!
Heroick! Which Excites, nay, more Commands!
Our Admiration, Homage, and Applause.

(27)

Manley imagines a truly new, truly heroic heroine: Almyna under-stands the fear that permeates all of the families in the empire and feels that she has personally been called forth to "save my Coun-try" from ruin, so she volunteers to marry the sultan and to sac-rifice herself for the greater good. She does not sit passively by, hoping that these desperate circumstances will change, nor does she take up arms against the sultan, meeting violence with vio-lence. Instead she trusts that her own exemplary act will carry the force of persuasion, a heroic sacrifice of that chastity. She kneels to her father, the Vizier, and begs him "to procure me, / The Honour of our mighty Sultan's Bed!" so that she might "save the innocent Live, / Of Virgin daughters and their Parent's tears / To stop the Course of such Barbarity" (28).

In her meeting with the sultan, she displays a presence of mind and a power of intellect impossible for him to ignore. Presenting him with a catalog of strong and accomplished women, includ-ing "the fam'd *Semiramis,* the Queen of Nations / Whom mighty *Alexander* emulated" and "our fair Neighbouring *Judith,*" she goes on to ask, "cou'd the *Roman* Ladies, their *Virginia, / Lucretia, Portia, Clelia,* thousands more, / Without a Soul, have gain'd such endless Fames?" (45–46). The sultan, moved by her beauty and the power of her arguments, agrees that she will be the last virgin he will marry and then kill: " . . . be our Queen / Our last and most be-lov'd, our Oath thus sav'd, / We the remainder of our Life will waste, / In penitence for our rash Vow, and thy fair Loss" (47).

After the marriage and the wedding night, two incidents about which the play is entirely silent, Almyna is ready to keep her word and die, and with equally heroic words on her lips, she faces her death with this prayer:

> Oh! holy Prophet! Take me to thy care
> And be my loss of Life, the last of our
> Great Emperor's wilful Crimes.
> Comfort my Father, for his Daughter's loss.
> And take Almyna's Soul to thy protection.
>
> (63)

By this point, the Sultan has begun to understand that his actions have caused his people distress, and he asks, "Are we become so monstrous to our People?" Moreover, he begins to fall in love with

Almyna's courage and dignity, so that at the fateful moment, rather than ordering her execution, he rushes to save her, saying, "Henceforth be it not once imagin'd / That Women have not Souls, divine as we, / Who doubts, let 'em look here, for Confutation, / And reverence with us *Almyna's* Vertue"[41] (64).

Thus Almyna's behavior saves not only herself but also *all* young women from the specter of being used and killed by the Sultan. Most startling of all, her actions force a very powerful man to re-write his favorite Islamic "truism"—"Women / Form'd as our Prophet says, without Soul" (9)—and accept woman as the spiritual equals of men. In doing so, Manley herself rewrites a set of Restoration conventions concerning female characters. Actively rejecting the passive and private virtues of women—silence, invisibility, and inactivity—she creates a heroine who makes a public display of her virtues: in short, she introduces a powerful, new, female heroic.[42]

Almyna could also be said to function as a kind of "monster of virtue"—a creature who embodies all of the excesses of the monster, who transgresses traditional boundaries in the ways monsters do, and who functions as one of Park and Daston's "powerful clarifying examples"—but this time through a benign, productive transgression.[43] She does not opt for the comic violence of the "vile Monster of Woman-kind," *The Woman-Captain,* nor is she a morally degenerate model for human emulation, not a "monster of prohibition," as was the Libertine. Most especially, she exists in opposition to the fragmented and abjected heroines, like Eurione and Morena, brought to excessive consciousness after trauma but simultaneously stripped of their agency. Instead, Almyna offers a new mode of self-definition that in its very monstrosity—still excessive, still liminal, still breaching boundaries—encodes its ultimate demise. But at the beginning of the eighteenth century, this female monster of virtue exists, if only for a moment, as the antithesis of the malevolent monsters of violent sexual assault.

6 Epilogue
Nation, Status, and Gender
on the Restoration Stage

IN THESE LAST FEW PAGES, I look to five plays that premiered along the time line that encompasses this study: the Earl of Orrery's *Mustapha, Son of Solyman the Magnificent* (1665); Aphra Behn's *Abdelazer; or, The Moor's Revenge* (1767); Dryden's *Don Sebastian, King of Portugal* (1690); Thomas Southerne's *Oroonoko* (1695), an adaptation of Behn's 1688 novella; and Nicolas Rowe's *Tamerlane* (1701), an eighteenth-century version of Christopher Marlowe's *Tamberlaine*. Each play features some of the same kinds of performances of identity that we have so far investigated, most especially in the representation of Moorish and Turkish characters set in remote and exotic landscapes. Rather than attempting to mix serious and tragic drama, I have limited this analysis to heroic and/or tragic plays, each one featuring a performance by Thomas Betterton, often accompanied by a performance from Elizabeth Barry, and almost all staging some form of attempted rape.

My focus in these final pages, on the interdependence among the categories of nation, status, and gender in these five plays, reveals some decided changes—and not necessarily for the better—for British women and non-British characters of both genders. One of the strongest barometers of status or class values in these plays is the degree to which women are vulnerable to sexual assault, for the more bourgeois the norm the more "rape-able" the female character is portrayed to be. This phenomenon is dependent on shifts recognized by students of early modern cultural history: during the seventeenth and eighteenth centuries, the qualities that define ideal aristocratic behavior move toward bourgeois virtues, while ideal gendered behaviors for *both* men and women shift toward the feminine. Bourgeois goodness rather than aristocratic worth begins to define the best of *both* aristocratic status and merchant class: merit and accomplishment replace heritage or birth. Discipline, careful management, and most especially the control that defines the classical rather than the grotesque body—in both the public and the private spheres—displace the old ideals of waste and excess in aristocratic display. This displacement functions equally powerfully in gendered terms: ideal behavior for both men and women becomes inflected by the traditionally "feminine" virtues. For men, that means a gentler persona, one less prone to violent public outbursts; for women, that means a continued movement into the passivity and seeming invisibility of the domestic realm. All of these changes depend for their efficacy on a particular representation of national others. In some cases, that means the reincorporation into the sanctioned fold a collection of European nationals, made benign through comedy or ridicule; in other cases, it means an exclusion of non-Europeans into the realms of the barbaric or grotesque through a subtext—and sometimes a very subtle one—of racial difference, a discourse unlike modern racist thinking, of course, but a representation of character that is still inextricably bound to racial and geographical differences. All of this means, for instance, at the beginning of this period, that the wife of the Turkish sultan is never positioned as the object of unlawful sexual advances; by the end of the era, the more tyrannous and cruel the Turk, the more liable he is to perpetrate sexual assault; at the beginning of this era, characters of high status act like royalty, peremptory and regal, filled with a sense of entitlement; by the end of this era, even monarchs themselves will describe the best ruler as humble and subject to the will of the people.

I acknowledge, by way of caveat, that the changes I have traced in the analyses throughout this text represent "uneven developments" at best, to adopt Mary Poovey's phrase in a different context. I recognize, for instance, that Indian queens, Turkish sultans, Moorish generals, Spanish pirates have all paraded across British stages during centuries of British drama. Threats of rape show up in the 1660s as well as the 1690s, that Almahide, perhaps the quintessential heroine in a heroic drama (Dryden's *Conquest of Granada*), must repeatedly suffer threats of sexual assault. Excesses in aristocratic behavior are also criticized in the earliest Restoration comedies: when Dorimant's shoemaker complains "'Zbud, I think you men of quality will grow as unreasonable as the women. You would ingross the sins of the nation; poor folks can no sooner be wicked by th'are railed at by their betters" (1.1.300–4), aristocrats in the audience would have understood that they were being ridiculed by one of their own, Sir George Etherege. But I will argue that a trajectory of changes in the identity categories can be plotted for the forty-five years of British drama under investigation here. And taken together, especially when seen in the light of those plays investigated throughout the whole of this book, these five plays allow us to chart sometimes problematic, and even contradictory, examples of the alterations in status-bound characteristics and the changes in ideal gendered behavior, both of which are dependent on changing representations of national characters found on the Restoration stage.

Orrery's *Mustapha, Son of Solyman the Magnificent,* the earliest of these plays (1665), features only Turkish characters, with the exception of the Queen of Hungary and her lords, and not much is made of their ethnic difference. Orrery's play premiered during the same year as Dryden's *Indian Emperour,* nine years after Davenant's *Cruelty of the Spaniards in Peru* (1656), and during a time of political recovery for England: Charles II had occupied his restored throne for only five years, and the royalists of old—aristocrats all—had assumed some of their old places in government and society; English imperial ventures were continuing apace, with greater and greater wealth and goods being supplied to aristocrats and merchants alike; and the second Dutch War (which would continue for two years) was just beginning to stimulate patriotic discourse and national feeling. *Mustapha* found a very receptive audience at this time, in part because of its exotic setting and in part because of its powerful central characters, especially its women characters.

The plot of *Mustapha* is a fitting complement to the age: an heroic drama with a tragic conclusion. The engine that drives this plot is a strong woman, Roxolana (played by Mrs. Betterton), mother to Mustapha and Zanger and wife to Solyman.[1] She is a woman strong enough to cross her powerful husband, and even to attempt to manipulate larger political power struggles, in the cause of protecting another royal woman and her royal son: after the death on the battlefield of the Hungarian king, Roxolana saves

the lives of the captured Hungarian Queen and her infant son
from the avenging impulses of the sultan. The Queen agrees to
take refuge in Roxolana's tent because she has heard of the Turkish
woman's goodness:

> You *Thuricus* on Embassy shall go
> To Roxolana's Tent, and let her know
> How much the common voice of Fame I trust,
> Which renders her compassionate and just;
> Whilst others say she all her Sex exceeds,
> They shew their Faith by words, but I by deeds;
> I by so strange a Trust may find relief,
> If she has Virtue equal to my Grief.

(9)

Roxolana must simultaneously attempt to contain the paranoia of
her husband, the sultan (played by Betterton), who fears that the
military prowess of their elder son, Mustapha, has made him the
darling of the army and a possible usurper. This part of the plot
turns on an English belief that Turkish political custom demanded
that the eldest son, once he assumes the throne, must murder all
of his brothers against the possibility of factions and division.[2]
Roxolana laments the custom this way:

> Oh cruel Empire! That does thus ordain
> Of Royal Race the youngest to be slain,
> That so the eldest may securely reign;
> Making the' Imperial Mother ever mourn
> For all her Infants in Succession born.

(25–26)

Orrery imagines a new, more "civilized" bargain made between
the brothers to disregard this dictate: they will not murder one another if offered the throne, and indeed they agree to active forms
of support of one another:

> *Mustapha:* By our great Prophet solemnly I swear,
> If I the *Turkish* Crown do ever wear,
> Our bloody Custom I will overthrow;
> That Debt I both to you and Justice owe.
> *Zanger:* And here I vow by all that's good and high,
> I'll not out-live the Day in which you die;

This which my Friendship makes me promise now,
My Grief will then enable me to do.

(11)

It is out of this bargain that Orrery stages the standard love versus honor conflict of heroic drama by setting up a contest between the two brothers who both fall in love with and who both end up supporting the other's pursuit of the virtuous captive Hungarian Queen, to the detriment of the other.[3]

In terms of the representation of national others, not even a suggestion of impropriety or division exists in the presentation of the love affair between these royal Turkish sons and the Hungarian Queen, except of course for the inevitable religious distinction made between them, a resistance presented as tepid at best. For instance, before Mustapha sees the Hungarian Queen and falls in love with her himself, he questions his brother's loyalty and even his sanity in loving an infidel woman: "What, love a Captive, and a Christian too? . . . Yet, *Zanger,* your Religion should prevail" (27–28). The Hungarian Queen also recognizes the differences in their religions, although she too apparently perceives the differences as anything but an impermeable barrier to a union: when urged by a cardinal to stop her grieving for her dead husband and to choose one of the brothers as a means of securing her safety, the Queen ticks off her options, none of which truly protects her:

I injure one, if I the other choose;
And keeping either I the Sultan lose.
Flying from both I from my Refuge run;
And by my staying shall destroy my Son.
Them for their false Religion I eschew,
Though I have found their Virtue ever true.
And when Religion sends my Thoughts above,
This Card'nal call them down, and talks of Love.

(45)

Most important, the Queen recognizes the virtues displayed by both brothers, not some stereotypical Turkish cruelty, tyranny, or violence. As an additional layer of irony, Orrery presents the person least committed to any transcendent principles as a religious leader, the cardinal.

In 1665 and in terms of the representation of characters of high status, kings and queens act like royalty. They may *be* national others, Turks or Hungarians, but they are easy stand-ins for British identification, for they perform their highborn status emphatically and without apology. During a tense interview between the sultan and Roxolana, for instance, when she pleads for mercy for the Hungarian Queen, the haughty discourse between these two royal characters positions them as equals in power:

> *Roxolana:* Had you not taught me, I had never known
> All Power to be fantastick, but your own.
> *Solyman:* I'll teach you now that Death's a serious thing,
> Call your Mutes, and for your little King!
> . . . .
> *Roxolana:* You rule enough, ruling the World and me;
> Pray let my Women, my own Subjects be.
>
> (16)

When the infant king is indeed brought forward, and when the Mutes make a move to take him, Roxolana offers up her strongest resistance to the sultan himself:

> Stay! *Zarma,* stay! If this, Sir, be your doom,
> Send me too where the Cruel never come;
> I'll bind him to me with my Arms and Hair,
> They try, Sir, if your Mutes or Visiers dare
> Enforce him from the Refuge of my Breast.
>
> (16)

In the end, Roxolana "conquers" the sultan's murderous impulses with her tears, and she compliments him on his decision to employ nonviolence: "By yielding you prevail, and your Recourse / Gains more than other Victors get by force" (17).

Gender boundaries work to support these changes, especially in the case of Orrery's lead female character, Roxolana: she is strong-willed, smart, able to manipulate political systems for her advantage, committed to protecting her own and the Hungarian Queen's royal children. Roxolana offers up a plan both to save her son Mustapha and to secure the Hungarian Queen's safety, but it depends on the Queen's pretending to love the elder son, Mustapha, and that would require some feigning:

Queen: I ever was without dissembling bred,
And in my open Brow my Thoughts were read:
None but the Guilty keep themselves unknown.
Roxolana: No wonder we so soon subdu'd your Throne;
. . . .
Queen: Madam, you teach what Christians are not taught
And seem to soar as high in Flights of Thought,
As now your Empire wide in compass swells.
Roxolana: Sure Christian Kings live not in Courts but Cells;
This is uncourtly, ill-bred Innocence,
Which cannot with dissembled Love dispense.
You must dissemble love to Mustapha,
And make him think, by what you often say,
That you for Love can mourn and languish too.

(50)

Not only are both of these women presented as courageous and strong but the plot elements also conspire not to undermine their positions. For instance, there is never even a hint of sexual violence in this plot, even though as a spoil of war the Hungarian Queen might be seen as vulnerable to sexual predation. And at the end of the play, when both her sons are dead through actions she could not control, Roxolana could have been stabbed or otherwise done away with in some bloody fashion, but instead she is punished according to her rank: treated as the sultan's equal in rank, she is forced to confess the part she inadvertently played in bringing about the deaths of her sons, divorced from the sultan, and banished forever from the presence of her weak-willed but powerful husband. She bears the weight of her misfortunes with great dignity and leaves the stage with this lament to the sultan: "I'll be Forgiveness beg for Love and Grief, / Since both offend you when they seek Relief / . . . . Sir, I'll depart / And at your Feet leave a forsaken Heart" (84).

Behn's *Abdelazer* (1676), an updated version of *Lust's Dominions* that powerfully echoes *Othello*, features both Spaniards and Moors as its central characters. Premiering a decade after *Mustapha* and during the decade that saw the production of Shadwell's *Libertine* (1675), *Virtuoso* (1676), and *Woman-Captain* (1679), and as well as the first part of Behn's own *Rover; or, The Banish'd Cavaliers* (1677), the action revolves around Queen Isabella of Spain who is presented as a rapacious, lust-driven lover of Abdelazer, a Moor.[4] In a plot that owes much to its Renaissance origins, the queen and the Moor work together—to the detriment of anyone who gets in the way, including her husband and children—to secure for themselves the throne. The historical Isabella was a devout Catholic, xenophobic about Northern Africans, and committed to producing a universal Catholic state; she would, of course, have been horrified by this presentation of her character, as a lustful villainess willing to engineer the demise of her husband, secure the death of her elder son, and label her second son a bastard and a product of a rape by a cardinal all in order to enjoy the illicit pleasures of her lover and to secure their mutual assumption of the Spanish throne. The play was produced two years after the conclusion of the Third Dutch War and, like *Mustapha,* during a time of growing stability in England, according to J. H. Plumb, a time of increasing populations, growing economic diversification—not just in the booming port cities but also throughout the home markets—and the "obliteration of local economic isolation," including increased economic activity among the gentry.

The character of Abdelazer, a potential usurper and clearly a political threat to the ruling power, thus presents a very interesting case for a 1676 audience. Also played by Betterton, the Moor initially seems a politically secure partner to the queen, supporting her schemes and satisfying her sexual desires. As the drama unfolds, however, he proclaims his love for the queen's daughter, Leonora, played by Elizabeth Barry, while trying to protect his lawful wife from the "unlawful" intentions of the queen's son, Philip. The plot—filled with lies, deceit, double-crossings, and the murder of friends and co-conspirators—is driven by multiple acts of "unlawful" love and desire for political ascendancy. Almost no one in the drama is a suitable focus of any audience identification, since most of the characters are deeply flawed and excessive.

Ethnic and national differences, however, abound, even though they are presented in highly ambiguous ways. In this case, the ambiguity works to undermine any straightforward assessment of racial or national difference. Abdelazer, for instance, when given to self-castigation, will sometimes use animal epithets to describe himself, "I am a Dog, and can bear wrongs" (1.2.190), or link himself with infernal images, "Who spurns the *Moor* / Were better set his foot upon the Devil—" (2.1.6–7). And yet understanding the power such language wields when others use it against him, he negates it with images of kingly power, aristocratic birth, and royal entitlement:

> The Queen with me! with me! a Moor! a Devil!
> A Slave of *Barbary!* for so
> Your gay young Courtiers christen me:—but Don,
> Although my skin be black, within my veins
> Runs Blood as red, and Royal as the best.—
> My Father, Great *Abdela,* with his Life
> Lost too his Crown: both most unjustly ravisht
> By Tyrant *Philip,* your old King I mean.
>
> (1.1.162–69)

At other times, degrading epithets are leveled against Abdelazer by less-than-admirable characters—most often by the hot-tempered Philip, son of the queen, who is committed to exacting his revenge on Abdelazer, an activity the Spaniard is especially keen to commence if it also allows him to injure and even kill his own mother in the process:

> I'de rather stay and kill, till I am weary;—
> Let's to the Queens Apartment, and seize this Moor;
> I am sure there the Mongrel's Kennell'd. . . .
> Mother—and Moor—Farewell,—
> I'll visit you again; and if I do,
> My black Infernal, I will Conjure you.
>
> (2.2.161–63, 166–68)

And yet the stereotypical charges of lasciviousness and sexual rapaciousness—which later in the seventeenth century and throughout the eighteenth century tend to be aimed at Moors, Africans, and other dark-skinned peoples—are here leveled at a European queen, a most Spanish character who cannot be charged with having been "infected" by the Moor, since early in the drama he is clearly tired of *her* excessive sexual impulses and ready to move on.[5] She is the one represented as driven by a lust that has exhausted the Moor, a fact about which he complains,

> Bawd, fetch me here a Glass,
> And thou shalt see the balls of both those eyes,
> Burning with Fire of Lust.—

That bloud that dances in thy Cheeks so hot,
That have not I to cool it
Made an extraction ev'n of my Soul,
Decay'd my Youth, only to feed thy Lust!
And wou'dst thou still pursue me to my Grave?

(1.1.52–59)

Behn's representations of these national others remains ambiguous and even contradictory.

Isabella and Abdelazer also possess an exaggerated sense of entitlement found in the worst elements of "bad" aristocratic behavior. An audience is *not* invited to admire these characters in the same way they are asked to feel some sympathy toward Roxolana, the Hungarian Queen, or even the misguided sultan in *Mustapha*. We might thrill to the ornate and elaborate qualities of Queen Isabella's lies, such as the moment when she spins an entirely false story of being raped by the cardinal, when even he is spellbound by the power of her narrative:

> *Queen:* In the absence of my King, I liv'd retir'd,
> Shut up in my Apartment with my Women,
> Suffering no Visits, but the Cardinals,
> To whom the King had left me as his Charge;
> But he, unworthy of that Trust repos'd,
> Soon turn'd his business into Love.
> *Cardinal:* Heaven's! How will this story end?
> ·
> *Queen:* Undress'd he came, and with a Vigorous haste
> Flew to my yielding Arms: I call'd him King!
> My dear lov'd Lord! and in return he breath'd
> Into my bosom in soft gentle whispers—
> My Queen! My Angel! lov'd *Isabella*!
> And at that word—I need not tell the rest.

(5.1.91–97, 112–16)

Abdelazer's devious schemes also fascinate, even as they horrify. For instance, at the moment that Queen Isabella dies after being stabbed by Roderigo and on Abdelazer's orders, the Moor pretends to lament her loss: "to find those Eyes, / Those Charming Eyes thus dying—Oh ye Powers!— / Take all the prospect of my future joys, / And turn it to despair,—since thou art gone—" (5.1.311–

14). The very moment she actually expires, however, Abedlazer's expression of grief transforms into joy:

> Farewell, my greatest Plague,—*[He rises with Joy.]*
> Thou wert a most impolitique loving thing,
> And having done my bus'ness which thou wert born for,
> 'Twas time thou shou'dst retire,
> And leave me free to Love, and Reign alone.
>
> (5.2.325–29)

In his willingness to dissimulate, and especially in the very skill-fulness of his performance, he is reminiscent of the very feminine Roxolana, who urged the virtuous Hungarian Queen to similar pretense. Such abilities suggest that this Moor, akin to his Moorish predecessors in Renaissance dramas, embodies "a dangerous but effeminate otherness that finally renders them safely inferior" to their European counterparts (113), according to Jean Howard's analysis of *The Fair Maid of the West*.

Queen Isabella and Abdelazer both die horrible deaths, with Abdelazer being stabbed by everyone gathered onstage in the last moments of the drama, as punishment for exceeding the legitimate behaviors allowed to modern monarchs. Experimenting with the elasticity of the boundaries of gender is usually the ideological element at the heart of Behn's dramas; in most of her work, she seems committed to exploring just how far she can push the limits of acceptable female, and some male, behavior. This drama, however, is different: gender distinctions are secondary to the requirements of the revenge form and to her examinations of issues of power. Played by Mrs. Lee, Isabella is a villainess of the old heroic mode, while Leonora, played by Mrs. Barry, emerges as perhaps the only admirable character. Upon closer examination, however, even she is revealed to be merely a pawn—a sexualized object of multiple male desires and ultimately only an object of exchange that functions to bring about closure at the end of the play.

Unlike the admirable Turkish monarchs in Orrery's *Mustapha*, who hold themselves still and who control even their deepest desires, the Spanish royals in Behn's play possess bodies too unruly, and in Abdelazer's case a body that is additionally too foreign and too dark, to function as anything other than as object lessons in the necessity to punish grotesque bodies and excessive behaviors. Behn surely has some fun presenting the pious Isabella in this scandalous light, satisfying the strong anti-Spanish feeling that would still have been present two years after the conclusion of the Third Dutch War. And while Abdelazer's blackness may not be presented as the standard that relegates him to the status of the nonhuman, in the contemporary racist sense, it is nevertheless a strong and de-fining element in his character; while a vile and ruthless Spaniard might be the one to call him "Dog," the dehumanizing effect lingers after its utterance.

Dryden's *Don Sebastian* premiered in December 1689, during a decade that saw the production of Lee's *Massacre of Paris* and *The Rival Queens*, Behn's *Widdow Ranter*, and Tate's *Dido and Aeneas*. It also premiered shortly after the Revolution and thus shortly after Dryden lost his position as laureate to Thomas Shadwell. His Ca-tholicism, which had forced him to move at least ten miles out of London, also doubled his taxes; that, along with his continued support for James II, contributed to the financial woes that drew him back to the stage. He chose as the vehicle for that return the story of Don Sebastian, the king of Portugal, who died in battle against the Moors in 1578. The differences between the two na-tional characters that populate this play—Moors and Portuguese exclusively—are presented, on the surface, not so much as a mat-ter of race but as a matter of religion; further investigation, how-ever, reveals that race plays a deciding part in the assignment of character.

In a plot that Dryden altogether fabricates, Don Sebastian is cap-tured by the emperor of Barbary, the lascivious and cruel Muley-Moluch, rather than slain on the battlefield. Brought onstage as a captive slave after the battle, Don Sebastian reveals his identity after drawing a black lot that signals his execution. In an imperial dis-course worthy of any hero of old from the heroic genre, Don Se-bastian imagines himself in possession of new lands, even in death:

> Now I have pleas'd my longing,
> And trod the ground which I beheld from far,
> I beg no pity for this mouldring Clay:
> For if you give it burial there it takes
> Possession of your Earth:
> If burnt and scatter'd in the air; the Winds
> That strow my dust, diffuse my royalty,

And spread me o'er your Clime; for where one Atom
O mine shall light; know there *Sebastian* Reigns.

(1.1.362–70)

When Muley-Moluch decides as punishment not to kill him but
to show him "for a Monster through my *Affrick*," Don Sebastian
picks up the metaphor but turns it against the emperor: "No thou
canst only show me for a Man: / *Affrick* is stor'd with Monsters;
Man's a Prodigy / Thy Subjects have not seen" (1.1.373–76). And
thus a captive king uses the epithet of "monster" to damn an entire
continent.

The plot itself centers around the love of these two enemies
from different geographical and religious backgrounds for the same
woman, a Barbary queen, Almeyda—a woman, earlier captured by
the Portuguese, who converted to Christianity, and a woman whom
Don Sebastian's father warned him that he may not love.[6] A member of the Portuguese party, she is equally haughty in her responses
to Muley-Moluch's attempts to possess her. When he orders that
her veil be lifted so that he can assess her beauty, she responds with
her own imperious command: "Stand off ye Slaves, I will not be
unveil'd . . . I am no Slave; the noblest blood of *Affrick* / Runs in
my Veins; a purer stream than thine; / For, though deriv'd from the
same Source, thy Current / Is puddl'd, and defil'd with Tyranny"
(1.1.425, 429–32). She becomes the object of Muley-Moluch's unlawful attentions after Don Sebastian and Almeyda steal away to be
married by a captive priest and to enjoy one night together, the
circumstance that sows the seeds of the tragedy in this tale.

By the conclusion of the play, Don Sebastian and Almeyda are
revealed to be siblings who have committed an act of incest: she is
the daughter of an adulterous affair between Don Sebastian's father
and the queen of the Moors. The play ends with each about to
journey to an undisclosed location and in discourses actually very
moving in their lament, anticipating the heightened pathos one
might find in the longing of Pope's "Eloisa to Abelard":

> *Almeyda:* For all things that belong to us are cruel.
> But what's most cruel, we must love no more.
> O 'tis too much that I must never see you,
> But not to love you is impossible:
> No, I must love you: Heav'n may bate me that;

Sebastian: Good Heav'n, thou speakst my thoughts, and I
speak thine.
Nay then there's Incest in our very Souls.
For we were form'd too like.

(5.1.588–90)

The Barbary emperor presents a very different case, however.
Lust-driven, politically tyrannous, and even willing to force his
religious adviser to authorize the rape of Almeyda after her marriage, Muley-Moluch is the uncontested villain of the piece. Before
the marriage, the emperor decides that he will marry Almeyda,
and that threat forces her to ask, "For what? To people *Affrick* with
new Monsters, / Which that unnatural mixture must produce?"
(2.1.458–59). Thus, for her, a character who is at least on the surface a Moor, there is nothing "unnatural" in her loving a European
man; rather, it is the mixing of her blood with the blood of a tyrannous, cruel, lascivious Moorish emperor that is the "unnatural"
pairing, a union that would produce "monsters," a word, as we
know from earlier analyses, that is code for rapists. The emperor
responds with an equally frightening prediction of offspring who
enact the very violence Almeyda fears, only this time as murderous
sibling rivalry:

Serpent, I will engender Poyson with thee;
Joyn Hate with Hate, add Venom to the birth;
Our Off-spring, like the seed of Dragons Teeth,
Shall issue arm'd, and fight themselves to death.

(2.1.464–67)

While Muley-Moluch might be presented as a monstrous figure,
he is not specifically figured in racial terms; indeed, while geographical references abound, they are never specifically attached to
color distinctions. Unlike Behn's Abdelazer, who calls himself
"devilish" or who is called by others "mongrel" or "dog," there are
no such epithets in this play. Nevertheless, the only "monster" in
this play—a drama filled with lies, bloody fighting, and incest—is
an altogether unruly Moor, a rapist and ruler terrifying out of control, the only creature positioned as a very powerful, *and* dark-
complexioned, *"Affrick"* monster.

Other characters of high status in *Don Sebastian* are relegated
to the "lower," comedic plot, and this is the structure I find most

192

intriguing, for it forces an audience to watch a noble character acting more like a lower-class servant or a wily trickster than a man of wealth and status. Most illustrative in this context is Antonio, a young Portuguese nobleman, captured in battle and sold into slavery to the mufti. While Antonio stands on the auction block, he is whipped, ridiculed, and forced to perform as if he were a prized horse. The following exchange with Mustafa, a creature of the mufti, creates a dehumanizing effect for the young nobleman:

> *Mustafa:* Learn better manners, or I shall serve you a Dog-trick; come, down upon all four immediately; I'll make you know your Rider.
> *Antonio:* Thou wilt not make a Horse of me?
> *Mustafa:* Horse or Ass, that's as they Mother made thee: ——
> But take earnest in the first place for they Sawcyness.
> *[Lashes him with his Whip.]*
>
> (1.1.508–13)

After being purchased by the mufti, Antonio spends the rest of the play trying to trick his master out of some of his wealth, by pretending to woo the mufti's wife in order to woo in earnest the mufti's daughter, Morayma—securing a small fortune in the process. After many disguises, much stage-play, and even a bit of slapstick, the young couple marries, and with promises of serenades, gallantries, foolish lovers, and rivals ringing in her ears, Morayma eagerly looks forward to the freedoms of her new life: "The best thing I have heard of Christendom, is that we women are allow'd the priviledge of having Souls; and I assure you, I shall make bold to bestow mine upon some Lover, when ever you begin to go astray, and, if I find no Convenience in a Church, a private Chamber will serve the turn" (5.1.108–12). Rose Zimbardo sees language such as this uttered by a supposedly cloistered Moorish woman as part of Dryden's overall presentation of "the sexual licentiousness of the Oriental woman" (164).

Dryden had experimented before *Don Sebastion* with mixing high heroic action and low comedy, in *Marriage a la Mode* and *The Spanish Fryar,* for instance. But the experiment here is of an entirely different order. Zimbardo, who presents one of the most interesting treatments of this play I have read, suggests that the differences emerge from a much larger epistemological shift that occurred in the late seventeenth century, a change in the very conception of selfhood that "grew out of a late-seventeenth-century coding that reformulated the idea of 'self,' invented 'interior space,' and related 'Truth' to that inner human arena" (19). Paradoxically, this movement inward allowed the thinker to project outward what he or she found inside and then to label it a universal standard; as a result, the "I" becomes "the discursive center from which all order arises, then to be projected and imposed upon the external world" (132–34). Writing at the end of this shift and in accord with its changes, Dryden necessarily fashions a play that "is vastly different from the heroic drama of the 1660s, which exist under the representational codes of pre-modern emblematic figuration," for he pens a drama that was filled with much greater "complexity of character, variety of detail, and irregularity of language, in short, a 'realism,' that strained the limits of heroic drama" (161–62). This epistemological shift had powerful implications for the construction of all the categories we have been investigating, but especially in terms of nations, national identities, and an English identity, for as Zimbardo argues "the distance from the end of the sixteenth to the end of the seventeenth century also marks the difference between seeing the 'Other' as different in external appearance but recognizably human and seeing that same 'Other' through the distorting lens of xenophobic fear and loathing" (156).

These changes are most visible in the most intriguing character Dryden creates in this play: Dorax, the renegade Portuguese who rebels against Don Sebastian, who lives among the Moors, who cynically distances himself from the new people and religion he supposedly embraces, and who thinks that he desires nothing more than to revenge himself on his old friend Don Sebastian and to obliterate forever his old identity as Don Alonzo. But Dorax's first words onstage point to his internal conflict. When Benducar asks him about his prowess on the battlefield, "cou'dst thou not meet *Sebastian*? / Thy Master had been worthy of they Sword" (1.1.84–85), Dorax hotly replies,

> My Master? By what title,
> Because I happen'd to be born where he
> Happen'd to be King? And yet I serv'd him,
> Nay, I was fool enough to love him too.
>
> (1.1.86–89)

Having adopted a Moorish name and having donned Moorish clothing for his new identity, Dorax enjoys a form of anonymity when he first comes into contact with his old ruler: he is able to stand among the Moorish soldiers without Don Sebastian's recognizing him; he is able to rescue his old king and provide him a sword for protection, without recognition; he is even able to return Almeyda to Don Sebastian's arms without the Portuguese ruler's recognizing him. Only when Dorax exchanges the material trappings of his new identity—when he takes off his "turbant" and puts on "a Peruque, Hat, and Crevat," according to the stage directions—does the king understand who Dorax *is,* his essential identity:

> *Dorax:* Now do you know me?
> *Sebastian:* Thou shouldst be *Alonzo.*
> *Dorax:* So you shou'd be *Sebastian:*
> But when *Sebastian* ceas'd to be himself,
> I ceas'd to be *Alonzo.*
>
> (4.2.657–61)

By the end of the encounter, the men embrace in friendship, and Alonzo/Dorax nearly runs "mad with extasy" when he learns that his Portuguese beloved is waiting at home for his return, "still indulging tears, she pines for thee" (4.2.921), Don Sebastian tells him.

By the end of the play, Muley-Moluch is dead. The incest between Don Sebastian and his half-sister Almeyda—and its peculiar form of "annihiliating sameness"—has been uncovered, and the two necessarily part forever. Only Alonzo/Dorax is rewarded, with a return to Portugal and a steadfast bride. On the surface, it appears that the "true" identity of Don Alonzo has re-emerged—a final embrace of an essential Portuguese identity. A closer look, however, confirms that identity throughout this play is much more fluid than it appears on the surface: with surprising ease, Don Alonzo "turns Mohametan," as he describes it, and wears the clothing of his new Moorish homeland and worships as good Muslims do; he puts off his Portuguese habits as easily as Don Sebastian fails to live up to his trust. With equal ease, the Barbary queen performs the same transformation, but in reverse: she becomes a Christian and loves a Portuguese man without qualms about racial or geographical difference, since both are royalty and born for an exogamous pairing.

But a final ideological lesson about racial purity and about the varieties of *"Affrick"* monsters alive in this play becomes clear in the last moments of the "upper," heroic plot: Muley-Moluch *must* die, for he is the ultraviolent, nightmare creature of European imaginations. Almeyda, however, only half-Moor and half-Portuguese, must also be sent away to live cloistered from view; Don Sebastian too is punished, for crossing both family and racial/ geographical lines, in his affection for Almeyda—his sister and a half Moor. Only Alonzo, who "returns" to his European origins, is rewarded with an appropriate, Portuguese bride. On the surface, one might want to read his character, the real hero of the piece, as representing the strengths that a mixture of cultures and identities can produce: a renegade, acting on principle, embraces the differences to be found in an "alien" culture. But in fact, he is the only Portuguese character of high status presented as ready to return "home" to his "real" nation by the end of the drama. Even Antonio—the character who began as a Portuguese slave, who turned into a successful wooer and lover of a Moorish girl in the middle acts, and who finally became a rich husband rewarded with half of the mufti's fortune in the final scene—cannot be said to be fully rewarded at the end of the play, for he too has "gone native," sent off with his Moorish wife to attend to Almeyda in the closing lines of the play. Derek Hughes has argued that the discrediting of Don Sebastian and Almeyda's heroic love "completes the discrediting of all the heroic ideals espoused in the play" (82); I would add that Antonio's marriage to a Moorish bride is the last straw.

Representations of national others extend beyond Europe and Africa to include New World indigenous peoples and colonists in Southern's *Oroonoko* (1696), a play that premiered in the same decade as Nicholas Brady's *Rape* (1692), Delariviere Manley's *Royal Mischief* (1696), and Mary Pix's *Ibrahim, the Thirteenth Emperour* (1696). The history of Southerne's "translation" of Behn's novella *Oroonoko* (1688) needs no rehearsal here, but a reminder about some of the most dramatic changes Southerne made is instructive. First, Southerne bifurcated the plot into the tragic story of Oroonoko's enslavement and the comic story of two English sisters, newly arrived in the New World and husband-hunting. As a result, the nuanced relations between and among national others, so powerful in Behn's work, disappear in Southerne's drama. Behn's narrator, who sheds such light on the relations between a European woman and two royal Africans, is herself bifurcated into two English sisters who have only the most tenuous relationship to Oroonoko himself. Southerne also rewrites the racial identity of Imoinda, from African princess to daughter of a white slave trader killed saving the life of Oroonoko, his trading partner in slaves. Thus Oroonoko's position as a slave trader, suggested in the novella, is made explicit, even insistent here.

Most important for our purposes, the Indians—so vital in Behn's text for setting up complex categories of friendship and threat, native values and courage—are nearly erased in Southerne's play. Their presence is felt only once, in an attack against the colony, where they are depicted as engaged in stealing the colonists' slaves, an attack that serves only to make concrete Oroonoko's bravery as he leads the charge against the native inhabitants. It is also an excuse for Imoinda to make this speech: "I am tossed about by my tempestuous fate, / And nowhere must have rest—Indians, or English! / Whoever has me, I am still a slave" (2.4.75–77). The Indians have become a backdrop, a part of the landscape against which the important action takes place. It is a powerful erasure of the representation of the group, historically, putting up some of the fiercest resistance to British colonization at the very moment Southerne's play was produced, and a powerful loss of the nuanced relations among colonists, slaves, and indigenous peoples.

The presentation of Oroonoko's blackness, as a tangible thing, first essentializes him in *opposition* to whiteness, an opposition that can be viewed as possessing its own power and status, but one removed from whiteness. Oroonoko himself speaks to that "equal but opposite" position in relating the sad tale of the loss of his beloved Imoinda to the vile clutches of his father back in Africa. Oroonoko describes Imoinda's father with special emphasis on *his* skin color: "There was a stranger in my father's court, / Valued and honored much. He was a white, / The first I ever saw of your complexion. / He changed his gods for ours and so grew great" (2.2.77–80). Imoinda's father dies in Oroonoko's arms, after having taken in his chest the poisoned dart meant for the prince, and Oroonoko returns to court to present a startling gift to Imoinda: "I presented her / With all the slaves of battle to atone / Her father's ghost" (2.2.94–96). More troubling, however, are those moments when Oroonoko's blackness is not presented merely "in opposition" to but as qualitatively different from the whiteness of the colonists, a descriptive marker that allows the plantation owners to position Oroonoko "below" or "outside" the power hierarchy in the New World. Such positioning can most tellingly be seen in the stage directions that describe Oroonoko's first onstage entrance: "Black slaves—men, women, and children—pass across the stage by two and two; Aboan and others of Oroonoko's attendants two and two; Oroonoko last of all in chains." In chains, he is visually different from Behn's Abdelezar whose blackness may be an excuse for other characters to call him a "mongrel" in an attempt to contain him, but whose power and status are clearly equal to those whom he deceives.

Southerne's Oroonoko also presents a particularly complex and complicated case for the interrelationships among gender, status, and nation.[7] Princely but black, enslaved, and separated from the woman he loves, Oroonoko is represented in both Behn's and Southerne's renditions as a man unjustly treated, but Behn's representation insists that the source of that injustice springs form Oroonoko's high status; he is first of all a prince; he is only secondarily black or African. In Southerne's much more colonialist view, Oroonoko is first of all a man racially different from the British colonists, an African transported to the New World, and thus, even though he speaks a princely rhetoric and refuses to bow down and accept his enslaved status, he is a much more difficult object of identification for a British theatergoer. He may be pitiable, a man who unfairly suffers, but he must inevitably be killed because he presents a powerful danger to the smooth workings of the colony. Hannah Arendt, calling the early modern era a time of "race-thinking before racism," characterizes the political conflicts of Europe as those of "a 'race' of aristocrats against a 'nation' of citizens (qtd. in Doyle 163). Southerne's *Oroonoko* speaks tangentially to this pattern. In a characteristic defense of slavery, Blanford—one of the admirable characters in this drama and one of the characters Southerne intends an audience to admire—justifies slavery with an argument about the birth or status of the Africans: "Most of 'em know no better; they were born so, and only change their masters" (1.2.207–8). Oroonoko himself is the character who most emphatically contradicts this facile argument. And yet when the colonists in America begin "naturally" to stare at the glorious sight he is, displayed in the marketplace, and when Blanford subsequently orders them to desist, Oroonoko proclaims,

> Let 'em stare on.
> I am unfortunate, but not ashamed
> Of being so. No, let the guilty blush,
> The white man that betray'd me. Honest black
> Disdains to change its color.
>
> (1.2.260–64)

As a man born of royal status, Oroonoko is quite comfortable being the center and object of others' gazes; here, however, he also calls attention to the single element of his life outside of Africa that has provoked his betrayal: the black color of his skin. His nearly insupportable doubleness of character emerges most strongly when Southerne again makes explicit Oroonoko's personal participation in the system that has enslaved him, this time when he seems to offer an argument that supports the enslavement of his himself and fellow Africans as the objects of a legitimate property exchange:

> If we are slaves, they did not make us slaves,
> But brought us in an honest way of trade;
> As we have done before 'em, bought and sold
> Many a wretch, and never thought it wrong.
> They paid our price for us, and we are now
> Their property, a part of their estate.
> To manage as they please.
>
> (3.2.107–13)

In these lines, Oroonoko loses some of his aristocratic luster, tarnished both by the metamorphosis of his royal status into that of a common trader in human flesh and by the emphasis on the color of his skin.

As seen above, status becomes complicated, contradictory, even confused in the case of the princely slave. Gender, however, is much less ambiguous in Southerne's presentation of Oroonoko's beloved, Imoinda, here metamorphosed into the white daughter of Oroonoko's slaving partner. The conventional language of love, distorted in Dryden's *Indian Emperour* when it is used as a tool of

imperial conquest, is similarly used *in Oroonoko* when the hero professes his love to Imoinda in the equally possessive language of empire. He says, upon discovering her alive on the Lt. Governor's
plantation,

> This little spot of earth you stand upon
> Is more to me than the extended plains
> Of my great father's kingdom. Here I reign
> In full delights, in joys to power unknown;
> Your love my empire, and your heart my throne.
>
> (2.3.242–46)

His claims to "reign," even as he wears the garb of slaves, and his
assumption of "powers" obviously denied him by his captive state
give to his statements the poignancy of a doomed love, while they
simultaneously make his actions seem nearly criminally naive.

Indeed, not even the reminder that his unborn child will be a
slave moves Oroonoko to violence, as it so powerfully does in
Behn's text. It is only Aboan's prediction that the new governor
will attempt to rape Imoinda that finally galvanizes Oroonoko, a
sexual violence that is played out for an audience in the form of
one of the worst characters in the play, the Lt. Governor, who tries
on two occasions to rape Imoinda. During one of the attacks, he
uses imperial language mixed with threats of sexual violence, a
discourse similar to that used by Dryden's Cortés, to suggest that
love has enslaved him, and in a most despicable promise he claims
that his rape of her will "liberate" her:

> And let me wonder at the many ways
> You have to ravish me.
> . . . .
> I come to offer you your liberty,
> And be myself the slave.
>
> (2.3.8–9, 16–17)

And yet a rape such as this would take a white woman permanently out of the embraces of a black man, even a black prince. It
would maintain racial boundaries for sexual conduct not found in
Behn's treatment of the story. For modern audiences, this scene
could suggest that Southerne not only marks the *limits* of race and
gender categories but also recognizes their *inseparability,* an interdependence also understood by Laura Doyle:

We need to see how fully a racial economy requires a supporting sexual economy. That is, the ability to maintain race
distinctions, including between nobleman and commoner,
requires the controlled circulation of women in marriages
within these racialized class borders. Control of women's
sexuality and reproductivity enables the institutionalization
of racial difference; and institutionalized racial differences, in
turn, empower the group claim to control of a woman's
reproduction—for it is within such groups that she finds her
economic base. In short, race hierarchies and gender hierarchies do not *simply* complicate or parallel one another; they
require one another. (169)

To maintain his control over the circulation of the body of this
white African woman, Oroonoko knows that he must kill Imoinda
so that the planters cannot capture and rape her. When Imoinda
asks to "assist" with her death by turning the dagger on herself, she
eagerly participates in prohibiting that circulation:

Nay, then, I must assist you.
And since it is the common cause of both,
'Tis just that both should be employed in it.
[Stabs herself.]
Thus, thus 'tis finished and I bless my fate
That where I lived, I die, in these loved arms.
[Dies.]

(5.5.319–23)

Oroonoko dies too, but only after stabbing and killing the Lt. Governor and thus securing his revenge on the man who would have
attempted to possess Imoinda's sexuality and, even more important
in a colonial context, her reproduction.

New images of Turkey bring us full circle in Nicholas Rowe's
Tamerlane (1701), a play that premiered five years after Manley's
Royal Mischief and Pix's *Ibrahim, the Thirteenth Emperour* and that
would be followed in five years by another powerful set of images
drawn from Islam, Manley's *Almyna* (1707). As J. Douglas Canfield has noted, Rowe took liberties both with history and with
Christopher Marlowe's representation of *Tamberlaine* in creating his
hugely popular eighteenth-century version, one that remained in
the repertoire throughout the century. The historical Tamerlane, or

Timur Lenk, was a Tartar who "savagely reestablished Mongol hegemony from India to Asia Minor, building towers out of the decapitated heads of his victims. In a single, decisive campaign in 1402 he defeated Bajazet, or Bayezid I, who had just led the Ottoman Turks to consolidate Anatolia behind Timur's back, so to speak," according to Canfield (38). Rowe distances his version of Tamerlane from the image of cruel and tyrannous Turks by making his eponymous hero—also played by Betterton—a Parthian, or Persian, a ruler trying to temper justice with mercy. Rowe reserves all his most extreme powers of representation for Bajazet (played by Verbruggen), a Turk spouting vile rhetoric and promising vicious acts of extreme violence leveled against Tamerlane, his family, and anyone who stands in his way.

Perhaps the most interesting element, for our analysis, is the political allegory contemporary audiences read into the struggle between the mild Tamerlane and the dyspeptic Bajazet—with each representing William III and Louis XIV, respectively, during the struggles of the War of Spanish Succession. Thus Rowe seeks and succeeds in getting an British audience to read a mild Persian ruler, given to moderation and measured forms of justice and mercy, as representing the contemporary English monarch, ruling with the consensus of Parliament and according to a constitution: in short, a ruler with perfect bourgeois sensibilities. Rowe displaces anxieties about bloodthirsty, tyrannous, and cruel rulers—allegorically their contemporary and most aggressive neighbors, the French—by drawing on powerful but anachronistic images of Turks, as a people who produce rulers vengeful by nature and delighted by others' fears, rulers who value birth above merit, rulers whose aristocratic sense of entitlement drives both their political and personal ambitions. In other words, it is a government looking back and not forward. Rowe presents his version of an ideal monarch as one profoundly influenced by bourgeois sensibilities and Whig politics, a ruler who could guide the country that would, a decade later in 1713, sign the Treaty of Utrecht that would secure the *asiento* and assure to England the exclusive rights to all slave trading in the Spanish West Indies, the first essential step in the production of a high seas hegemony and global empire.

Tamerlane also offers up the sharpest instances of the use of sexual violence as a political and ideological force, an activity increasingly found on the Restoration stage both in its number and in its emotional intensity. Never is there even a hint of sexual violence launched against the highborn, public women in Orrery's *Mustapha,* our earliest play. The issue of rape is raised, twice, but never acted on in *Abdelazer:* once, the king openly and emphatically insists to Florella, Abdelazer's wife, that he is not and will not be her rapist; later, the more "private" Leonora, and thus a more likely candidate for such violation than the strong and public Queen Isabella, is nearly assaulted by Abdelazer, but the attack is interrupted.[8] In *Oroonoko,* the aristocratic white African princess Imoinda, once she has metamorphosed into a private slave, becomes the object of her oppressor's desires and the reason for her husband's "sacrifice" of her. In *Tamerlane,* however, an actual rape occurs—even if there is a feeble attempt to call it a marriage—and the action becomes a pivotal point in the development of Rowe's arguments about preferred forms of power and governance.

The figure of the "rape-able" woman functions both as the vehicle by which the playwright demonstrates the rapist's rapaciousness, a tyranny easily translatable into political terms, and as the pathetic object of audience sympathy and desire. In this case, Bajazet "rapes" Arpasia, played by Elizabeth Barry, who describes the violence of the incident this way to her beloved, Moneses:

> Scarce hadst thou left
> The Sultan's camp when the imperious tyrant,
> Soft'ning the pride and fierceness of his temper,
> With gentle speech made offer of his love.
> Amazed, as at the shock of sudden death,
> I started into tears and often urged
> (Though still in vain) the difference in our faiths,
>
> . . . .
>
> Then bade the priest pronounce the marriage rites,
> Which he performed whilst, shrieking with despair,
> I called in vain the Pow'rs of heav'n to aid me.
>
> (2.2.336–42, 354–56)

After the sexual assault, Arpasia becomes in effect "a Turkish wife," women whom she calls "monstrous" and whom she dismisses with the label reserved, as we have seen, for both the rapist and his victim: "Greece, for chaste virgins famed and pious matrons, / Teems not with monsters like your Turkish wives, / Whom guardian eunuchs, haggard and deformed, / Whom walls and bars make honest by constraint" (4.2.157–60).

Rowe's hero, however, provides the most telling difference of all: the metamorphosis of the ideal leader from one whose qualities are those bestowed by birth and heredity to those earned through merit and just action. The Prince of Tanais describes Tamerlane this way:

> No lust of rule (the common vice of kings),
> No furious zeal inspired by hot-brained priests,
> Ill hid beneath religion's specious name,
> E'er drew his temperate courage to the field.
> But to redress an injured people's wrongs,
> To save the weak one from the strong oppressor,
> The sword to punish, like relenting Heav'n,
> He seems unwilling to deface his kind.
>
> (1.1.24–31)

In this, he is clearly juxtaposed to the evil Turk, Bajazet, also described by the prince as "proud," "impatient," "Fond of false glory, of the savage pow'r," "ruling without reason," and "confounding just and unjust by an unbounded will" (1.168–76). Bajazet condemns himself when he seeks to inflict additional injury on the already traumatized Arpasia:

> Yes! I must have her.
> I own I will not, cannot go without her.
> But such is the condition of our flight
> That, should she not consent, 'twould hazard all
> To bear her hence by force. Thus I resolve, then,
> By threats and pray'rs, by every way to move her.
> If all prevail not, force is left at last,
> And I will set life, empire on the venture
> To keep her mine.
>
> (5.1.30–38)

Once Tamerlane finally imprisons Bajazet, he does not order an execution; instead, tempering justice with mercy, he orders the public humiliation of the Turk: "I'll have thee borne about in public view / A great example of that righteous vengeance / That waits on cruelty and pride like thine" (5.368–70). As an example of just how significant the changes in ideal male, aristocratic, and even Turkish behavior have been, notice the language Bajazet uses in response, a strong, haughty, and proud discourse similar to that employed by Dryden's Don Sebastian when he was threatened by public ridicule:

> It is beneath me to decline my fate.
> I stand prepared to meet thy utmost hate.
> Yet think not I will long thy triumph see:
> None want the means when the soul dares be free.
> I'll curse thee with my last, my parting breath,
> And keep the courage of my life in death.

(5.371–76)

Compare this with Tamerlane's parting pronouncement on the necessary kingly virtues:

> But justly those above assert their sway
> And teach ev'n kings what homage they should pay,
> Who then rule best when mindful to obey.

(5.383–85)

This is a stunning prescription for political stability: by 1701, kings will pay homage, if they wish to rule.

These images, then, of national others—Turks, Spaniard, Indians, and Moors, in particular—provide figures that provoke desire as well as repugnance in English audiences and, while their representations persist, they also change throughout the decades under investigation here. Turks, who were always at least potentially a threat throughout most of this period, move from admirable aristocratic rulers, with destructive and peculiar political laws, to cruel and tyrannical despots eager to rape the innocent and pillage valuable lands, all before they effectively disappear by the middle of the eighteenth century. Spaniards, who begin as demonized figures of otherness—imperial, greedy, rigid, and thoroughly implacable—end as fraternal Europeans enfolded into British consciousness as failed imperialists who provide lessons in proper colonial behavior or who function as harmless figures of delight and ridicule, as benign creatures lost in their own distant dreams of an impossible Catholic hegemony. Moors, Africans, and Indians, on the other hand, are the objects onto which Europeans displace their anxieties about more local struggles: either they are erased, in the way that the Indians disappear from Southerne's *Oroonoko,* or they are turned from princes and mighty rulers into rowdy rabble or, worse still, slaves. By the end of the eighteenth century, when England has footholds all over the globe—in North America, Asia, and India—Richard Cumberland's *West Indian* (1771) arrives on the London stage to demonstrate that labels for national others have metamorphosed into descriptions of *English* men and women *returning* from colonial "outposts," and not the inhabitants who originally occupied the lands Europeans were settling; indigenous peoples, like the Indians in Southerne's *Oroonoko,* disappear.

Behavior once demanded of aristocrats, a conspicuous consumption necessary to maintain their status within their communities, according to Lawrence Stone, comes to be seen as a matter of a bad domestic economy. Aristocrats living in "the old style" are represented as libertines and wastrels, men committed to the production of waste and not to the production of profit.[9] Shadwell's Don John is the strongest example, of course, but Behn's Abdelazer and Rowe's Bajezet are equally powerful illustrations. Ideal gendered behavior works to support and even to rewrite these shifting boundaries of status. Orrery's strong Turkish women, and even Dryden's outspoken Almeyda, metamorphose into pathetic objects of sexual assault by the end of the seventeenth century—into Rowe's Arpasia who barely whispers: "Forgetting all the toils and troubles past, / Weary I'll lay me down and sleep till—oh!" (5.208–10), and with that she dies. The figures of kings in these plays, such as Rowe's Tamerlane, however, demonstrate the most startling metamorphosis, for they abandoned the iron fist in exchange for a gentleness that seeks justice and not revenge; a king must be willing to bow to the will of his subjects and, like a good wife, "to obey."

This collection of plays also contributes to our broader understanding of the ways identity functioned more generally as a locus of powerful interest to Restoration playwrights. Restoration drama is so rich in moments that feature identity as the playwright's thematic focus or as an essential plot ingredient for the development of character that it appears nearly compulsory. When playwrights experiment with the possibilities for the redefinition of old categories, exploiting the new elasticity in old boundaries, they position identity as shifting and fluid, rather than fixed and stable. This in turn allows a playwright such as Aphra Behn to explore the liberating pleasures of pushing the limits of the new possibilities, while it leads a playwright such as William Wycherley to attempt to contain his anxiety by marking the limits of the old boundaries.

Such a strategy of containment has emerged from this analysis as the predominant process playwrights used in their attempts to mute the threat that performed identities always produce.[10] Of the works examined here, the tragedies present the most troubling acts of containment, since the containment process is dependent on acts of violence, often specifically launched at the bodies of women, for their efficacy. Whereas the early narratives of European encounter and conquest were comfortable with traditional notions of the transformation of female identity as a result of marriage— the body of Dryden's native Cydaria simply joins with that of Cortés to effect a transfer of land from New World inhabitant to European—the stories of settlement and colonization cannot permit such assimilation: native bodies are threatening to a status quo that perceives land occupied to be land owned, and thus any lability of native identity in later plays must be contained, as in the case of the death of the Indian Queen. That same act of containment occurs in the violence done to the bodies of rape victims whose resulting trauma forces them into a heightened subjectivity, because they are without the power to correct and redress the wrong, a wrong so powerful and so anxiety-producing that playwrights finally offer up acts of suicide to obliterate the pain and to quiet the broken body. In these cases, identity is not temporarily divided, doubled, or multiplied in favor of a new, performed identity; in these tragedies, unstable identities produce chaos and confusion.

In comedy, the performance of various identities resonates with much greater joy and potential liberation than the pain and pathos of performances found in tragedy. But even here, seeming attempts at containment are present in moments of the conservative reinscription of a singular, even an essential, identity—attempts that almost always fail to contain the excesses that such performances produce. This attempt to contain and its failure is nowhere more visible than at the conclusion of Behn's *Feign'd Curtizans,* the play that features Cornelia—a young, virginal heroine who masquerades as a prostitute throughout much of the drama—whose delight in and potential danger from "feigning" we saw in the first pages of this book. The ending of this play, a seeming return to a supposedly more "stable" reality for all the "feigning" characters, features the uncovering of all the "real" social identities of the characters and the sorting out of all the amorous affairs. The sisters, Cornelia and Marcella, are "revealed" to be young, marriageable women of quality. Marcella confesses to Fillamour that she deceived him into thinking her a courtesan, and he responds with a most courtly apology for his interest in the courtesan: "How ere my eyes might be impos'd upon, you see my heart was firm to its first object, can you forget and pardon the mistake[?]" (5.4.691–92). This sorting out of the "confusion of women" at the conclusion turns out to be a relief and a delight for him.

Galliard, on the other hand, beloved of the cross-status- and cross-gender-dressed Cornelia, is aghast at this young woman's "feigning" of her "dishonesty," and he responds with a belittling and less-than-kind question about her activities once her "true" status is uncovered: "have I been dreaming all this Night, of the possession of a new gotten Mistress, to wake and finde my self nooz'd to a dull wife in the morning?" (5.4.703–05). Eager and witty as ever, Cornelia responds to that unkindness with the performer's answer: "I do here promise to be the most Mistriss-like wife,—you know Signior I have learnt the trade, though I had not stock to practice, and will be as expensive, Insolent, vain, Extravagant, and Inconstant, as if you only had the keeping part, and another the Amorous Assignations, what think ye Sir[?]" (5.4.708–12). Even though to a modern reader's ears this sounds like a most ominous, if pleasantly addressed threat to overspend his money, speak to him uncivilly, pursue only her own egocentric desires, and even engage is unsanctioned love affairs, Galliard is pleased with the response and accepts her with these words, "She speaks Reason! And I'me resolved to trust good Nature!—give me thy dear hand" (5.4.714–15). Cornelia, unlike her sister, has not abandoned the possibilities that performance generates, and indeed, she describes her marriage, with an actor's term, as a "part."

The actions of these two young heroines will serve as the last examples in this book of the ways that Restoration playwrights explored and often attempted to contain the performance of new identities on the Restoration stage. Marcella's happy ending indicates that sometimes the performance is liberating, in that it allowed her to seek out and attain her desires. At other times, the performance of a new identity becomes a riskier proposition, as it was for Cornelia, betrothed to a man doubly disappointed in her "honesty," for it not only prevented a consummation of his unsanctioned sexual desires but it also demanded the sanctioned—and permanent—bonds of matrimony. For one sister, "feigning" has been a temporary, if aggressive, act of manipulating the external, material signifiers of identity that returns to the stability of marriage and a singular identity at the conclusion of the play; for the other sister, "feigning" has been a rehearsal for all her new, and maybe even riskier, roles to come. These actions serve as only one of many examples of playwrights' exploration of the expanding and newly various opportunities for performing identities found on the Restoration stage.

Notes
Works Cited
Index

Notes

1. Introduction: New Identities on and off the Restoration Stage

1. Unlike many of Behn's comedies, *The Feign'd Curtizans* was not based on a known source. What we do know is that the play was first acted in the Duke's Theatre in 1679 and that Elizabeth Barry's role as Cornelia was favorably received. For more information on the production history, see Jane Spencer's "Deceit, Dissembling, and all that's Woman."

2. Laura Rosenthal has written very persuasively on this subject in "'Counterfeit Scrubbado'" and in "Reading Masks."

3. Deborah Payne, also noting the discrepancy between the tone of the speaker and the reputed reputation of the recipient, places the discourse in the proper literary context: "The marked disparity between Gwynn's public persona and the ethereal creature hovering in these lines mocks the speaker's courtly pretense to Platonic lover" ("'Poets'" 113).

4. The most influential scholar of what has been called "the performance school" of identity is Judith Butler, who draws on psychoanalytic models for her groundbreaking argument that identity is the *effect* of performance, not its *cause*. Thus gender (and by extension any identity category) is revealed to be a cultural fiction, one that members of the culture agree, consciously or unconsciously, to perform and to produce. See Butler's *Gender Trouble*. Other scholarly works that treat the issue of the performance of gender include Diana Fuss's *Essentially Speaking* and her essay "Fashion and the Homospectatorial Look" and Sue Ellen Case's *Performing Feminisms*. For critics of this position, such definitions of the performative run the risk of offering up a thoroughly relative identity, one entirely unanchored. Critics of the performative model argue that identity is never shaped by individuals entirely through individual will, that other forces—psychological, sexual, geographical, historical—must also be taken into account. For an argument about "the deficiencies of the performative model of subjectivity," see Molly Anne Rothenberg and Joseph Valente's "Fashionable Theory and Fashionable Women."

   I find each of these positions to be at opposite and extreme ends of one continuum of behavior. I prefer to work from the premise that individuals have the capacity to choose certain behaviors, that individual will is an important element in determining some human actions. At the same time, the forces of both culture and nature work to shape those individual choices, in ways sometimes conscious, sometimes unconscious. The analyses that follow display a number of ways that these choices and forces function on the late-seventeenth-century stage. I also share Katharine Maus's suspicions about the usefulness of the application of psychoanalytic theory, especially in terms of our understanding of subjectivity, to the early modern era. Arguing that "'subjectivity' is often treated as a unified or coherent concept when, in fact, it is a loose and varied collection of assumptions, intuitions, and practices that do not all logically entail one another and need not appear together at the same cultural moment" (29), Maus suggests that psychoanalytic criticism has become increasingly irrelevant to the problem of subjectivity in the early modern period. Her concerns—and my own as well—are primarily epistemological, asking how one person can know another, rather than psychoanalytical, asking primarily developmental questions such as how does a person know himself or herself, often as part of a family (*Inwardness* 29–31).

5. Freddie Rokem describes the relationship between bodies and texts this way: "Every production of a play (and consequently every performance of it) is a concrete bodily realization of the presence of the human body in the dramatic text that draws our attention to the cultural and aesthetic codes of bodily behaviour" (222). These bodily realizations helped to produce category crises that must have been particularly intense for a spectator sitting in a Restoration playhouse that featured new movable onstage scenery, an atmosphere as changeable as the lability of identity present in the onstage characters. For more on the Restoration playhouse, see Jocelyn Powell's *Restoration Theater Production* and Peter Holland's *Ornament of Action.*

6. Other important works on the body and identity include Thomas Laquer's *Making Sex: Body and Gender from the Greeks to Freud* and, with Catherine Gallagher, Laquer's *The Making of the Modern Body;* Elaine Scarry's *Body in Pain;* Lori Hope Lefkovitz's collection *Textual Bodies,* Suzanne Scholz's *Body Narratives.*

7. Stallybrass and White offer up a succinct contrast between Elias and Bourdieu: "Thus whilst Bourdieu connects the regulation of manners to the operation of the whole metaphysical and ideological outlook of a culture, Elias connects manners to the internal construction of the subject, to the historical formation of self, repudiating any possibility of a separation of the psychical and the social" (90).

8. Megan Matchinske's argument about such changes during the Renaissance is a good one:

> Printing presses, changes in market and land use, revisions in church policy and practice, redistribution of property and title, a bureaucratization of royal government and civil service, all of these allowed for and insisted on a multitude of differing registers with the 'state' to monitor behavior and determine acceptable codes of conduct for English people. (3–4)

About migration to the city and the new demands on individuals, Katharine Eisaman Maus writes "the new urbanite needed to learn to manage a wider spectrum of familiarities: from almost anonymous interactions with unknown persons, to casual attachments with acquaintances, to the intimate relationships among family members and close friends" (*Inwardness* 24).

9. See also Jones DeRitter's *Embodiment of Characters* and Susanne Scholz's introduction to *Body Narratives* for cogent summaries of the socioeconomic, demographic, political, and sociopolitical changes taking place during the seventeenth and eighteenth centuries.

10. I do not mean to imply that, during the Restoration, England had a full-blown discourse of nationalism similar to that found during the nineteenth-century heyday of British imperialism. But clearly discourses concerning *national identities* were alive at this time, discourses that had as their boundaries both geographical and cultural markers.

11. Nabil Matar notes that when Britons encountered Muslims in the Eastern Mediterranean and in North Africa they encountered a "powerful religious and military civilization which viewed them as an inferior people with a false religion," people who unabashedly stared at them, in an attempt to humiliate them, or who were reminded, by the redness of their European skin, of pigs: "From whatever angle a Briton reflected on the Muslim perception of the Christian, he realized the Muslims saw themselves in power and certitude" (*Islam* 3–4).

12. Matar also argues that "the most famous and publicized visitor of [Charles II's] reign was the Moroccan ambassador Mohammad bin Hadou, who arrived on 29 December 1681 and departed on 23 July 1682. There were poems written about the occasion, descriptions in private correspondence and diaries, and most importantly, news reports about the ambassador in the *London Gazette*" (*Turks* 38).

13. C. J. Heywood cites Carl Gollner's *Turcica: Die europäischen Türkendrucke des XVI. Jahrhunderts* as an attempt to provide a bibliography of sixteenth-century European writings on the Ottoman empire. That research reveals that from 1501–1550, over 1,000 titles were printed; another 2,500 titles were printed in the next half century; and the seventeenth century would find at least as many, if not more, titles published (56n. 1). For an examination of later, eighteenth-century representations of Turks on the British stage, see W. Daniel Wilson's "Turks on the Eighteenth-Century Operatic Stage."

14. As early as 1603, however, Knolles records a lessening of Turkish power that in hindsight reveals his wishes as much as an accurate description; in an extended metaphor that likens the growth of an empire to the aging of a human being, Knolles sounds the death knell for the Ottoman empire: "Now as this aged Empire hath many in-bred diseases, so it is threatened abroad by the Persians on one side, by fear of the Egyptians and Arabs getting head on another [*sic*]; by the Christians on a third, of which the Polander is of most danger, as being nearest in place and oftenest provoked" (30).

15. The controlled classical republican, according to Michele Cohen, has been called by John Barrell "the most authoritative fantasy of masculinity in early eighteenth-century Britain" (75). Cohen cites Barrell's "'Dangerous Goddess': Masculinity, Prestige, and the Aesthetic in Early Eighteenth-Century Britain," which appears in *The Birth of Pandora and the Division of Knowledge*.

16. For stimulating analyses of powerful eighteenth-century instances of the beginnings of the culture of narcissism and of a society of spectacle, see Stewart Crehan's "*The Rape of the Lock* and the Economy of 'Trivial

Things'" and Guy Debord's *Society of Spectacle;* an analysis of more modern instances can be found in Jean Baudrillard's *Simulcra and Simulation.*

17. Helen Deutsch and Felicity Nussbaum go even further and call this increased observation "a fetishization of difference, its need to know difference through envisioning it," even as that very curiosity also, and paradoxically, "affords the opportunity for new forms of potentially subversive subjectivities and interiorities" (18). Mr. Spectator, a later eighteenth-century creation in whom is deployed "an unprecedented technology for reform of London's manner and morals" has been said to "anticipate precisely the 'Eye of Power,' the voyeuristic gaze which disciplines subjects by observing them"; but according to Scott Paul Gordon,

   > the superhuman technology devised to accomplish reform testifies less to the success of the spectatorial regime than to the intractability of the readers it hopes to control. The *Spectator's* gaze represents a disciplinary *fantasy,* and it is only in this sense that Mr. Spectator anticipates Bentham's panopticon or the cinematic apparatus of recent film theory. (4)

18. During defines "self-specularisation" as related to a similar process called "self-othering"—"a means for construction or finding a self as another or by identification with others"—and he offers advice from a 1740s *London Tradesman* as an example: "A tradesman must be a perfect Proteus, Change Shapes as often as the Moon, and still find something new" (60–61). Other forms of "real-life" disguise were also available in the eighteenth century: women cross-dressed as men, especially to gain work, or the poor dressed "up" simply by acquiring their clothes as cast-offs or through theft (61). In this context, David Garrick's genius becomes his constant display of a "lack of localness," a phrase that beautifully encapsulates the possibility of being other than oneself (Diderot appreciated Garrick's ability to produce an identity that was "never himself" [qtd. in During 57]).

19. One may easily substitute past tense verbs, as I have done, in the following sentence penned by Llewellyn Negrin about the twentieth-century fashion industry to produce a sentence equally descriptive of the late-seventeenth-century one: "Commodities [were then] consumed not because they ostensibly [satisfied] some practical need but because they [served] as ways of differentiating individuals within the social hierarchy. In the context of capitalist society where one's social position [was] no longer fixed at birth, commodities [did] not so much reflect but rather [created] status distinctions" (113).

20. See Deborah Laycock's essay, "Shape-Shifting," for more on credit as female: "The economy of desire as facilitated by credit is depicted as a feminine economy; mutability is inscribed on the very character of credit, the symbol of the new economics" (132).

21. For a most provocative argument about "the radical shift under way since the eighteenth century from a text-based to a visually based culture," see Barbara Stafford's *Body Criticism.*

22. James Thompson has argued elsewhere that

   > as money is fully capitalized, that is, as it is reconceived from a thing to a process, from wealth to the representation of wealth, from inert hoard to the means of making wealth, there is a similar shift from an objective

conception of money to an instrumental or functional definition. And as money is dematerialized, so its function as sign or representation is reemphasized. (" 'Sure' " 286)

Paradoxically, female characters in the plays of the late eighteenth century undergo the opposite process: "it is the female character whose value is subject to fluctuation and must be verified by one method or another, and so fixed. . . . the method of valuation shifts from extrinsic to intrinsic, from name to face, while monetary theory moves in the opposite direction" (" 'Sure' " 301). This interior form of identity was about to be fully exploited in the new and what would prove to be the defining literary form of the eighteenth century: the novel. For more on the relationship between gender and interiority, see Thompson's *Models of Value*. Laura Brown's *English Dramatic Form, 1660–1740* offers another compelling argument about the relationship between dramatic forms and the emerging novel.

23. Will Pritchard has analyzed the part that cosmetics played in the debate between authentic and inauthentic identities for women: "Painting injected an element of behavior (doing) into what ought to have been pure, bodily 'being.' It made the otherwise authentic face a site for counterfeiting" (41).

24. One result of this dividedness is a new modern relationship to the body: from "the spectacular semiosis of the Renaissance body," as Barker puts it, modernity fashions a new body for its own "labour-intensive and empirical epoch," one body that is actually two—the body as mere flesh, as "dead meat," or as a thing "out there" in the world, "rather than 'in here' in the charmed circle of sovereign but self-appointed consciousness" (vi). Barker's most powerful insight concerns the relation of surface to depth in early modern dramas: This theatrical world achieves its depth by "a doubling of the surface"—a layering of spectacle upon spectacle, one without increased depth but increased surface, one that serves to expand time rather than "excavate a hidden level of reality" (*Tremulous* 25).

2. Imperial Identities: Encounter, Conquest, and Settlement

1. For a cogent summary of the development of British trade in the colonies, see Jeremy Black's *System of Ambition*.

2. For a dated but fascinating argument about British and American anti-Hispanism (from a strong supporter of Spain and its achievements), see William S. Maltby's *Black Legends in England*.

3. In *Colonial Writing and the New World, 1583–1671*, Scanlan details the publication history of the *Brevíssima relación* and its influence on English politics. Translated and published in English in London four times between 1583 and 1699, the text provided English Protestants with

    justification for both their foreign policy toward Spain and their colonial policy in the New World. The cruelty so graphically described in the *Brevíssima relación,* which the English figured as typically Catholic and Spanish, enabled the English to see colonial endeavor as a means of defining what it meant to be English and what it meant to be Protestant. (8)

4. Citing the work of Tommaso Campanella *(Della monarchia di Spagna)* and Jose del Campillo y Cossio *(Nuevo sistema de gobierno económico para*

la *América*) as critical of the Spanish imperial worldview, Anthony Pagden writes, "Like most of her European critics, Campanella and Campillo believed that Spain was trapped in a mental condition of something we, if not they, might legitimately describe as pre-modernity" (*Lords* 122).

5. In one of the strangest moments in a generally strange play, this panto-mime follows the "Sixth Speech": While a "wild Ayr" plays, a Spaniard comes onstage, loaded down with gold ingots and "wedges" of silver, and falls asleep. "Two Apes come in from opposite sides of the Wood, and dance to the Ayr. After a while, a great Baboon enters, and joyns with them in the dance. They wake the Spaniard, and end the Antiqiue Measures with driving him into the Wood" (113). In one very real sense, then, it is not the British who drive out the Spaniards but native creatures. A spectator sensitive to iconographic stand-ins, however, is forced to see some similarity between the baboon and the British.

6. *The Indian Emperour* was a hugely popular play that remained in the repertoire for nearly half a century. It premiered in April 1665, alongside the Earl of Orrery's *Mustapha, Son of Solyman the Magnificent,* another heroic drama, set this time in remote and exotic Turkish regions. Other plays produced during the 1664–65 season included Davenant's *Rivals,* Orrery's *Generall,* Shakespeare's *Macbeth,* and Jonson's *Volpone.* By June 1665, there were such dangerous increases in the plague that the theaters were shut down; they opened again in October 1666 with *Mustapha* and *The Indian Emperour* forming two staples of that and succeeding seasons.

7. That these two, contradictory sets of discursive strategies are often employed by imperial writers can be seen in Simon Ryan's arguments about similar descriptions of Australia: "The first was a repetition of already colonized 'native' civilizations, with villages and a recognizable culture, and the second, a waste/emptiness needing filling in by European expansion. . . . either the land is full of the kind of 'native' cultures already known to Europeans, or it is empty. The 'blank map' trope creates Australia as a place that is in reality (and not just in representation) blank" (238–9). Moreover, the land is equally often imagined as a passive female body that requires male investigation and control.

8. In a highly speculative account of what the Indians in the region of the Jamestown settlement might have thought of the British settlers, Jeffrey L. Hantman writes, "I am convinced that Indians perceived Europeans in a category analogous to that which Western intellectuals term 'the other.' Centuries of continent-wide social and economic exchange led Amerindians to be generally aware of one another's differences, but the European stranger was something fundamentally different" ("Caliban" 74).

9. John Loftis's classic *Spanish Plays of Neoclassical England* chronicles the close relationships between the playwrights of England and Spain. He argues that "in their parallel development, the English and Spanish dramas have more in common than either has with any other of the national dramas of Europe" (ix). In 1660, the English would have known the works of Lope de Vega, Tirso de Molina, and Calderon, and they would have had "a generalized understanding of a brilliant Spanish Renaissance literature" (2). Loftis cites British "Spanish plot" plays as evidence—those plays that portray Spanish or Portuguese characters in their native country or the parts of Italy controlled by Spain. English playwrights would also

have regarded Spanish drama as "a reservoir of plots available for use on the English stage" (162). French settings, we know, were much rarer. By the time Aphra Behn begins her career, "the later phase of Spanish plots," as Loftis calls it, the forms had become part of traditional Restoration plot patterns, resulting in *The Dutch Lovers,* "a Restoration comedy of Spanish romance in one of its most highly developed forms, graceful and entertaining" (147).

10. Verena Stolcke disputes the traditional descriptions of the "conquest" of the Americas. She writes that "historians have read these chronicles in a highly selective way. The conquest of America has therefore been presented as a an affair between men, as an aggression and dispossession realized by a few men (the Spaniards) against other men (the Indians)," when in fact "the assault on indigenous women was not simply a matter of pleasure forced from the women of the vanquished; it was a definitive way of sealing the Spaniards's victory through the appropriation of that which, in the conquerors' reasoning, constituted the most valuable possession of the defeated" (272–73).

11. The English translation I use, *The Discovery of the New World by Christopher Columbus,* has no line numbers. I therefore cite only page numbers parenthetically in text.

12. Anthony Pagden describes the *Requerimiento* (requirement) as a peremptory document that came in the form of a declaration:

> This document—surely the crassest example of legalism in modern European history—began with a brief history of the world since its creation, laid out the grounds for the Castilian monarchs' claim to be the true rulers of the Americans, and then promised the Native Americans all manner of hideous punishments, including, of course, their enslavement and the seizure of their lands, if they resisted the "ambassadors" of their new ruler. When he read it, Bartolomeo de Las Casas once said, he did not know whether to laugh or cry. (*Lords* 91)

Stephen Greenblatt, too, sees the absurdity of the event: "a strange blend of ritual, cynicism, legal fiction, and perverse idealism, the *Requerimiento* contains at its core the conviction that there is no serious language barrier between the Indians and the Europeans" (*Learning* 29).

13. Pagden writes the following about the historical accounts of marriage between Europeans and Native Americans:

> The Spaniards, whose native populations had entered the historiography of the empire as noble, if primitive, warriors, were seen, at least at first, as potential marriage partners, although the crown did nothing to encourage such unions. Some members of the *conquistador* class even attempted liaison with what they identified as a native aristocracy. (*Lords* 150)

Pizarro's brother, for instance, "threatened" to marry an Inca princess and declare himself king of Peru. Cases such as these rarely occurred, and by the eighteenth century marriages between Spanish men and aristocratic Native American women had evolved into "a series of metaphors which preserved, as far as possible, the greatest possible distance between true *criollos,* the now mythologized 'Aztec' and 'Inca' past on the one hand, and the grim realities of the mestizo underclass and the still autonomous American peoples on the other" (150).

14. Historically, the Taxallans, traditional enemies of the Mexican empire, fought alongside the Spanish only when it gained them a direct advantage. Presented in the *Indian Emperour* here as subordinates, or "vassals" as Cortés actually calls them, they were in fact fierce rivals of Montezuma and in no way inferior subjects. For more on the Taxallans, see Clendinnen's "'Fierce and Unnatural Cruelty': Cortés and the Conquest of Mexico."

15. Clendinnen argues that the "returning god-ruler" theory was powerfully reinforced by Sahagun's *Florentine Codex,* a "late-dawning" story that appeared nearly thirty years after the conquest. It presents Montezuma as paralyzed by fear on first meeting Cortés, but Clendinnen suggests that the tale "bears the hallmarks of a post-Conquest scapegoating" (16).

16. J. M. Armistead has argued that the play stages "a confrontation between two rather similar men [Cortés and Montezuma] representing two nations whose cultures differ more in degree than in kind, more in customs than in social or political structures" (139). This seems to be a much too optimistic reading, one that is seduced by the seemingly commensurate structures Dryden sets up, whereas indeed the differences in power (on the other side of real history) are enormous. See Armistead's "The Occultism of Dryden's 'American' Plays in Context."

17. Clendinnen writes that

    siege was the quintessential European strategy: an economical design to exert maximum pressure on whole populations without active engagement, delivering control over people and place at least cost. . . . For the Mexicans, siege was the antithesis of war. . . . the deliberate and systematic weakening of opposition before engagement, and the deliberate implication of noncombatants in the context, had no part of their experience. (30)

18. A mid-seventeenth-century publication, Thomas Gage's *A New Survey of the West-Indias: or, the English American his Travail by Sea and Land,* is typical of the British descriptions of the Cortés encounter. Focusing very little, if at all, on the actual moments of encounter, Gage concerns himself with the effects of famine and want in the city: "the Citizens were in great necessity, and so many dead with hunger and sicknesse; that there were heaps of dead bodies in the houses . . . [as the Spaniards later walked through the streets] the very barks of trees and roots gnawn by the hungry creatures, and the men so lean and yellow that it was a pitifull sight to behold" (48).

19. *The Widdow Ranter* was a posthumous production, even though the exact date for the premiere is not known; the prologue and epilogue, which were printed separately, bear a licensing date of November 20, 1689, according to *The London Stage,* and the dedication of the 1690 edition complains "Had our Author been alive she would have Committed it to the Flames rather than suffer'd it to have been Acted with such Omissions as were made." The play was not revived. Concurrent productions included Lee's *Massacre of Paris* and *Rival Queens,* Tate's *Dido and Aeneas,* and Dryden's *Sebastian.*

20. For more information on the historical events of Bacon's rebellion and for an especially useful bibliography of the history, see Margaret Ferguson's "Miscegenous Romance."

21. David Kramer recognizes these same impulses in Dryden:

    The minds and aims of imperialist and subject are, at this stage in Dryden's drama, depicted not only differently from each other, but with differing degrees of artistic and imaginative success. Dryden almost always depicts the expansionist urge of the imperialist in terms of the characteristically male vocabulary of energy, vigor, glory, heroism, and poetic splendor, and even when a manifestation of this urge is unequivocally despicable, as in the racking scene, Dryden's poetic and dramatic representations of imperial activity flicker with a light that chills as it illuminates. (79)

22. Anthony Pagden writes of the differences between the Spanish (and to a lesser degree Portuguese) and the English and French conquests. The Spanish overran large native populations, but "both the English and the French were, for a number of related causes, driven either to exclude the Native Americans from their colonies, or to incorporate them as trading partners. Despite the abortive attempt by the British to enslave the populations of Carolina, nowhere did they become, as they did throughout Spanish America, 'vassals.'" Or as Montesquieu declared, the Spaniards looked upon the Americas as "objects of conquest" while the others saw them as "objects of commerce" and treated them as such (*Lords* 65, 68).

23. Janet Todd describes Cromwell's 1658 funeral as "a magnificent affair," for which many of the bills were never paid. She speculates that Flirt's father either supplied the mourning cloth, for which he was not paid, or he speculated on the commodity (Behn, *Widdow* 452).

24. Thomas Scanlan reminds us that, during this time, English national identity was "very much in flux," and he argues that "the colonial project became one of the primary ways that the English used to articulate and define their own emerging sense of nationhood," with native populations functioning in complex ways to contribute to the definition of Englishness (3).

25. For another analysis of the ambiguity one finds in Behn's treatment of identity, see Liz Bridges's "'We Were Somebody in England.'"

26. Anthony Pagden suggests that this maintenance of the status quo was later replaced by fears about a shift in the balance of power, perhaps a permanent shift, between the metropolis and the colony, from conquest to settlement: "the Spanish hildalgo in Mexico and an English gentlemen in Virginia may well have had more in common with each other than with merchant and artisan settlers from their own native countries when it came to envisaging the form of community they wished to establish" (6). In the case of Spain in the early eighteenth century, the power relations between colony and metropolis had not merely changed, they "had been inverted. 'The Indies and Spain are two powers under the same master,' observed Montesquieu in 1748, 'but the Indies is the principal one and Spain nothing but an accessory'" (152). In the end, the successful British began to experience the same fears as the less successful Spanish, according to Pagden:

    Migration, which could perhaps be checked, was not the only, or even the most unsettling, danger presented by imperial expansion. Far more serious was the possibility that over-reaching might finally result in the collapse of the metropolis's own political and moral culture, the dissolution of its ethical values, even—the most alarming prospect of all—its final absorption by the very empire it had itself created. (*Lords* 106)

27. Nabil Matar has argued that the following idealization and containment of the Indian took place during this era: "It is no wonder that as soon as the American Indian was brought under control, Britons and other Europeans proceeded to invent him as the Noble Savage and the Edenic Indian; once he was domesticated or annihilated he could safely be imagined in a favorable manner" (*Turks* 106). Moreover, by the end of the seventeenth century, Matar argues that the Muslim "Savage" and the Indian "savage" had become completely "superimposable" on English thought and ideology. Only in the eighteenth century did "a colonial discourse against Islam in the full sense of the term" evolve (*Turks* 170).

28. The threat the Indian Queen poses is muted a bit by the casting in the original 1689 production: Anne Bracegirdle, famous for playing blushing virgins and for being the soul of excellent English womanhood, would have presented another instance of the oscillations that colonial impulses inspire.

29. Joseph Roach also reads the death of the queen in terms of race: "the prenuptial sacrifice contributes to the fiction of the originary whiteness of the Virginians and thus to the 'safer repose' of the Anglo-Americans' 'country'" (*Cities of the Dead* 127).

3. National Identities: Merchants on and off the Restoration Stage

1. *The Gentleman Dancing-Master* was produced by the Duke's Company and premiered in Dorset Gardens, February 6, 1672. A fire at the King's Theatre may have caused Wycherley to transfer the play there. While little is certain about the production, we do know that Edward Angel played Don Diego and James Nokes played Monsieur Parris. These facts make act 2, with the raillery at the French and the celebration of the clownish abilities of the English actors Angel and Nokes—lines spoken, of course, by Angel and Nokes—even funnier. The play lasted a respectable six nights. See B. Eugene McCarthy's biography of Wycherley for additional details.

2. *The Dutch Lovers* premiered on February 6, 1673. Also produced during this season were Shadwell's *Sullen Lovers* and *Epsom Wells,* Shakespeare's *Macbeth,* Duffett's *Spanish Rogue,* and Settle's *Empress of Morocco.*

3. Jacqueline Pearson has argued that this play shows Behn "questioning the stereotypes commonly associated with Dutchness even as she seems to use them" ("Slave Princes" 225). I would agree with her that "Haunce as Other is the least threatening to the women of the play's male characters," but I would suggest that his good humor in discovering his being tricked into marriage is a confirmation of a status stereotype rather than a questioning of a national one.

4. Wycherley's own family status was a matter of contentious debate during the 1670s. His biographer, B. Eugene McCarthy, reports that the Wycherley family's right to claim gentleman status was publicly challenged three years after the play premiered: "a search was made on [Wycherley's father's] claim to the rank of gentleman at the insistence of a number of

Shropshire gentry who apparently disbelieved his ostensible rank and thought it worth challenging, and this search, made during the years 1676 to 1679, settled the status of the Wycherley family and their arms, as well as the locale and state of their residence."

5. Addison's *Spectator No. 435* contains a complaint specifically about English women who return from France dressed in men's attire and generally about all Britons who return from abroad "infected" by French fashion: "I must observe that this Fashion was first of all brought to us from France, a Country which has Infected all the Nations of Europe with its Levity. . . . Modesty is our distinguishing Character, as Vivacity is theirs."

6. In this context, Gail Ching-Liang Low's argument about race in nineteenth-century colonial literature provides an interesting contrast: "it is the white man who dresses up and the native who reveals his body for consumption by dressing down"; she also argues that an appeal to the surfaces of the body, found in a number of nineteenth-century descriptions of African warriors, "is strategic to a discourse of racism" (108). For a different kind of argument, one concerning the insistently "theatrical" nature of this play, see W. Gerald Marshall's "The Idea of Theatre."

7. For a fascinating examination of the relationships among trade, nationalism, and literary production, see Robert Markley's "Violence and Profits on the Restoration Stage."

8. For more information about the trade relations between England and Spain in the seventeenth and eighteenth centuries, see an old but still useful text, Jean O. McLachlan's *Trade and Peace with Old Spain, 1667–1750.* McLachlan argues that

> an additional advantage of the Old Spanish trade, from the point of view of the British merchants and statesmen, was that it was carried on in British bottoms, and this provided an opportunity for British shops to secure a considerable part of the carrying trade to Spain. . . . In 1662 an Act of Parliament had been passed to encourage the use of moderately large and well-armed ships in the trade to Old Spain. Thereafter English merchants made considerable profits by carrying a great deal of Spain's foreign trade. (7)

McLachlan's information about British imports from Spain is also enlightening in the context of Don Diego's trade: "In England strict mercantilists might frown on the import of wines and fruit since these commodities were unproductive, but since the public demanded sherries and Canary wine, grapes, almonds, and oranges, [J.] Cary asserted that 'since we must drink wines, 'tis better to have them from the Spaniard than from the French'" (17).

9. J. H. Plumb writes about the relatively easy movement from one class to another during this period:

> Toward the ends of their careers, ["the merchant princes"] often bought up great estates to endow themselves with the social prestige which went with land ownership and which would enable their sons and daughters to marry into the aristocracy or to acquire a title in their own right. These were the men who controlled the Bank of England and the great chartered companies. . . . With property came standing in society and a future for one's children, for in the early part

of the century it was relatively easy to pass from one social class to another—a fact which amazed Voltaire and others. (*England in the Eighteenth Century* 14, 17)

10. Plays produced during this same 1705–06 season included Vanbrugh's *Relapse;* Behn's *Rover; or, The Banish'd Cavaliers;* Centilvre's *Gamester* and *Basset Table;* Dryden's *Indian Emperour, Aurenge Zebe, All for Love,* and *Spanish Fryar;* Tuke's *Adventures of Five Hours;* Otway's *Venice Preserved;* Shakespeare's *Othello;* Southerne's *Oronooko;* and Rowe's *Tamerlane.* For an interesting and persuasive argument about why Pix's play should be dated 1706, rather than 1709 as some scholars would have it, see Susan Garland Mann and David D. Mann's "The Publisher William Turner, Female Playwrights, and Pix's *The Adventures in Madrid.*"

11. Juliet McLaren points to an element in Pix's comedies—her focus on women characters—that may be overstated in this quotation, but which is generally true: "Her plays were about women: ordinary, middle-class, sometimes middle-aged women, not about men. She had male characters in her plays, but her real interest was not in the men at all. She had funny, meaty parts for three, four, sometimes five, actresses, in an era when plays tended to list two—occasionally three—substantial roles for women" (113).

12. Forty-four years later, the naval officer's account of his *Trip to Spain* (1704) makes no mention of Spanish New World atrocities; indeed, it is palpably absent. Instead, it is almost exclusively an attack on the "ridiculousness" of Spanish material culture. And the difference is startling: on page after page, one finds descriptions of Spanish men's cloaks and cuffs, ribbons and doublets, sleeves and swords but not a word about their New World excesses. The author locates his ridicule in material culture, believing, like Wycherley's Don Diego and Monsieur Parris, that fashion alone can signify essential difference. Gomez then—rather than being strangely out of place in a world saturated with questions of fashion and gender (a world that has moved out of that old, aristocratic, hypermasculine role)—is the focus of the most intense ideological work performed in the drama.

4. Discursive Identities: Actresses on and off the Restoration Stage

1. Roberts adds that the boxes were there "for display, for luxury, or private company; the galleries for economy and, occasionally, business; and the pit for society and the spectacle of the stage and its most eminent patrons." Moreover, he claims that most women did not feel the need for a male escort, nor did they fear that theater-going would damage their reputations (94). For additional discussion of the Restoration audience, see Allardyce Nicholl, *A History of English Drama,* vol. 1; Emmett Avery, "The Restoration Audience"; Harold Love, "The Myth of the Restoration Audience" and "Who Were the Restoration Audience?"; and Ann Thompson, "Women/'Women' and the Stage."

2. Ros Ballaster argues a slightly different point concerning the possible "confusion" of playwright, prostitute, and actress:

> Ironically the performance of their plays with women acting female parts seems to have forced a constraint on women playwrights that the aristocratic women writers of "closet" drama rarely had to confront; they explore in print the question of their "difference" from two proximate professions for women, that of the actress and that of the

prostitute. In all three professions women display their talent for material profit. While the presence of the female body on stage might be understood as a useful analogy for the woman playwright, in fact, who more often sought to distinguish her own image from that of the actress. (269)

3. I draw attention again to Laura Rosenthal's most insightful article "Counterfeit Scrubbado" and its refutation of the claim that actresses were actually engaged in prostitution. Professor Rosenthal's own argument is compelling—that "the actress-as-whore identitification performs the cultural work of attempting to maintain shifting and unstable distinctions between marriageable and unmarriageable women for the class of men who dominated the theater audience" (4). I fully agree with this analysis and provide, as my own argument, a claim that the essentializing discourses, fixated on the sexual activities of the women players—not just the "the actress-as-whore identification"—generally served the larger cultural function of maintaining an essentialized, and thus exclusive, aristocratic-class status quo.

4. For the best discussion of the problems encountered and presented by the first actresses to take the British stage, see Elizabeth Howe's incomparable *First English Actresses*. For other enlightening treatments, see also Kristina Straub's *Sexual Suspects*, Deborah Payne's "'And Poets Shall by Patron-Princes Live,'" and Peter Holland's *Ornament of Action*.

5. I very much take Deborah Payne's point when she argues that Gould, et al., probably do not represent widespread and unvarying cultural norms and that attributing too great a power to his and others' "ravings" (as she rightly calls Gould's attacks) is a mistake. Payne's point that Elizabeth Barry, in conjunction with Betterton, managed to ruin Gould is indisputable evidence of the vulnerability of his position. Payne's overarching argument is also a powerful one: "perspectivism and professionalism spawn a complex dynamic whereby perfectly ordinary women become simultaneously the object of collective attention and the practitioner of an 'art,' a doubly powerful yet circumscribed position. The fascination with the lives and skills of actresses can be situated at the intersection of civic prominence, virtuoso display, and professional anxiety" (35). I maintain, however, that part of the phenomenon of late-seventeenth-century celebrity depends on what Payne has called "gossip," a discourse that she rightly distinguishes from commodification, and the new printed extratheatrical discourse that inevitably accompanied the performances of Restoration actresses, a discourse more interested in the private activities of women's bodies than in those of men's bodies.

6. Catherine Gallagher described the process clearly: "If prostitution, then, was often imagined as acting, to unmask an actress as a prostitute was simply to reveal her as an actress. What was essential to both arts, indeed what collapsed them into one, was the successful maintenance of a gap between self-representation and the 'real' woman" (*Nobody's Story* 30).

7. In his essay "'As If (She) Were Made On Purpose,'" Thomas A. King offers a powerful argument about actresses' "two bodies," when he writes that the art of acting for Restoration women "was the ability to present *both* bodies [the body of the character and that of the "actress"] to their audiences, [to present] any tension between the two underlying

and reinforcing the conflicts of the dramatic text" (82). My argument suggests that actresses were accompanied by an additional body, the body of extratheatrical discourse alive in the world.

8. Katharine Maus writes with insight about the close relationship between accusations of sexual misconduct and what she calls "the celebrity industry": "Surely the lucrativeness of this industry rests upon its claim to represent a 'private' and therefore more authentic life presumed to reside behind the glittering surface of the celebrity lifestyle. At the same time the account of celebrity inwardness is endlessly revisable, and thus remarketable, because few of the consumers of such truths have any way of verifying them" (*Inwardness* 214).

9. Behn's *Rover; or, The Banish'd Cavaliers* and *The Emperor of the Moon* were her most popular plays, and productions of each continued consistently throughout both the Restoration and the eighteenth century.

10. In "'Once a Whore and Ever'?" Nancy Copeland argues that an initial difference between Angellica Bianca's and Hellena's advertisement of themselves is that Hellena's blazoning of herself begins as private, even though Willmore finally takes possession of her beauty in his own blazon, and thus Hellena loses control of the public representation of herself—very like the Restoration actresses who played her.

11. See also Jocelyn Powell's *Restoration Theater Production*, especially chapter 3, "Music and Spectacle," for a more detailed description of the modified Restoration playhouses that provided the possibility for new, more spectacular productions.

12. Catherine Gallagher puts it in succinct terms: "Everyone knows that Aphra Behn, England's first professional female author, was a colossal and enduring embarrassment to the generations of women who followed her into the literary marketplace" ("Who Was That?" 23). There is no evidence that Manley ever saw the *Rover; or, The Banish'd Cavaliers,* which premiered in 1677 (with Barry playing the part of Hellena) and which was again performed in 1680, in 1685 (twice), in 1687, and in 1690. However, *The London Stage* does suggest that the play might have been revived in 1696 (the same year that *The Royal Mischief* premiered), for it was reprinted again that year. In any event, Manley was aware that she was writing in the same tradition (and under the same constraints) as Behn.

13. *The Royal Mischief* premiered in April 1696, after the division of the playhouses and during the first year of rather fierce competition between them. A number of familiar plays were produced that season, some of the most important are the following: Southerne's *Oroonoko;* Trotter's *Agnes de Castro;* Banks's *Cyrus the Great;* Cibber's *Love's Last Shift;* Behn's *Younger Brother;* Manley's own *Lost Lover;* Dryden and Howard's *Indian Queen;* Pix's *Ibrahim, the Thirteenth Emperour* and *Spanish Wives.*

14. Lady Mary carried copies of *The Embassy Letters* with her throughout her lifetime, very likely revising and embellishing her descriptions of the lives of Turkish women for the last forty years she herself lived. For more on these letters and all of Lady Mary's extraordinary correspondence, see my *Lady Mary Wortley Montagu and the Eighteenth-Century Familiar Letter.*

15. Barry and Bracegirdle acted together not only in this play but also in Pix's *Adventures in Madrid* and Manley's *Almyna,* which is examined in chapter 5, "Monstrous Identities." The other parts in the first production of *The*

Royal Mischief included these: The vizier Osman was played by Thomas Betterton; the vizier's wife, Selima, by Mrs. Bowman; Acmet, the eunuch, by Mr. Freeman; and the evil Ismael by Mr. Hudson.

16. Manley used *The Travels of Sir John Chardin Into Persia and the East Indies* as her source. Chardin's original contains many of the gruesome incidents Manley retains: the princess lives with her nephew who sends his legitimate wife back to her family home with her nose, ears, and hands cut off (because, he claims, she engaged in an adultrous affair with the vizier, who is himself shot alive out of a canon). The nephew in Chardin's account is bloodthirstier, for he racks servants, poisons the sons of his first wife, and has his own brother's eyes gouged out. For a truly wonderful reading of the play as satire, see Melinda Alliker Rabb's "Angry Beauties": "Manley's *Royal Mischief* is a satirical revision of tragedy and heroism, a female mock-heroic, limited by its historical context and framed without benefit of feminist theory" (142).

17. For claims that "the logic of Western thought is too rooted in the visual," see Evelyn Fox Keller and Christine R. Grontkowski's "The Mind's Eye," where the authors trace such logic to Cartesian theory that severs the mind from the body—a division that safeguards knowledge (which is linked to seeing) from a desire that is intimately associated with both the body and the female.

18. The principle of identification is so strong, according to Roger Scruton, that in portraiture, "representation and denotation are the same relation. . . . Denotation is the special case of reference exemplified by proper names and portraits—that case where a symbol labels an individual" (qtd. in Brilliant 26).

19. Peter Brooks offers up an interesting feature of this paradox:

    If the male body in patriarchy becomes the norm, the standard against which one measures otherness—and thus creates the enigma of woman—one might expect the male body to be more openly displayed and discussed. But a moment's reflection allows us to see that the paradox is merely apparent. Precisely because it is the norm, the male body is veiled from inquiry, taken as the agent and not the object of knowing. (15)

20. Ernst Kris and Otto Kurz have investigated the connection between visual images and magic. They write of anecdotes concerning people who fall in love with representations:

    Here we come upon the most common practice associated with the equation of picture and depicted, namely, the belief in magic, especially effigy magic—the belief that "a man's soul resides in his image, that those who possess this image also hold power over that person," . . . The shadow whose outline is traced is deemed to be part of the person himself. This idea is reminiscent of a common notion of magical thought, according to which possession of a part of, or the paring from, a person's body lend one power over him. (*Legend, Myth, and Magic* 73, 74)

    For a criticism of Kris and Kurz's arguments, see David Freedberg's *The Power of Images,* especially pp. 201–5.

21. Citing examples from modern films that feature women who actively

look, Mary Ann Doane writes, "There is always a certain excessiveness, a difficulty associated with women who appropriate the gaze, who insist upon looking. . . . [they are] constructed as the site of an excessive and dangerous desire" (140). The over-possessiveness and excessive desire of the female protagonist of *Leave Her to Heaven* (1945), a woman—like Princess Homais—revealed to be the murderous epitome of evil, "are signaled from the very beginning of the film by her intense and sustained stare at the major male character" (140). Such women are always punished, Doane concludes, because "the woman as *subject* [emphasis mine] of the gaze is clearly an impossible sign" (141). For additional discussions of women spectators, the female gaze, and its rewards and punishments, see "The Spectatrix," a 1990 special issue of *Camera Obscura;* Constance Penley's *Feminism and Film Theory;* and Tania Modeleski's *The Women Who Knew Too Much.* For a powerful and persuasive reading of the inadequacies of feminist film theory when applied to the theater, see Deborah Payne's "Reified Object or Emerging Professional."

22. A fascinating analysis of a related phenomenon—that of "the spectatrix" in the Restoration theater, herself a woman who gazes and is gazed upon—can be found in Laura Rosenthal's "Reading Masks." Her discussion of the mask, as a garment that covers the area around the eye but not the eye itself and is thus emblematic, is particularly compelling.

23. Christopher Pye provides a particularly provocative explanation for the narcissism present in spectatorship. He suggests in his reading of the sovereign on the frontispiece of the first edition of *Leviathan* that "the spectacular figure enables us to complete a fantasy of absolute visibility, of sight seeing itself. Through the doubled gaze, we are able to see in the eye that looks directly at us, not just a secondary reflection of our eye, but the fully distinct and objective embodiment of our sight. In a sense we are made the spectators to our own powerful vision" (103). For more on aristocratic spectacle, see Paul Hammond's "The King's Two Bodies."

24. In this context, Jocelyn Powell's remarks about the artificiality of the Restoration stage take on new meaning:

> The actors appeared in front of the painted scenes, their disjunction from them undercutting the illusion of the stage as the writer's wit undercut the heroics of their plots. It is significant that when Brecht adapted *The Recruiting Officer,* he employed the same kind of disjunction for his own purposes, sharpening the artificiality of the action to point [to] the question it raises by the juxtaposition of flesh and blood actors with a two-dimensional, painted scene. (60)

25. For additional discussion of the sexualization of the actresses, see Kristina Straub's *Sexual Suspects.* For contemporary accounts of the players, see Anthony Aston's *A Brief Supplement to Colley Cibber, Esq.;* Betterton's *History of the English Stage;* Thomas Brown's *Works;* Colley Cibber's *Apology;* John Downes's *Roscius Anglicanus;* and Charles Gildon's *Life of Mr. Thomas Betterton.* For collections of contemporary attacks on the players, see Montagu Summers's *Restoration Theatre* and J. H. Wilson's *Court Satires of the Restoration.* For a look at the ways two mid-eighteenth-century actresses—Charke and Fenton—were represented, see Cheryl Wanko's "The Eighteenth-Century Actress and the Construction of Gender."

26. For a fascinating discussion of the ways that "sovereignty is an irreducibly theatrical phenomenon" (86) and the ways a monarch comes to possess an awesome and always visible presence, see Christopher Pye's "Sovereign."

27. Kristina Straub argues that an actress's marrying respectably was the exception, rather than the rule (155); yet it is the public perception—the persistence of a discourse connecting actresses with aristocrats—that forms the focus of my concern.

28. Wilson cites an even more fascinating incident of the blurred lines between player and aristocrat in an anecdote concerning Kynaston's impersonation of Sir Charles Sedley:

    > When Edward Kynaston, who closely resembled Sir Charles ("a handsome plump middle sized man") had the effrontery not only to get "some laced cloathes made exactly after a suit Sir Charles wore" but to appear so dressed on the stage, Sedley was annoyed and promptly hired "two or three" bullies to chastise the player. The bravos accosted Kynaston in St. James's Park, "pretending to take him for Sir Charles," picked a quarrel with him, and beat him so savagely that he was forced to take to his bed. (*All the King's Ladies* 29)

    Sir Charles, however, refused to sympathize with Kynaston, claiming his own reputation had suffered more than "Kynaston's bones." (*All the King's Ladies* 29)

29. When Pepys describes Charles II's entry into London, according to Paul Hammond, he says nothing of the significance of the event; he reports only spectacle: using the word "show" five times, Pepys is primarily interested in what people wore: "So glorious was the show with gold and silver, that we were not able to look at it—our eyes at last being so much overcome with it." Hammond concludes, "Evidently, the conspicuous display of wealth was itself an effective demonstration of the power of the new monarchy; it dazzled, and that was enough" (20).

30. Dr. Doran writes of one such incident involving Barry and the wife of James II: "Mary of Modena testified her admiration by bestowing on the mimic queen [Barry] the wedding-dress Mary herself had worn when she was united to James II, and the queen of the hour represented the Elizabeth, with which enthusiastic crowds became so much more familiar than they were with the Elizabeth of history" (53).

31. The gender-based, not class-based, form of this display of difference occurs in female cross-dressing. As Pat Rogers, Kristina Straub, and others have pointed out, an actress's failure to pass herself off as a man was the source of pleasure for eighteenth-century audiences; it was the revelation of her *essential* femaleness that relieved the anxiety. Laura Mandell puts it this way: "The cross-dressed woman on stage who cannot be manly proves the rule that women are not like men, and it was this reinforcement of the law that gave audiences such pleasure" (77).

32. Erika Fischer-Lichte writes that "the particular mode of [the actor's presentation of the body] onstage may contribute to this ongoing process by representing and propagating new models of self-presence and self-presentation for audience imitation" (23). For a more detailed discussion of the relationship between stage representations and larger cultural self-definitions, see "Theatre and the Civilizing Process."

33. Shadwell's *Virtuoso* presents another such "confusion of women" in a moment when Sir Samuel remarks to Hazard, "These are very angry ladies, Hazard. Just now we met two were very kind to us. Pretty rogues, they had delicate hands, arms, and necks, and they were women of quality, I'm sure by their linen." To this naive and unworldly view of the material performability of Quality, Hazard replies, "That's no rule, for whores wear as good linen as honest women. Fine clothes and good linen are the working tools of their trade" (5.4.28–32).

34. A later eighteenth-century incident, drawn from Thomas Davies's accounts and concerning Anne Oldfield, is equally telling in this regard: "Notwithstanding these [her sexual liaisons with Maynwaring and Churchill] were publicly known, [Oldfield] was invited to the houses of women in fashion, as much distinguished for unblemished character as elevated rank" (*Dramatic Miscellanies* 2.434).

5. Monstrous Identities: Excess, Sexual Assault, and Subjectivity

1. Ambroise Paré's *Des monstres et prodiges* was originally published in 1573 and was frequently reprinted thereafter.

2. For a skeptical reading of Park and Daston's thesis about this movement from prodigy to pathology, see Stephen Pender's "'No Monsters at the Resurrection.'" For other readings of eighteenth-century monsters, see James Aubry's "Revising the Monstrous" and Judith Hawley's "Margins and Monstrosity."

3. Park and Daston offer the compelling argument that monsters are valuable because they demonstrate the ways that nature's aberrations reveal its regularities. Seventeenth-century natural philosophers believed that "the most penetrating insights into the inner workings of nature were to be gleaned from the close study of anomalies"; this belief directed seventeenth-century experiments towards singular phenomena (45). By the eighteenth century, monsters provided biologists "clarifying counter examples to normal embryological development," so that by the end of the century "the canon of prodigies [had] been dissolved . . . Nature's activity was regular and monolithic, and her ordinary workmanship was prized above her extraordinary productions" (53). Thus by the mid-eighteenth century, "an appetite for the marvellous had become, as Hume declared, the hallmark of the 'ignorant and barbarous,' antithetical to the study of nature as conducted by the man of 'good-sense, education and learning'" (54).

4. In a play set in Madrid and filled with excessive characters (including a new character—La Nuche, a Spanish courtesan, played by Elizabeth Barry—as well as old characters familiar from the first part, such as Ned Blunt and Willmore, the Rover himself), the "monsters" are unique. The play premiered in January 1681; other plays of note produced that season include Dryden's *Spanish Fryar,* Lee's *Lucius Junius Brutus,* Tate's *Tyrant of Sicily* and *King Lear,* and Otway's *Soldier's Fortune.*

5. It would appear from clues in the text that the Giant was "composed" of two players, one on the shoulders of another. For instance, later in this scene and during what must have been a very funny moment, Smith, playing the part of Willmore, invites Hunt, playing part of the giant, to pass through a door too small; the Giant claims that, "by way of Inchantment,"

"she" can pass through such a too-small opening, and the stage directions read this way: "Hunt being all Doublet, leaps off from another Man who is all in Britches, and goes out, Britches follows stalking." I assume that the part of the Dwarf was played by a child, as was the case later in the eighteenth century.

6. Susan Owen argues that the whole play is an unusual instance of Behn's "anatomization of libertinism": "The function of 'these Lady Monsters' is to show the monstrousness of libertinism itself; its object is so irrelevant that it can even be a freak (in Restoration terms), so long as there is the spice of novelty. In Act V, the poor giant is pushed and pulled to and fro by the various men as if she were literally an object" ("Sexual Politics" 26, 21).

7. Pearson also argues that the monsters make political points about Europe during the Interregnum. When Willmore says, "better to be Master of a Monster, than Slave to a damn'd Commonwealth," Cromwellian rule becomes monstrous and, I suspect Behn would argue, as large as the giant in its ambitions and as small as the dwarf in its talents ("Slave Princes" 223).

8. This is quite a change from the drama presented just a few years before. We need only remember Dryden's *Aboyna* or Davenant's *Cruelty of the Spaniards in Peru* to remember that the Spanish were likely to be portrayed as being loathsome and vile.

9. *The Woman-Captain* probably premiered in September 1679, during the same season that saw the productions of Behn's *Young King; Rover; or, The Banish'd Cavaliers; Feign'd Curtizans;* and *Revenge;* D'Urfey's *Virtuous Wife;* Etherege's *She Would if She Could* and *Man of Mode;* the premieres of Otway's *Orphan;* and Settle's *Female Prelate.*

10. For a very fine reading on the uses of force in the play, see John P. Zomchick's "Force, Contract, and Power in *The Woman-Captain.*"

11. The play was produced in May 1676 by the Duke's Company and so could have featured Mrs. Barry and Mrs. Bracegirdle. All we do know for certain is that Underhill and Leigh, two of the most famous comedians, played Sir Formal and Sir Samuel. Other plays produced during that season include the premiere of Otway's *Alcibiades,* Dryden's *Aureng-Zebe,* and Etherege's *Man of Mode,* Behn's *Abdelazer,* and Webster's *Duchess of Malfy.*

12. Perhaps Susan Staves's remarks about attempted rapes are relevant here: "Attempt is simultaneously a natural topos of comedy and a jurisprudentially difficult idea. Unsuccessful attempts are intrinsically comic because villains who huff and puff with all their might and main but only give themselves coughing fits and never actually blow the house down are silly villains who do no real harm" ("Fielding and the Comedy of Attempted Rape" 87).

13. In some ways, this position echoes the admittedly more extreme position of Catherine MacKinnon, who has written the following:

> If sexuality is central to women's definition and forced sex is central to sexuality, rape is indigenous, not exceptional, to women's social condition. In feminist analysis, a rape is not an isolated event or moral transgression or individual interchange gone wrong but an act of terrorism and torture within a systemic context of group subjection, like lynching. The fact that the state calls rape a crime opens an inquiry

into the state's treatment of rape as an index to its stance on the status of the sexes. (42)

14. It is no accident that Anne Bracegirdle figures prominently in so many scenes of sexual assault. See chapter 3 for an extended reading of the ways that the focus of the discourse on the supposedly private aspects of the actresses' lives had an influence on the roles they played and how they played them.

15. Kristina Straub and Jean Marsden both offer compelling arguments of this kind. Straub claims that the discourse of rape surrounding eighteenth-century actresses was an attempt to exclude the idea of feminine control from the spectacle of feminine desire: "Rape attempts to subject a 'feminine' desire to the domination of a 'masculine' desire" (104), but she concludes that the metaphor of rape in its very excessiveness points to the failure of that exclusion: "Representations of the actress's desire suggest, however, that this subjection is incomplete; the actress's desire exceeds the models for feminine sexuality implicit in the discourses of prostitution, domesticity, and professionalism" (104). Marsden describes scenes of rape as "fictions designed as erotic spectacle for an audience that is tacitly assumed to be male" (185–86), and she concludes that the real-world result of such spectacle is the arousal of the desire of the (male) members of the audience:

> As represented on stage, the motivation for the rape is blatantly, even crudely sexual, and to emphasize the erotic potential of the rape itself, the rapist's desire is explicitly stated. Coupled with the physical display of the actress, these descriptions, often expressed at length and in near-pornographic detail, operate to arouse the audience's desire. (187)

16. First performed in June 1675 but showing up again in 1676 and 1697, this eponymous character had a long stage history. It is generally agreed that the first real Don Juan is Tirso de Molina's *El burlador de Sevilla y convidado de piedra* (published 1630), followed by Moliere's *Dom Juan ou le festin de pierre* (published 1665). For an examination of the four-hundred-year history of the various Don Juan stories, see J. Douglas Canfield's "The Classical Treatment of Don Juan in Tirso, Moliere, and Mozart." The first London production was put on by the Duke's Company and thus Barry and Bracegirdle could have taken the parts of Maria and Leonora. Other plays of note produced during this season include Shakespeare's *Tempest, Hamlet, Macbeth,* and *Othello;* Dryden's *Indian Emperour;* Villiers's *Rehearsal;* the premiere of Wycherley's *Country Wife;* Crowne's *Calisto;* and Lee's *Sophonisba.*

17. Scholars still attempt, in the language of modern literary criticism, to find an explanation for the "comedy" of sexual assault and "ridiculousness" of criminal behaviors: Don John as well as Antonio and Lopez are "but caricatures intentionally exaggerated, made grotesque and wildly comic," according to Anthony Kaufman, who goes on to argue that "the very extravagance of [Don John's] career insures that the play is finally comic. The very rapidity and the mechanical repetition of violent crime distances us from the action and the result is laughter" ("Shadow" 248). The "grotesque fantasy" of *The Libertine* Kaufman ultimately judges a failure because Shadwell turns Don John into a "heroic" figure at the end: "[P]erhaps it is the nature of the myth, with its subtle invitation to identify with peer aggression, and sexuality, that led Shadwell to belie his satiric conception of Don John in favor of an almost romantic figure," an appeal

that is ultimately "to the subconscious self—to the dream of power and the perfect freedom to act out aggression" (249–50). Refusing to fit into any tidy generic categories, the play also invites modern audiences to laugh at these behaviors we find utterly repellent. Susan Owen refuses the invitation and argues that "disgust at the promiscuity and the venereal disease which lurks beneath the facade of nobility" is the attitude that has "authorial sanction" in *The Libertine* (177), and she concludes that "hypocrisy, bad faith, double standards, predatoriness, and sexism are at the heart of libertinism" (*Restoration* 159).

18. Staves argues that, through the course of the century, these questions were worked out in such a way that notions about fundamental human nature changed: by the end of the seventeenth century, it was decided that "Man was not essentially a creature of lust and vengeance, but a tranquil social animal animated by benevolence. The nature by which he is to order his behavior is not a transcendent and hierarchical nature of abstract forms, but an immanent nature of the passions and sensations familiar to himself within himself" (*Players' Scepters* 302).

19. Richard Braverman has argued that the development of the libertine can be divided into three distinct phases. In the first, which runs through the early 1670s, the libertine appears "as a broadly comic figure who breathes new life into a society recently freed from the Puritan yoke" and who behaves according to an "extravagant" code of manners. In the mid-1670s extravagance turned into cynicism as the Cavalier transformed into "the predatory rake-hero who exploits wit and sexual presence at the expense of comic potential." In a comeback made in the 1690s, the libertine showed signs of being a changed man, "particularly in the hands of Whiggish revisionists who in due course transformed him into an *honnête homme* as they reconfigured a new, postrevolutionary erotics of power" (142–43). Shadwell's *Libertine* would then be a product of the cynical 1670s, and its protagonist the "predatory rake-hero" who, I would like to argue, could be said to function as a monster of prohibition. For another useful treatment of the libertine, see James G. Turner's "The Properties of Libertinism."

20. Barbara Benedict offers up a provocative analysis of the 1790s case of Renwick Williams, a man found guilty of a series of violent attacks against women—he stabbed women in their lower bodies—and thus was labeled "The Monster" in the popular press. Benedict argues that, in its unregulated sexual hostility, "this monstrosity seemed very like masculinity itself. . . . This monstrosity usurps civilized sexual relations, exposing men as predators" (129–31).

21. Steintrager also argues that

In addition, moral monstrosity appears against the background of eighteenth-century sensationalism and its concerns: the eyes interface directly with affects. Objectivity, that is, emotional indifference to the spectacle of suffering, rather than enjoyment or pity, is not an option—or rather, it is an option that will be increasingly foreclosed as the century develops. (115)

22. In Shadwell's *Woman-Captain,* Sir Humphrey and his two profligate friends, Bellamy and Wildman, indulge a different, but equally excessive appetite: they love food and participate in their own veritable hymns to

the pleasure of culinary delights, excessive and monstrous appetites that
blot out all other desires:

> *Sir Humphrey:* My chief Cook has a Book drawn up by these Gentle-
> men and my self. Read and be learned.—There you shall find what is
> in season still—the youngest Meat always most nourishing.—The new
> faln Lamb, The tender Kid, and young fat Pigs. Veals fed with Milk,
> Whitebread, and new-laid Eggs, with young fat Beefs, and smallest
> Forrest Mutton, fat Bucks for Summer, Barren Does for Winter.
> *Wildman:* Fawns out of their Dams Bellies ript, Gelt Goats, Bruis'd
> Venison, Sucking Rabbits, Leverets, Dousets, White Haws, Velvet Head
> and Ears, Shoulders of Venison in the Kell with blood.

(1.114)

This list continues beyond even this point, to be followed throughout the
play by other such lists of luxurious items—all to excess. And as John P.
Zomchick has argued, when the bawd arrives to offer the gentlemen
"three Maidenheads," these become commodities to be added to the list
of consumer goods (178).

23. A number of scholars argue that male sexual excess in the eighteenth century was, paradoxically by modern standards, described as "effeminate"—
that is, like women generally, the effeminate man acted on his excessive
emotions. But Todd C. Parker has countered that this effeminacy ultimately became the sign of superior masculinity in the seventeenth century (9), while Thomas A. King provides this qualification: "The behaviors
characterizing 'effeminacy' became 'privacy,' while the spectacularity or
publicness of the aristocratic body became 'effeminacy' and 'queerness.' . . .
This understanding of effeminacy as an exercise of selfhood lacking public utility provided the basis for the seventeenth-century critique of the
courtly aristocracy. The dependence of sovereign and court power on
spectacularity and the conspicuous circulation and consumption of commodities and labor became 'effeminate' against the development of the
utilitarian, rationalist, and critical looks enabling the explosion of techno-
logical and bureaucratic power" ("Displacing Masculinity" 120, 122). See
Todd C. Parker, *Sexing the Text,* and Thomas A. King, "Displacing Masculinity." Deutsch and Nussbaum also cite the early modern descriptions of
excess in this context: For men, "deformity is often associated with over-
sexed effeminacy or impotence. Since the female condition would seem to
be aligned with natural defect, men fear that 'defect' is an emasculating
contradiction to the empowering and mutually constitutive character
traits of aesthetic taste and civic humanism" (12).

24. In an interesting twist, this Don John monster performs in a fashion contrary to the monster's norm. Jeffrey Cohen argues that "As a vehicle of
prohibition, the monster most often arises to enforce the laws of exogamy,
both the incest taboo (which establishes a traffic in women by mandating
that they marry outside their families) and the decrees against interracial
sexual mingling (which limit the parameters of that traffic by policing
the boundaries of culture usually in the service of some notion of group
'purity')" ("Monster Culture" 15). Here, Don John is happier preying on
his own family members and enforcing the enactment of taboos, a reflection of the degree of his monstrousness.

25. Wheatley also invokes Coleridge's response to Shadwell to explain the drama: Coleridge wrote, "nothing of it belongs to the real world," a sentiment echoed by Wheatley himself, "Don John is an abstraction of pure materialism," a figure who offers to a Restoration audience a moral lesson about how "materialism bars him from virtue because the only worthy ends available to the materialist are the satisfaction of appetites" (90). Laura Brown will argue that the play is "an exaggeration of the Don Juan story so outrageous as to be almost ridiculous but so vehement as to constitute a clear moralistic condemnation of the reigning comic protagonists. . . . *The Libertine* presents sexual license as a violent attack by the upper class upon the lower, morally equivalent to and accompanied by the most heinous and bloody crimes, and properly subject to the worst of metaphysical punishments" (105–6).

26. As Pearson notes, a raped woman was not allowed to survive; instead she might commit suicide or be murdered or just fade away (*Prostituted Muse* 98). But the rape plot could offer a more sinister message: when comedy, Pearson argues, assumes that women say no when they actually mean yes and when both men and women accordingly end up cynical about the very possibility of rape, it is more dangerously assumed that "no woman need suffer rape: she can always choose to die instead, so that if she survives she must be guilty of 'so vile, so base a Crime'" (96). She might also participate in "masochistic self-abasement" (98). For information on actual eighteenth-century rape laws and rape statistics, see Antony E. Simpson's "Vulnerability and the Age of Female Consent" and Lynn A. Higgins and Brenda R. Silver's *Rape and Representation*. For detailed discussions of plays containing rapes or attempted rapes, see Pearson's *Prostituted Muse,* Howe's *First English Actresses* and Susan Owen's "'He that Should Guard My Virtue Has Betrayed It.'"

27. Brady's *Rape* was first produced in 1692 but was subsequently "updated" for a 1730 production that contains a host of fascinating changes. The most important are the changes in time and geography: rather than Vandals and Goths, the 1730 version features the Spanish and Portuguese. Whereas there are innumerable references to ravishment and even the use of the word "rape" in the 1692 version, the 1730 production contains no such "coarse" language: *ravish* becomes *dishonor; lustful* becomes *hateful;* and most important, the use of the word *rape* in 1692 becomes *crime* in 1730. The very graphic scenes describing the rape are simply excised in the later version; the extended stage directions concerning Eurione's disordered state after the rape become the curt, "Emilia [Eurione] discover'd bound" (41). Both versions contain Eurione's self-description after the rape as "contagious," and both contain her line: "And all chaste hand will blister that but touch me" (41). And most tellingly, the cross-dressed woman remains in the later version, but the cross-dressed man (even a young one) is apparently too much for later, finer sensibilities to bear. Other plays produced during the initial 1692 season include Behn's *Emperor of the Moon;* Dryden's *Indian Emperour;* Otway's *Orphan;* and Settle's *Fairy Queen.*

28. Deborah Burks makes the following distinctions:

> Rape, which seems to be derived from the Latin, *rapere,* of which *raptus* is also a form, meant in English "the act of taking anything by

force[, the] violent seizure (of goods), robbery" *(OED)*. Ravishment, from the French, *ravissement,* a form of the verb *ravir,* may derive from the same Latin root as *rape.* Drawing on the idea of transportation, both "rape" (rapture) and "ravishment" develop the additional meaning, "to transport with delight." The conjunction of meanings embedded in these words corresponds to an ambivalence about the crime: it was simultaneously understood to be a violent theft and a sexual dalliance. The first was certainly reprehensible; the second might be open to interpretation. (769)

29. Genselaric's remarks suggest that he thinks Eurione finds his assault a "pleasing rape," a phrase Duane Coltharp has coined; he argues that what is at stake in the notion of a "pleasing rape" and in the fictions of libertinism in general is "civilization, repression, and their attendant discontents," and that Almanzor and other heroes of heroic drama repeat the same characteristic libertine themes: "primitive freedom from civic belonging, erotic struggle, and the consequent patriarchal impotence" (17, 24).

30. Thomas DiPiero has argued that a profound connection between libertine violence and the obliteration of subjectivity exists:

> The libertine search for pleasure can properly be described as an inscription or writing of violence performed not just on the victim's body but on her entire subjectivity. . . . The libertines strive, in fact, to attain a state of phallic *jouissance* predicated on the obliteration of subjectivity. . . . Libertine pleasure derives in part from the annihilation of victims' subjectivity, but it seems to require the demolition of libertine subjectivity as well. (255–56)

As we see above, the very opposite occurs in these Restoration dramas, where acts of violence precipitate a short-lived move into traumatized subjectivity.

31. Settle's *Female Prelate* (1680) features a female monster, Pope Joan, who uses sexual violence to overstep social, political, and religious boundaries, and the play features a double-rape plot, as Joan and her compatriot Lorenzo each employ a bed trick to secure sexual relations with the Duke and Duchess of Saxony respectively. The play provides interesting contrasts to those above. After the Duke is assaulted, he wonders whether he has been turned into "some incarnate Devil, doom'd to walk / Deaths burning plains" (52). Tainted by evil, he does not question, as Eurione did, whether his body has been invaded or breached but whether his fundamental nature has been transformed into evil incarnate. More important, unlike Eurione, he can still imagine himself as a sexual creature—it is just that now his partners are evil spirits of the night. Most important, again unlike Eurione, he does not experience himself as fragmented or shattered. He maintains his integrity, albeit in tainted form, because his violation was not the result of force or violence; he was deceived into acting on his own, albeit misdirected, desires. When he discovers that his beloved Angeline has been similarly tricked, his reaction is very different: a wave of rage accompanied by a lament for *his* loss. But in some respects, Saxony has actually been violated, and thus to his credit, he opens his arms and invites his raped beloved into his embrace the first time he sees her, even though he describes her as "poor ravisht sweetness" (62). Angeline herself responds to being assaulted with a truly painful set of images: she produces

a description of the monstrous raped woman as all wounds and breaches: "Oh my vast Wounds! there's a wide breach of ruine / In this one breast, will let in death enough / To break both hearts" (62–63).

32. *Ibrahim, the Thirteenth Emperour* premiered in May 1696 (a month after the premiere of Manley's *Royal Mischief*) after the division of the playhouses and during the first year of rather fierce competition between them. A number of familiar plays were produced that season, some of the most important are the following: Southerne's *Oroonoko;* Trotter's *Agnes de Castro;* Banks's *Cyrus the Great;* Cibber's *Love's Last Shift;* Behn's *Younger Brother;* Manley's own *Lost Lover;* Dryden and Howard's *Indian Queen;* and Pix's own *Spanish Wives.*

33. Since this play was first produced by Rich's company, neither Mrs. Barry nor Mrs. Bracegirdle would have acted in it. The title page shows that Mrs. Rogers took the part of Morena.

34. Another important question of luxury, linked to the effeminization of a powerful man, occurs in Shadwell's *Woman-Captain.* There, Sir Humphrey, who has just come into his inheritance, is squandering it on food and other sensual delights, the kind of complaint usually lodged against women; as we know, eighteenth-century discourse often described women as too fond of luxury, especially as it was linked with lust and lasciviousness. Shadwell's understanding of the term is an older one, untainted by the changes brought about by a modern mercantile economy; Beth Kowaleski-Wallace nicely summarizes the difference: "luxury as lasciviousness slowly disburdens itself [during the eighteenth century] from the moralistic inclination that had associated it with the sinful indulgence of the body" (76). Sir Humphrey's excessive love of luxury is of this older kind but still locates him, status and all, outside of the masculine norms: he says, "what e'r the Globe afford I'll have to satisfie my Luxury" (21).

35. Ros Ballaster argues that the contrast between Sheker Para's "duplicitous agency" and Morena's "passive valour" displays that fact that "women's political agency or success in the heroic tragedy by women is more often than not achieved *at the expense of* their opposite, the virtuous woman. To be political agents in the drama, female characters in Restoration dramas by women are required to play with and manipulate the ideologies of femininity that constrain them, rather than eschew them completely" (286–87).

36. Copp Elia Kahn cites Ellen Rooney's remarks about female resistance and its place in the way rape is read:

> the *absence of feminine desire* in rape is read as simple (unequivocal) passivity. . . . Because the "object" of rape is finally helpless, her defeat is read as passivity, and her passivity is totalized. As a consequence, her *resistance* (her *activity*) *goes unread.* Ironically, it is this activity—the resistance of the victim—that makes rape rape. (qtd. in Kahn 154)

37. Elizabeth Howe provides a fascinating speculation:

> Restoration audiences would, of course, be more accustomed to spectacles of naked women suffering violence because of public floggings and pillories. It has been suggested that such experiences, combined with "inattention and dim lights," must have made blood-covered

heroines seem far less shocking than they seem when abstracted by the modern reader. (43)

38. Laura Mandell offers up a compelling psychoanaytic reading of scapegoating, rape and female subjectivity:

    A woman who is a flat character will not serve as an effective scapegoat. In she-tragedies, being raped endows the female figure with a sense of personhood because a raped woman is someone who had an invisible intention made visible in its violation, who has an inner volition differing from outer actions, and therefore who is a person with psychological depth. . . . Self-murder makes visible that she did not consent to rape, and thus that her mental intention differed from her (forced) sexual. (41)

39. Reading Shakespeare's story of Lucrece, Copp Elia Kahn has argued that rape functioned in that story to produce a powerful political "rape authorized revenge; revenge comprises revolution; revolution establishes legitimate government" (141). Linked to the political is the problem of subjectivity, as unified and powerless or as fragmented: "In contrast to Tarquin, Lucrece . . . is superbly unified; all that she says and does coheres around her chastity, and she dies in order to purify and reassert it. It is also this unity, however, that keeps Lucrece from attaining (as it were) the subjectivitiy that is Tarquin's" (147), and even though being raped grants Lucrece a voice, hers must necessarily be the voice of the victim (152).

40. *Almyna* premiered in December 1706, a very busy season, and ran for three nights. A small sampling of the plays produced during that season include Dryden's *Spanish Fryar* and *Indian Emperour;* Shakespeare's *Hamlet;* Behn's *Rover; or, The Banish'd Cavaliers* and *Emperor of the Moon;* Steele's *Tender Husband;* Southerne's *Oroonoko;* and Farquahar's *Recruiting Officer.*

41. In her stoicism, Almyna is reminscient of the figures Mary Beth Rose has defined as offering a new form of the heroic: "that which privileges not the active confrontatiion with danger, but the capacity to endure it—to resist and suffer with patience and fortitude, rather than to confront and conquer with strength and wit" (84). Examples Rose uses are Milton's *Samson Agonistes,* Behn's *Orronoko,* and Mary Astell's *Some Reflections Upon Marriage.*

42. This play also features a character, Morena's sister, who is very much the stereotypical passive and victimizable woman. Having fallen in love with the wrong man, she ends the play lying dead on the stage, a victim of her own and her lover's overpowering sexual desires.

43. Leonard Tennenhouse has argued, in his examination of *The Duchess of Malfi,* that "lust doubles the woman. In that it produces either a desirous or a desiring self, lust makes her monstrous in some way" ("Violence Done" 89). And he goes on to describe the cause of that monstrosity as an excess: "The monstrous woman also possesses an extra member. Women subjected to punishment are those who either bring an extra member into the body politic or else take on the features of masculine desire themselves" (89–90). Certainly the Duchess of Malfi brings an extra member into the body politic: she brings a human being, her husband, as well as her lust. But I suggest that in the 1690s, emotions other than lust, and Almyna's courage is the best example, are equally excessive and produce their own

forms of doubling: Almyna is after all both potential victim and finally savior. Her eager embracing of the possibilities of an heroic death is itself an introduction of an extra member into the body politic—not an excessive sexual desire but excessive intellect and excessive courage.

6. Epilogue: Nation, Status, and Gender on the Restoration Stage

1. One of the few scholars to take an interest in Orrery's *Mustapha, Son of Solyman the Magnificent* is Laura Brown, an astute critic who complains of the rigidity of Orrery's dramatic formula and the simplicity of his repeated and explicit maxims, but who also calls the play "the significant example of a heroic actions with a tragic conclusion" (8).

2. Richard Knolles, for instance, writes the following about Turkish brothers who chose not to follow the custom of fratricide: "For the mercie shewed by *Achmet* to his brother *Mustapha,* so much differing from the Ottoman custome, begot such disorder, that it became pernicious, almost to the utter dissolution of that State" (28). Justin McCarthy speculates that the mothers of the sultans helped to end the practice of fratricide:

   > Upon coming to the throne a sultan would immediately order the assassination of his brother. From the accession of Mehmet II (1451) to Mehmet III (1595) scores of unfortunate siblings were murdered "to ensure peace in the world." . . . the sense of morality of even a hard-hearted ruling class was revolted by the practice. The powerful women of the harem were a particular factor in putting an end to it. (160–61)

3. The verbal fencing of Mustapha and Zanger, as they debate whose claim to the Hungarian Queen is stronger, could have been lifted directly from Dryden's *Indian Emperour.* The same language of discovery and conquest, of prior claims and stronger attachments, of seeing and possession is spoken by the Indian brothers, Guyomar and Odmar, only in this Turkish exchange there is the strength of "belated" (i.e., English) claims to an empire fully positioned as the stronger:

   Zanger: As of the fair new World he claim'd a Right,
   Who chanc'd to have it first within his Sight;
   So since to me she did the first appear,
   I claim the Right of a Discoverer.
   Mustapha: The first Discov'rer only saw the Shore;
   The second claim'd Possession seeing more

   . . . .
   You but the Beauty of her Face did find;
   I made the rich Discovery of her Mind.
   You of the Borders of *Elysium* boast
   Her Mind is all the In-Land to that Coast,
   I by a second Voyage finds more
   Of Beauty than was ever found before.

   (Mustapha 40–41)

4. Joyce Green MacDonald argues that what makes *Abdelazer* so fascinating "is the ideological weight and resonance the play attaches to the figures of women, particularly of mothers. The conduct of motherhood, and not of fatherhood, is what holds the fate of Spain in the balance" (68–69). I would add that a similar heroic theme punctuates Orrery's *Mustapha, Son of Solyman the Magnificent,* a structure Katherine M. Quinsey sees at work

in Dryden's two-part *Conquest of Granada,* "the play is notable for the centrality given its female characters: leadership roles—though clearly qualified and limited—are given to almost all its women" (129).

5. I thus disagree with Joyce Green MacDonald's argument that "race is everything" (69) in *Abdelazer* and subscribe to Jacqueline Pearson's argument that race, and cultural differences more generally, provide "useful tropes for gender differences," such as in the case of Pix's rewriting of *Othello* "to carry further its problematization of stereotypes of difference" ("Blacker" 17). Susie Thomas, too, argues that Behn's revision of *Lust's Dominion* "reveals a consistent concern to minimize the racism of her source" ("This Thing of Darkness" 18). Nabil Matar's work on Renaissance stereotypes about Spaniards and Moors is also useful in this context: "in the popular imagination and in the plays [of the English Renaissance], the lust and darkness of the Spaniard often takes precedence over the assumed evil of the villainous Moor. Moreover, the fact that at least some white, European Christians could be portrayed as lustful, intriguing devils served to complicate the neat compartmentalization of national, religious, and racial types, and to add depth to the representation of Moors," for in 1599 (the approximate date of the production of *Lust's Dominion*), "an Elizabethan audience might have harbored stronger prejudices against Spanish Catholics than against a Barbarian prince" (*Moor* 7–8, 107).

6. Derek Hughes points to the fact that, in the years preceding *Don Sebastian,* Dryden had written *Absalom and Achitophel* (1681) and *The Hind and the Panther* (1687), poems "both influenced by Milton and both concerned with the quest for stable values in a fallen and mutable world; . . . In 1689, he was ready to demonstrate with elaborate dramatic subtlety what he had so baldy and homiletically stated in 1674: that heroic prowess and heroic love are alike tainted by the corruption of the Fall" (73).

7. Much more could be said about the comic plot: Southerne's New World setting allows him to comment on the different power dynamic of gender at play in the Americas. The result is a drama where a woman, Charlotte Weldon, controls all the action of the comic plot. She goes aggressively out into the world—to perform, to masquerade, to produce her desires, including arranging a marriage for her sister. About the breeches she dons, she says, "they have assisted me in marrying my sister, and have gone a great way in befriending your cousin Jack with the Widow. Can you forgive me for pimping for your family?" (5.1.70–73). As Charlotte's "pimping" makes clear, Southerne makes explicit the relationships among husband-hunting, the selling of women in the marriage market, and the putting of slaves on the auction block. Laura Rosenthal, recognizing the parallels between Charlotte's "pimping" and the selling of Oroonoko and other slaves, writes that "Behn's *Oroonoko* problematizes human commodification, while Southerne's seeks complex ways to justify it. . . . instead of confronting the problem of human commodification, Southerne deflects this public controversy into the private terms of erotic possession" (133, 150).

8. The word "monster" is absent from this play, until Abdelazer's attempted rape of Leonora. Once she is rescued by Ozmin, she urges him away, by using that epithet and a reference to disease, the two metaphors most likely to surface after sexual assault: "That Monster's Presence I must fly, as from

a killing Plague" (466). Philip, too, after he is caught and enchained by Abdelazer, calls him "dreadful Monster" (468).

9. Elena Russo offers just such a status-based argument about the libertine: "In its rejection of the ethos of politeness, in its nostalgia for archaic forms of social interaction, and in its defense of individual integrity against and above all, libertinage is one more aspect of that generalized reaction against the commercial, polite society that developed under absolutism—one of the most flamboyant, if confused, ones" (396).

10. For an interesting analysis of the issue of containment, especially as it is intimately linked with subversion, see Jonathan Gil Harris's argument that it is precisely "the historical freight attaching to containment in the late twentieth century that makes it a potentially useful tool for the materialist critic of early modern literature and culture" ("Historicizing Greenblatt's 'Containment'").

Works Cited

Aksan, Virginia H. "Is There a Turk in the Turkish Spy?" *Eighteenth-Century Fiction* 6.3 (Apr. 1994): 201–14.

Armistead, J. M. "The Occultism of Dryden's 'American' Plays in Context." *The Seventeenth Century* 1.1 (July 1986): 127–52.

Armstrong, Nancy, and Leonard Tennenhouse. Introduction. *The Violence of Representation*. Ed. Nancy Armstrong and Leonard Tennenhouse. London: Routledge, 1989. 1–20.

Aston, Anthony. *A Brief Supplement to Colley Cibber, Esq.; His Lives the late Famous Actors and Actresses*. N.p.: n.p., n.d.

Aubry, James. "Revising the Monstrous: Du Plessis' *Short History of Prodigies* and London Culture in 1730." *Studies in Eighteenth-Century Culture* 23 (1994): 75–91.

Avery, Emmett. *The London Stage, 1700–1729*. Vol. 2. Carbondale: Southern Illinois UP, 1959. 5 vols.

———. "The Restoration Audience." *Philological Quarterly* 45 (1966): 54–61.

Backscheider, Paula R. *Spectacular Politics: Theatrical Power and Mass Culture in Early Modern England*. Baltimore: Johns Hopkins UP, 1993.

Baldwin, Frances Elizabeth. *Sumptuary Legislation and Personal Regulation in England*. Baltimore: Johns Hopkins UP, 1926.

Ballaster, Ros. "The First Female Dramatists." *Women and Literature in Britain, 1500–1700*. Ed. Helen Wilcox. Cambridge: Cambridge UP, 1996. 267–90.

Barish, Jonas A. *The Antitheatrical Prejudice*. Berkeley: U of California P, 1981.

Barker, Francis. *The Culture of Violence: Tragedy and History*. Manchester: Manchester UP, 1993.

———. *The Tremulous Private Body: Essays on Subjection*. Ann Arbor: U of Michigan P, 1995.

Barker, Francis, Peter Hulme, and Margaret Iversen. Introduction. *Colonial Discourse/ Postcolonial Theory*. Manchester: Manchester UP, 1994.

Barrell, John. *The Birth of Pandora and the Division of Knowledge*. London: Macmillan, 1992.

Works Cited

Baudrillard, Jean. *Simulcra and Simulation*. Trans. Sheila Glaser. Ann Arbor: U of Michigan P, 1995.

Behn, Aphra. *Abdelazer. The Works of Aphra Behn: The Plays 1671–1677*. Ed. Janet Todd. Vol. 5. Columbus: Ohio State UP, 1996.

———. *The Dutch Lover. The Works of Aphra Behn: The Plays 1671–1677*, Ed. Janet Todd. Vol. 5. Columbus: Ohio State UP, 1996.

———. *The Feign'd Curtizans. The Works of Aphra Behn: The Plays 1678–1682*. Ed. Janet Todd. Vol. 6. Columbus: Ohio State UP, 1992: 83–160.

———. *The Rover; or, The Banish'd Cavaliers*. Ed. Frederick M. Link. Lincoln: U of Nebraska P, 1967.

———. *The Second Part of The Rover. The Works of Aphra Behn: The Plays 1678–1682*. Ed. Janet Todd. Vol. 6. Columbus: Ohio State UP, 1996.

———. *The Widdow Ranter. The Works of Aphra Behn,: The Plays 1682–1698*. Ed. Janet Todd. Vol. 7. Columbus: Ohio UP, 1996: 285–354.

Belsey, Catherine. *The Subject of Tragedy: Identity and Difference in Renaissance Drama*. London: Methuen, 1985.

Benedict, Barbara M. "Making a Monster: Socializing Sexuality and the Monster of 1790." *"Defects": Engendering the Modern Body*. Ed. Helen Deutsch and Felicity Nussbaum. Ann Arbor: U of Michigan P, 2000. 127–53.

Betterton, Thomas. [Printed by Edmund Curll.] *The History of the English Stage, from the Restauration to the Present*. London: n.p., 1741.

Bianchi, Marina. "Consuming Novelty: Strategies for Producing Novelty in Consumption." *Journal of Medieval and Early Modern Studies* 28.1 (Winter 1998): 3–18.

Black, Jeremy. *The Rise of the European Powers, 1679–1793*. London: Edward Arnold Pub., 1990.

———. *A System of Ambition? British Foreign Policy, 1660–1793*. London: Longman, 1991.

Bourdieu, Pierre. *Outline of a Theory of Practice*. Trans. Richard Nice. Cambridge: Cambridge UP, 1977.

Brady, Nicholas. *The Rape. A Tragedy*. London: n.p., 1730.

———. *The Rape: or, the Innocent Imposters, a Tragedy*. London: n.p., 1692.

Braudel, Fernand. *Civilization and Capitalism, 15th–18th Century: The Perspective of the World*. Trans. Sian Reynolds. Vol. 3. New York: Harper and Row, 1979.

Braverman, Richard. "The Rake's Progress Revisited: Politics and Comedy in the Restoration." *Cultural Readings of Restoration and Eighteenth-Century English Theater*. Ed. J. Douglas Canfield and Deborah C. Payne. Athens: U of Georgia P, 1995. 141–68.

Bridges, Liz. "'We Were Somebody in England': Identity, Gender and Status in *The Widdow Ranter*." *Aphra Behn: Identity, Alterity, Ambiguity*. Ed. Mary Ann O'Donnell, Bernard Dhuicq, and Guyonne Leduc. Paris: L'Harmattan, 2000. 75–80.

Brilliant, Richard. *Portraiture*. Cambridge: Harvard UP, 1991.

Brooks, Peter. *Body Work: Objects of Desire in Modern Narrative*. Cambridge: Harvard UP, 1993.

Brown, Laura. *English Dramatic Form, 1660–1760*. New Haven: Yale UP, 1981.

Brown, Thomas, ed. *Works*. 3 vols. London: n.p., 1715.

Burks, Deborah G. "'I'll Want my Will Else': *The Changeling* and Women's Complicity with their Rapists." *English Literary History* 62 (1995): 759–90.

Butler, Judith. *Bodies that Matter: On the Discursive Limits of "Sex."* New York: Routledge, 1993.

——. *Gender Trouble: Feminism and the Subversion of Identity*. New York: Routledge, 1990.

Canfield, J. Douglas. "The Classical Treatment of Don Juan in Tirso, Moliere, and Mozart: What Cultural Work Does It Perform?" *Comparative Drama* 31 (1997): 42–64.

——. "Introduction to *Tamerlane*." *The Broadview Anthology of Restoration and Early Eighteenth-Century Drama*. Ed. J. Douglas Canfield. New York: Broadview Press, 2001. 38.

Caruth, Cathy. "Traumatic Departures: Survival and History in Freud." *Trauma and Self*. Ed. Charles B. Stozier and Michael Flynn. Boston: Rowman and Littlefield, 1996. 29–44.

Case, Sue Ellen. *Performing Feminisms: Feminist Critical Theory and the Theatre*. Baltimore: Johns Hopkins UP, 1990.

Castle, Terry. *Masquerade and Civilization: The Carnivalesque in Eighteenth-Century English Culture and Fiction*. Stanford: Stanford UP, 1986.

The Character of Spain: Or, an Epitome of Their Virtues and Vices. London: n.p., 1660.

Chardin, John. *The Travels of Sir John Chardin*. London: n.p., 1686.

Cibber, Colley. *An Apology for the Life of Mr. Colley Cibber, Comedian, and the Late Patentee of the Theatre Royal*. London: n.p., 1740.

Clarke, Janet. "The Production and Reception of Davenant's *Cruelty of the Spaniards in Peru*." *Modern Language Review* 89.4 (Oct. 1994): 832–41.

Clendinnen, Inga. "'Fierce and Unnatural Cruelty': Cortés and the Conquest of Mexico." *New World Encounters*. Ed. Stephen Greenblatt. Berkeley: U of California P, 1993. 12–47.

Cohen, Jeffrey Jerome. "Monster Culture (Seven Theses)." *Monster Theory*. Ed. Jeffrey Cohen. Minneapolis: U of Minnesota P, 1996. 3–25.

——. Preface. *Monster Theory*. Minneapolis: U of Minnesota P, 1996.

Cohen, Michele. *Fashioning Masculinity: National Identity and Language in the Eighteenth Century*. London: Routledge, 1996.

Coles, Paul. *The Ottoman Impact on Europe*. London: Thames and Hudson, 1968.

Colley, Linda. *Britons: Forging the Nation, 1707–1837*. New Haven: Yale UP, 1992.

Coltharp, Duane. "'Pleasing Rape': The Politics of Libertinism in *The Conquest of Granada*." 21.1 (Spring 1997): 15–31.

Congreve, William. *The Way of the World*. *British Dramatists from Dryden to Sheridan*. Ed. George H. Nettleton and Arthur E. Case. Rev. by George Winchester Stone. Carbondale: Southern Illinois UP, 1969. 307–48.

Copeland, Nancy. "'Once a Whore and Ever'? Whore and Virgin in *The Rover* and Its Antecedents." *Restoration: Studies in English Literary Culture 1660–1700* 16.1 (Spring 1992): 20–27.

Crehan, Stewart. "*The Rape of the Lock* and the Economy of 'Trivial Things.'" *Eighteenth-Century Studies* 31.1 (1997): 45–68.

Curran, Andrew, and Patrick Graille. "The Faces of Eighteenth-Century Monstrosity." *Eighteenth-Century Life* 21 (May 1997): 1–15.

Dale, Leigh, and Simon Ryan. "Introduction: The Body in the Library." *The Body in the Library*. Ed. Leigh Dale and Simon Ryan. Amsterdam: Rodopi, 1998. 1–14.

D'Amico, Jack. *The Moor in English Renaissance Drama*. Tampa: U of South Florida P, 1991.

Davenant, William. *The Cruelty of the Spaniard in Peru*. *Playhouse to Be Let*. Part 4. London: n.p., 1663. 103–14.

Davies, Thomas, ed. *Dramatic Miscellanies*. 3 vols. London: n.p., 1784.

Davis, Lennard J. "The Fact of Events and the Event of Facts: New World Explorers and the Early Novel." *The Eighteenth Century* 32.3 (1991): 240–55.

Davison, Roderic H. *Turkey: A Short History*. 3rd ed. Huntingdon, England: The Eothen Press, 1998.

Debord, Guy. *Society of Spectacle*. Detroit: Black and Red, 1983.

De Certeau, Michel. "Travel Narratives of the French to Brazil: Sixteenth to Eighteenth Centuries." *New World Encounters*. Ed. Stephen Greenblatt. Berkeley: U of California P, 1993. 323–28.

Defoe, Daniel. *A Plan of the English Commerce, Being a Compleat Prospect of the Trade of this Nation*. 2nd ed. [1730]. New York: Augustus M. Kelley, 1967.

———. "A True-Born Englishman." *Selected Poetry and Prose of Daniel Defoe*. Ed. Michael F. Shugrue. New York: Holt, Rinehart and Winston, 1968.

DeRitter, Jones. *The Embodiment of Characters: The Representation of Physical Experience on Stage and in Print, 1728–1749*. Philadelphia: U of Pennsylvania P, 1994.

Deutsch, Helen, and Felicity Nussbaum. Introduction. *"Defects": Engendering the Modern Body*. Ann Arbor: U Michigan P, 2000. 1–30.

Diamond, Elin. "Gestus and Signature in Aphra Behn's *The Rover*." *English Literary History* 56 (Fall 1989): 519–41.

DiPiero, Thomas. "Disfiguring the Victim's Body in Sade's *Justine*." *Body and Text in the Eighteenth Century*. Ed. Veronica Kelly and Dorothea Von Mucke. Stanford: Stanford UP, 1994. 247–65.

Doane, Mary Ann. "Film and Masquerade: Theorising the Female Spectator." *Feminist Film Theory: A Reader*. Ed. Sue Thornham. New York: New York UP, 1999. 131–45.

Dolan, Frances E. *Whores of Babylon: Catholicism, Gender and Seventeenth-Century Print Culture*. Ithaca: Cornell UP, 2000.

Doran, Dr. *Their Majesties' Servants, or Annals of the English Stage*. London: William H. Allen and Co., 1864.

Douglas, Mary. *Purity and Danger: An Analysis of Concepts of Pollution and Taboo*. London: Routledge and Kegan Paul, 1969.

Downes, John. *Roscius Anglicanus, or an Historical Review of the Stage*. London: n.p., 1708.

Doyle, Laura. "The Folk, the Nobles, and the Novel: The Racial Subtext of Sentimentality." *Narrative* 3.2 (May 1995): 161–87.

Dryden, John. "Annus Mirabilis." *Selected Poetry and Prose of John Dryden*. Ed. Earl Miner. New York: The Modern Library, 1969.

———. *Don Sebastian, King of Portugal. John Dryden: Four Tragedies*. Ed. L. A. Beaurline and Fredson Bowers. Chicago: U of Chicago P, 1967. 281–408.

———. *The Indian Emperour. The Works of John Dryden*. Ed. John Loftis and Vinton A. Dearing. Vol. 9. Berkeley: U of California P, 1966.

Duffy, Michael. *The Englishman and the Foreigner: The English Satirical Print, 1600–1832*. Cambridge: Chadwyck-Healey, 1986.

Duncan, Carol. "The Aesthetics of Power in Modern Erotic Art." *Feminist Art Criticism: An Anthology*. Ed. Arlene Raven, Cassandra L. Langer, and Joanna Frueh. Ann Arbor: U. M. I. Research Press, 1988.

During, Simon. "Rousseau's Patrimony: Primitivism, Romance and Becoming Other." *Colonial Discourse/Postcolonial Theory*. Ed. Francis Barker, Peter Hulme, and Margaret Iversen. Manchester: Manchester UP, 1994. 47–71.

Elias, Norbert. *The Civilizing Process: History of Manners*. Trans. Edmund Jephcott. Vol. 1. New York: Urizen Books, 1978.

Elliott, John H. "Introduction: Identity in the Atlantic World." *Colonial Identity in the Atlantic World, 1500–1800*. Ed. Nicholas Canny and Anthony Pagden. Princeton: Princeton UP, 1987. 3–13.

Etherege, Sir George. *The Man of Mode; or, Sir Fopling Flutter. British Dramatists from Dryden to Sheridan*. Ed. George H. Nettleton, Arthur Case, and George Winchester Stone. Carbondale: Southern Illinois UP, 1969. 153–96.

The Female Wits. The Female Wits: Women Playwrights on the London Stage 1660–1720. Ed. Fidelis Morgan. London: Virago, 1981. 390–433.

Ferguson, Margaret. "Juggling the Categories of Race, Class, and Gender: Aphra Behn's *Oroonoko*." *Women, "Race," and Writing in the Early Modern Period*. Ed. Margo Hendricks and Patricia Parker. London: Routledge, 1994. 209–24.

———. "News from the New World: Miscegenous Romance in Aphra Behn's *Oroonoko* and *The Widdow Ranter*." *The Production of English Renaissance Culture*. Ed. David Lee Miller, Sharon O'Dair, and Harold Weber. Ithaca: Cornell UP, 1994. 151–89.

Works Cited

Ferris, Lesley. *Acting Women: Images of Women in Theatre*. New York: New York UP, 1989.

Fischer-Lichte, Erika. "Theatre and the Civilizing Process: An Approach to the History of Acting." *Interpreting the Theatrical Past: Essays on the Historiography of Performance*. Ed. Thomas Postlewait and Bruce A. McConachie. Iowa City: U of Iowa P, 1989. 19–36.

Foucault, Michel. *The Foucault Reader*. Ed. Paul Rabinow. New York: Pantheon Books, 1984.

Freedberg, David. *The Power of Images: Studies in the History and Theory of Response*. Chicago: U of Chicago P, 1989.

Furtado, Peter. "National Pride in Seventeenth-Century England." *Patriotism: The Making and Unmaking of British National Identity*. Ed. Raphael Samuel. Vol. 1. London: Routledge, 1989. 44–56.

Fuss, Diana. *Essentially Speaking: Feminism, Nature and Difference*. New York: Routledge, 1989.

———. "Fashion and the Homospectatorial Look." *Identities*. Ed. Kwame Anthony Appiah and Henry Louise Gates, Jr. Chicago: U of Chicago P, 1995. 90–114.

Gage, Thomas. *A New Survey of the West-Indias: or, the English American his Travail by Sea and Land*. London: n.p., 1655.

Gallagher, Catherine. *Nobody's Story*. Berkeley: U of California P, 1994.

———. "Who Was That Masked Woman? The Prostitute and the Playwright in the Comedies of Aphra Behn." *Women's Studies* 15 (1988): 23–42.

Garber, Marjorie. *Vested Interests: Cross-Dressing and Cultural Anxiety*. New York: Harper-Perrennial, 1992.

Gilbert, Helen. "Responses to the Sex Trade in Post-Colonial Theatre." *The Body in the Library*. Ed. Leigh Dale and Simon Ryan. Amsterdam, Rodopi: 1998. 261–71.

Gilder, Rosamond. *Enter the Actress: The First Women in the Theater*. London: George G. Harrap, 1931.

Gildon, Charles. *The Life of Mr. Thomas Betterton*. London: n.p., 1710.

Gill, Patricia, and Thomas DiPiero. "Introduction: Illicit Determinations." *Illicit Sex: Identity Politics in Early Modern Culture*. Athens: U of Georgia, 1997. 1–19.

Goffman, Daniel. *Britons in the Ottoman Empire, 1642–1660*. Seattle: U of Washington P, 1998.

Goldberg, Jonathan. *Women Writing: English Renaissance Examples*. Stanford: Stanford UP, 1997.

Gordon, Scott Paul. "Voyeuristic Dreams: Mr. Spectator and the Power of Spectacle." *The Eighteenth Century* 36.1 (1995): 3–23.

Gravdal, Kathryn. *Ravishing Maidens: Writing Rape in Medieval French Literature and Law*. Philadelphia: U of Pennsylvania P, 1991.

Greenblatt, Stephen. *Learning to Curse: Essays in Early Modern Culture*. New York: Routledge, 1990.

———. *Marvelous Possessions: The Wonder of the New World*. Chicago: U of Chicago P, 1991.

———. *Renaissance Self-Fashioning: From More to Shakespeare*. Chicago: U of Chicago P, 1980.

Hammond, Paul. "The King's Two Bodies: Representations of Charles II." *Culture, Politics and Society in Britain, 1660–1800*. Ed. Jeremy Black and Jeremy Gregory. Manchester: Manchester UP, 1991. 13–48.

Hantman, Jeffrey L. "Caliban's Own Voice: American Indian Views of the Other in Colonial Virginia." *New Literary History* 23 (1992): 69–81.

Harris, Jonathan Gil. "Historicizing Greenblatt's 'Containment': The Cold War, Functionalism and the Origins of Social Pathology." *Critical Self-Fashioning: Stephen Greenblatt and the New Historicism*. Frankfurt am Main: Peter Lang, 1999.

Harth, Erica. *Ideology and Culture in Seventeenth-Century France*. Ithaca: Cornell UP, 1983.

Hawley, Judith. "Margins and Monstrosity: Martinus Scriblerus his Double Mistress." *Eighteenth-Century Life* 22.1 (Feb. 1998): 31–49.

Hendricks, Margo. "Civility, Barbarism, and Aphra Behn's *The Widdow Ranter*." *Women, "Race," and Writing in the Early Modern Period*. Ed. Margo Hendricks and Patricia Parker. London: Routledge, 1994. 225–349.

Heywood, C. J. "Sir Paul Rycaut, A Seventeenth-Century Observer of the Ottoman State: Notes for a Study." *English and Continental Views of the Ottoman Empire, 1500–1800*. Los Angeles: William Andrews Clark Memorial Library, 1972. 33–59.

Higgins, Lynn A., and Brenda R. Silver. *Rape and Representation*. New York: Columbia UP, 1991.

Hill, Christopher. *The Century of Revolution: 1603–1714*. Vol. 1. New York: Norton, 1961. 3 vols.

———. *The Collected Essays of Christopher Hill: Writing and the Revolution in Seventeenth-Century England*. Vol. 1. Amherst: U of Massachusetts P, 1985.

Hill, John. *The Actor: A Treatise on the Art of Playing*. London: n.p., 1750.

Hobbes, Thomas. *Leviathan*. Ed. Richard Tuck. Cambridge: Cambridge UP, 1991.

Holland, Peter. *Ornament of Action*. Cambridge: Cambridge UP, 1979.

Howard, Jean E. "An English Lass Amid the Moors: Gender, Race, Sexuality, and National Identity in Heywood's *The Fair Maid of the West*." *Women, "Race," and Writing in the Early Modern Period*. Ed. Margo Hendricks and Patricia Parker. London: Routledge, 1994. 101–17.

Howe, Elizabeth. *First English Actresses: Women and Drama, 1660–1700*. Cambridge: Cambridge UP, 1992.

Hughes, Derek. "Dryden's *Don Sebastian* and the Literature of Heroism." *Yearbook of English Studies* 12 (1982): 72–90.

Hulme, Peter. *Colonial Encounters: Europe and the Native Caribbean 1492–1797*. London: Routledge, 1986.

Works Cited

Jed, Stephanie. *Chaste Thinking: The Rape of Lucrece and The Birth of Humanism*. Bloomington: U of Indiana P, 1989.

Jones, J. R. *Britain and Europe in the Seventeenth Century*. New York: Norton, 1966.

——. *Britain and the World, 1649–1815*. Sussex: Harvester, 1980.

Jowett, Claire. "Radical Identities? Native Americans, Jews and The English Commonwealth." *The Seventeenth Century* 10 (Spring 1995): 101–19.

Kahn, Copp Elia. "*Lucrece:* The Sexual Politics of Subjectivity." *Rape and Representation*. Ed. Lynn A. Higgins and Brenda R. Silver. New York: Columbia UP, 1991. 141–59.

Kamen, Henry. "Spain." *A Dictionary of Eighteenth-Century World History*. Ed. Jeremy Black and Roy Porter. Oxford: Blackwell, 1994.

——. "Spanish Succession, War of." *A Dictionary of Eighteenth-Century World History*. Ed. Jeremy Black and Roy Porter. Oxford: Blackwell, 1994.

Kaufman, Anthony. "'The Perils of Florinda': Aphra Behn, Rape, and the Subversion of Libertinism in *The Rover, Part I*." *Restoration and Eighteenth-Century Theatre Research* 11 (Winter 1996): 1–21.

——. "The Shadow of the Burlador: Don Juan on the Continent and in England." *Comedy from Shakespeare to Sheridan: Change and Continuity in the English and European Dramatic Tradition*. Ed. A. R. Braunmuller and J. C. Bulman. Newark: U of Delaware P, 1986. 229–54.

Kehres, Jean-Marc. "Libertine Anatomies: Figures of Monstrosity in Sade's *Justine ou les malheurs de la vertu*." *Eighteenth-Century Life* 21 (May 1997): 100–113.

Keller, Evelyn Fox, and Christine R. Grontkowski. "The Mind's Eye." *Discovering Reality*. Ed. Sandra Harding and Merrill B. Hintikka. New York: D. Reidell, 1983. 207–24.

Kelly, Veronica. "'Who's the Bigger Dill'? The Madhouse in Recent Australian Drama." *The Body in the Library*. Ed. Leigh Dale and Simon Ryan. Amsterdam: Rodopi, 1998. 167–84.

Kelly, Veronica, and Dorothea Von Mucke. Introduction. *Body and Text in the Eighteenth Century*. Ed. Veronica Kelly and Dorothea Von Mucke. Stanford: Stanford UP, 1994.

King, Thomas A. "'As If (She) Were Made On Purpose To Put the Whole World Into Good Humour': Reconstructing the First English Actresses." *The Drama Review* 36.3 (Fall 1992): 78–102.

——. "Displacing Masculinity: Edward Kynaston and the Politics of Effeminacy." *The Image of Manhood in Early Modern Literatures*. Ed. Andrew P. Williams. Connecticut: Greenwood Press, 1999. 119–40.

Knolles, Richard. *The Generall Historie of the Turks*. London: n.p., 1638.

Kowaleski-Wallace, Elizabeth. *Consuming Subjects: Women, Shopping, and Business in the Eighteenth Century*. New York: Columbia UP, 1997.

Kramer, David. *The Imperial Dryden: The Poetics of Appropriations in Seventeenth-Century England*. Athens: U of Georgia P, 1994.

Works Cited

Kris, Ernst, and Otto Kurz. *Legend, Myth, and Magic in the Image of the Artist*. New Haven: Yale UP, 1979.

Laquer, Thomas. *Making Sex: Body and Gender from the Greeks to Freud.* Cambridge: Harvard UP, 1990.

Laquer, Thomas, and Catherine Gallagher. *The Making of the Modern Body.* Berkeley: U of California P, 1987.

Las Casas, Bartolome de. *The Devastation of the Indies: A Brief Account.* Trans. Herma Briffault. Baltimore: Johns Hopkins UP, 1974.

Laycock, Deborah. "Shape-Shifting: Fashion, Gender, and Metamorphosis in Eighteenth-Century England." *Textual Bodies: Changing Boundaries of Literary Representation.* Ed. Lori Hope Lefkovitz. Albany, New York: State U of New York P, 1977. 127–60.

Lefkovitz, Lori Hope. Introduction. *Textual Bodies: Changing Boundaries of Literary Representation.* Albany, New York: State U of New York P, 1977. 1–18.

Leinwand, Theodore B. *Theatre, Finance and Society in Early Modern England.* Cambridge: Cambridge UP, 1999.

Lewis, Bernard. *Islam and the West.* New York: Oxford UP, 1993.

Liss, Peggy K. *Atlantic Empires: The Network of Trade and Revolution, 1713–1826.* Baltimore: Johns Hopkins UP, 1983.

Lloyd, T. O. *The British Empire 1558–1983.* Oxford: Oxford UP, 1984.

Loftis, John. *The Spanish Plays of Neoclassical England.* New Haven: Yale UP, 1973.

Love, Harold. "The Myth of the Restoration Audience." *Komos* 1 (1967): 49–56.

———. "Who Were the Restoration Audience?" *Yearbook of English Studies* 10 (1980): 21–44.

Low, Gail Ching-Liang. "His Stories?: Narratives and Images of Imperialism." *New Formations* 12 (Winter 1999): 97–124.

Lowenthal, Cynthia. *Lady Mary Wortley Montagu and the Eighteenth-Century Familiar Letter.* Athens: U of Georgia P, 1994.

MacDonald, Joyce Green. "Gender, Family, and Race in Aphra Behn's *Abdelazer.*" *Aphra Behn: Identity, Alterity, Ambiguity.* Ed. Mary Ann O'Donnell, Bernard Dhuicq, and Guyonne Leduc. Paris: L'Harmattan, 2000. 67–74.

MacKinnon, Catharine A. "Rape: On Coercion and Consent." *Writing the Body: Female Embodiment and Feminists Theory.* Ed. Katie Conboy, Nadia Medina, and Sarah Stanbury. New York: Columbia UP, 1997. 42–58.

Maltby, William S. *The Black Legends in England: The Development of Anti-Spanish Sentiment, 1558–1660.* Durham: Duke UP, 1971.

Mandell, Laura. *Misogynous Economies: The Business of Literature in Eighteenth-Century Britain.* Lexington: UP Kentucky, 1999.

Manley, Delariviere. *Almyna: or, the Arabian Vow.* London: n.p., 1707.

———. *The Royal Mischief.* London: n.p., 1696.

Mann, Susan Garland, and David D. Mann. "The Publisher William

Turner, Female Playwright, and Pix's *The Adventures in Madrid.*"
RES: Review of English Studies 44.184 (1995): 531–34.

Markley, Robert. "Violence and Profits on the Restoration Stage: Trade,
Nationalism, and Insecurity in Dryden's *Amboyna.*" *Eighteenth-
Century Life* 22.1 (Feb. 1998): 2–17.

Marsden, Jean. "Ideology, Sex, and Satire: the Case of Thomas Shadwell." *Cutting Edges: Postmodern Critical Essays of Eighteenth-Century
Satire.* Ed. James E. Gill. Knoxville: U of Tennessee P, 1995. 43–58.

———. "Rape, Voyeurism, and the Restoration Stage." *Broken Boundaries.* Ed. Katherine M. Quinsey. Lexington: UP of Kentucky, 1996.
185–200.

Marshall, Cynthia. "Wound-man: *Coriolanus,* Gender, and the Theatrical
Construction of Interiority." *Feminist Readings of Early Modern Cul-
ture.* Ed. Valerie Traub, M. Lindsay Kaplan, and Dympna Callaghan.
Cambridge: Cambridge UP, 1996. 93–118.

Marshall, W. Gerald. "The Idea of Theatre in Wycherley's *The Gentleman
Dancing-Master.*" *Restoration: Studies in English Literary Culture, 1660–
1700* 6.1 (Spring 1982): 1–10.

Matar, Nabil. *Islam in Britain, 1558–1685.* New York: Cambridge UP,
1998.

———. *Turks, Moors, and Englishmen in the Age of Discovery.* New York:
Columbia, 1999.

Matchinske, Megan. *Writing, Gender and State in Early Modern England.*
Cambridge: Cambridge UP, 1998.

Maus, Katharine Eisaman. *Inwardness and the Theater in the English Renaissance.* Chicago: U of Chicago P, 1995.

———. "'Playhouse Flesh and Blood': Sexual Ideology and the Restoration Actress." *English Literary History* 46 (1979): 595–617.

McCarthy, B. Eugene. *William Wycherley: A Biography.* Athens, Ohio:
Ohio UP, 1979.

McCarthy, Justin. *The Ottoman Turks: An Introductory History to 1923.*
London: Longman, 1997.

McKendrick, Neil, John Brewer, and J. H. Plumb. *The Birth of a Consumer Society: The Commercialization of Eighteenth-Century England.*
London: Europa Pubs, 1982.

McKeon, Michael. *The Origins of the English Novel: 1600–1740.* Baltimore: Johns Hopkins UP, 1987.

McLachlan, Jean O. *Trade and Peace with Old Spain, 1667–1750.* Cambridge: Cambridge UP, 1940.

McLaren, Juliet. "Presumptuous Poetess, Pen-Feathered Muse: The
Comedies of Mary Pix." *Gender at Work: Four Women Writers of the
Eighteenth Century.* Ed Ann Messenger. Detroit: Wayne State UP,
1990. 77–113.

McNay, Lois. "Gender, Habitus and the Field: Pierre Bourdieu and the
Limits of Reflexivity." *Theory, Culture and Society* 16.1 (1999):
95–117.

Works Cited

Meltzer, Francoise. *Salome and the Dance of Writing: Portraits of Mimesis in Literature*. Chicago: U of Chicago P, 1987.

Modeleski, Tania. *The Women Who Knew Too Much: Hitchcock and Feminist Theory*. New York: Methuen, 1988.

Montrose, Louis. "The Work of Gender in the Discourse of Discovery." *New World Encounters*. Ed. Stephen Greenblatt. Berkeley: U of California P, 1993. 177–217.

Mulcaire, Terry. "Public Credit; or, The Feminization of Virtue in the Marketplace." *PMLA* 114 (Oct. 1999): 1029–42.

Munns, Jessica, and Penny Richards. "Introduction: The Clothes that Wear Us." *The Clothes that Wear Us: Essays on Dressing and Transgressing in Eighteenth-Century Culture*. Newark: U of Delaware P, 1999. 1–36.

Murray, Timothy. *Theatrical Legitimation: Allegories of Genius in Seventeenth-Century England and France*. Oxford: Oxford UP, 1987.

Negrin, Llewellyn. "The Self as Image: A Critical Appraisal of Postmodern Theories of Fashion." *Theory, Culture and Society* 16.3 (1999): 99–118.

Newman, Gerald. *The Rise of English Nationalism: A Cultural History 1740–1830*. New York: St. Martin's Press, 1987.

Nicholl, Allardyce. *A History of English Drama: Restoration Drama, 1660–1700*. Vol 1. Cambridge: Cambridge UP, 1952.

Ogilby, John. *Africa: Being an Accurate Description of the Regions of Egypt, Barbary, Lybia and Billedulgerid, the Land of the Negroes, Guinee, Ethiopie, and the Abyssines*. London: n.p., 1670.

Orrery, Roger Boyle, Earl. *Mustapha, The Son of Solyman the Magnificent*. London: n.p., 1734.

Owen, Susan J. "'He that Should Guard My Virtue Has Betrayed It': The Dramatization of Rape in the Exclusion Crisis." *Restoration and Eighteenth-Century Theatre Research* 9 (Summer 1994): 59–68.

———. *Restoration Theatre and Crisis*. Oxford: Clarendon, 1996.

———. "Sexual Politics and Party Politics in Behn's Drama, 1678–83." *Aphra Behn Studies*. Ed. Janet Todd. Cambridge: Cambridge UP, 1996. 15–29.

Pagden, Anthony. *Lords of All the World: Ideologies of Empire in Spain, Britain and France, c. 1500–1800*. New Haven: Yale UP, 1995.

A Pageant of Spanish Humours, Translated out of Dutche [sic] by H. W. London: n.p., 1599.

Paré, Ambroise. *On Monsters and Marvels*. Trans. Janis L. Pallister. Chicago: U of Chicago P, 1982.

Park, Katharine, and Lorraine F. Daston. "Unnatural Conceptions: The Study of Monsters in Sixteenth- and Seventeenth-Century France and England." *Past and Present* 92 (1981): 20–54.

Parker, Todd C. *Sexing the Text: The Rhetoric of Sexual Difference in British Literature, 1700–1750*. Albany: State U of New York P, 2000.

Payne, Deborah. "'And Poets Shall by Patron-Princes Live': Aphra Behn and Patronage." *Curtain Calls: British and American Women and*

Works Cited

the Theater. Ed. Mary Anne Schofield and Cecilia Macheski. Athens: Ohio UP, 1991. 18–34.

———. "Reified Object or Emergent Professional? Retheorizing the Restoration Actress." *Cultural Readings of Restoration and Eighteenth-Century English Theater.* Ed. J. Douglas Canfield and Deborah C. Payne. Athens: U of Georgia P, 1995. 13–38.

Pearson, Jacqueline. "Blacker Than Hell Creates: Pix Rewrites *Othello.*" *Broken Boundaries.* Ed. Katherine M. Quinsey. Lexington: UP of Kentucky, 1996. 13–30.

———. *Prostituted Muse: Images of Women and Women Dramatists, 1642–1737.* New York: Harvester, 1988.

———. "Slave Princes and Lady Monsters: Gender and Ethnic Difference in the Work of Aphra Behn." *Aphra Behn Studies.* Ed. Janet Todd. Cambridge: Cambridge UP, 1996. 219–34.

Pender, Stephen. "In the Bodyshop: Human Exhibition in Early Modern England." *"Defects": Engendering the Modern Body.* Ed. Helen Deutsch and Felicity Nussbaum. Ann Arbor: U of Michigan P, 2000. 95–126.

———. "'No Monster at the Resurrection': Inside Some Conjoined Twins." *Monster Theory.* Ed. Jeffrey Cohen. Minneapolis: U of Minnesota P, 1996. 143–67.

Penley, Constance. *Feminism and Film Theory.* Ed. Constance Penley. New York: Routledge, 1988.

Peters, J. S. "The Novelty; or, Print, Money, Fashion, Getting, Spending, and Glut." *Cultural Readings of Restoration and Eighteenth-Century English Theater.* Ed. J. Douglas Canfield and Deborah C. Payne. Athens: U of Georgia P, 1995. 169–94.

Philips, John. *Tears of the Indians.* London: n.p., 1656.

Pile, Steve, and Nigel Thrift. Introduction. *Mapping the Subject: Geographies of Cultural Formation.* London: Routledge, 1995. 1–12.

Pincus, Stephen. "Republicanism, Absolutism and Universal Monarchy: English Popular Sentiment During the Third Dutch War." *Culture and Society in the Stuart Restoration.* Ed. Gerald Maclean. Cambridge: Cambridge UP, 1995. 241–66.

Pix, Mary. *The Adventures in Madrid.* London: n.p., 1706.

———. *Ibrahim, the Thirteenth Emperour of the Turks.* London: n.p., 1696.

———. Preface. *Royal Mischief.* Delariviere Manley. London: n.p., 1696.

———. *The Spanish Wives.* London: n.p., 1706.

Plumb, J. H. *England in the Eighteenth Century.* New York: Penguin, 1950.

———. *The Growth of Political Stability in England, 1675–1725.* London: Macmillan, 1967.

Postlewait, Thomas. "Autobiography and Theatre History." *Interpreting the Theatrical Past: Essays in the Historiography of Performance.* Ed. Thomas Postlewait and Bruce A. McConachie. Iowa City: U of Iowa P, 1989. 248–72.

Powell, Jocelyn. *Restoration Theater Production.* London: Routledge and Kegan Paul, 1984.

Pratt, Mary Louise. *Imperial Eyes: Travel Writing and Transculturation.* London: Routledge, 1992.

Prescott, Anne Lake. "The Odd Couple: Gargantua and Tom Thumb." *Monster Theory.* Ed. Jeffrey Cohen. Minneapolis: U of Minnesota P, 1996. 75–91.

Pritchard, Will. "Masks and Faces: Female Legibility in the Restoration Era." *Eighteenth-Century Life* 24.3 (2000): 31–52.

Pye, Christopher. "The Sovereign, the Theater, and the Kingdome of Darknesse: Hobbes and the Spectacle of Power." *Representations* 8 (Fall 1984): 85–106.

Quinn, Michael. "Celebrity and the Semiotics of Acting." *New Theatre Quarterly* 6.22 (May 1990): 154–61.

Quinsey, Katherine M. "Almahide Still Lives: Feminine Will and Identity in Dryden's *Conquest of Granada. Broken Boundaries.* Ed. Katherine M. Quinsey. Lexington: UP of Kentucky, 1996. 129–49.

Rabb, Melinda Alliker. "Angry Beauties." *Cutting Edges: Postmodern Critical Essays on Eighteenth-Century Satire.* Ed James E. Gill. Knoxville: U of Tennessee P, 1995. 127–58.

Reeve, John. "Britain or Europe? The Context of Early Modern English History: Political and Cultural, Economic and Social, Naval and Military." *The New British History: Founding a Modern State, 1603–1715.* Ed. Glenn Burgess. London: I. B. Tauris, 1999. 287–312.

Ribeiro, Aileen. *The Art of Dress: Fashion in England and France, 1750–1820.* New Haven: Yale UP, 1995.

Roach, Joseph. *Cities of the Dead.* New York: Columbia UP, 1996.

Roberts, David. *The Ladies: Female Patronage of Restoration Drama, 1660–1700.* Oxford: Clarendon, 1989.

Rokem, Freddie. "Slapping Women: Ibsen's Nora, Strindberg's Julie, and Freud's Dora." *Textual Bodies: Changing Boundaries of Literary Representation.* Ed. Lori Hope Lefkovitz. Albany, NY: State U of New York P, 1997. 221–44.

Rose, Mary Beth. " 'Vigorous Most/When Most Unactive Deem'd': Gender and the Heroics of Endurance in Milton's *Samson Agonistes,* Aphra Behn's *Oroonoko,* and Mary Astell's *Some Reflections upon Marriage." Milton Studies, 33: The Miltonic Samson.* Ed. Albert C. Labriola and Michael Lieb. Pittsburgh, U of Pittsburgh P, 1997. 83–109.

Rosenthal, Laura. " 'Counterfeit Scrubbado': Women Actors in the Restoration." *The Eighteenth Century* 34.1 (1993): 3–22.

———. *Playwrights and Plagiarists in Early Modern England.* Ithaca: Cornell UP, 1996.

———. "Reading Masks: The Actress and the Spectatix in Restoration Shakespeare." *Broken Boundaries.* Ed. Katherine M. Quinsey. Lexington: UP of Kentucky, 1996. 201–18.

Rothenberg, Molly Anne, and Joseph Valente. "Fashionable Theory and Fashionable Women: Returning Fuss's Homospectatorial Look."

Works Cited

Identities. Ed. Kwame Anthony Appiah and Henry Louise Gates Jr. Chicago: U of Chicago P, 1995. 413–23.

Rowe, Nicholas. *Tamerlane. The Broadview Anthology of Restoration and Early Eighteenth-Century Drama.* Ed. J. Douglas Canfield. New York: Broadview Press, 2001. 38–74.

Russo, Elena. "Sociability, Cartesianism, and Nostalgia in Libertine Discourse." *Eighteenth-Century Studies* 30.4 (1997): 383–400.

Ryan, Simon. "Ludwig Leichhard: Australia's Missing Penis." *The Body in the Library.* Ed. Leigh Dale and Simon Ryan. Amsterdam: Rodopi, 1998. 237–48.

Sahlins, Peter. *Boundaries: The Making of France and Spain in the Pyrenees.* Berkeley: U of California P, 1989.

Samuel, Raphael. Introduction. *Patriotism: The Making and Unmaking of British National Identity.* Vol. 3. London: Routledge, 1989.

Scanlan, Thomas. *Colonial Writing and the New World 1583–1671.* Cambridge: Cambridge UP, 1999.

Scarry, Elaine. *The Body in Pain: The Making and Unmaking of the World.* New York: Oxford UP, 1985.

Schoenfeldt, Michael C. *Bodies and Selves in Early Modern England.* Cambridge: Cambridge UP, 1999.

Scholz, Susanne. *Body Narratives: Writing the Nation and Fashioning the Subject in Early Modern England.* London: Macmillan, 2000.

Scott, Thomas. *The Spaniards Perpetual Designs to Universal Monarchie.* N.p.: n.p., 1624.

Settle, Elkanah. *The Female Prelate: Being the History of the Life and Death of Pope Joan.* London: W. Cademan, 1680.

Shadwell, Thomas. *The Libertine. The Complete Works of Thomas Shadwell.* Ed. Montague Summers. Vol. 4. London: Fortune Press, 1927.

———. *The Virtuoso.* Ed. Marjorie Hope Nicolson and David Stuart Rodes. Lincoln: U of Nebraska P, 1966.

———. *The Woman-Captain.* A Critical Old-Spelling Edition. Ed. Judith Bailey Slagle. New York: Garland Publishing, 1993.

The Shorter Pepys. Ed. Robert Latham. Berkeley: U of California P, 1985.

Simpson, Antony. "Vulnerability and the Age of Female Consent: Legal Innovation and Its Effect on Prosecution for Rape in Eighteenth-Century London." *Sexual Underworlds of the Enlightenment.* Ed. G. S. Rousseau and Roy Porter. Manchester: Manchester UP, 1988.

Sommer, Doris. *Foundational Fictions: The National Romances of Latin America.* Berkeley: U of California P, 1991.

Southerne, Thomas. *Oroonoko. The Broadview Anthology of Restoration and Early Eighteenth-Century Drama.* Ed. J. Douglas Canfield. New York: Broadview P, 2001. 379–427.

"The Spectatrix." Spec. issue of *Camera Obscura.* 20–21 (1990).

Spencer, Jane. "Deceit, Dissembling, and all that's Woman: Comic Plot and Female Action in *The Feign'd Courtesans." Rereading Aphra Behn.* Ed. Heidi Hutner. Charlottesville: UP of Virginia, 1993. 86–101.

Stafford, Barbara. *Body Criticism: Imaging the Unseen in Enlightenment Art and Medicine.* Cambridge: MIT P, 1993.

Stallybrass, Peter. "Patriarchal Territories: The Body Enclosed." *Rewriting the Renaissance: The Discourses of Sexual Difference in Early Modern Europe.* Ed. Margaret W. Ferguson, Maureen Quilligan, and Nancy J. Vickers. Chicago: U of Chicago P, 1986.

——. "Time, Space and Unity: the Symbolic Discourse of *The Faerie Queene." Patriotism: The Making and Unmaking of British National Identity,* Ed. Raphael Samuel. Vol. 3. London: Routledge, 1989. 199–214.

Stallybrass, Peter, and Allon White. *The Politics and Poetics of Transgression.* Ithaca: Cornell UP, 1986.

Staves, Susan. "A Few Kind Word for the Fop." *Studies in English Literature* 22 (1982): 413–28.

——. "Fielding and the Comedy of Attempted Rape." *History, Gender and Eighteenth-Century Literature.* Ed. Beth Fowkes Tobin. Athens: U of Georgia P, 1994. 86–112.

——. *Players' Scepters: Fictions of Authority in the Restoration.* Lincoln: U of Nebraska P, 1979.

Steele, Richard. *Tatler No. 25. Selected Essays from "The Tatler," "The Spectator," "The Guardian."* Ed. Daniel McDonald. Indianapolis: Bobbs-Merrill, 1973.

Steintrager, James A. "Monstrous Appearances: Hogarth's 'Four Stages of Cruelty' and the Paradox of Inhumanity." *The Eighteenth Century* 4.1 (2001): 59–82.

——. "Perfectly Inhuman: Moral Monstrosity in Eighteenth-Century Discourse." *Eighteenth-Century Life* 21 (May 1997): 114–32.

Stillman, Robert E. "Hobbes's *Leviathan:* Monsters, Metaphors, and Magic." *ELH* 62 (1995): 791–819.

Stone, Lawrence. *The Crisis of the Aristocracy: 1558–1641.* Oxford: Clarendon, 1965.

Straub, Kristina. *Sexual Suspects: Eighteenth-Century Players and Sexual Ideology.* Princeton, Princeton UP, 1992.

Summers, Montagu. *The Restoration Theatre.* London: Keagan Paul, 1934.

Tennenhouse, Leonard. "Playing and Power." *Staging the Renaissance: Reinterpretation of Elizabethan and Jacobean Drama.* Ed. David Scott Kastan and Peter Stallybrass. New York: Routledge, 1991. 27–39.

——. "Violence Done to Women on the Renaissance Stage." *The Violence of Representation.* Ed. Nancy Armstrong and Leonard Tennenhouse. London: Routledge, 1989. 77–97.

Thomas, Susie. "This Thing of Darkness I Acknowledge Mine: Aphra Behn's *Abdelazer; or, The Moor's Revenge." Restoration: Studies in English Literary Culture, 1660–1700* 22.1 (Spring 1998): 18–39.

Thomas, Tobyas. *The Life of the Late Famous Comedian Jo. Hayns, Containing His Comical Exploits and Adventures, both at Home and Abroad.* London: n.p., 1701.

Thompson, Ann. "Women/'Women' and the Stage." *Women and Litera-*

ture in Britain, 1500–1700. Ed. Helen Wilcox. Cambridge: Cambridge UP, 1996. 100–116.

Thompson, James. "Dryden's Conquest of Granada and the Dutch Wars." The Eighteenth Century 31 (1990): 211–26.

———. Models of Value: Eighteenth-Century Political Economy and the Novel. Durham: Duke UP, 1996.

———. "'Sure I Have Seen That Face Before': Representation and Value in Eighteenth-Century Drama." Cultural Readings of Restoration and Eighteenth-Century English Theater. Ed. J. Douglas Canfield and Deborah C. Payne. Athens: U of Georgia P, 1995. 281–308.

Todd, Dennis. Imagining Monsters: Miscreations of the Self in Eighteenth-Century England. Chicago: U of Chicago P, 1995.

Todd, Janet. The Works of Aphra Behn. Ed. Janet Todd. Columbus: Ohio State UP, 1992.

Todorov, Tzvetan. The Conquest of America. Trans. Richard Howard. New York: Harper Perennial, 1984.

A Trip to Spain: or, A True Description of the Comical Humours, Ridiculous Customs, and Foolish Laws of that Lazy Improvident People the Spaniards. London: n.p., 1704–5.

Turner, Brian S. "The Rationalization of the Body: Reflections on Modernity and Discipline." Max Weber, Rationality and Modernity. Ed. Scott Lash and Sam Whimster. London Allen and Unwin, 1987. 222–41.

Turner, James G. "The Libertine Sublime: Love and Death in Restoration England." Studies in Eighteenth-Century Culture 19 (1989): 99–115.

———. "The Properties of Libertinism." 'Tis Nature's Fault: Unauthorized Sexuality During the Enlightenment. Ed Robert P. Maccubbin. Cambridge: Cambridge UP, 1987. 75–87.

Turner, Terence S. "The Social Skin." Reading the Social Body. Ed. Catherine B. Burroughs and Jeffrey David Ehrenreich. Iowa City: U of Iowa P, 1993. 15–39.

Uebel, Michael. "Unthinking the Monster: Twelfth-Century Responses to Saracen Alterity." Monster Theory. Ed. Jeffrey Cohen. Minneapolis: U of Minnesota P, 1996. 264–91.

Van Lennep, William. The London Stage, 1660–1700. Vol 1. Carbondale: Southern Illinois UP, 1963. 5 vols.

Vega, Lope de. The Discovery of the New World by Christopher Columbus. Trans. Frieda Fligelman. Berkeley: Gillick Press, 1950.

Wallace, Beth Kowaleski. "Reading the Surfaces of Colley Cibber's The Careless Husband." SEL: Studies in English Literature 1500–1900 40.3 (2000): 473–89.

Wanko, Cheryl. "The Eighteenth-Century Actress and the Construction of Gender: Lavinia Fenton and Charlotte Charke." Eighteenth-Century Life 18.2 (1994): 75–90.

Wells, Marcia. Persephone's Girdle: Narratives of Rape in Seventeenth-Century Spanish Literature. Nashville: Vanderbilt UP, 2000.

Wheatley, Christopher. Without God or Reason: The Plays of Thomas

Works Cited

Shadwell and Secular Ethics in the Restoration. Lewisburg: Bucknell UP, 1993.

Williams, Andrew P. "Soft Women and Softer Men: The Libertine Maintenance of Masculine Identity." *The Image of Manhood in Early Modern Literature.* Ed. Andrew P. Williams. Connecticut: Greenwood P, 1999. 94–118.

Williams, Eric. *From Columbus to Castro: The History of the Caribbean 1492–1969.* London: Andre Deutsch: 1970.

Wilson, J. H. *All the King's Ladies.* Chicago: U of Chicago P, 1958.

———. *Court Satires of the Restoration.* Ed. J. H. Wilson. Columbus: Ohio State UP, 1976.

Wilson, W. Daniel. "Turks on the Eighteenth-Century Operatic Stage and European Political, Military, and Cultural History." *Eighteenth-Century Life* 9.2 (Jan. 1985): 79–92.

Winn, James A. *John Dryden and His World.* New Haven: Yale UP, 1987.

Wycherley, William. *The Gentleman Dancing-Master. The Plays of William Wycherley.* Ed. Peter Holland. Cambridge: Cambridge UP, 1981. 117–344.

Zimbardo, Rose. *At Zero Point: Discourse, Culture, and Satire in Restoration England.* Lexington: U of Kentucky P, 1998.

Zomchick, John P. "Force, Contract, and Power in *The Woman-Captain.*" *Restoration: Studies in English Literary Culture, 1660–1700* 20 (Fall 1996): 175–87.

Index

Index

Index

Haynes, Joe, 115
Hendricks, Margo, 66, 71, 74
heroines: and female identity, 238nn. 41, 43; mothers as, 181–85, 239n. 4; rape and, 174; as strong, 32, 176–78; victims as, 164, 169, 171–72
Heywood, C. J., 12, 215n. 13
Hill, Christopher, 10, 38, 137
Hill, John, 114
Hill, Richard, 117
Hispaniola, 38, 40
Hobbes, Thomas, 3
Holland: ascendancy of, 8; colonialism of, 69; English wars with, 76, 80–81, 85–87, 99, 181, 186; France and, 10, 95; merchants of, 94–95; ridiculing of, 84–85, 87–92; Spain and, 39; trade and, 38, 85, 94–95. See also *Dutch Lovers, The*
Holland, Peter, 118
Howard, Jean, 8, 189
Howe, Elizabeth, 155–56, 237n. 37
Hughes, Derek, 196, 240n. 6
Hughes, Margaret, 138
Hulme, Peter, 49, 57
Hungary, 14

IBM, 78
Ibrahim, the Thirteenth Emperour (Pix), 31, 168–74, 196
identity: changes in, 6, 214n. 8; definition of, 3–5, 19, 20, 74, 213n. 4; fluidity of, 3–4, 20, 25, 138, 195, 206–7; interiority and, 5, 26–27, 194; violence and, 28, 29, 34. See also gender identity; identity, containment of; monsters; national identities; status
identity, containment of: 207–9; aristocratic identity and, 74–75; and class mobility of, 101; gender and, 152, 164, 184; imperial identity and, 34, 65; national identity, 79–80, 92, 96–99, 103–4; status and, 34, 74–75, 103. See also identity
imperialism: Christianity and, 61–62; colonialism and, 15–16, 69; Davenant on, 36, 40–42, 58, 63, 94; Dryden on, 36–37, 42–44, 54–56, 60, 63–64, 221n. 21; justification for, 41–42, 53, 58–63, 218n. 7, 219n. 12, 221n. 21; Nabil Matar on, 17–18, 71; miscegenation and, 207, 219n. 13; Montrose on, 16, 35–36, 58; Pagden on, 40, 66, 217n. 4,

219n. 12. See also England, imperial identity of; Spain, national identity of
incest, 191, 195–96
Indian Emperour, The (Dryden): analysis of, 65; colonialism and, 32; contested women in, 57–60; and imperial identity, 55–56, 62, 64, 207; natives and, 36, 37, 61, 75; on the New World, 43–48; as propaganda, 39, 83; the romance of conquest and, 29, 48–51, 53–54, 63–64, 199–200; staging of, 181, 218n. 6
Indian Queene, The (Dryden), 45
Indians. See natives
interiority: female identity and, 31–33, 119, 122–23, 136, 165, 216n. 22; identity and, 5, 26–27, 194; spectators and, 27
"In the Bodyshop" (Pender), 146
Inwardness and the Theater in the English Renaissance (Maus), 168, 214n. 8, 226n. 8
Isabella, Queen of Spain, 185–86
Islam in Britain (Matar), 11, 14–15, 215n. 11

Jamaica, 38, 40
James I, 90
James II, 140, 190
James III, 10
Jamestown, Virginia, 66, 67
Jed, Stephanie, 163, 174
Jennings, Frances, 142
Jowett, Claire, 40
"Juggling the Categories of Race, Class, and Gender" (Ferguson), 64, 67
Justine (Sade), 159

Kahn, Copp Elia, 237n. 36, 238n. 39
Kamen, Henry, 11
Kaufman, Anthony, 155, 232n. 17
Kehres, Jean-Marc, 159
Kelly, Veronica, 6
Kempe, 115
King, Thomas A., 121–22, 225n. 7, 234n. 23
Knolles, Richard, 11–13, 15, 215n. 14, 239n. 2
Kowaleski-Wallace, Beth, 237n. 34
Kramer, David Bruce, 48, 63, 221n. 21
Kris, Ernst, 227n. 20
Kurz, Otto, 227n. 20
Kynaston, Edward, 115

La Salle, 50
Las Casas, Bartolome de, 39, 40, 93–94

Index

Index

Montesquieu, Baron de, 221nn. 22, 26
Montezuma: conquest of, 220n. 15; Cortés and, 36, 47, 53, 55, 220n. 15; human sacrifices and, 45; love plots and, 59, 60
Montrose, Louis: imperialism and, 16, 35–36, 58; on masculinity, 55–56; on New World, 42; on Spain, 8, 108
Moors: cross-national dressing and, 194–96; Europe and, 8, 11, 16; identity of, 197–99, 240n. 5; as monsters, 186–92, 196; natives and, 17–18, 222n. 27; plays about, 179, 185–96, 203, 206, 239n. 4, 240n. 5; Spain and, 16, 49
Mountfort, William, 117
Mulcaire, Terry, 25
Munns, Jessica, 24, 139, 141
Murray, Timothy, 129–30
Muslims, 12–14, 215n. 11; and Islam in Britain. See also Moors
Mustapha, Son of Solyman the Magnificent (Orrery), 179, 181–85, 189, 218n. 6, 239nn. 1–2

national identities: boundaries of, 19, 79, 96, 98–99; class mobility of, 87, 101–3, 138, 223n. 9; clothing and, 23–24, 139; colonialism and, 28–29, 39–42, 215n. 10, 217n. 3, 221n. 24; containment of, 31, 79–80, 92, 96–99, 103–4; and cross-national dressing, 87–93, 95–99, 101–3, 105–6, 194–96; patriotism and, 80–83; refinement of, 5, 18, 20–22, 180, 233n. 18; status and, 19, 28, 101; theater and, 78; wealth and, 28. *See also* aristocratic identity; class; England, imperial identity of; gender identity; Spain, national identity of
Native Americans. *See* natives
natives: colonialism and, 66, 68–70, 73–75, 197; as contested women, 49–50, 57–59, 63, 67–69; cross-dressing by, 74–75; depictions of, 42–43, 45–48, 220n. 18, 222n. 27; discovery of, 36; England and, 47–48, 54–55, 63–64; identity of, 8, 17–18, 53, 75, 207; internal conflicts of, 63, 64, 67; miscegenation with, 67–68, 75; as monsters, 60–62; Moors and, 17–18, 222n. 27; otherness of, 45, 47–48, 58; romance of conquest, 29, 48–51, 53–54, 63–64, 199–200; Spain's imperial identity and, 17–18, 40–43, 48, 193–94, 217n. 3,

219n. 10; specular women and, 49–51, 53; treatment of, 40–41, 48, 94, 221n. 22. See also *Discovery of the New World by Christopher Columbus, The; Indian Emperour, The*
Negrin, Llewellyn, 216n. 19
Newman, Gerald, 80, 83
New Survey of the West-Indies, A (Gage), 220n. 18
Nussbaum, Felicity, 145, 216n. 17, 234n. 23

Ogilby, James, 16
"'Once a Whore and Ever'?" (Copeland), 226n. 10
Oroonoko (Behn), 89, 179, 203, 240n. 7
Oroonoko (Southerne), 179, 196–201, 206, 240n. 7
Orphan, The (Betterton), 142
Orrery, Earl of, 179, 181–85, 189, 206, 218n. 6
Othello (Shakespeare), 185
otherness: of Africans, 197–99, 240n. 5; ambiguities of, 186, 222n. 27; of Europeans, 92, 95, 205, 218n. 8; of men and women, 149; of monsters, 60–62, 144, 186–92, 196; of natives, 37, 45, 47–48, 58; notions of, 205–6; xenophobia and, 194
Ottoman Empire: in *Almyna*, 31–32, 168, 175–78, 201, 227n. 16, 238n. 40; bibliography on, 215n. 13; decline of, 124–26; England and, 11–12, 15, 182; fear of, 13–15, 124; France and, 202; fratricide in, 239n. 2; harems in, 125–26; in *Ibrahim*, 31, 168–74, 196; Muslims and, 12–13; in *Mustapha*, 179, 181–85, 189, 239nn. 1–2; national identity of, 12, 125, 202; and Spain, 12; in *Tamerlane*, 179, 201–5, 206, 224n. 10; women in, 12–13, 125–26. See also *Royal Mischief, The*
Owen, Susan, 155, 231n. 6

Pagden, Anthony: on colonialism, 221n. 26; on European history, 37; on imperialism, 40, 66, 217n. 4, 219n. 12; on natives, 221n. 22; on Spain, 38–39, 41–42
Pageant of Spanish Humours, A (H. W.), 94
Paradise Lost (Milton), 63
Paré, Ambroise, 145
Park, Katharine, 145, 146, 178
Parker, Todd, 234n. 23

Index

Index

CYNTHIA LOWENTHAL is an associate professor of Restoration and eighteenth-century British literature and dean of Newcomb College at Tulane University. Her most recent book is *Lady Mary Wortley Montagu and the Eighteenth-Century Familiar Letter.*